Dem Mikhailov

NULLFORM

Thank you for reading my books! The adventure begins! Dem Mikhailov

Book 9

Magic Dome Books
in collaboration with 1C-Publishing

Nullform
Book 9
Copyright © Dem Mikhailov 2025
Cover Art © Sergei Kolesnikov 2025
English translation copyright © Colin Parker 2025
Published by Magic Dome Books in collaboration with 1C-Publishing, 2025
All Rights Reserved
ISBN: 978-80-7702-502-7

This book is entirely a work of fiction.
Any correlation with real people or events
is coincidental.

All Books
by Dem Mikhailov:

Clan Dominance: The Sleepless Ones LitRPG Series
Books 1-9

Heroes of the Final Frontier
(The World of Waldyra LitRPG Series):
Books 1-5

Nullform RealRPG Series:
Books 1-10

The Crow Cycle LitRPG Series:
Books 1-4

Crossroads of Oblivion
A Portal Progression Fantasy Adventure Series
Books 1-5

TABLE OF CONTENTS:

CHAPTER 1

HE WAS WAITING FOR US downstairs. And he was magnificent. Yet simultaneously repulsive, depending on which aspect of him you looked at. If you admired his clothes — snow-white shirt with splendid silvery lace collar; spangly black pants; brown boots buffed to a bright sheen, adorned with a multitude of golden rivets, and resting on the table; and large sunglasses resting on his hummocky forehead — then he was magnificent like an opulent medieval court dandy. But if you looked at the man himself, then he was a piece of old and recently drenched shit, red speckled with black, which had sprouted arms and legs, and whose carefully brushed mane of black hair cascaded down onto the silvery collar.

Taking a seat opposite him, and not concealing my interest, I made a close inspection of the fourth-rank hero Wormeus Magmus. He clearly did not care much for this, although to give him his due he did tolerate it stoically for the first few minutes. Then:

"What are you gawking at, macaque?" he asked in a slightly gravelly voice as he removed his boots from the table and leaned forward.

"It talks as well." I blinked in shock before staring at Little Miss Green Eyes as she sat down beside me. "It's amazing how technology has progressed around here."

"Elb!" the girl barked. "We agreed you would be calm and well-mannered. Yes, Wormeus looks like an unwrapped but still uneaten chocolate bar, but tone down your excitement."

"Chocolate bar?" I asked in surprise. "What are you talking about? All I see is a piece of shit in sunglasses that has crawled from a jagged asshole."

I blocked Wormeus's strike with two hands, while simultaneously pushing off with my feet and flying backwards along with the chair. The chair legs scraped along the floor before coming to rest, while I snorted, wiped the blood from my lips, and inspected my reddened hand. Wormeus's blow had been forceful enough to it slam into my face.

"Macaque," Wormeus hissed disdainfully. "Are your little hands intact? Can you eat?"

"Intact they are," I smiled, standing and taking hold of the chair back. "But being the dumb macaque I am, I have managed to misplace my utensils."

Blinking, Wormeus stared at the table in an

attempt to understand where my knife and fork had gone.

"Your hand, Worm," Green Eyes tittered softly.

"Oh shit!" the fourth-rank hero announced with feeling as he glanced at his right hand, from which protruded the deeply sunken knife and fork. "You freaking macaque!"

"Why are you not shrieking and rolling around the floor in pain?" I inquired, disappointed, before waving to the innkeeper, who stood pressed against the wall in clear expectation of a heroic brawl kicking off.

"My nerve endings are hyposensitive," sighed the pimply monstrosity, cautiously extracting the knife from the wound between his knuckles. "Fuck."

"You need to be more aware of your surroundings," I said, sincerely sympathetic.

"Now then. Stop jousting with words, boys," said Teulra, whose face was still concealed by a thin gauze half-mask. "That is not why we came here, Worm."

"Indeed," agreed the other, slamming the bent fork down on the table and turning his head towards Bugnar, who had sidled up. "Fine. Innkeeper, spread the table. Plenty of meat. Fried! With golden crackling. And you, Elb, would be better off not calling me a piece of shit."

"Chocolate?" I offered, looking suggestively at his silvery collar. "Unwrapped—"

"I do not care for such words from a man. I am Wormeus. Worm, to my friends."

"That's a relief," I said, sighing that relief. "Wormeus... Worm, you look like a section of earthworm chopped off and baked in the oven."

"Quite right." The fourth-rank hero nodded and adjusted his collar. "Just so. Not a piece of shit!"

"Do you like meat?" I asked, changing the subject and reaching for the dish of over-browned and obviously overcooked meat which had been set before Wormeus. "Do you like the crunch of muscle fibers between your teeth?"

"I adore meat," replied Wormeus in a squeaky voice as he slowly clenched his right hand into a fist and squeezed thick blood from the wound. "I am fucking crazy about meat, fried meat with tantalizingly crunchy crackling, no spices required, just a pinch of salt, and maybe a shake of black pepper for added aroma."

"That is exactly how it has been cooked," the innkeeper mewed timidly as he brought the next dish.

"So why aren't you eating, if everything is cooked just as it should be?" I asked without especial interest, taking my neighbor Teulra's knife and fork and helping myself to a big fat chunk of meat.

"He can't," Green Eyes said with another titter.

"Teulra!" Wormeus shouted. "Are you having a laugh at my expense?"

"He eats only plant-based food," Teulra explained, recovering herself. "His body categorically rejects anything else."

"Did that happen after the change?"

"It did." The musclebound worm sitting opposite me shook his lumpy head and stabbed his fork with disgust into a green lettuce leaf. "After the change. I'm not complaining, mind. I gained more than I lost. Much more."

"I can see that," I said, glancing at his right fist.

Spotting my glance, Wormeus put quite some effort into stretching his thin and nigh unnoticeable lips into a wide grin, took a tissue from the table, and wiped his right hand.

The wound was gone.

All that remained were two barely distinguishable marks on the slightly lighter skin where it had been spiked by the knife and fork a couple of minutes ago. And I had buried those table implements deep.

"Regeneration is a terrific thing," said Wormeus, chuffed with the effect he'd produced and the ill-concealed expression of envy on my face.

"And that is not all," added Teulra, fingering her gauze half-mask as she looked indecisively at a plate of wonderful-smelling and still sizzling fried eggs. "This high-society dame is shilly-shallying. Fuck shit. I so want to dip some bread into that salted and peppered yolk."

"Everything is cooked just as it should be, madam!" shouted the innkeeper joyfully as he placed some condensation-beaded pitchers on the table. "Tuck in!"

"Shit," Teulra repeated, tugging her half-mask from her face.

"Afraid of catching something?" I asked, chewing noisily. "Or are you bulimic? You're not that ugly."

Wormeus was lost to a fit of laughter and nearly knocked his loathsome salad onto the floor. Giving me a vicious look, Teulra made her decision and divvied up the fried eggs before prodding the yolk with a piece of aromatic rye bread.

"Supreme fucking etiquette," she exclaimed, before stuffing her mouth and squinting in bliss.

"Etiquette," the wincing Wormeus echoed, returning to picking dejectedly at his salad while inhaling through his nose with all his might to saturate himself with the aroma emanating from the plate of meat. "It is indeed strange etiquette for a real lady to be forever concealing her surely fine face behind a half-mask or, at worst, a veil. If you fuck such a lady in a dark corner of a nighttime rose garden, she might be butt naked, but so long as she is wearing a half-mask, no one will judge such sweet spontaneous behavior from two people in the grip of passion. But should she be unveiled, and should you so much as brush her with your little finger..."

"Then she is a cheap whore," said Teulra, licking egg yolk from her lips. "Emphasis on the word 'cheap'."

"Do you give a shit about their opinion?" I asked as I poured myself some lemonade.

"Everybody gives a shit if they really want to

make it to the Lands of the Covenant one day."

"I heard something about a certain Allurdos…"

"Allurdos Delurdos. An immortal Sacrifice. Don't ask what language it is, I have no idea. I only know how to pronounce it correctly and what it means. There are two interpretations. Many consider the correct translation to be 'In the name of immortality,' and that these words are taken from the language of the Highers, which in turn is an amalgam of all known languages in the world."

"We're all chatting in the same language here."

"Now, yes," Teulra agreed, and squeamishly she pushed away a hodgepodge of various fruits and berries topped with a suspicious-looking viscous thin pink jelly. "Poor me a small shot of vodka, the cranberry one."

"Just a second," I said, reaching for the decanter. "Somewhere out in the prairie is a whole herd of wandering minoses and fauns that call themselves Allurda Lurda or something like that."

"Those words are forever being distorted," said Wormeus, waving a dismissive hand. Then, leaning over the dish, he sniffed greedily like a junkie, before crunching down angrily on a cabbage leaf. "The minoses. The problem with that herd just grows and grows, while the heroes in these parts just wait and wait for the red rag to be waved."

"What does that mean?"

"Do you know about the restrictions?"

"Restrictions of what?"

"Of *whom*," Teulra corrected me, then looked at Worm and asked, "You're talking about heroes, right?"

"That's right. I am talking about those shitting heroes who are higher than third rank. You made the right decision, Elb, when you hung back and didn't hurry to Crontown. Not that I would have let you cross the line and enter, mind."

"If only I could allow so many gaps in my health," I said with a shrug.

"I like your chutzpah, little one," Wormeus said, grinning, "very much. I see that at least five percent of the tales told about you are not simply idle gossip. Do not take this the wrong way. I am not one to create difficulties for newbies who are striving for something, whatever it be. I myself came here in ripped trousers and a vest gray with dirt, and carrying on my shoulder just one thing of value: Killrada. I came here alone, and on my way I ran into quite a number of motherfuckers who did everything to make me either leave, losing sta-tus, or die. But I survived, flourished even."

"And killed all your ill-wishers, even the really tiny ones," the girl chuckled.

"I did," Wormeus confirmed. "What's the use of abiding by something as cheap and overrated as absolution? Fuck forgiveness! Vengeance is what you need. Stabbing an old offender in the liver with a rusty spike brings instant relief. So I killed them slowly and only when I was in a very bad mood. Savvy? It's like mint candies: sweet yet cooling. Squeeze the soul out of a wheezing mongrel, and feel lightened, your mood instantly improved. The rest of the frightened sweeties you don't have to touch yet; they can wait their turn. And you know, I noticed they stopped spoiling my mood. Quite the opposite, they really tried to make sure my spirits were always raised."

"Maybe you could show me your memoirs about your graying balls? What do they say about red rags and the line?"

"I did warn you about his personality," Little Miss Green Eyes snorted, grinning widely and displaying the cute dimples in her cheeks and the tiny twinkling rocks on several of her teeth.

"That freaking line, the boundary of no return," grumbled the sentient worm in the inexpensive shirt. "It's on the road. You should have seen something like it on the border of the Crontown zone."

"The one about responsibility?"

"The very same. There is a second line on the road somewhere in the middle of Hello. If it's crossed by anyone with hero status no lower than second rank, Mother will cease giving him tasks outside the Crontown zone. The zone here might be very big, but the line is nonetheless a limit, and a strict one. You can, of course, lose status and drop down to first rank, but then as punishment you will be kicked out of the zone, and you will not be able to return until you get back up to second rank and then wait six months. Such is the penalty for refusing a task or failing to complete one."

"So Crontown heroes aren't issued tasks outside the Crontown zone?"

"Correct."

"And if I complete the day's task? I can take a walk wherever I like, yeah?"

"Certainly. But twice a day Mother will check your location and the status of tasks issued. And even if your crew has completed her mission but you are not in the Crontown zone when the next one is issued…"

"No punishable crime has been committed," I noted. "The previous task is completed. You are not slaves to the system."

"Slaves to the system. How grand that sounds. We are heroes of the system, and that is worse. Mother keeps records of everything. Did you know that?"

"Uh-huh."

"It's pretty much the same system here. Every task completed is a tiny bonus and helps you move up the ranks. You are rank two."

"That's right."

"In order to make rank three, you will have to complete at least a hundred tasks. In a row. No failures."

"How routine."

"Teeth-grindingly so," Wormeus agreed. "Maddeningly so. But what options are there? None. Except for doing a heroic deed, if you catch my drift?"

"I get it. A hundred mundane system tasks completed on the trot allows you to move up one rank."

"Correct. There are more than enough heroes here to go around, so it is very rare to be issued more than one task per day."

"A hundred days to move up one rank?" I frowned weakly. "That sounds shit."

"Optimist!" Teulra blurted. " No way, goblin. Who would let you, a filthy ass newbie, build up a winning streak of a hundred tasks? Those fuckers would stop you."

"They would do anything to stop you," Wormeus concurred.

"And how would they do that?"

"Well, let us suppose you and your crew get a task to kill a group of prisms or beastfolk with negative criminal statuses, that have entered the Crontown zone. You set off gaily to take them out, and when you get there, tired, you see Teulra smiling contentedly having just whacked the bastards and wiggling her tush in joyous anticipation of your grieving and bellyaching. Savvy?"

"The system would mark the task down as failed?"

"No. That would mean a drop in status followed by exile. Mother would mark the task down as not completed for, let's say, an almost legitimate reason. So there would be no harsh penalty, but it would cut short a series of successfully completed tasks, and you would be back to square one. Now imagine completing ninety-nine tasks, and the next one, the hundredth, theoretically granting you the next rank of hero."

"Hmm."

"That is why there is an unspoken rule not to fell random beasts you come across, without truly solid grounds. Mother might have entrusted those beasts to someone else, and without even meaning to, you do someone else an ill turn and earn his bitter hatred forever, along with his bloody revenge. Shitting on someone else's dandelions is more trouble than it's worth. Never a truer proverb."

"What strange proverbs you have around here. Heartfelt though."

"Everything is driven by intrigue here in Crontown. Complex political games, goblin. You're not going to get anywhere near your goal if you go at it like a bloodthirsty drill bit. You will get bogged down in sticky shit and drown."

"Are you going to keep frightening me with your odious smile for long?"

"We have been boiling away in this broth for many a long year." Wormeus paid not the slightest attention to my question and ruefully pushed away the now cold meat, which had ceased giving off such a strong aroma. "We know every VIP ass around here not only by smell, but also by taste. Teulra and I have been working in tandem for a long time. She may be a lone wolf and I the leader of a crew, but we still work well together."

"Sometimes," Green Eyes added.

"Sometimes," Wormeus agreed.

"And not in every situation."

"Not in every situation."

"And there's no way Crontown heroes can leave the zone for any period of time?" I asked, staring once more at Teulra.

"Why not?" she smiled sweetly. "Vacations haven't been prohibited. Once every six months, third-rank heroes are given three days off. Fourth rankers get a week."

"And fifth rankers?"

"Are you kidding? They stop doing regular jobs. Mother does not send rank-five heroes on random tasks. They spend nearly all their time training and waiting for the Scarlet Signal."

"My head's beginnings to hurt," I announced, "again."

"Ignore the pain and continue remembering," Green Eyes advised.

"What's it got to do with me? What's a line on the road to Hello got to do with anything? And what do you need from me, you fourth-rank heroes?"

"Hold your horses!" said Teulra, behaving just as an eternally hungry hero should and stuffing herself with as many calories as possible, without a hint of embarrassment or pointless false modesty. "We haven't finished scaring you get."

"What with? Wormeus's mug?"

"If nothing else," said Wormeus, grinning with teeth of little use to a herbivore. "Be afraid of my mug, goblin. By the way, what news of those goosed tunny fish? Rumor has it all amphibious prisms are keeping a low profile. Never mind not dipping their butts in the ocean, they're afraid of even taking a bath. What if they get fucked? And then have to ferry someone over seas and oceans? Huh?"

"It's the only way we know," I sniggered in reply, casting a meaningful sidelong look at Green Eyes. "Although we hope to find more."

Swallowing a piece of meat with enormous difficulty, she said hoarsely:

"Perhaps. Innkeeper! Fuck the lemonade. Wine, red wine. Red wine so tart it's astringent."

"I've got just the thing. It's not only your lips will pucker." The forgotten Bugnar beamed a smile, but immediately checked himself when he clocked Teulra's cold stare. "Ahem, I'll just bring it, madam."

"So what are you going to frighten me with?" I repeated my question.

"All the usual stuff, goblin. Without us you will soon be eaten here. And before you counter, I know what you're going to say. Something ultimately obvious and pretentious, the sort of thing favored by aggressive scumbags, something like, 'Just let them try,' or 'Let them choke on it,' or 'I'll go in through the mouth with my sword and come out through the asshole,' or even my favorite, 'They can shit me out, and I will bounce right back.' Ain't happening! They will try, and they will not choke. They will eat you, and you will not bounce back. No way. They will definitely do everything in their power to kill you and all those who limp behind you. For one very simple reason: the more fourth-rank heroes there are, the lower the chances of receiving a really hardcore task. And the fewer hardcore tasks you complete, the lower your already negligible chances of promotion to the highest rank, five. And if you're not a fiver, you're not getting Allurdos Delurdos. Which means you don't get to become immortal and you don't get anywhere near the Lands of the Covenant or the highest of the Highers. So what have they been hard at work here all these years for? And, goblin" — Wormeus leaned forward, resting his hands on the table and dipping his shirt in his salad — "they have a special score to settle with you."

"But I haven't been here for a day yet."

"Precisely. All the other Crontown zone newbies go barely noticed for months, sometimes even years, while you are a shitting rising star, famous throughout half the world. Elb the goblin. Fuck those tunafish, and come breezing in to shore. Fuck Zombieland, and receive the unique Blue Light reward. Two hero ranks in forty-eight hours! And here you are in Crontown, not gathering dust, not tarrying, but what now? Fuck the local beauty queen and go galloping into the Lands of the Covenant on her sleek back? And no, do not look at Teulra with your jaw dropped. She is a skank by local standards."

"What did you say, you piece of shit? Eaten too much salad and it's gone to your head?" A knife was stabbed into the tabletop.

I ignored it, slicing thoughtfully into a piece of overcooked meat. Placing the wine on the table, the innkeeper suggested meekly:

"Should I char some more pork? For the aroma?"

"Char away!" Wormeus replied.

"That's enough spoiling the meat!" I said.

"Too right!" said Teulra in my support. "Turnip eater! Rutabaga sucker! May you be forced to suck a strawberry one day."

"Hey, that's not even something to wish on your enemies."

"You'll get your heroic vacation. And you'll eat. And fall into a coma again."

"I can't wait." All of a sudden, Wormeus became deflated and melancholy, squeamishly pushing his salad away and eyeing the fried meat with longing. "Yeah, I can't fucking wait. I'm fed up of chewing leaves, sucking roots, and humbly swallowing a single bean at a time."

"What about when you're on vacation?" I asked in sincere surprise. "Does your body not, like, recover?"

"Nothing's ever going to recover inside me. But I eat. Kilos and kilos' worth."

"On the first day of his vacation he chuffs killer doses of ferments and has a couple of injections before scoffing kilos of seriously fatty meat and falling into a lethargic sleep," Teulra explained. "And I have to fucking look after him. He doesn't trust anyone else. And before falling into his coma he takes everything off and climbs into a bath of warm running water. There he lies for two days, excreting liquid foamy shit. And he fondles himself, all over, stroking and tugging with a beatific smile. It's pretty grim. When he recovers himself, he eats again, less than before but he still puts away three kilos of chicken burgers. And then he's out again for another two days. Then for a snack he chuffs half a kilo of meat and veg, veal and whatever, then enters a shallow coma for twenty-four hours. And his vacation is over."

"A week in paradise," Wormeus sighed bitterly. "And the dreams, ah, the dreams."

"Yes, I know about your dreams, you lover of your own body."

"Are we going to keep talking about your modest masturbation? Or shall we return to the subject of my fright? Although I get the gist already. To begin with, I'll require protection and explanations from you. And you will need my help in a certain matter."

"That's right."

"And as I understand, you think I'm going to hang around here for a while, and that's why you value your services so highly."

"Meaning?"

"Hang around here for a hundred days?" I said, raising my hands. "Why the fuck would I do that?"

"At the very least. And that only if everything goes smoothly, which never happens. But basically, in roughly four months, with our help, you will—"

"I'm not interested." I shook my head.

"Have you lost it, Elb?" Green Eyes fixed me with a stare.

"I'm not interested," I repeated. "I am not about to spend months in Crontown and its environs. I need to go that way." Raising my knife, I pointed it out of the window, beyond which could be seen the other, "fashionable," side of a huge basin. "I need to get to the Lands of the Covenant. Preferably tomorrow."

"You are an absolute psycho," Wormeus announced with conviction. "Teulra, we are wasting time with this naïve island halfwit. No offense, Elb. You are a psycho, and I like psychos, but you need to have at least a loose grip on reality."

"You're in a hurry, Elb," added Teulra.

"But," I said, pausing briefly before continuing, "I'm still interested in hearing about this shit you wanted me to clear up. And if it really does interest me, is it far?"

"In the Crontown zone."

"Will any killing be necessary?"

"Naturally."

"Sounds good already. What are these tasks the system issues to newbies like us?"

"You did not cross the line into Hello. The tasks will be routine: patrol the roads, patrol the roads, and patrol the roads. Incidentally, many of those who want to live in places like that deliberately tarry in the Crontown zone but do not cross the line. You can do enough there to get by."

"But statistics for climbing up the ranks...?"

"Naturally, they don't count. Mother is strict."

"The system is skewed," I said, disagreeing, "but we're talking about something else here. One task per day per crew, right?"

"As a rule. Additional tasks do crop up, but they are not obligatory."

"Thank heavens for small mercies."

"You have seventy-two hours from the moment you enter the Crontown zone. Acclimatization, as it were."

"Uh-huh. So tell me everything. But only the facts. Tell me everything you know, and what you want from me. If I'm interested, or agree because I consider it advantageous to me or my crew, then I will demand something. And if I do it, you will owe me. Big time."

"Even me?" Teulra lay her breast softly on my shoulder.

"Even you," I said, skewering another piece of meat with my fork. "And I will demand that the debt is paid, you can be sure of that."

"How unkind your eyes are," Wormeus said admiringly and, pulling at his chin, nodded sharply. "Fuck it. It's worth it. But mind you don't encroach upon my ass, goblin. You understand. Moderation, everything in moderation. I am not Teulra, to squeal loud enough for the whole tavern to hear."

"You fucker! You piece of shit!"

"Ugly bitch!"

"Let's get down to business," I said, interrupting their friendly compliments. "And order some more lemonade."

CHAPTER 2

"FREAKING MARE!" Flapping his massive arms, the roaring orc flew from the horse's shimmering back and crashed down onto the grass. By twisting and turning, he managed to land relatively softly, before raising his head and, choking on his words, barking, "It isn't a mare anyway! Why the hell was it forged in the first place? And why so huge?"

"Just because," said Jorann, stroking the neck of her chestnut — and real — stallion. "Don't be jealous."

The redhead handled herself like an absolute natural in the saddle, as though she were born there, and bending down low from it, she would pick flowers from the long grass and run her flask along in the crystal-clear streams running over rocks.

I also felt very at home, rocking back and forth in the comfortable leather saddle fixed to the steel croup of my hooved robot. That was why I preferred robots, and had advised the orc to choose likewise. It was a more relaxed ride, predictable and even. Anything was better than perching on the back of a sensitive animal. But something wasn't quite right with Wreck and his steel stallion, and this was the orc's second fall.

"They should have put this cock on the withers, not under the belly. That way it would be close at hand." Wreck continued his blustering as he rose to his feet and hurried after the imperturbable metal racehorse moving with ease up a steep slope.

"A cock on the withers? Close at hand?" said a gray-haired girl with big ears, her pouty lips rounded in non-comprehension. "What would be the point of that, militarily speaking, Sergeant Wreck? It's made of metal. It can't feel anything."

"Idiot girl! Not as a cock, as a handle! To hold on to!"

"Ah, that's what I thought."

"Hold on to a horse's cock?" said Jorann, eyes wide in innocence. "So that's your fantasy, is it?"

"Fuck off! Commander, can I walk?"

"Get your ass up onto the horse and sit proud," I ordered, without turning around. "Squad! Keep away from the edge. It's better to be bitten than to fall down a cliff and spill your brains on the rocks."

We were riding along a narrow winding path through a deep gorge. The view all around was one of stunning beauty. Streams, grass, and flowers, and rock faces wound with wild grape vines. And the place was heaving with snakes. They were everywhere. As were mice, which occasionally came whizzing out of cracks in the cliff wall, clearly involuntarily. They whizzed out on jets of water, squeaking plaintively, before hurriedly scattering to hide, only to die here sooner or later from the overabundance of writhing scaly vermin.

Ten riders. Three live horses, with acceptable wear and tear, and seven shabby steel ones. All ten obedient and calm, with the exception of Wreck's robot steed, which just refused to get along with its rider, listlessly displaying the remaining dregs of its former strength and some strange idiosyncrasies of computer code. But that was enough for an incompetent rider like the orc to go flying from the saddle. Although nobody risked laughing at him, apart from the catty Jorann, whose stallion was pulling behind it a yawning chitinous cocoon from which Gabby was beginning to hatch.

"I've squished a grass snake, commander," said Gabby, his voice resounding. "Is that okay? Will Mother Nature not be offended?"

"It's fine," Wreck answered for me, "nothing to worry about. Although the thing which just grabbed the squished snake and dragged it back inside your butt with a dull visceral growl, that has made me a mite jumpy. And Mother Nature as well."

"Yeah right. Are you kidding?"

"He's not kidding," I said, looking pensively at the cracked cocoon.

"Eat your proteins quietly, sweetie" Jorann

purred. "With any part of your firm athletic body."

Serpentary Landfault.

Beautifully named. Apt, too. Now what we needed was not to die in this backwater fifteen kilometers from our favored inn, the Shiny Shack. And to die here would certainly be easy. Although not from snake venom, for which we had antidotes aplenty for both us and the live horses. No. It would be easy to die here, by falling into the gorge, or by a boulder falling on your head from the greenery-rich cliff face hanging over us.

But I was not complaining. I had, after all, agreed myself to take part in this crazy scheme.

We were making our way and hurriedly to the promised land.

We were on a direct route to paradise.

To those very same pastures of heaven, or whatever they call those places where you can sample anything that is meant to be sampled, and not only will you not be held accountable, but you will also be smiled at affectionately, perhaps even encouragingly, by someone with a gentle and homely message in their eyes: "Come on, weasel, go on shitting, go on…" And then bang! You fly out of the golden gates head over heels, with the remains of a not overly sweet fruit in your teeth.

Random nonsense was creeping into my weary head again. Not even nonsense, but mere snippets of nonsense. Snippets of something confused, part drug-induced recollection, part deduction, part invention. But these associations were not with the *word* "paradise," but with the *theoretical place known as "paradise."*

And that was precisely how our destination was labeled on the old hand-drawn map spread out over the saddle. The place we were heading for was called Paradise Promised. Jeez.

To begin with, when Teulra, sometimes pressing her scantily covered breast against me, sometimes letting out raspy sniggers, poured moonshine and lemonade down her throat... *I just knew the heroic nobility stole booze recipes from the swinish goblins. Add a cocktail cherry, and there you have it, an aristocratic cocktail instead of scumbag pig swill* ...So anyway, when the nuzzling Teulra Green Eyes suddenly mentioned that our destination was Paradise, I laughed. By this time we'd been joined at table by a number of my veterans and the tigers, so I was not laughing alone. But without batting an eye, Teulra simply produced a map — from where, I could not tell — and spread it out among the plates, pinning the edges down with glasses. And yes, the name Paradise Promised was there, looking like a large green ink blot fallen onto a gray-black board.

Cliffs, cliffs, barren lands, more cliffs, disorderly weavings of ravines, mountains, dunes, and basically anything that nature could make to look darksome, unwelcoming, and unable to feed even a couple of emaciated goblins. And slap bang in the center of all this splendor was the green blot of Paradise. Satisfied that we believed her, Teulra began to speak, Wormeus helping her, although from time to time he would glance predatorily at the bandaged Tigrala, boldly ignoring Tigr's angry snarlings.

Just like in the heavily thumbed ancient books, entering Paradise was no mean feat, for some even impossible. When, at the very beginning of her tale, Teulra hinted at some heavenly divine power, I puckered my brow and told her to provide exclusively facts and nothing but. No cock and bull.

After a moment's thought, Green Eyes shrugged and, mechanically coiling and uncoiling her fork, which was pliable like plasticine in her hands, began to speak in facts.

Paradise Promised was the official name of a specific group of territories given over freehold by the system, for ever and ever, or until such time as this world ceased to exist. Given over to whom? Some community. Some large and fanatically religious community that did not acknowledge technology after a certain level. Horse-drawn or hand carts were good; the heavenly host would not be angered. Whereas a powered wagon, be the engine petrol-driven or electric, was a sin. A horse-drawn mower or plow was a superb contraption. But a motor-powered field-tilling machine? That devilry must be dismantled and burned this instant!

It went without saying that the substantial chunk of ground was not given for gratis. This was not some tiny little island to be gifted to rawtarians or some other insignificant group of museum-dwelling ethnics.

The lands were sold. And for an incredible

sum, if you were to believe the gobbets of information that had long since begun to filter down from the Lands of the Covenant. The community had agreed to pay the demanded sum without question, but had also stated particular terms of its own. When these were refused, the community smiled sweetly and suggested an amount three times bigger. Only to be refused again. Then five times bigger. At which point the answer was affirmative.

For the insane sum paid, the community was given a huge area of ground for its exclusive use, as well as a guarantee of the total absence of any external control whatsoever.

No flying drones.

No observation domes.

Fuck the automatic trade points!

No more fucking steel horses! (Although this hadn't actually worked out very well for them.)

No motorized carts, no electric cables, no satanic means of communication, no books containing more than one black-and-white picture, no recreational sex, and none of the latest chemical reagents. Anyone who thought otherwise should be burned at the stake.

The list of demands was so long that nobody knew it in its entirety.

Yet the essence was simple: this was a closed territory, separated from all other lands by a ring of boondocks. Snakes and other beasts were welcome; sentients not so much.

The perimeter of Paradise was marked by a

steel palisade fitted with well-armed observation domes. The area outside was patrolled by flying drones.

Visitors were categorically unwelcome. If you tried to enter, the system would stop you. Most definitely.

The people of the commune, known as the Ammnushiti, were very peace-loving, yet at the same time insanely severe, disciplining their own people with steel-wire gauntlets sprayed with sulfuric acid And there were no outsiders there.

Paradise Promised was open to visitors just twice a year. This rule was haggled for by the system — or the Highers — in ancient times, and justified by the need for infrequent yet necessary control. After all, who knew what a large group of deeply religious people would be getting up to, isolated there like that? What if their collective consciousness had yesterday entertained the cheerful thought that all the other inhabitants of this world were freaking shitbags? And had begun doing push-ups and practicing pitchfork lunges together, with the intention of going to war against the rest of the world. And again there was the possibility of an epidemic; what if something suddenly began to spread? Initially they had tried to make their visits more frequent, but the ammnushiti had resisted, and the upshot was that twice a year a group of seven riders could pass through their lands. No wheeled technology. Even regular horse-drawn carts were not allowed. Because, why the fuck would they want their blessed lands carved up by the filthy wheels of something alien and diabolical? Hooves were less of a problem, for beyond the palisade ran the wide but shallow circuitous Silver Stream, whose waters would cleanse the sinners that came here. Yes, washing was necessary. People and horses alike needed a good scrubbing, and then you could move on. Why could the carts not been washed as well? Who knew? The ammnushiti with their meek smiles were clearly not planning to enlighten any half-wits. Nobody particularly argued with them, and they really had paid an insane sum of money, up in the billions, as well as handing over most of their assets, keeping only their holy relics. And technically they demanded nothing in return, no constant medical assistance, no protection, no food. They asked only to be provided with fertile lands and forest. Which they were granted.

And who would refuse such a generous offer?

I will give you everything. Just leave me alone!

And so they did.

There was just one problem: in the past year, not a single group dispatched on a routine monitoring visit had returned.

And then we show our faces, goblins from the asshole of the world, along with a ragtag collection of the toothed, the clawed, and the maniacal that had attached themselves to us along the way.

The thing was that you could not get at the ammnushiti if you were, according to their code, a blackened evildoer. And that included anyone who had gained hero status higher than second rank.

Why? Because heroes killed. They killed anything that stood in their way. You did not become a hero by picking flowers and gently massaging koalas' butts. To rise in status from kindheart, you had to kill, kill, and kill again. The ammnushiti considered, for reasons known only to them, that those who had never been higher than second rank were not yet so accursed and soaked in sin that their mere presence could poison these radiant promised lands. How could they possibly know the heroes' backstories? Easy: the system knew. The ammnushiti did not have to check everything, for they knew that the system would not let them be approached by any diablos, whether in their animal or human guises.

Who puts together an inspection team of five riders?

The task was not exactly key, but it was nonetheless important. Hence its solution was trusted exclusively to heroes of at least fourth rank.

In the past year, two such heroes had received a system task to get together an inspection team which would dive into Paradise and return with a report. Both heroes fucked up, received a good knuckle-rapping, and were instantly relieved long-term of the opportunity to climb up to the highest rank.

The next one whom the system designated as responsible (a month after the last fiasco) was Wormeus Magmus. And when he, feeling out of sorts, chewed on his finely chopped grass, looking angrily around (after all there was a reason why it was he who had been stitched up in such a fashion; some louse must have suggested Worm by name), the green-eyed lifesaver had suddenly sat down next to him. And she had said to him, "Don't take it to heart, bastard. You still have the chance to save your shitty rank, and you might not even have to do anything damp and smelly. Wormeus' spirits were lifted and he began to listen more attentively.

And this was how the story came to involve Elb the goblin, who crawled from the asshole of the world and crossed the ocean on goosed tunny fish, before kicking up a fair spot of bother in Zombieland on the way to lighting the legendary blue night-light.

My back story and the later-verified facts so impressed Wormeus that he decided to chance his arm with the thug that I was. I mean, what if?

The terms of the task were simple: you could only be accompanied as far as the security ring, the border with the lands of the ammnushiti; entrance was permitted to a maximum of seven heroes, whose rank could be no higher than two; and the heroes had to return within forty-eight hours, counting down from the moment of entrance.

The system had to trust the glorious heroes, or at least their leader, since there had been instances of people appointed by the system choosing members for a squad, only for the system to dismiss their candidates without any explanation.

On the way they were bound to brush against a number of sensors disguised as rocks, which did not allow the system to monitor the lands, but did let it know that the squad which had entered was actually doing something, as opposed to sunbathing behind the fir trees. The ammnushiti considered it a sort of ritual for outsiders, and those rocks had long been surrounded by buildings protecting them from any nastiness, and incense burned close by. Uh-huh. They closed the door to the stinking bathroom and sprayed it with flower-scented freshness.

No sinful intercourse. Yes, that's right, no screwing among the heroes. No way. Impossible. It was a great sin.

Obviously you must display total respect for the precious traditions of the ammnushiti. Among the dozen or so of these traditions that were listed for me was the prohibition of even partial exposure of any "lady bits," and the insistence on men looking like men. This last requirement mystified me somewhat, but I thought it best not to go there.

Weapons. Yes, clearly there was no shortage of danger, but nonetheless weapons should not be overly wicked. For which reason only break-action shotguns, revolvers, and single-charge rifles were allowed. No automatic weapons, and categorically no needle guns. No freaking inventions of Satan such as a medkit affixed beneath the left tit, and categorically nothing electronic or automatic. The sole concession that the system was able to force was the steel racehorses. The ammnushiti were not about to give their own horses to any filthy guests, and while there were sometimes live horses, it wasn't always a given, etc. etc. Basically, bring them, but be very careful. Leave them outside the village walls, etc. etc. And if at all possible, try to give those beasts the look of the living. Perhaps that was why the robot had been enhanced with a steel dick?

If after forty-eight hours the seven controllers — strictly the full complement thereof — did not exit with a report, then whoever sent them in there could expect a hefty penalty of a drop in status of two ranks. The returning squad members did not all have to be alive. If one had died or been killed, it was enough to bring his body out, or at least some vital part of it. Basically, if I made it out alone, a string of my comrades' heads slung over my shoulder, the system would chalk it up as a success.

So there you go.

The ballsy seven.

The tenacious seven.

The magnificent seven controllers.

I consented.

I didn't really know why, but I consented because I felt it would be something truly interesting. Scarcely had I given my consent and confirmed it than Wormeus asked me for a list of those who would be accompanying me. Which I provided. And the lump-of-dried-shit hero immediately relayed the names to the system, presenting them as his trusted squad of controllers. The response was instantaneous: accepted. Be at the border no later than six hours from now. Sigh of relief breathed.

Before listening further, I demanded an advance which included free accommodation, food, laundry, etc. for my squad in the Shiny Shack for the entirety of next week. I would also require a supply of specific munitions and weapon parts. And a bag of my favorite tart sweets, my stocks of which were running low.

When I received their promise that everything would be delivered within the hour, I went back to listening to the tales of the ugly worm who was afraid to lose so much due to someone's evil streak.

And there was plenty to listen to.

The system afforded the ammnushiti enormous respect for a rather odd reason: it did not consider them part-enablers of the death of the old world. Crudely speaking, they had a positive karmic balance. What was balance? Wormeus shrugged his shoulders. Who knew? The word just sounded good. But anyhow, there were different ways to say it, although the essence remained the same: the ammnushiti, who just like all other goblins had settled in this new world with the sole aim of survival, despite life before this having been almost ideal by system and Higher standards, had also paid for their sojourn here.

It was the equivalent of a rental apartment being taken by someone who was not only rich, but also had a scrupulous "green" reputation and paid for a lifetime in advance.

That was why the ammnushiti had the right not only to live in this world, but also to have some sort of influence on its future.

Meaning?

Fuck knows. Wormeus smiled again. The system just issues a small flat steel container holding some papers. The container can be opened by only a very restricted number of the ammnushiti, known as elders. If possible, each of the elders must open the container, read the contents, and tick the item he considers the truest. If it's impossible to get the container to all of them, then at least one of them must open it. A task within a task. And the more elders who give their opinion, the more bonuses awarded by the generous system, which is very pleased when everything goes as ideally as possible.

What's in the container?

Papers. Pictures, graphs, and text.

And what's it all about?

Nobody knows. The papers are inspected in private and a decision made quickly, and the ammnushiti spill no beans. What is espied obliquely is espied, and also disseminated by rumor among the hero class.

But what could possibly be the point of making decisions concerning the future of the world?

Again, fuck knows. Perhaps there's just a shitty poll asking questions like: what do you think about replacing our dying oak trees with yews, or simply planting more oaks? Or maybe we should just challenge tradition and plant camphor trees everywhere?

Okay.

Okay.

Just then, the delivery service showed up with gifts.

I spread my personal "advance" out in front of me and set to dismantling a revolver. My fighters, taking their commander's lead, quickly ran to snatch the remaining guns and do the same thing with them. Clocking our actions with ill-concealed encouragement, Wormeus opened his maw and was about to mutter some grudging praise. But when he saw the scorn in my gaze, he thought better of it and instead looked out of the window, bitter and offended. Then he announced unexpectedly that if we didn't fuck up, much would change in the political picture of Crontown. He would be able to climb higher, pull a couple of important levers, shift a few dusty cogwheels, gag a dozen poisonous mouths, and perhaps even poke out five impudent eyes. Much would be received by many. And very much would be lost by many. So very much that they would want to feel the gift of amnos on themselves once more.

Wait.

The gift of amnos?

That's right, the gift of amnos.

A little bit of detail, perhaps, worm?

Maybe you'd like a fork in your throat, monkey? Hmm, what a picture that would be!

Here Teulra jumped in, pink with drink and food and clearly in the highest of spirits, and occasionally reminded Wormeus that they were not just friends anymore. Now he owed her a big debt.

He replied that the task had not even begun yet, so it was too early for the raggedy cat to start purring. When she stopped hissing at the hero, Green Eyes explained:

In one of the darkest and narrowest side streets in the Crontown suburb of Hello, there is a large picture drawn on a brick wall. Drawn masterfully, to be sure. So masterfully that it is impossible to look at it without emotion. No matter how hard you might try, you will not be able to maintain detachment.

A picture of what?

People. People with overblown zits in place of heads. Zits with painted faces. Thin overstrained necks bearing huge disgusting red bubbles with white crowns of pus, and purulent streaks crisscrossing faces distorted with pain and suffering. Holding on to these zits with their hands to support the unbelievable weight of subcutaneous reservoirs of pus and grime, people are emerging from the terrible reddish twilight onto a narrow path, and as the path becomes lighter and straighter, they stride towards a golden twinkling cloud up ahead. Difficult to make out inside the cloud are thin gentle hands stretching towards the poor pustule-headed wretches approaching. Hurrying, pushing, kicking, and stepping over their own kind, the unfortunates fight their way through to the golden cloud, each in his own manner, some chanting and pointing at epaulets decorated with big fat stars, some waving golden visiting cards under others' noses, and some smiling sycophantically through the pain while simultaneously tripping up others. Many of them are looking not forwards but backwards — alarmed, frightened, and regretful — at the thick crimson twilight which appears to be charging forwards to swallow up not only the path and the zit-folk, but also the golden glow itself. One way or another, all the unfortunates are marching along the path and into the golden glowing cloud.

That is just one half of the picture, the left half.

While the right half... Exiting a golden-white haze are happy people with grotesquely narrowed and shrunken heads. No pus, no inflamed and painfully red zits, just regular heads with neatly combed hair and absolutely calm content faces. No one shoving, running, or shouting. Everyone walking calmly, smiling, and supporting each other. The thing that first catches the eye is that nobody is looking backwards. Nobody. They are all looking straight ahead, to where a blinding white archway is visible in the calm gray twilight, a ray of sun falling inside it.

Beneath the picture is the legend: The Great Gift of Amnos.

Basically, that is all. One small detail is that all the children walking towards the golden cloud have their faces deleted, while on the path leading away from the cloud, there are no children at all.

The picture is guarded around-the-clock, as well as being covered with a large sheet of Plexiglas and fitted with a steel canopy and lighting. At least three hardcore heroes protect the picture at all times, responsible for its preservation. There have been attempts by idiots to destroy the anonymously painted canvas. And that is the news from the world of art. That is the gift of amnos.

I see.

So, what else about this ammnushiti commune?

That is basically all.

Go, goblins, to the promised land, don't get anything dirty, don't get jiggy with each other, you lascivious mares and stallions, and do not get hammered. Run past the monitor stones, show the papers to the old-fart elders, wait for those wrinkly retards to put their crosses, then have a good look around and head for the exit. You have forty-eight hours from the moment you enter the territory of Paradise Promised.

Totally acceptable terms.

And a totally acceptable reward. Not the one where, in the event of a successful mission, Wormeus shitting Magmus would be heavily in my debt. No, that was a mere trifle. On the other hand, the system would be party to yet another weighty argument that Elb the goblin, who had crawled from the asshole of the world along with his equally filthy and stinking associates, could be absolutely trusted. What did that give us? Something, sure, but what? There was no way of knowing, but I was convinced of one thing: one good thing about computer logic was its consistency. This had recently been confirmed when Wormeus received a positive response from the system concerning the membership of our squad. No contemplation, no checks of each squad member, just immediate green light as soon as the smart machine clapped eyes on the name Erikvan-Elb.

And I wanted that to continue, so that no sooner did the name of Elb the goblin light up as a candidate, than the system would give the joyful go-ahead.

Squad...

I took almost everyone with me, leaving our gear in the capable hands of Rox, who began to dig around in the asshole of Hippo the exoskeleton, mangled in the explosion. He was aided in the inspection by our wounded, and those who had already been patched up but whose health I assessed as still pretty ropey.

Moving out from the Shiny Shack was a large mixed squad of about twenty-five bright-eyed, bushy-tailed, and well-armed mugs, which made its first stop at a safety area located at the end of a path which finished at Serpentary Landfault. Three heavily scratched trade points, tilting slightly, and one gas-powered campfire, which took some lighting and sputtered for a while, ejecting air. Here we left behind the troops we didn't need, including Klappa and Tigrala. Equipped with weapons, ammunition, medkits, other trappings of civilization, their brief was to keep an eye on the location until our return, maintaining control of it and exterminating any suspicious-looking bastards according to my favorite principle of chew-and-swallow. At the first sign of anything out of the ordinary, they were to put lead in heads. Otherwise, they wouldn't get out alive, what with being relative newbies. Klappa and Tigrala were experienced, but not that experienced. And I wanted to be sure that upon our return — bearing in mind that we might be on our last legs — we would be greeted by assistance rather than enemy fire. I also ordered them to conduct at least two field training sessions per twenty-four hour period, at least one of which should be at night. And if it should suddenly start bouncing down with rain, they were immediately to begin an extraordinary training session. Fighters must be able to act in any situation, at any time of day or night, and in any weather conditions. They must be able to act capably, taking out the enemy and not themselves. I also discussed smoke signals with Klappa. They may have been primitive, but sometimes it was the most reliable means of sending a distress signal or an urgent rallying cry. You just try to smother a fat gray column of smoke rising into the sky! Klappa accepted his fate with pride and outward nonchalance, as befits any warrior. But nonetheless I advised him to stick to the rules of their interesting game, which involved stones, knives, and nipples. After all, when something interesting and important was up for grabs, all too often Klappa would lose to the cunning-ass orc. Stroking the handle of his sword, Klappa fell into deep thought as he stood by the campfire, which at long last had caught alight and was burning with an even flame.

That left seven of us continuing along the narrow path, which soon wound its snakelike way upwards before running along the edge of a deep gorge.

Me, Tigr, Wreck, Jorann, Steak, and Burger, with Gabby being dragged behind. One of the horses was pulling a couple of heavy packs of food, water, ammunition, blankets, and other sundry items. And our horses were laden with more than just their riders, for I was not planning to eat or drink anything local to the ammnushiti territory. Nor was I going to use their poultices for treatment, or sleep in their houses or in any conditions proposed by them.

The past year had seen the traceless disappearance of a number of battle groups. It would be naïve to think those groups had consisted solely of blundering runts who'd all tripped over the same stone, scratched their heads against one another's, and died as one from the stench and concussion. No. They had not died here just any old how. You could not ignore the potential danger presented by a squad of seven battle-seasoned war dogs. And just when I was tired of being told tales of peace-loving violence-hating bearded sheep roaming the area. Well, yes.

*　*　*

The metal palisade was low and way more effective. In fact it was no mere palisade. It was two parallel lines of chain-link fencing, three and a bit meters high and topped with coils of barbed wire, the strip of land between them dotted with dome-bearing posts that looked like hideous mushrooms. No sooner did our sweaty mugs appear at the top of the path winding up the side of the gorge, than one of the domes caught us in its laser beams. The beams scanned, studied, winked, and were extinguished.

Access granted

How sweet and ordinary.

With a light squeaking and scraping sound, the first gates opened before us, their bottom edges sweeping away fallen leaves and litter from the concrete area in front of them. I entered the gates first, coolly moving deeper into the fenced lock and paying no heed to the decomposing corpse that lay ten meters away, beavering away over which were some large rabbits skillfully tearing off dangling fibers of torn flesh and greedily swallowing them. After briefly checking us out with beady red eyes, the big-earses returned quietly to their feast. Slowly the gates closed, leaving us in a cage full of predators. Though not for long. The second gates opened even more squeakily.

The road was open.

Access granted
Welcome to Paradise Promised

What did paradise look like?
Rotten. It looked rotten.

I had seen no duller place in this world since I'd forced open my swollen eyes on the island of the rawtarians. But there had at least been something there.

Whereas here…

Well, there seemed to be everything here. But there was one problem: everything had been arranged by someone dogged, meticulous, and in no hurry.

Moving away from the wall, we found ourselves on the banks of a small stream. I forbade everyone from swimming, but nobody was exactly dying to dip their tush in the paradise waters anyway. So the horses alone got their feet wet, and I ordered Gabby to be carried, slung over the rump of one of the steel horses. I doubted there would be anything deadly in the water, but why the fuck risk it? If somebody suggests you bathe your hands in the lands of a potential enemy, spit in his face and rub the gob in with the sole of your boot.

After overcoming the insignificant water obstacle, we entered a forest split in two by a glade and, winding our way among young overgrown bushes and saplings, we went another two hundred meters before the landscape changed sharply and we found ourselves in a park.

At first I didn't notice, blissing out in the shade for a few seconds, but then I realized that all the trees without exception were growing in strict rows. And it was a mixed forest, coniferous and deciduous trees together. Several rows of pines and a couple of rows of firs, followed by two rows of something broadleaf with thick trunks, before more broadleaves, but different ones. It was as if we were moving between ranks of different soldiers on a parade ground: infantry, artillery, intelligence, sappers, etc.

Bringing my horse to a halt, I dismounted first, and the heavenly ground struck the soles of my boots. Taking a few steps and picking up a gloveful of leaves, I exchanged glances with Jorann, who nodded her understanding and said:

"This ain't no forest. It's a reserve plantation."

"Reserve?"

"Supplies. A living store of timber for various life situations. These trees are arranged in sections, large groups of similar kinds of tree planted as far as possible from each other to prevent the spread of pests or disease. Considering the ammnushiti build everything themselves and are suspicious of progressive technology — the pathetic fools! — they'll be in constant need of lumber."

"Have they done a good job?"

"Hell yeah," confirmed the redhead from her saddle as she surveyed the endless rows of old trees. "Titanic work has been conducted here."

"I can see that," I said, before scrambling back onto my impassive robot. "Move out."

In earlier times there had been a forest here, the same as the one we'd left behind. But later the wild scrub had been chopped out and uprooted, and everything taken away, before earthworks had begun, judging by the relief, which was too even, just perfect, as though the hills had been leveled first and the gullies filled in, and only then the saplings planted.

Jorann was absolutely right when she spoke of the titanic work that had been done.

This was the groundwork for life a very long way into the future. The ammnushiti were planning to live in these lands forever, and were concerned with the long-term needs of their descendants.

The plantations were easy to move through, though the journey was sickeningly boring. The rustling treetops stretched for miles, the only obstacles being the occasional windfallen branch. And there was next to no animal life, which was understandable. You just try and live in such a gut-wrenching place! What we did spot was a few wolves, a she fox, and a black bear lolloping past in the distance. We also heard the stirrings of tiny animals in the foliage. We came across snakes as well, three large creeping vermin. Jorann steered her stallion skillfully so that the yawning Gabby was drawn over their scaly bodies. He did not let this gastronomic chance go to waste, gripping the squished meat with some unknown part of his body and shoveling it into another one.

The apotheosis of the tedium was a neat sign with an arrow pointing towards the "Modest and Glorious Town of Holy Haven."

"Jeez," I said through gritted teeth as we trotted past.

"Quiet waters run deep with infected whores,"

said Wreck, seconding my motion.

"Sharks," said Jorann, correcting him.

"Juicy to fuck in a backyard overgrown with lavender," sighed Burger, a sassy and outgoing middle-aged chick who was having difficulty getting used to her ill-tempered commanders and the weight of her equipment.

"Really?" Wreck perked up and turned cautiously towards her, trying not to fall from his feisty steel stallion. "Gimme details, fighter. Did the lavender scratch your behind?"

"Now then," I added to my previous comment and dismounted for a second time.

Stepping away from the barely noticeable path running down the middle of the glade, I hunkered down and parted some thorny branches which all but concealed something interesting from view.

Doubled over on the ground, hands gripping his belly, lay a dead goblin. Average-length fair hair, blue eyes frozen in deathly surprise, clearly defined cheekbones and angular chin. The abrasions, scratches, and blood covering his face could not hide the fact that the goblin was surprisingly young.

"Tigr?"

"Fourteen years old, give or take."

"I'm not talking about that. Take Burger and Steak and run in a circle around us at a radius of three or four paces. Look for his tracks, and the tracks of whoever was following him."

"Whoever *plural?*"

I removed the kid's already limp hands from

his belly, revealing two crossbow bolts buried deep in it, one painted red, the other yellow. And it was paint, to be sure, a mark of sorts. And it was unlikely that the same archer had fired different-colored bolts. Although… Pulling the bolts out, I compared their tips. They were identical, flat and serrated. They would be good against soft unprotected flesh, but against armor they would bounce off, inflicting no harm. Taking these two bolts to the stomach, the goblin had not stood the slightest chance. It was amazing he'd managed to run this far. And run he had, testament to which was the trampled undergrowth seven or eight paces further on. He'd been fleeing.

"Fine," said the beastfolk Tigr, "but maybe I should go alone? They'll only slow me down."

"Don't kick against the pricks. And keep out of sight," I said after a moment's thought. Tigr vanished, lost instantly among the trees.

Turning the corpse onto its back, I took a closer look at it. White homespun shirt with laced collars, voluminous sleeves, no seams or anything else of the sort. Coarse black pants, held up with braces and tucked into ankle-high leather boots. Half a yard away lay a crumpled and blood-soaked rag. The redhead turned it over, revealing a waistcoat from whose pockets spilled a number of multicolored beads and stones. That was all. No sack, no bag, no weapons, not even a pocketknife.

"What forest-dwelling monstrosity is this?" I barked, standing dumbfounded over the corpse. "Who wanders the woods empty-handed?"

"Maybe he's a halfwit?" suggested Burger.

"Or he dropped everything while he was running," Jorann retorted.

I turned around and aimed my shotgun at the trees. Then I lowered it. Emerging from the tree line, one paw held to his mouth as if to say, "Shhhhh, goblins!" Tigr beckoned us with the other paw. Then, repeating the silencing gesticulation, he made more hand signals to the effect that we should not bring the horses with us. And that went for Gabby as well.

"Keep an eye on the horses, louse," I ordered quietly as I stepped over the helpless prism enfettered in its cocoon.

"Huh?"

"I don't want to see so much as a scratch on my horse's ass!" Wreck ordered, stepping unnecessarily on the prism as he walked over him. "And I will check."

"Steak, Burger, stay with Gabby," I ordered without turning back.

"Yes, Commander!"

After following Tigr for a short time (I was less adept than him in maneuvering through the forest terrain), we came to a low hill overgrown with pines, which looked more out of place than it would in the middle of a wheat field. Why had the locality been planed down to the evenness of a table top, but the hill left intact? Although that wasn't the most interesting thing. Tigr indicated that last time he'd skirted around the hill and stopped beneath an enormous broken pine bough close by. Now he wanted to climb higher. Thinking for just a second, I nodded, realizing nothing truly menacing awaited us under that branch, and the scout simply wanted to take up a convenient position, which was absolutely normal for his tribe.

When I reached the pine, having rounded the hill, I heard a loud reproachful voice break into a shout before regaining its weary huskiness. The reason we hadn't heard voices before was that they were very reliably blocked out by the hill and the pines. That was also why they hadn't heard us, and why Tigr was not taking great pains to keep hidden, and had not explained everything. What was there to explain? Everything was clear enough as it was.

The hill was almost horseshoe-shaped, an arc of sorts, high at the toe and descending towards the heel. Good protection from bad weather. A tiny cabin built from dark logs, its roof new and covered with wooden boards like tiles. The grass around it had been mown and bundled together into a haystack, which was now being thoughtfully chewed by a dozen saddled horses. The cabin door was wide open, and in front of it was another pile, this time of meat. All that was missing for perfect harmony with the horses' haystack was some large predators expertly tearing and swallowing the dead flesh.

"Fuck-a-doodle-do!" Jorann exhaled, clinging to my wrist.

Twisting my wrist to free my hand, I nodded and quietly agreed:

"Most unexpected."

Teenagers. Actually, still children. But what, or rather who, was the pile of meat made up of? The dead bodies dragged here by the horses had been left in a heap, and the ropes that bound their hands and feet not untied. Variously colored — yellow, red, and green — crossbow bolts protruded from wounds. Many of the dead beardless faces had never been introduced to a razor. The same clothes: black pants and jerkins, white shirts, boots. That was the boys. The girls wore long blue dresses, from beneath whose hems stuck legs in stockings and stout boots, and headscarves. Fuck. The youngest one, who was looking at me with his one intact eye (the other eye socket was full of crossbow bolt) was no more than thirteen, maximum. I was being stared at by a child who had been killed violently.

And judging by the voices we had already heard, the children had not merely be killed. These teenagers had first been set free, chased around the woods like game animals, shot, bound, and dragged here to this cabin, where they were thrown in a pile. Then the hunters had sat down to rest on logs, setting their longbows, crossbows, and axes on the ground.

Strewn to the side of the pile of corpses were identical light-colored shoulder bags spotted with blood and bullet holes.

Just fifteen adult hunters, and already graying. They were dressed roughly like their victims, except that some of them also wore long canvas capes which were sure to be good at fending off rain, while others wore coats of the same material.

A thin and frightened girly shriek came from the cabin, followed by a dull thud. A minute later a grayish and reasonably thickset old man appeared from the dark doorway pulling a naked dead body by its arm. The first thing I noticed was the axe wound to the forehead and the rolled-back eyes, but I was not remotely surprised to see the quivering breasts. A number of corpses in the pile were also naked. And they were all girls.

"Big-titted sinner." The old man produced a somber sigh and thwacked the bloodied axe into a log. "Lend me a hand, will you, Hauns?"

"Sinful and sweet," said a man with a thin fair beard as he rose to his feet. "That's why I sinned with her twice. The temptation was too much."

"You shall pray for forgiveness."

"Yes, I shall. Oh, how I shall pray for forgiveness."

Together they took the girl's corpse — she was at most fifteen — skillfully by the hands and feet, chucked it onto the pile, and stepped away. It turned over and slipped from the top of the pile, the breasts flopping onto the face of another child.

"They're all squirming," croaked the old man with ill-concealed irritation. Squinting at whoever had been speaking before his emergence from the cabin, he said encouragingly, "You keep talking. You speak the truth. True words, kind words, edifying words, enlightening words."

"That's right, uncle Jacob, that's right. Thank

you for noticing. Encouragement from an elder of the Holy Haven is a great honor."

"Carry on, Theodore. Carry on with your enlightenment."

Theodore bowed his head in reverence. He was about forty, neat haircut, gray temples and beard, top lip shaved clean, just like all the other hunters.

"Why sin? What for?" Theodore raised his hands then theatrically grabbed his head. "Have you at least thought about it, you sinful progeny? Where are you hurrying to? I'll tell you where: to Hell! You are hurrying directly to hell. And what will you find there? I'll tell you that as well: death! Free, sleazy sex. There is no hope of paradise there. So? You have experienced the same here, in our blessed lands. You have experienced death, sex, and the loss of hope. Do you like it?"

A threesome of teenagers, almost hanging, with arms akimbo, was silent and did not raise their bloodied chins from their chests. Two boys, one girl. The girl had a crossbow bolt in her leg. Another two or three years, and she might have become a real beauty. Her hair hung loosely over her chest, covering her rude bits and smashed-up face.

"All your friends, who you crippled at the rumspringa for rejecting the pure life, are lying over there, mutilated. And who is to blame for that? You! Because of you, the young and glorious saplings died. Because of you!"

"All we wanted to do was leave, that's all! According to our ancient right, nobody is held against their will," hissed a dark-haired lad, quietly but furiously, throwing his head back unable to contain himself.

"Silence!"

"You raped them! Rape!"

"They were sinners."

Turning to my fighters, I muttered:

"When I start the ball rolling, kill the ones sitting on the logs. Don't touch the elder."

After waiting for their nods, I stood up.

"All they wanted to do was leave!" the kid yelled, looking at the victimizers with eyes full of hate. "They chose freedom. You led us on a path to a different life. You collected supplies for us. Then you caught us up and—"

"I won't argue. It was a deception, pure and simple." Theodore smiled gently. "May my viscera howl if it isn't true."

"It's worse there, you jerk-off," I said, striding out from behind a pine and raising my shotgun, which had already killed so many dumb motherfuckers that it was time to think of a stinging name for it. *Viscera? Yes, why not?*

The buckshot unloaded at point-blank range literally folded Theodore in half. Throwing his arms out wide, he flew backwards. With my next shot I blew apart the beater's head as he reached for his crossbow. The ensuing firefight left no chance for the lovers of sweet sin. Two of them, it was true, had managed to avoid serious injury and attempted to flee, but Tigr came crashing down upon them, trampling them under him and thrashing around with his taloned paws.

"Tsk-tsk." I shook my head and aim my revolver at the space between the elder and Hauns. "Tell me, just how sweet was it?"

"I..." Hauns exhaled with a deep grunt, grabbed at his perforated crotch, collapsed, and rolled around in the pine needles.

"Good fucking day to you, uncle fucking Jacob." I smiled widely at the elder of Holy Haven. "We have brought you some papers. Some amendments have been made according to worldwide practices. You need to put some ticks."

"This is..." The old man was smart and cunning, and tried very hard to wriggle out of the situation. A million thoughts whizzed around inside his gray head. He was trying to find a path that led to life, and in doing so he began to bore me. He would put up no resistance.

But how?

Which faith could explain that?

"Put some ticks," I repeated, placing my hand on his shoulder and forcing his ass back down onto its log. "Put them where you like, and we can continue our conversation."

"And if I don't want to?"

"Don't want to do what?" I asked in surprise, looking into the old man's raised eyes.

"Put any ticks next to the amendments."

"But you have no option. " I smiled softly and shot him right in the left ear, but not from too close. "No option."

When every last scream had died down, silence

hung over the hill and the cabin, and I, holding the twitching old man down with my boot on the remains of his ear, asked in concern:

"Are we not violating the principles of your faith overly? Are we not sinning by not knowing—"

"We fall shamelessly short of their sanctimony, lead!" The orc's mug contorted grievously as he slit the throat of one of the men. "Look at what they do with such relish. But what about us?"

Jorann lurched forward.

"You killed children, you monsters!"

The redhead's strike made Theodore wheeze and blank out for a couple of seconds. He came around to find himself straddled by a real beauty, his arms pinned to the ground by her knees. And the reason the unashamed sinner came around was the knife thrust into his bullet-wrenched balls and immediately withdrawn, before making a deep furrow in his cheek from his temple to his chin. It was the first stroke, a trial stroke, before Jorann set to shredding his face good and proper. I did not interfere, but continued to trample the elder's head into the pine needles, while observing the real Jorann, her face distorted in ire and pleasure at once.

"I'll tell you everything and do anything you need." From beneath the sole of my boot, the elder's voice sounded distant, like some deity. It had become impassive and confident. The old man had made his choice.

"Just kill me quickly. Not like—"

"You need raping with a club before you die," I hissed with undisguised hatred. "And then that club needs shoving down your throat. But you are a respected elder of the tenderhearted pacifist ammnushiti. Surely there is no sin on you? Yes, you killed a herd of youngsters, and before that you tortured and raped them. But is that really a sin?"

"It's a sin! A great sin! But—"

"Take that, motherfucker! Any more buts?" shouted the incensed Jorann as she stabbed her blade again and again into the remains of Theodore's crepitating face.

I caught Tigr's attention and quickly described a circle in the air with my finger, upon which the sagacious beastfolk set off at a run to check if we were alone in the locality, or if there were more ammnushiti on the way, desirous of something sweet.

"Where would they have gone?" the old man said, his head twitching beneath my foot. Interested, I removed it and looked at him as though at a roach. "Where would they have gone? You are living proof of the stinking villainy that inhabits the big world. You are a crazy ginger beast scraping the face from a living person. You started killing us without the slightest hesitation. What for? Because we saved the souls of wayward lambs? We saved their souls! They left chastened. They left as martyrs. And the golden gates of paradise will open before them."

"Nicely put," I said, enthusing. "Did it take you

long to think that up?"

"But it's the truth! You are worse than us. You came here and started killing straightaway. Just look!" The elder pointed at the hunters lying on the ground. "Each of them was a father. Every one of them! Each of them had two or three children, raised correctly. Children who cultivated the fields, gathered the harvest, tended to the gardens and livestock. Day and night. We toil! We think about our children's future. But what will happen if we let them go one day?" The hand now indicated the threesome beneath the tree. "They will leave, become impregnated with savagery and sin, then return here, according to their birthright, and begin sowing vice and flustering the minds of the innocent youth. It is better that we butcher them now, like hungry beasts, and fling their remains into the undergrowth, than release them and have them come back here later, leading Satan himself by the hand. We sacrifice the small for the greater good. Rumors of their deaths, albeit not one hundred percent true, will spread quickly throughout our lands and subdue the minds of the other juveniles, return them to the path of the righteous. So, what am I wrong about, uncharitable stranger?"

"Put some ticks!" I barked, throwing the flat steel container down in front of the old man. "Steak, Burger, untie the prisoners, take them just over there, and tie them back up. Then give them an injection."

"Yes, commander!"

"It will be done!"

"So you're the big baddie," uncle Jacob sniggered wanly, "sent by the iron god to our blessed lands."

"About your speech…"

"What did I say wrong? Nothing!"

"Everything," I said with a chuckle. "If three troublemakers muddy the clear water, do not wait for the consequences, but fling them immediately over the steel wall into the big world. And drop the hint that should they ever so much as think about returning… You get the picture. The only thing is that it seemed you were waiting especially, old man."

"What for? The wrath of God?"

"No. You were waiting for more girls to join their group. Young flesh that is so to your taste. What was it you croaked back then when you were dragging the dead kid from the cabin? Big-titted sinner? I reckon you had your eye on her before, right? Your mouth had been watering over the girl for ages? And there it was, at long last, the opportunity to get your putrescent teeth into that sweet candy."

A single fleeting glance at me made clear that I was not mistaken.

"I'm done." The elder briefly waved the paper at me to demonstrate the thick ticks. Then, as though obeying an old instinct, he quickly returned it to the container and slammed the lid shut, before looking me hopefully in the eye and saying, "Can we talk? I'll show you the grain of truth in my words and the mistakes in yours."

Picking up the container, I retrieved the axe from the log and threw it at the feet of the dark-haired lad, asking casually:

"Can you cope? Or aren't you big enough even for this?"

"I can cope!" The lad's strong hands took up the axe, and he strode purposefully forward.

"What are you doing!" the elder yelled. "I held you in my arms when you were three days ol... AAAAA!"

When a killer is unskilled and hateful, he throws all his strength into each skewed strike, oftentimes removing patches of skin and flesh, but not touching internal organs or vital arteries. Strike upon strike, strike upon strike. The old elder expired after the ninth strike. Standing over the corpse, breathing heavily, a viselike grip on the blood-spattered axe, the kid glowered at me and said:

"Are you going to go after the rest of the elders? If you are, count me in!"

"First, let's go have a little chat about your idyllic lifestyle." I beamed a smile and fearlessly turned my back to him. "I am Elb the goblin. And you are...?"

"I am Steard."

CHAPTER 3

AT FIRST EVERYTHING was good. Then everything became simply excellent.

Steard, just like everyone else born here in Paradise Promised, knew the history of his people inside out.

Their ancestors — the first settlers — together with their children, belongings, and some cattle, arrived here at the same time as the land, forests, hills, and even rivers were handed to them.

While it may be a sin to think so, everything was just as it was in the book describing the creation of the world: on the first day the light was separated from the dark, on the second appeared the stars, etc. etc. Or something like that. They didn't know for sure, since the elders did not let the books out of their hands, did not let anybody read them, and did not even speak their titles. They themselves, however, studied the books constantly and regularly quoted excerpts from them at prayer meets.

But he digressed.

Their ancestors landed here the day the new world was created. They saw the stars and the sunlight overhead; they saw the trees lowered down from the sky, huge clumps of soil around their roots; and they saw whole sections of forest dropped imperiously into place from the same sky. They watched as all around was submerged under water which began as a sea, before partly draining into the land, and partly running into cavities which would later become the beds of streams and rivers. Their ancestors saw the first rains fall, and with them the first winds blow, and those days merged into a windy, wet, and cold week. They observed cages being lowered from the sky, then their doors opening to allow frightened beasts to shuffle timidly out or fly out like bats out of hell. Some animals were delivered asleep, the bears, for example, who took a long time to regain consciousness, unable to lift their massive heads from the ground.

But there was no time to take it all in, for they found themselves surrounded by pyramids of heavy crates hammered fast together and covered in sailcloth. And using those crates, which contained their personal possessions, seed banks, tools, and so forth, the ancestors constructed the first sturdy shelters to protect their women and children from the wind and rain. Armed with spades, they dug deep ditches into the earth of the valley they were settling, to drain water away from the shelters. They hung cauldrons over campfires and erected canopies above them. Then the women got to work, and soon above the valley, above their new world, drifted the smells of porridge, tea, and fried eggs and bacon. Hearty meals were required, because a lot of heavy work lay ahead.

Thus the foundations were laid. And tales of this foundation were handed down from generation to generation, and no one could stop it, although attempts were made to do so, by the elders and their henchmen. It wasn't as though the elders tried to eradicate the story of their appearance here, the chronicles of their feats of labor, but they did try by all means possible to distort history and bring the elders to the forefront, zealously glorifying them as inspired leaders of people, no less inspired builders, and epic toilers who carried five sacks of sand at a time, etc. etc. Tellingly, it had been a hundred years since the previously elective post of elder became hereditary. And thus appeared the clans of elders, soon losing their humility, although that happened much later. To begin with everything was very good and rosy.

The ammnushiti. The name for the people appeared later.

Here, in Paradise Promised, gathered a number of large communities with faiths that often differed from one another. They believed in the same god, but their methods of worship were not the same, and many aspects were in conflict concerning acceptable technologies, prayers, the raising of children, the language of communication, and other important details. No few spears were broken in slanging matches and raucous arguments before differences were settled and the fragmented fraternities blended together into a harmonious and unified people of peaceful farmers.

Plots of land were allotted for villages, and construction began. Roads were laid, trees chopped down, rocks dug out, boulders broken, houses and barns quickly built, and allotments sown, and the first green shoots sprang up on the carefully and skillfully tilled land.

Those were happy times. But the following centuries were happier, the golden years, the years to be alive if you wanted to feel the happiness God sent every day. It was Paradise in its truest sense, and nobody stopped them existing according to the holy covenant.

The only exception to the covenant were the clear instructions concerning proportions and rules, according to which the lands of the ammnushiti had to consist of sixty percent woodland and another five percent uncultivated meadow. The ammnushiti did not have the right to change the locations of the sources of the rivers running through their lands and out through the steel fence. Neither did they have the right to start fires to burn off dead grass. These strict rules, spelled out and imposed from on high, were called the Balance, and were a constant reminder of the fact that the people were under constant observation, albeit from afar and no doubt by means of the metal mushrooms protruding from the ground, but nonetheless under observation. For which reason they had no business poking about by the palisade. Why expose yourself to the heavy gaze of sinners? There was no need for that.

Any other interference from the iron god? None. The agreement concluded was religiously honored. The ammnushiti lived quietly and nobody came anywhere near them. With the exception, that is, of the seven alien horseback sinners who rode fast along the paths and roads to their villages, where they powwowed briefly with the elders before leaving, also fast. But that was nothing. It was even necessary, and it would always be good for the youth to see a bunch of truly cheerless sinners whose souls would definitely go to hell. And here they came, malodorous, malicious, ferocious, saturated with dark, marked with the seal of hell, and reeking of death. That was how all the ammnushiti described them, since they did their utmost to avoid direct contact, leaving that burden to the much-suffering elders.

That was when the troubles began, as was noted by a now long-deceased old toiler.

And the big troubles began with this "nothing."

At first the elders simply mediated arguments and broke up fights, and knowing the wisdom of these elected old man, the people turned to them whenever help was needed. The election process was a long one. When an elder died, after his burial the people of his village would ruminate for weeks, even months, before electing his successor. After all, they did not want to choose the wrong man. But then the elective elders took on the burden of communication with the outsiders, reading through the papers they brought, on which each of them could put one of two marks: a tick or a cross. Nobody particularly understood this, but everyone knew it concerned the wider world and not just Paradise Promised. The elders grew in importance in the people's eyes, for they had a hand in the fate of the world and surely that would bring them closer to God.

But the elders soon became over-revered. Exceedingly over-revered. And this led to the current situation. After generations and generations, the elders had turned from kind wise advisors into blackhearted kings.

And, naturally, it was the elders who had begun working with the younger generation at that critical adolescent age when they had to participate in an ancient custom: first they lived for a week with their peers in special buildings which were to be found on the outskirts of every village; then they were given the choice of remaining or leaving. Nobody was ever kept in Paradise by force. Quite the opposite, it was driven into them from birth that getting in was unimaginably hard, while finding yourself deprived of the right to live here was a piece of cake, so it was best not to sin. This was a place for pure and lamblike grafters whose thoughts were only of God, family, and plowing. It was a place for those whose days were humdrum, whose days began and ended identically for the duration of their entire lives, whose routine never changed, which only added to their contentment.

Who needed uncertainty? No one. Not knowing what tomorrow might bring gave rise to worry, which led to perturbation, and if the soul became perturbed, a trapdoor would be opened to hellish whispers inciting you to strange thoughts and deeds. And that is why uncertainty was a sin. Every ammnushiti knew that the day after tomorrow, in a week, or even in a year's time, he would still be swinging his hoe rhythmically in the allotment, feeding the cattle, raising his children, and chatting with his wife in exactly the same way, and all this at strictly regulated times of the day. Late evening and nighttime? That was a time for sleep. Everyone had to be in his bed two hours before midnight, resting peacefully until the following morning. And if you were raising a ruckus at midnight, that was the time to award yourself a couple of whips with a willow cane, weep uncontrollably, and repent, before going to bed and contemplating the salvation of your soul. For rosy souls did not raise a ruckus at night. It was with good reason that the elders reminded them of the terrible punishment dealt to the sinful souls of nighthawks in bygone days: they were made to dress in ingloriously bright rags which all but denuded their bodies, then gathered together and heavily intoxicated with liquor, before being made to dance along to unbearably loud music. Then for the most egregious sinners, the process was repeated over and over, sometimes until morning, by which time they would be bawling their eyes out from the pain in their heads and the burning shame at the righteous humiliation the punishment had dealt them.

And so they lived happily from day to day.

And the elders gradually amassed power, while simultaneously gathering a cortège of sycophants each. The first alarm call came when it proved impossible to remove a flagrantly sinning elder from his elective position. Just impossible. His flunkies would not allow it. Of course no brute force was employed, admonishment being preferred, which involved each of them being taken aside for a private chat, which in turn might involve some entreatment or even some beseeching if necessary.

And how do we know this? The chronicles. Every family held a significant store of information that was handed down from the old to the young. And families communicated among themselves. It stood to reason that much of it was distorted by time and retelling, but be that as it may, the story of the ascent of the elders was identical in each family.

First their list of duties would expand.

Then their authority was widened and deepened.

Next they each gained the right to single-handedly judge any ammnushiti who committed a wrongdoing.

And so the elders became not only advisors,

but also judges, and the mass of regular ammnushiti were deprived of their right to judge.

And then —

"I'm fed up with this," I said, interrupting the dark-haired lad's inconsistent account. "It's all clear anyway. Then the elders seized what power was left with their dry wrinkled hands and started raping and killing the kids, right?"

"Right. Except we say that wolves ate the sinners."

"Meaning?" I asked in surprise.

"For centuries fathers have been finding their children rotting in the forest after they decided to leave," said Steard gloomily. "So viciously mauled it's disgusting. That's where the saying comes from. Sinful children are eaten by wolves. And..."

"And?"

"And we believed it. We believed savage wolves were roaming the borders of Paradise, sent by an iron god. Maybe not even a god, may be sent by Satan himself. But some, it is said, managed to slip through the steel fencing and escape, to find there were no wolves, only a safe road leading to the big sinful world."

"And you believed that bullshit?"

"What is bullshit?"

"You believed all that, but you don't know what bullshit is? It's what your head is full of," I barked, finishing up the cleaning of my revolver and returning it to its holster on my belt.

It was an open holster, leather and somewhat tight. On the way here I'd had to spend hours trying to learn, or rather relearn, how to draw the revolver, cock the hammer, aim, and fire in a single flowing movement. I was slowly getting the hang of it, but it was still far from perfect.

"I detect a lie."

"You wanted to believe, so you believed. But I don't believe all ammnushiti are that dumb. Surely you can't be such an imbecile as to believe in fierce man-eating wolves roaming the borders, without connecting the disappearance of teenagers to the simultaneous absence of an elder and his stooges? That's your main evidence right there. A lascivious old fart leaves the village with his beaters, following the kids who've fled to freedom, and a few days later their mutilated bodies are found and it's all put down to the wolves? Yeah right!"

"There's a lie rattling around inside my head."

"Here, take a drink." I gave him a flask of moonshine mildly diluted with lemonade.

"What's this?"

"The blood of a sinner mixed two-to-one with the ass slime of a saint!" Wreck growled, giving the lad a clip around the ear. "Drink, you spineless dipshit!"

"Hmph."

"Gimme some!" A girl lying on a blanket, her bullet-riddled leg covered in medicinal glue, extended a demanding hand, grabbed the flask, and took a no-nonsense swig. Despite coughing and her eyes goggling, she took another slug before passing the flask to her girlfriend sitting next to her. The girlfriend had the figure of a boy, a morose look on her face, and almost barbarian, carelessly hacked chestnut-brown hair, which she ran her fingers through while gazing somberly anywhere but at the dead bodies. After taking a glug from the flask, she returned it to her partner-in-misery, who took an even bigger glug of the clearly unfamiliar drink. Mistake.

"So that's where the real character and brains are," I snickered, placing my hand on Steard's shoulder and pushing him away. "While you're nothing but a marathon chronicler."

"A what?"

"Go away and pray," I ordered, turning towards the girls, "while I have a chat with the real leader."

"I want to go with you! To fight!" said Steard sulkily.

"Piss off," I replied.

Then the lad, with the aid of the orc's enormous paw, flew aside and landed on the pile of dead bodies.

Jumping straight back up, he made as if to say something, but I cut him off:

"Dig some graves for your guys."

"But—"

"Dig graves, bitch!" I shouted. "Fucking dig! Why are you alive anyway? Your girls got fucked in every orifice, and all you got was a couple of slaps round the face and a lecture about your life of sin. You should have been the first to die, before that old bastard stuck his flaccid cock in a child. Where were you then, huh? Never mind. If you tell me right now that you were knocked out, and tied up already unconscious, I won't call you a pathetic cocksucker. Were you knocked out? Were you unconscious?"

"I… I was… They rounded us up. We were surrounded. They were adults, strong angry adults, and I didn't know what they wanted to do."

"What didn't you know? You were getting killed, and the girls were getting groped! And I guarantee they were talking out loud, and shouting after you as well. That tribe of scumbags is always the same. They can't resist shouting after you that they're going to catch you up and fuck you!"

"Yes, but we thought it was some kind of test."

"That's one hell of a test. And what about when the first bolts got someone in the back? When the first girl started screaming? When they started tearing her clothes off and forcing her legs apart? When an adult piece of shit shoved his stinking member in her, did you still think it was some strange kind of test?"

"I couldn't think anything! I was frightened. I didn't understand. I didn't understand anything!"

"And you allowed yourself to be tied up? If you'd fought back, if you'd ripped out their throats with your teeth, or at least gotten your teeth into their boots, maybe one of the girls would have been able to escape and would still be alive now."

"Then they would have killed me!"

"That's right," I said, "they would have killed you. I get the initial shock which allowed you to get tied up. But why did you then not thrash around like a madman when one of your girls was being raped in the shack by uncle Jacob and the others?"

"I—"

"Dig graves! Bury the ones that didn't get rescued by outsiders reeking of death and sin! And start with that poor big-titted wretch."

"Her name was Hannah."

"I don't give a shit. Get digging!"

"Steard speaks sweetly, but that's all," the girl said with a sigh. "But he didn't incite us to leave. That was me."

"I see. Name?"

"Amnushka."

"Amnushka," I repeated after her, as I watched Steard take an old hoe, which the orc had found by the shed, and start digging the first grave. The orc approached the lad, stopped him, and offered him the flask of moonshine again. This time the sobbing boy did not refuse and took a couple of huge bittersweet swallows. "Can you tell me, Amnushka, what happened to the terrible sinful strangers who came here before us?"

"There are seven of them every time."

"Go on."

"And every time they are so... extraordinary," Amnushka added, sliding her attentive gaze over me.

You could understand her. Compared to them, we looked like aliens from a distant future. They wore homemade clothes, while we had twinkling cuirasses and other battle garb, firearms, helmets with transparent visors, and heavy backpacks on our backs.

It was a serious oversight on the part of the system. A big mistake. You couldn't go around introducing fugitives from a sweet and sinful future to a pastoral past. Want to introduce some controllers? Go ahead. But first make a few demands: they must all have beards; no prisms or beastfolk; dress the selected few in identical clothing; give them only live horses; and arm them with spears and crossbows. That's the kind of outsider who won't attract the attention of the unsophisticated ammnushiti.

"So where are these extraordinary people?"

"Some are dead, some are in the Forbidden Garden," Amnushka replied readily.

"I see," I said with a chuckle. "Dead or in the Forbidden Garden. Could you be a tad more specific, feisty girl?"

"I'll tell you everything. If you give me that rattling thing and show me how to use it properly."

"Why?"

"Because if you do, I will lay down with you, sinner. I may be young, but I am also ripe."

"And dumb," I added, wincing. "Don't overrate yourself. What do you want with a sawn-off?"

"I'm from another village, and we who chose sinful freedom were sent here by our elder, uncle Dooch. He's very old, and very kind and wise, but he must have known where he was sending us."

"Must have," I agreed. "They must be in league

together, all the Paradise elders. He must have consciously sent you to be raped and killed."

"So will you give me the gun?"

"Tell me about the Forbidden Garden. And don't worry about your elder. We'll be paying your freaking uncle a visit anyway. He still hasn't fucking voted, the sinner."

"He is a sinner," Amnushka concurred, exchanging glances with her silent trembling friend. "A fucking sinning elder! A fucking elder! Am I right?"

"You are. Now, tell me about the Garden. Otherwise I'll send you to dig graves."

"The Garden. The great Forbidden Garden."

The hooch was distorting her speech, but also disinhibiting her brain and loosening her tongue, so her story began to flow like a river during the spring melt.

The name of the Forbidden Garden was in no way connected with anything negative or sinful. Quite the opposite, the garden was more often called the Paradise Garden or the Garden of Purity. This was for the simple reason that it was created in the dim and distant past by the ancestors of the ammnushiti, who had chosen as its location a central and very fertile plot of land. In the center of the garden rose some rugged rocks, also not without reason. The garden was surrounded by a wall of rock, constructed by everyone mucking in together in their free time to split boulders, dig the ground in search of stones, and make bricks with a clever mixture of clay, dry grass, and ash. The wall was made of whatever materials they could find, and was seriously big. Well, it had to be, to stretch all the way round the enormous garden. In the wall were a number of wooden gates which were almost always carefully shut, and flowing out through it were a number of high-flowing streams. The garden was open to the sun and wind.

Many moons ago the wise ancestors, who lived by the experience of previous generations, realized that the plants might one day be devastated by a certain blight, which they apprehensively and variously named "white rot," "root rot," or "black slime." The affliction itself could be beaten, just so long as it didn't spread throughout all the villages and lands. For which reason the Forbidden Garden was created, to contain safely within it an abundance of fruit, berries, and other crops. Every year in springtime the garden was planted with dozens of new saplings. The fields were tilled, the bushes pruned, new beehives cobbled together, and flowers transplanted. In a word, a bunch of gardening was done. During summer and autumn the fruits of the gardeners' labors were harvested, some being given to the "little world," as the inhabitants of the Garden called the lands of the ammnushiti, and some were eaten by the gardeners. Some, the best and largest part, were conserved in a specific way and stored long-term in a special place right in the heart of the garden, beneath those unwelcoming rocks. There, in cool, dark, dry conditions, the ammnushiti's food stores were carefully preserved. Now they weren't afraid of any kind of plant blight, for they could all be eradicated. All sick trees and other plants would require destroying, and diseased soil removed to a safe distance, before new cultures from the Forbidden Garden were planted in the sad-looking abandoned patches. This practice justified itself at least three times, after serious outbreaks of disease among the plants.

Where were these diseases coming from?

Well, they may have been imported by stray land animals or airborne feathered ones. Or perhaps on the boots of sinful outsiders, if they omitted to wash thoroughly in the ring-shaped moat, which had been constructed in such a way as to not come into contact with any other streams or rivers entering Paradise, bypassing them via underground stone pipes. However, an animal might drink from, or take a dip in, the moat and then carry the infection into the forest and beyond. Basically, outsiders were to blame for any troubles. At least twice in the last five years an explosion of white rot had followed directly from the visit of a seven. And one time the outsiders arrived sick, after which a lot of pigs died, though not a single ammnushiti became infected. This produced an outcry among the poor folk, for apparently the righteous men did not get sick from swine diseases.

In any case, the Forbidden Garden saved everything that had to do with plants and seeds. It also contained ponds full of large healthy fish, as well as poultry houses, but apart from this, no other animals were kept in the Garden. Except, that is, for goats, which were used to clear away the old dead grass in the meadows and between the old trees. After all, it was not for no reason that goats came into this world with such a fearful sinful eyes: they were greedy, eating anything and everything, good or bad. But that was it. Various birds and fish, plus goats.

In the Garden toiled the old, the infirm, and the crippled, and naturally they went there exclusively of their own accord. Those who didn't want to would always be cared for by their children and grandchildren. You simply did as much useful work as you were able, and nobody would say a single bad word if all an elderly man could manage in a day was to carve a single wooden spoon or make a couple of twig brooms. Their business was to turn gray and die after a long and peaceful twilight surrounded by loving relatives.

Though many preferred to leave for the Garden.

Why "leave"? Because there was no way back. That had been decreed long ago. Someone had also applied the label of "druid" to those who left to live and toil in the Forbidden Garden. The elders searched long and hard for the joker, but in vain, afterwards declaring that such indecent words were not to be used. They were not druids. They were ammnushiti just like everyone else, only a touch more holy due to the fact that they decided to devote the twilight of their lives to working for the good of the whole community. Upon which, entry to paradise was guaranteed.

Why was there no return from the Garden?

Precisely because it was the Forbidden Garden. After all, what was a person? A person was restless, sticking his nose in where it wasn't wanted, touching things he wasn't supposed to, poking about in whatever he came across, rubbing, trampling, tasting, inhaling, disturbing the dust, and then visiting all manner of infection upon his house. And thus infections spread, from those who particularly liked to wander, spend the night abroad, and generally...

Yes, you could wash thoroughly, but nobody was insured against a tiny field mouse scurrying into the garden and spreading disease. Although as we all know, God helps him who helps himself. So surrounding the Garden was a wide strip of land with no large plants, where the grass was mown regularly, and large encroaching beasts were stopped in their tracks by volunteer patrols from each village, and small animals as well if possible. And everyone prayed that, along with the water, nothing entered the Garden which...

So far God had been merciful, and the Forbidden Garden had on numerous occasions saved the ammnushiti people from great disaster.

The druids, i.e. God's gardeners, toiled continuously, and appeared at the Garden gates regularly, communicating from a distance and exchanging news both bad and good, receiving the same in return. They also had their own cemetery right there in the Garden.

I see. Well, that's as maybe. But what have outsiders got to do with anything?

They sinned very grievously. So grievously that even reconciled ammnushiti couldn't reconcile themselves with it. The first of the sevens that weren't allowed to leave caused drunken devastation, getting lashed on the hellish hooch they'd brought with them, eating strange stuff, some even snorting stuff or putting drops in their eyes and under their tongues. The only thing they didn't do was shove lubricated sticks up their butts. They were totally off their heads. No respect whatsoever for ammnushiti. And with their loss of inhibition came undisguised lechery. They started hitting on the girls, whose husbands and fathers stepped in peacefully only to be viciously beaten. The hot-headed outsiders decided to cut off their hands. And so they did, at the same time shouting that it was okay and they wouldn't chop anything else off, so the dumbass ammnushiti could make it to the nearest medblock on their own two feet, where "Mother" would sew on new ones.

Who could sew on hands and feet?

If you lost them, that was it forever. Fashion a hook or pincers to replace your lost hands, strap a whittled wooden stump to your leg, and get on with your life.

Nineteen ammnushiti lost their hands that fateful day. Another two were killed. That made twenty-one in total. When the outsiders crashed out, full of booze and drugs, the elders gathered hastily and decided their behavior must not go unpunished. God would not forgive them if they allowed these devil's delegates to leave. Although killing them was also not on, of course. So let them atone for their filthy sins by working in the Forbidden Garden. The aliens were shackled in leg irons as they slept, their hamstrings cut, and their unholy possessions confiscated. Then they were sent to the Forbidden Garden, where they were greeted by the forewarned and woebegone druids. Or gardeners, rather.

The next seven left by the same route: into the Garden. Upon entry they were plied hospitably with alcohol, namely a particular kind of cider infused with herbs, which first tranquilized them, relieving them of their restlessness and clarity of mind, and then sent them to sleep. They drifted off in the cabin of sin in the first village, and awoke in the Forbidden Garden. Thenceforth the process only got easier, and, which was surprising, the gardeners acquired a taste for it and announced openly that there was still room for another fourteen sinners.

News of these events was not hushed up, instead spreading throughout all the lands of the ammnushiti. At a general assembly, everyone was ordered not to utter a word concerning recent events should they come across any outsiders. Not a single word! Whatever happened was for the good of the people. May the garden yield fruit! And for the imprisoned outsiders, may this portion be only for their benefit, to wash away their sins, if only in part. There was nothing to worry about, for what was twenty lost dark souls to a bunch of sinners? Nothing. Nobody was going to be overly concerned about them, and nobody was going to search for them. Everyone was to keep their traps shut, and escort any outsiders to the elders, who knew what to offer guests with a penchant for drunkenness and debauchery.

After listening to the last part of the now drunk girl's story, I laughed and shook my head.

Dumbass hillbillies.

Catching the girls' uncomprehending look, and Steard's, who had stopped digging, I spat on one of the corpses and explained the reason for my levity.

Would nobody be especially concerned for the disappeared sinners?

No. It was an important system task, and not just anyone was allowed in here. And the isolated incident of the drunken orgy and subsequent slaughter only served as proof. Before that, everything was okay. If any of the rednecks had their bearded faces punched every so often, it was no cause for concern. Basically, it wasn't junkies and boozehounds who came here, but serious goblins, and what is more, goblins sent by a no less serious hero. A hero who investigated any blunder hawkishly and would not listen to petty excuses such as "We had some dodgy moonshine and everyone lost the plot." Instead he would start slashing faces. And he wouldn't omit to make inquiries concerning his fighters.

That was the norm. That was the rule. That

was his duty.

I did not consider myself a righteous person, but if I lost seven fighters in one go, I would find out what happened to them. Even if it killed me, I would find out, because they were my fighters and I was responsible for them, and I would get to the bottom of it. If they'd done something shitty and been minced with good reason... well, the truth would probably come out sooner or later. And if, like the second and all subsequent sevens, they were plied with alcohol and had their tendons cut just for the hell of it, and were enslaved for nothing, I would arm myself with a sickle, slice every second ammnushiti's throat, and cut off every third one's balls. Those freaking gardeners would be uprooted.

Pretty much anyone would do the same in my shoes.

Conclusion? It wasn't immoral indifference that spared the ammnushiti, but the system's strict protection, which did not permit anyone to organize search parties to come here. If it did, the souls of the locals would long since have been shaken out, and the bearded sheep would not have hesitated to show where their former buddies were now crawling around on all fours.

Interrupting the inebriated teenager, I stood up and shouted at the dark-haired coward:

"Stop fucking around. Pick up your friends' corpses and load them onto the hunters' horses. Wreck, help the milksop."

"I am not a milksop!" Without even asking why

the hell he'd been wasting time with his hoe, the lad cast the instrument aside and, his eyes sparkling, continued, "We are raised to live in peace, not to retaliate, and to accept our fate with humility!"

"You're kidding, right?"

"No, I certainly am not!"

"In that case, why the hell did you chop up helpless old uncle Jacob with your axe, huh, pacifist?" I asked.

"Um…"

"Um," I parroted, drawing myself up tall and frowning. Hours in the saddle had taken their toll, turning my thigh muscles into lumps of pain. After all, the saddle had been on a metal horse, so I'd been sitting still, not kicking my heels into its sides or making it jump wildly. "Bind your friends' corpses and strap them to the saddles. Load your buddies onto the cart. Look into each one's eyes before closing them, and remember you are guilty of their deaths."

"Why are you saying all this?"

"Think about it," I sniggered maliciously before turning to the girls. "And what are you looking at so aggrievedly? That goes for you as well. Don't sell yourselves short. Fight for every breath, for every second. And if you don't want to, stay here in your peaceful stagnant swamp, live a quiet life, have some children, grow old, and become gardeners. Don't hanker after the big world!"

"You are very wicked," said Amnushka.

"Get your wounded ass up and onto a horse.

Do you know anything about this Haven?”

“Yes.”

“Do you know who the second in command after Jacob is, who would have known about what happened?”

“Yes.”

“In that case, you will be riding alongside me and telling me all about it.”

“Will you refrain from touching the peaceful and the honest, the noble and the kind?”

“Has that hooch gone to your head?”

“Yes. But tell me you won’t touch them.”

“I have no interest in the peaceful and the kind,” I chuckled, taking my inanimate animal by the reins. “And I don’t give a shit for the honest and the noble. But tell me in as much detail as you can about the others. Jump to it, fighters! Mount your steeds. We move out for the noble and honest village of Haven. Widen your smiles.”

“Are we going to do any killing?” asked the orc in hope.

“Not immediately,” I replied, glancing at the waggling head of the dead big-titted sinner. “Not immediately. We’ll wait and see if they offer us some cider first.”

“Cider with special herbs?”

“Uh-huh.”

“I mean, we don’t even know. I was just asking for dumbass Gabby.”

“Uh-huh.”

“Gotcha. I shall enlighten the others. It’ll put a smile on their faces. What about the corpses?”

"Don't you fret, orc. All in good time."

"Gotcha. By the way, Gabby's started hatching. Another hour or two, and a scary louse will come crawling out."

"It's just one piece of good news after another," I said, climbing up into my saddle. "Get him to shake a bony-ass leg."

"I'll pass it on."

CHAPTER 4

HOLY HAVEN GREETED US dumbfounded.

The emergence from the forest of six grim riders was a complete shock for the merrymakers in the arcadian green meadow. The ammnushiti were playing ball, their jolly whoops filling the spectators' ears with a sense of peace. It was bona fide existential bliss. The crops were beginning to ear, the children were frolicking, and the adults were smiling tenderly. But all the while, a good half of them knew that right now, somewhere beyond the trees, in a dark secluded corner of the forest, teenagers just like these were being raped and murdered.

I would not have been surprised if this raucous public merriment had been organized with the exclusive goal of distracting the community's attention from the plight of the kids who had left to pursue a different fate, and to get away from the hunters who had followed the obstinate youngsters.

Not far from the field abutting the village, which I was not going to inspect yet, began a paved road wide enough for two carts moving in opposite directions to pass each other easily. When my steel steed clanked its hooves on the first flagstone, the surface was not remotely agitated, merely responding with a sardonic ring.

The road was a piece of quality workmanship. But who gave a shit? I was more interested in the living.

And here they came, running with one hand covering their faces, in the manner of approaching goblins frightened they might be struck in the face. Unfortunately this meant that their balls were open to attack.

"Hehe," said the first ammnushiti to arrive, hastily wiping his mouth on his jerkin.

"Is that meant by way of greeting, goblin?" I asked with a yawn, looking down from my saddle on the crowd frozen in the field, whose forgotten ball was now rolling away, and the stupefied woman with a laundry basket who stood by the building closest to us.

"Welcome!" proclaimed the ammnushiti, snapping out of his stupor and managing to catch his breath. "You are the seven!"

His eyes ran over the six of us in turn, stopping for a second on the riderless horse laden with bags, and for ten seconds on Gabby's cocoon, which lay covered with dusty rags on the paving stones.

"The seven controllers," the ammnushiti added. "We are glad to see our foreign guests. We thank you for visiting us. And we thank you for your concern about us. Once again I welcome you to our quiet and peaceful land. Allow me to show you to our guesthouses. The womenfolk will immediately prepare a glorious and bountiful feast."

He was obviously repeating someone else's words learned by heart, and it would not have surprised me if these precise same platitudes, sweet and clearly atypical for a perverted puritan, had been used to greet the previous seven before they were poisoned with cider. But despite his attempts, this ammnushiti, an obedient student and teacher's pet, was doubtless one of those whose head was always dunked in the toilet during recess. He may have memorized his speech, but he was still a shit actor. However, this would surely have been enough for regular weary outsiders coming here more to rest than to fight, lulled by news of a tribe of enlightened pacifists.

"Are you an elder?" I inquired with a smile as I moved forward.

Remaining where he was, the man nearly snapped himself in two at the waist as he bent backwards, shaking his head.

"No no! Our elders and many of our other venerable members have departed on an urgent matter. But they will soon return. I have merely been appointed, with the approval of the elder, to watch over our village in his absence."

"They're not here," I concluded in disappointment. "Curses."

"They will be back soon. I know the elder has some important papers to look at before you are able to continue your journey. Please follow me, respect guests. I shall show you to your ample and comfortable lodgings, where you can wash your exhausted bodies and—"

"Papers? I don't give a shit for any papers. Your elder is a man of law, right? A judge?"

"That is c-correct."

"We've got some bastards we would like to present to him, for which we would like to demand a reward. We tensed our exhausted buns to the limit to put a stop to a crime. And not in just any old place, but right here in this freaking Paradise of yours. We helped you. And you poor little lambs are surely indebted to us now."

"A crime? Here in Paradise?" His lips formed into a sincere and beaming smile for the first time.

Forgetting his unsurety and fear, and probably his modesty and piety to boot, the ammnushiti displayed open jollity.

"There are no such sinners here in Paradise. Nobody steals. Nobody—"

"Rapes or murders?" I returned his smile in the same manner and nodded to Wreck. Then I raised my voice sharply and altered the tone to a gruff and direful snarl. "How fucking bizarre! Bizarre! Here we are, traveling at a leisurely pace and taking in the paradisiacal beauty, when suddenly we catch sight of stirrings in the bushes. We look closer and see bare-assed rapists fucking, torturing, and killing teenagers. What is more, they are master craftsmen. And they are preaching moralistic sermons to their victims."

"Um... um..." He understood, but he didn't yet understand that he understood.

Something didn't quite add up in his neatly coiffured head. The same could be said for a number of other elderly and well-seasoned men who were stepping closer. They had cottoned on. They realized who we'd seen back there, but they were still refusing to believe in such evil.

"It goes without saying that we hacked those motherfuckers to pieces," I said, my gentle smile making the chief ammnushiti step back a couple of paces and cover his face with his hands again. "We tortured them viciously, extremely viciously, and then we slowly slit their croaking throats. We brought those bastards' heads here with us, to stand trial in front of the kind wise elder, who must surely condemn their crimes."

Wreck pulled the drawstring of his sack and the severed heads tumbled out onto the road. Burger repeated the trick with her sack, adding more balls to the fun children's game while smiling sweetly at a girl frozen on the spot at the edge of the green field, to whose feet one of the heads now rolled.

"Can you kick it back?" Burger asked.

Bending over, the girl sprayed everything in front of her with a fountain of vomit, creating a fleeting rainbow which she stared at transfixed.

The orc then deliberately kicked another couple of balls along the road towards the men. Nearly running up against the boot of the main man, the head of the dead elder uncle Jacob looked upwards to the clouds, grinning joyously and gripping his own penis between his teeth. It was my idea to decorate the gifts in this fashion, and I'd ordered Steak and Burger to do the job, making them return briefly to the scene of the bloodshed.

"Aaaaa," the ammnushiti croaked.

Taking a step backwards, he tripped over, crashed down onto his butt, and began to crawl, scraping his boots on the paving stones and not taking his eyes from the severed heads.

"Those are the rapists!" I thundered, leaping down from my saddle and drawing my sawn-off shotgun from my belt. "So crimes are committed in your paradise after all. Those kids were dressed just like you. The astonishing thing is that when we, outraged by your filth, shoved a pine tree up his ass" — I pointed at Jacob's head — "as he croaked and gurgled and sprayed revolting shit from every orifice, for some reason he suddenly declared himself the elder of the village of Holy Haven. Can you imagine such effrontery? He, a mongrel rapist and revered elder, besmirched you. He smeared you with filth and ass slime. Well, obviously we were disgusted, and we thrust the tree in the even further, to mask the smell of shit with the scent of pine."

"Ummm."

Many of those gathered were retching by now, and some running away. Others, the hardier of soul, were hurrying to lead their children away. Doors and gates banged shut, and wailing could be heard. The field, bedecked for celebration, rapidly emptied.

"I... I..." Shaking his head, the ammnushiti continued crawling, rubbing his ass on the perfectly paved road that ran among the green meadows and fields.

I smiled a kind and pacifying smile.

"Do you know who these bastards are? Are they from your village?"

Silence in response. Even those still barfing suddenly managed to overcome their goblin weakness and freeze on their knees or in their double-over poses, immersing themselves in deep thought and staring at the faces of the dead.

"Well?" I pressed, leaning down to the eldest of the fuckers. "Do you recognize their faces, goblins? Maybe I should remove their cocks from their mouths?"

"I..."

"Yes?"

"I didn't... We didn't..."

"We don't know them!" came the decisive bark of a bent-over granddad with a thick cane in his hand and a malicious dastardly fire in his eyes. "We don't know them!"

"Cross yourself! " Jorann said with a sonorous laugh as she raised her shotgun and shot a hole in the old man's chest. "Lying old fucker!"

Shouts and howls were raised to the heavens. Rocking back and forth on my heels, I waited a short while before waving a hand and continuing with interest to observe the genuflecting ammnushiti men, the women wailing in the distance, and the howling children. The children were super anxious, the older among them eyeing us with anything but resignation, their hands clutching not gifts of fruit, but clubs and axes. For these twelve-year-olds didn't know that one day the time would come when they would be able to choose their destiny. And if they chose freedom, similarly fucking humble old men would appear in the forest to rape and dismember them before strewing their limbs around the nearby woods, before spreading tales of diabolical wolves chowing down on the recalcitrant youths.

I gave a hand signal and a cart appeared, trundling from around a bend in the road hidden by trees. Sitting in it were the surviving teenage ammnushiti. Or rather they were not sitting, but standing at full height and glaring at the village with unconcealed animosity.

"You sent us to our deaths!" came the shouts from the approaching cart. "You sent us to our deaths!"

So much tragedy. Had I, at fifteen or sixteen, lived such an emotional life and considered that anyone in this shitting evil world had cared about me? Unlikely.

"You're stupid," I said, leaning over and grabbing the deputized village elder by the scruff of his neck and pulling him towards me with ease. "You are unbelievably stupid. I told you we saw them raping and killing. How come it didn't occur to you, you fuckwit, to ask if we'd saved any of them? Huh?"

His eyes displayed no comprehension. Which was why, with a heavy sigh, I smashed my helmet into the bridge of his nose, threw the now unconscious piece of shit to the side, and turned to the next local, my attention attracted by his reticence and pensiveness. He too was frightened. Very frightened. Yet at the same time other emotions flickered alternatingly in his eyes. He was thinking hard, at pains to find a way out of this shitty situation. And he wasn't thinking only of himself, otherwise he would have slipped away quietly long ago. He was trying to figure out what he could do so that the apoplectic interlopers would not destroy the entire village.

I beckoned him with a finger. Forcing his stubborn legs into action, he staggered forward a couple of paces before stopping dead still with his arms stretched defiantly down by his sides. His expression was serious. No tears, no stupid smile, no traces of vomit around his mouth.

"I speak, you act," I suggested.

He nodded.

"You have been doing shitty business here, facilitating hunts for young goblins."

"I was always against it," he countered. "I had no problem with them leaving for the big world. But I made no decisions—"

"You could have killed all the bastards and established a kind punitive dictatorship."

"I'm not that strong and resolute."

"Clearly not. Listen here, mister weak and irresolute. You've all got five hours. And when I say 'all,' that means the entire ammnushiti people. Do you understand?"

"Yes."

"In five hours' time, all the elders must be here, without exception. Every last one of those old bastards. They are the founding fathers, right? And a founding father must surely be prepared to sacrifice himself for the sake of his people. And together with the elders, I want to see all the old folk who are in the authorities' pocket. There are approximately five of them in each of your villages. Trying to hide anyone will be useless, because those survivors have already provided me with a bunch of names. And you are a tight-knit community here. Nobody has any secrets. You know everyone's names."

"I understand. Five hours. All the elders and their inner circle of old folk."

"Your calmness surprises me."

"I am trying to make sure you don't start killing and burning."

"Good. But I haven't finished yet. I also want to see everyone who has taken part in at least one child hunt. Every one of those bastards. And let them know they will be killed. That goes for the elders too. I am just a goblin from the asshole of the world, and there's lots I don't give a shit about. If I'm being honest, I don't give a shit about anything, but I hate it when children are raped and murdered. Maybe it's the remnants of some vestigial fatherly instinct. What do you think?"

"I... I don't know. Oh God. Are you proposing I call them all to their deaths? And forewarn them about it?"

"Uh-huh," I snarled. "Every last fucking one of them. Warn them. And tell them they've got five hours. And if they're not all here then, I will obliterate your shitting paradise. I will shoot the entire adult population and take all the children away. And at the border of your lands I will inform the system that the innocent children of Paradise Promised are being corralled, raped, and murdered. As proof of that, I will take all survivors to the nearest medblock for questioning, and with their help I will find a couple of those motherfucking rapists who are still breathing and trembling, and take them there for questioning too. And they will reveal all. They will confess to everything. And that will mean your own personal end of the world, the end of your Paradise. Then more people like me will come here to seek out the rest of the population and send them for interrogation, and all those found guilty will be punished. All the children will be taken into care, and those ammnushiti who have done nothing wrong will simply be sterilized. After all, why should you have the opportunity to bear children if you send them to the slaughter so easily?"

"Oh God."

"Those who have spent years raping and killing must be held accountable for their sins, for the edification of their offspring. If they want to save their Paradise and their people, make sure they show up. In doing so, they will show you their fidelity to their principles. You've got five hours, and the clock is already ticking. Now go!"

"Yes!"

"Get a move on!"

"Yes!"

The ammnushiti, however, dazed and bemused, found himself unable to move.

Just then, with a deafening crack and a wave of stench, Gabby's cocoon split, filthy rags flying to the side, and a spiky leg broke through the chitinous shell, followed by an arm working its way through the stiff crimson slime. Then a familiar voice was heard over the croakings and gurglings:

"Sticky shit! Every crevice full of it! Fuck!"

With these words the combat prism stretched up to his full height, and with a roar, shattered the now vacant cocoon with his hands.

"Gabby!" Jorann squealed with joy, throwing herself at the praying mantis and locking her lips on his mandibles.

"Pincers on his tush," said Wreck, turning to me with envy. "Why do they get everything and we get nothing? He's got pincers on his tush, commander!"

"It's a tail with pincers," I corrected him, scratching my chin pensively. "Looks good. And everything else is bigger."

I took a quick glance over my shoulder and snickered. We were alone, not a single ammnushiti in sight, just a cloud of dust slowly settling on the road.

"Are we going to the freaking Garden, commander?" inquired Steak.

"Why the hell would we do that?" I asked, shrugging my shoulders.

"Well, the prisoners are there, washing radishes and licking turnips."

"They are heroes. Let them fight for their freedom."

"I suppose so."

"That said, I haven't decided yet," I admitted, surveying our surroundings. "Jorann! Stop sucking slime! Let's gather up the heads and hang them on the cart in garlands. Then we go to the village, make ourselves at home, get washed, and prepare some food. But only using our own produce. Then we wait."

"Do you think they'll come?" asked Wreck croakingly. "The elders and all the other flakes?"

"They've got no choice."

"Well they could just not show up. Go off and hide in the woods instead."

"So let them," I replied. "They've adhered to their principles for years, Wreck. If they reject them now, and don't want to sacrifice themselves for the greater good..."

"That's political suicide," grunted the redhead as she wiped her mouth.

"And physical suicide," I added. "Imagine you're a father who's killed his own daughter, justifying it as an act in the name of the greater good.

The time comes for him to expose his own wrinkled ass to an axe strike in the name of that same shitting greater good. And he suddenly refuses, gets scared, doesn't want to die for the benefit of others. What would you do, Wreck?"

"I wouldn't give up my daughter in the first place. She's my daughter. I'd kill any fucker, and I wouldn't give a shit for anything they said."

"Absolutely right." I shrugged again and turned my gaze back on Gabby. "Hmm."

I wouldn't say the prism's changes were absolute. The second wave of his evolution had left some kind of filthy foam on certain parts of his body. The first thing that caught the eye were his mandibles, which had become longer and bulkier. It wasn't hard to imagine such facial pincers breaking bones. His head was larger and more bulbous, and a dozen tiny sharp spikes had appeared on the curved plate of his forehead. Were he to headbutt someone's unprotected face... Spikes also protruded from his shoulders. They'd been there before, of course, but they now formed an ugly hulking stakewall. His re-grown arms seemed thinner, yet at the same time they were way more armored and spikier, which made them much closer to real insect limbs. Gabby kept flexing and unflexing them, clenching and unclenching the digits to test his new acquisitions. Nuzzling up to him again, the redhead observed these manipulations with acute fascination. Several feet away, an old man, forgotten by all, raised himself from the tall grass, picked up his hat, turned around, and a wink later his long gray-bearded face found itself a yard from the prism's disgusting armor-plated back. The mantis turned his head almost 180 degrees in the direction of the noise without moving his body. A clack of mandibles, and the old man produced a thin protracted whine, a dark wet patch spreading over his festive blue pants.

"And you, grandpa, were you also party to the torture and rape of little children in the forest?" I inquired as I looked at the frightened old man. "Or are you clean?"

"They are sinners. The punishment is meant purely to cleanse their stubborn souls," the old man squeezed out mechanically, clearly not understanding what his trembling lips were actually saying. "To lie is to sin. I can scarcely remember how many times me and my late brother went hunting, how many times we caught the runaways and pinned their thrashing bodies to the ground. But I vividly remember telling her, 'Repent and accept it as absolution. It'll be easier to — '"

"Absolution of sin by a meaty rod?" I chuckled. "Gabby, kill him."

The prism twitched a shoulder, but he didn't have time to turn around before the tail growing from the small of his back twitched and snapped its pincers, and with a gurgling sound the old man sat slowly down again, clutching his blood-reddened neck with his hand.

"The garlands are ready!"

"Move out!" I ordered as I took a closer look at

the tail of the prism stumbling uncertainly along the road.

It looked like a thick chain whose links were visible through the skin stretched over it. It wasn't very long, just a meter or so, and as the mantis walked, the tail either drooped, or suddenly rose with surprising ease and pressed itself against his back, the closed pincers resting just below the nape of his neck. The bloodied pincers looked just so, the thick serrated chitin grotesque and scary. Wave it in the face of a frightened kindheart, and he'd give you everything he had and tell you everything he knew. Judging by the smell, the ammnushiti had not only pissed himself but also shat himself.

"We'll have to fit you out for a new cuirass and other combat gear," I said to Gabby.

"Uh-huh," he replied, beginning to step a little more confidently now. "Jorann, I'm okay. Where's my backpack? I want something heavy to carry. Commander!"

"Yes?"

"Can I explore my abilities again? Jumping, bending, crawling, and whatnot?"

"Why, of course you can," I replied encouragingly, glancing at the approaching village and paying no attention to the squeaking cart full of young ammnushiti peering anxiously at their former ancestral home.

I did not have time for that right now.

Entering the village unhindered, we passed down a short street and found ourselves on a neat

rectangular square paved in gray stone. It was surrounded on all sides by the façades of houses with
windows shuttered fast, doors and gates closed,
and a small plot of land in front of each, enclosed
within a low fence and sown with flowers. Climbing plants decorated the walls and roofs with fra-
grant flowers, as well as the latticework arches
over the side streets and the large awnings sheltering a multitude of food-laden tables and
benches. It was clearly here that the gaggle of pacifists were meant to come, after playing ball to
their hearts' content, to park their butts on the
benches and eat their fill of the spread. And over
to the side were piles of brightly painted sticks,
hoops, and balls. Evidently playtime was to last
deep into the night. Well, yes. The children's heads
had to be knocked empty of all memories of the
teenagers who'd made so bold as to choose an alternative life path for themselves.

I could not but accept that such an apparently
idyllic village really could seem like paradise to
some. For which reason I put my boot into the
kneecap of the slack-jawed Steak, who had been
standing there for several minutes mesmerized by
the delicately reared sweet-smelling local beauties.
Gasping, he collapsed to the ground, where he
rolled around in feigned pain, before springing
back up and reaching for his weapon. When he realized who'd kicked him, he released his grip and
stared at me with quizzical non-comprehension.

"As soon as the thought enters your head that
you wouldn't mind a house like that, a beautiful

roly-poly wife, and a covey of kids, the wolf dies and a buffalo is born. Do you know the difference between those two beasts?"

"Um, a wolf eats meat and a buffalo chews grass?"

"A buffalo kills exclusively to protect itself and its herd. A wolf kills constantly and without contemplating why. Do you understand?"

"Yes."

"What do you understand?"

"That I don't want to be Steak. Because it's like a piece of buffalo butt taken down by wolves."

"You're learning," I said approvingly. "Earn yourself a new name."

"Yes sir. But my name is actually—"

"Earn another name."

"I understand, lead. Screw paradise! Give me hell! To live with wolves is to mince people."

Knitting my brow, I waved him towards the cart and ordered him to help with the unloading, the food, and everything else. There were too few of us for me to assign just one job to each fighter. I was not about to make my veterans do the cooking, because peaceful pacifists or not, these were the locals' lands, their motherland. Even a worm would try to bite you if you stepped on it. And not only had we walked over them with our steel-soled boots and hooves, but we had also issued a blinding ultimatum. We were like demons appearing straight from hell, and the false holy men would definitely try to send us back there.

"Lead?"

"Don't relax, orc," I said, with a nod up at the roofs. "Get Big Ears and Burger up on that roof, lying down and facing in opposite directions to keep an eye on the rooftops and side streets."

"What are these dumb bastards going to do?" the orc asked, his brow knit with a certain frustration. "They're mental insipid spackers, good for nothing. All they can do is pray."

"I agree," I concurred.

"They've plowed up everything around here," Jorann noted, trying to pry something from a gap in Gabby's armor with a knife. "They've changed the landscape."

"That wasn't them," the orc retorted.

"It was their ancestors who did the planning," I said. "All these slugs do is live according to a historical set of strict rules and regulations for life. This is when to till the earth, this is when to sow the wheat, this is when to gather the berries and mushrooms, this is when to rape and murder the sinful teenagers, this is when to sing sweetly in the chapels. Wreck?"

"I'm on it."

After passing on my commands, Wreck turned and dropped his jaw in astonishment. Looking at the side-street entrance framed with luxurious white flowers, I chuckled knowingly. It wasn't every day you saw and heard things like that.

"Cursed sinners! Defilers! Murderers!" Running at us yelling was a man in a helmet with the visor lowered, brandishing a sawn-off with extreme lack of skill. The howling fool was thirty paces away, but closing rapidly as he sprinted over the flagstones of the square.

It was his undoing. Flagstones were not concrete. Cobblestones were not concrete. You had to lift your feet higher if you didn't want to trip.

And then it happened, the sinners' menace did trip, pulling the trigger as he fell, and we watched as he transformed his right foot into a clump of shredded flesh.

"AAAAAAA!" As he tumbled over the cobblestones, his helmet clattering resonantly against them, the screaming miscreant looked...

How I laughed. Looking at the bleeding idiot, I chortled to realize my reaction was too emotional, and that the reason for this was an oncoming flashback. Once again I was overwhelmed by the half-forgotten sensation of impending delirium loaded with snippets of frayed recollection. Although for now I managed to reign it in.

"What are you laughing at, you monsters?" The piercing squeal came from a woman running out of the same side street, who threw herself down on her knees next to the wounded man. "He's a human being! He's badly wounded. He's bleeding. And you're laughing. He needs help."

"Wreck."

"Yes."

"If that bawler's still here in ten seconds, shoot him in the other foot."

"Gladly," the orc replied, before shouting at her, "Hey, you goody-goody whore! Tense your buns, shut your cake hole, and get your husband or your stupid son back in the asshole he crawled from! I'm going to count to five, and then I'm going to shoot him in his dumbass head."

"Who are you to—"

"Five! Four!"

"Oh God! Oh God!" Grasping the hand of the injured man, the woman got a grip on herself and dragged him back into the side street with surprising strength and speed. They made it within the allotted time frame and hid behind a fence. Somewhere down there a gate banged shut, before everything went quiet. For about five seconds.

Then from the next side street came another prolonged howl, a thin and trembling mouse-squeak battle cry.

"He's packing an axe," Tigr warned from the edge of the roof, gently stroking the rifle lying by his side. "And there's another pacifist running silently behind him, with a shotgun in his left hand and a pitchfork in his right. Permission to—"

"Knock yourself out," I said, gesturing with one hand while taking my water flask from my belt with the other.

A shot rang out, followed by shouts from the street. Then silence. Then another grating quivering "Aaaaa!" this time filled with much more terror and surprise. Then an absolutely enchanting:

"The bullets of sinners beget steel from hell. Steel from hell begotten in our loins. Steel from hell. Oh, mother of mine. Oh, father of mine. Burning hellish steel is begotten in our loins and our wombs. Their sinful seed. Their accursed seed has entered me and spawned. Spawned. Oh God!"

Then another couple of seconds' silence, before another shout, from someone else this time:

"What have I done? What have I done with his rump? What have I done with my neighbor's rump?"

Without waiting for an answer, the beastfolk, snorting with laughter and reloading his rifle, explained:

"I was aiming for his belly, but I hit him lower down. The smarting pain made him stop quickly, but the guy running behind him with the pitchfork didn't stop, and he sunk the pitchfork into his tush at such an angle that all three prongs came out of the bullet's exit wound. And he decided—"

"That the bullet had burst in his belly. Shoot that other bawler. But don't kill him, just wound him enough to make him suffer."

"Belly or balls?"

"Sounds good. The more wounded there are, the more trouble there is with them, the more fear there is, and the less the desire to attack the sinners. Keep a constant eye on them. I'm going to rest for a bit."

"Yes sir, lead!"

"All of them! They've only got shotguns and pitchforks. There might be the odd rifle confiscated from previous sevens, and they might find revolvers or even pistols as well. Maybe even compact automatics, easy to hide in the pants. Get up close and put a close-range volley in any heroic halfwit who reckons himself overly hardcore. Basically, don't relax. Don't remove your armor, and keep your visors down so no one pops a cap in your faces. Don't let anyone get close to you."

"Yes sir!"

"Compact automatics in the pants? You mean small and rapid-firing?" Wreck asked, surveying the now noiseless houses. "Ha! Just as I thought. Dumb bastards. Shitting rabbits. If one more armed scumbag shows up, we'll fell the freaking lot of them!"

The sound of another round being fired. Followed by another shout from the street, which morphed into a moan of real pain before fading away to silence.

Settling down against a wall so I was concealed by the carts on one side and a woodpile on the other, I fell silent and zoned out in a flash.

Crimson-lime isocitrate.

My pocket held something else recommended by Leo Skinflint. I'd received it lieu of an advance, but I decided not to use it just yet. I would wait and see where the flashback took me.

*　*　*

Working expertly with a heavy hammer, he was skillfully affixing a picture to the wall of an old brick building. The snuggly abutting municipal boxes of "cozy economy-class social housing" had been built as close together as possible in a place where a desolate promontory had once stretched, now transformed into a stifling humid littoral.

Thirty yards away the sea roared, encroaching closer and closer with every passing day. Very soon everything would disappear into the water, and tens of thousands of paupers would become vagabonds. Then social care would disappear, along with the regular government drone deliveries of medicines, food rations, and vitamins that helped children grow up not totally deformed by lack of fresh fruit and vegetables. Then there was fiber. Fiber was delivered by the hundredweight by the caring government, for it was important that poop moved along the bowels rather than just sitting there turning sour, which would have unhealthy and putrescent consequences. But how did poop appear in the bowels anyway if most of the citizens of this coastal town only ate once a day?

Lowering myself noiselessly from the wet roof, I leaned against the wall five paces from the wide and once muscular, though now merely fleshy back of the hammer-wielding heavyweight. Of course my descent could not have been totally silent, and I was acting out of firmly ingrained habit, although I knew that the even tapping of the hammer would be decent enough sonic camouflage for my movements.

As was customary for a serial killer, the presence of such a noisy instrument allowed for calm and unhurried action.

The naked dead woman fastened to the wall with steel spikes was about forty. Her saggy flabby belly, and full hefty breasts with their enormous nipples sucked off by her children, shuddered with every strike of the hammer. Her head was not moving anymore, for the spike through her left eye had pierced the back of her head and fixed her skull to the wall, and at such an angle that the corpse seemed to be staring into the sky. Her arms were spread out and raised, and her legs parted wide, too wide. Over the body flickered an almost dead LED lamp, the likes of which were a common sight around the town.

After hammering home the last spike, the heavyweight decided to take a breather. I did not disturb him, continuing with interest to observe him breathing heavily and grunting as he massaged his lower back and biceps. After holstering his hammer in a loop on his belt, he took a piece of paper from his breast pocket, and illuminating it with a tiny flashlight, he read from it, mumbling and snivelling, while draining the remaining contents of a bottle in a few greedy glugs. The smell of moonshine added to the stench of the place. I waited patiently. Finishing his reading and catching his breath, the man took something else from his belt bag. It was a can of white paint, which he now sprayed generously along the wall under the dead woman's arms, drawing a most artless pair of angel's wings with dismally drooping feathers. Putting the can away, he then unsheathed a kukri and sliced it across the woman's belly, opening it and allowing her innards to spill out and hang there in a huge crimson-black lump. Swallowing heavily, cussing, gagging, and clearly at pains not to vomit, the heavyweight adjusted the bloody clod with the tip of the blade, before producing more items (I could guess what) from his breast pocket, and tinkering with the entrails. Then he stepped hastily away with relief, leaned a shoulder against the wall, and admired his masterpiece by the light of the dying lamp.

Hung on the wall, with her legs, arms, and wings outspread, was a dead eviscerated angel. A number of purposefully thick and bright-orange cocktail straws and five similarly bright cocktail umbrellas protruded from her now external guts.

"Oh Lord," gurgled the heavyweight, and quickly covered his mouth with his hand. "Okh Lorshd."

"You are a remarkable serial killer, Rana Djang," I said, not moving from my spot. "Most remarkable. And you obviously love your difficult business."

"Oh Lord!" The startled heavyweight jumped, and turned sharply around to face me. "Son of a bitch!"

I pulled my half mask down and moved forward, leaning slightly away from the wall that had been camouflaging me so well with its shades of orange, brown, and green that were so close to the settings of my smart clothes. Looking me over, Rana Djang, a brooding thickheaded businesslike giant, shut his trap and froze. Only his massive hands were still moving, slowly away from his tactical belt, his fingers spread in a clear display that he was unarmed.

"Normally serial killers get a kick out of their business," I continued, returning my half mask to its position in order to filter out the stink that was collecting in the narrow alleyway. "But for some reason you are quite the opposite. Talk straight, motherfucker. Are you the much-feared Angel Ripper, or whatever he's known as by the locals and the press? Are you the one who's plunged this shitty little town into terror by stealing ladies from their boudoirs? The one who forces their menfolk stay at home, making them give up their urgent and vital contract work, which in turn has forced a mighty corporation to hire me? And what about the children? Do you kill them as well? Have you created the same freaking bloody horrors with infants as well?"

"I don't touch children! Never! I only ever slice women. And anyway, are these real women? They're whores. Cheap whores who will suck you off for a cigarette and a slug of bourbon. Why should such tarts be allowed to live?"

"I see. So it is you after all, the Ripper of Angels, yes?" I asked, taking a couple of steps towards the wheezing grunting heavyweight, who had sometime been a powerlifter, but had turned into a fat hog yet still retained some of his former strength.

"It's... complicated," Rana Djang uttered hoarsely, pulling a small silver object from his belt and launching it in my direction. He followed this up by jumping at me with his bloodied kukri held out in front.

* * *

"Jeez," I sighed, and was immediately overcome by the urge to vomit.

Suppressing the urge with enormous difficulty, I stood on all fours for a while, then slowly straightened up, drank the remains of the water in my flask, and repeated, "Jeez."

I recalled the flashback I'd just had. I remembered it! Perhaps not all of it, but at least now it wasn't a mishmash of snatches retrieved from who knew where. Moreover, I remembered the whole miserable scary story from the island town, from the very moment I arrived there to how it had all ended. There were gaps, but I sensed nothing major had been lost.

Standing motionless, I hurriedly flicked over and over through the recollections in my head, trying to fix them in my consciousness so as not to forget them again. Catching myself about to make a dangerous move, I forced myself to withdraw my hand from the pocket containing the bag of tears. Not now. But definitely later. Together with the recommended tablet.

"Dead Devilkins," I whispered, mentally reading a newspaper headline that flashed before my eyes.

Everything had begun with a call, an enormous reward, a request to hurry in return for a fantastic bonus, and meager slivers of information and huge power.

I remembered. That time I'd conducted the investigation in my trademark fashion, quickly and mercilessly.

And Rana Djang, who had lunged at me with his curved hatchet, hadn't lied: everything was very, very complicated.

"What did I miss?" My question was addressed to Gabby, who stood motionless in a somewhat strange pose nearby, obviously protecting his comatose commander.

The strangeness of the pose was that he sat using his tail for support, the pincers stuck into the ground. His legs were even crossed, and he seemed perfectly comfortable. His unblinking eyes were concentrated on his new clawed digits, located on his new hand in a strange indentation in his bony blade. When he straightened his fingers and closed them together, they formed a continuous blade.

"Fighter," I said, reminding the impudent louse of my presence.

Snapping out of his reverie, the prism shook his ugly head and announced joyfully:

"I can hold a cup of coffee in my hand again."

"Now that is an achievement," I said. "But can you hang from your fingers?"

"Yes! My grip is firm. I've already tried. I've even done some pull-ups."

"One-handed?"

"Uh-huh."

"How many?"

"After forty-eight I got bored of counting. And

pull-ups."

"I see. So, what did I miss?"

"One attack. Eleven locals, clumsily armored and bedecked with weapons. Firearms. Felling them was a joke. Jorann counted the trophy guns. Counting one revolver and one rifle, or one revolver and one shotgun, for each heroic mug, we captured about fifteen heroes' worth of weapons. So the locals are now mildly less armed, which makes life easier for us."

Thinking for a second or two, I shook my head and said:

"We still can't relax."

"Agreed."

"What else?"

"In terms of loot? Eleven sets of armor: cuirasses, helmets, load-bearing vests, boots, and even the backpacks they... This'll make you laugh, commander."

"What will?"

"Their backpacks were stuffed to the brim with bandages, herbal ointments, and needles and threads for stitching wounds. What the fuck? I get the impression they thought they could dress their wounds in the heat of battle. Bandage them with a squirt of holy unguent, and Bob's your uncle, no more injury. Hurrah! Oh yes, they also had strips of fabric with prayers or something written on them. What do they need those for? And why the hell did others come running to them, unarmed fools shouting those same prayers and at the same time cursing us? It's nonsense! Lousy nonsense!

They're all rotten around here, heads full of pus and shit."

"You seem strangely cheerful."

"I've got fingers again, commander. It might not seem much, but it's so nice to be able to scratch my ass again."

"Good reason," I said, accepting the weightiness of his argument. "Get ready to take charge of your own personal dirty dozen, louse. It will be a mixed dozen, three or four goblins, and all the rest miserable ugly fuckers like you."

"Gotcha."

"Your authority over them will be absolute."

"Gotcha."

"No, you don't got nothing, louse," I said with a shake of my head. "When I say absolute authority—"

"I understand, commander," Gabby said, interrupting me. "And it'll be easy."

"Really?"

"I'll just copy you. Lots of humiliation. And pain, pain, and more pain. And a drop of praise every seven days, and even then not to everyone, so that the others die of envy."

"You've almost got it," I said encouragingly, before casting a glance at the louse's "shooting stick." "Comfortable?"

"Perfectly. A proper multifunctional item. There's also this..."

Standing up, the louse turned his back to me, stretched his tail towards me, and unclenched his pincers. Then he twisted them slightly, and from out of them came a five-centimeter-long thick chitinous spine, the tip of which produced a drop of thick yellowish liquid.

"Did you forget to shake after taking a piss?" I asked, looking with interest at the truly snazzy appendage. I was even a little bit jealous.

In appreciation of my joke, the prism clacked his mandibles, one of which was adorned with a painted red smiling face, and then withdrew the spine back into the pincers, saying:

"A wicked bit of kit. I reckon it's poison. It needs testing out."

"Haven't you tested it on the idiot pacifists yet?"

"I only discovered it myself three minutes ago. There's something else as well."

"And what might that be?"

"Well, the way I discovered the spine hidden in my tail, it was like someone had told me." The prism's unblinking eyes stared at me. "Someone sitting inside me. A second…"

"Insect?"

"Uh-huh. She somehow tipped me the wink about the spine, and I even learned exactly how to twist the half-opened pincers slightly before striking, so the spine pokes out."

"She?"

"She!" Gabby said confidently. "The gluttonous dumb bony bitch living inside me. I've decided to call her Clash."

"Don't tell Jorann," I said with a chuckle, "or she'll dig Clash out of you with a spoon and a nail file."

"Well, yes. Just don't laugh, commander. It's just the feeling I get. And she seems so kind and smiley, caring and brave. She lives somewhere here." The louse's new hand described a circle on the left side of his chest.

"Think less, act more," I barked, stretching. "Get your cuirass on."

"It doesn't fit."

"I don't give a toss, get it on. Cover your head first."

"Gotcha."

"Was I out for long?"

"Four hours. The first hour you were twitching and muttering something about sliced-up dancing children and some angel chick with a decorated Christmas tree up her tuckus. You were saying something about dark streets as well, asphalt flooded with blood, and how rinsing fleeced human skin is easiest in a washing machine with a couple of capfuls liquid soap, but preferably unscented, because it's unnerving when dead skin smells of coconut. Then you were quite and slept for the next three hours."

"Good."

"Did you have a nightmare?"

"Nah." I shrugged my shoulders. "Just something about daily life before. Who's this coming to pay us a visit?"

"All the same lot," came a voice from above. "Don't even bother getting up, lead, we can cope by ourselves."

"Again." Gabby was obviously trying to frown, but his chitinous face wouldn't allow it, and he could only express his emotions by clacking his mandibles angrily. "Squad dead ahead!"

"Squad dead ahead," I agreed, taking up my sawn-off. "Looks more like shit on legs actually. And…" Freezing in midstep, I lowered my overly dangerous weapon. "Shit! Everybody put your shot guns away. I repeat, no fucking shot, of any size! Shit!"

A squad of thirty ammnushiti were heading towards us, all of them armed. Ten of them were senile old fuckers who lived in the resignation of knowing what shit went on here. Another ten were girls between thirteen and sixteen, clearly inexperienced in handling the axes and pitchforks they wielded. And the last ten were mere children, the oldest about eleven, if that. A dismal scowl on his face, he was lugging an axe that was too big for him.

"This is paradise?" I asked into space, looking for an observation dome out of habit. "Is this fucking paradise? Children on the attack?"

As though in response, a quavering nasal voice from behind the houses came:

"They killed your parents. Mercilessly. Those heathen sinners killed innocents. Look at those innocent bodies lying there. Vengeance is a sin! Vengeance is prohibited. But it is our duty to cleanse our sacred lands of the sinful rabble. It is the duty of every ammnushiti. We shall banish them. We shall banish that filth from Paradise

Promised!”

“Tigr!” The word came out like the hiss of a snake.

“Lead?”

“Go fetch the loudmouth.”

“Yes sir.”

“Don’t kill him. Bring him here in one piece. And look lively.”

“Yes sir. Burger, follow me.”

“Fuck!” Jorann shouted as she jumped out from around a corner. “Have those idiots lost it? Sending children into battle?”

“Start praying meekly, boys and girls. Pray, old men. Pray before you start chasing and beating. Pray to the tyrants with tears in your eyes!” The loudmouth just wouldn’t shut up.

“Sinners!” the discordant squad members struck up in chorus. “Killers of our parents and grandparents, we beseech you to leave, you sinners. You murderers of our parents and grandparents.”

“You killed my daddy!” One of the ammnushiti girls, about thirteen, bit her lip and raised her shotgun.

The blast knocked the weapon from her hands, striking her in the face and throwing her backwards. Peppered with the resulting shot, Jorann screamed and squirmed. Gabby moved quickly towards her, picked her up in one hand and removed her to safety. The cussing ginger idiot girl was grasping at her thigh. Apparently a single pellet had slipped between her protective pads.

Another two shots rang out, but the barrels were aimed too high, and one rifle bullet and a bunch of shotgun pellets were unleashed into the sky. I sprinted forwards. Slipping past an old man struggling to make a backswing, I gave him a short stab in the throat. Picking a shotgun from the ground, I leaped over a groaning girl and crashed down with all my weight onto a gaggle of human bodies trying to retreat. My helmet took a weak swiping blow from a pitchfork, following which my belly received a similar strike. I tore an axe from a little boy's grip with my free hand, knocked a couple of kids over with my shoulder, trying not to cripple them, and then, dodging back a step, I allowed one old man coming at me with his axe raised to bring it down on the head of another. Ignoring the dazed gray-haired old fool now on his knees with an axe in his head, I pushed aside anyone who was in my way and collected up the remaining firearms, before dashing in a wide arc back to my position, where I angrily threw the trophies down at the foot of the wall. Shit! Rolling around on the ground were the children wounded by the angry old sinner. Someone pulled the axe from the old man's head, before the involuntary killer laid a wrinkly hand on his shoulder and asked warily:

"Are you okay, Lazarus?"

After mumbling a response, the injured man collapsed. Taking a seat on the ground and not removing her furious gaze from me, a girl wiped blood from her shotgun-shot-riddled face. Hardcore. Very hardcore. If I were younger, I wouldn't be able to let such a potentially natural born fighter slip away.

"Aaaa!" A quavering nasal scream was raised to the heavens. Three shots rang out, followed by more shouts and Tigr's wild animalistic roar.

The vengeance squad remained where they were, and a minute later Tigr returned, the fool slung over his shoulder and kicking about in an amusing manner.

Dropping him at my feet, Tigr retreated, and everyone close by watched the man jump to his feet and freeze in fright. He wore a goatee beard with no mustache.

"Why didn't you come out to fight?" I inquired with a smile, not looking at the man. I was still looking at the "fighters" who'd been sent to their deaths. "Why did you send children into battle?"

"I didn't send them to their deaths," said the little man, stirring from his stupor. "We do have a grain of sanctity in us, you know! I would never raise a hand to a child."

"You are a master wordsmith," I snorted, unholstering my revolver.

"Wait, stranger, wait! We only want one thing: for you to—"

Entering his belly, and surely his stomach too, my bullet cut him off midsentence. I quickly rattled off another four shots, aiming deliberately to shatter the bones in his shoulders and pelvis. Unsatisfied, however, I lay my boot into his right side, digging the steel toe cap in as deep as possible and feeling something inside give a horrible crunch. Then I put a fifth bullet in his nut sack, so that the bastard who sent kids to their deaths would think twice about having children of his own. Mutilated, he didn't even cry out, having passed out after the first bullet. Pity.

Surveying the enemy forces, I shouted angrily:

"All you children go home! If you don't, I'll kill all the adults, all your mothers and grandmothers, all your brothers, fathers, and grandfathers who are still alive. I'll burn your houses and your flowering gardens. I promise. In three minutes' time, I don't want to see a single infant or teenager! Get to your homes! MOVE!"

The thunderous clanging steel in my voice made them leap into action. Leaving their weapons behind, the "warriors," pale with fright, ran away lickety-split, while I continued shouting after them:

"If I see a single child outside, I'll kill you all! I'll slice up every last one of you. If you don't want any more trouble, keep your children locked up at home. Hey, you murderous old fart, take this one with you," I said, nodding at the scumbag writhing at my feet.

"Who needs this shit?" the old man asked huskily as he struggled to his feet. "What am I doing here? Why did I trick the children? What an old fool! Lord, may my soul burn in hell. Not for killing my friend, but for the children I urged forget their shyness and just go. No amount of praying can atone for that. I can never forgive myself. That loquacious devil confused me, muddled me, bathed me in black sin. Oh well, it's time to face the music."

The old man's first axe strike was to his left wrist, where it made a deep cleft. The second was to his neck, where it cut easily through the sagging flesh and severed an artery. Reeling, he dropped the axe and collapsed next to Lazarus, whom he had just killed. He had gone to face the music.

"Okay," I said. "Okay, you old fart, you have regained a smidgen of respect for your people. Tigr, what can you see from up there?"

Back up on the roof, the beastfolk pointed a beclawed finger in the direction away from the road which had carried us here.

"There's a crowd on the way. Half a hundred mugs."

"Any children?"

"Nope."

"Weapons?"

"Nope. Old people at the front. All wearing white, simple pants and shirts. Barefoot. They seem to be chanting a prayer. A jolly life they live around here."

"Live*d*," I corrected him, "live*d*. These shiteaters' independence is now a thing of the past. Jorann! How're you doing over there?"

"I'm in position," she replied, her voice still trembling from the anger bubbling inside her. "Is that bastard loudmouth hatemonger still alive?"

"You may consider him dead," I replied, reloading my revolver as I observed the motherfucker twitching in his death throes in a spreading pool of his own blood.

"Thanks, Elb! Thank you on behalf of the children. I was beginning to think—"

"Everyone up on a roof!" I commanded, cutting off her revelations. "Trophies in the cart! Hey, combat kids! Yes, that means you, rape survivors. Get out of here!"

"Where to?" asked a frightened dark-haired girl sticking her head out of the cart.

"Go join them," I said, pointing towards the houses. "Join them in their houses and tell them everything."

"Tell them what?"

"Everything! All the juicy gory details. Tell them how your friends cried, shouted, and prayed. How they were raped and murdered. As much shocking detail as you can. Mimic your rapists' laughter as you tell them how your holy old men and elders took turns with teenagers driven mental by such disgusting behavior."

"Oh God. Why do they need to know all that?"

"So they don't go to their own deaths for the sake of those scumbags," I replied harshly, waving a commanding hand. "Go! Everything must be paid for, kids. Salvation from penises and knives. And your payment is to convince the mental population here not to die for an unworthy cause. Consider it your... your..."

"Fucking penance!" yelled the redhead. "Run! Save the children, pacifists! Get a move on!"

"So this is paradise," I said, shaking my head.

"Freaking shitting paradise. Hell's better than this."

"So why did we leave home in the first place?" asked Wreck, who was surprisingly quiet today. "We should have stayed at home in our native asshole."

"Less of the philosophy," I barked, "and more killing."

"My favorite credo," said the orc with a grin as he drew a loving hand over his rifle.

Settling into a convenient position on a roof, and covering myself with a couple of trophy cuirasses sporting traces of blood, I waited patiently, gazing up into the serene blue sky. It was so exquisite and almost real, you just knew the paint was seriously expensive. There were even clouds, undoubtedly generated artificially by special machines. After all, you couldn't spray paint the whole world. I gazed into the sky and listened. At first I heard the familiar voices of the teenagers we'd saved and sent to the local houses, as they shouted and tried to get through to the people in the houses, which were shut fast. They weren't really houses, more like sticky roach traps. From the outside they were bright, modest, and decorous. Whereas on the inside they were pasted with strong religious glue that had a psychedelic vise-like grip on the souls of fanatical fools. There was no getting through to people like that. But the number of bloody deaths recently crashing down on this village of fools must surely have made them more open-minded. Perhaps it would be possible to convince the half-wit mothers and fathers it really wasn't such a good idea to send their children to their deaths.

After several minutes of shouting, intermingled with the extremely unskilled, one might even say embarrassing, use of such words as "fuck," "asshole," and "shit," the negotiators began to make headway. You had to give them their due: the students were turning out to be quite capable, and with each new sentence they were using more and more artful and tasteful language. It now flowed from the mouths of the speakers and was chewed over with relish in the ears of the stupefied listeners. Then everything went quiet. Not for long, mind, for soon the multitudinous snow-white delegation of voluntary suicide assassins rolled into the village.

Casting a quick glance at the crowd making its way onto the blood-washed square, I rose to my feet, stood up tall, and looked down on the vacillating ammnushiti, slowly taking them all in. There were approximately a hundred of them. Not many. Seriously not many. Deceptive dumbass twats. Deceptive.

"Are all the child rapists and murderers here?" I asked, loudly enough that not only those on the square heard me, but also the occupants of the surrounding houses.

"We are pure in our intentions, as we were pure in our terrible but necessary deeds." The response came with breathtaking and practiced ambivalence from a tall, if not towering, old man in the middle of the crowd.

"Have you been training all your life, blood-sucker?" I inquired casually, as I made another headcount of the douchebags. "You must have spent years polishing that verbal arsenal of yours."

"I don't understand."

"You don't fucking need to," I said dismissively, pointing a finger at the old man. "You! Lie down in that puddle!" My finger moved down to the largest puddle, a mixture of water, blood, and tantalizingly yellow vomit.

"I—"

"Do it!" I barked. Cracking, the old fart in the pristine snow-white robes began slowly to lower himself into the puddle, his face expressing true martyrdom.

Jumping down from the roof, I was by his side in a flash and putting the full weight of my boot on the back of his gray head, forcing his face into the muck. After holding him like that for a short while, I kicked him in the side, forcing him to roll over.

"On your feet!"

The dirty red-and-black figure stood up on trembling legs, yellowish streams dripping from his wizened face, and his lips all of a tremble, making the strands hanging from them quiver as well.

"Next!" I ordered, pointing at the man next to him. "Lie down! In the puddle!"

"We came for a peaceful discussion about—"

"Silence! All of you!"

Satisfied I'd gotten my message over, I waved to Wreck, Gabby, and Tigr. The trio looked like the evilist of the evil who had burned in the hell of the ammnushiti's nightmares.

"Help them atone in the proper fashion. There isn't enough blood around here, so fetch up some more. But don't kill them."

"Don't kill them?" asked Wreck, his mismatched eyes goggling in uncomprehending chagrin. "Umm…"

"They won't resist," I said. "The last thing we fucking need is the system's karma for the mass murder of a bunch of hereditary pacifist perverts."

"I suppose so. Although in that case I don't see why the fuck we need them all here."

"Do it! And be quick about it!"

"Gotcha."

Soon everything was moving along just fine.

Shitting human nature.

As soon at the ammnushiti realized they weren't going to be killed or harmed just yet — poking, spitting, and kicking aside — they immediately perked up, and moreover they began to do everything themselves, voluntarily and calmly bathing in the blood of their fellow tribesmen. Many puked — especially when Gabby found a new source of fresh blood — and we were able to give them a good roll around in their own surprisingly bright vomit. The new source of blood was a dozen cows which Gabby drove from their enclosure to the square, where he organized a whirligig meatgrinder which flung clumps of flesh out from the center of the square.

When this stage of the procedure was over, I

summoned Jorann and explained the next part of my plan, which she and Wreck then put into effect. I ordered Gabby and Tigr to fetch more livestock. I needed blood. Lots of blood.

One by one the ammnushiti on the square fell to the ground, where the growling ginger lass, temporarily forgetting her hatred, laboriously spread them out them. Returning with more cows and sheep, the fighters set to cutting the innocent animals' throats. The sheep proved to be the easiest to deal with. A single short gash, hold underarm, squeeze, and walk around spraying the tightly closed ranks.

Half an hour later we were done.

Back up on the roof, I examined the results of our doings and beamed a wide grin.

Not bad. And most importantly, copious.

"Will it work though?" asked the pensive Steak.

"There is no Mother here," said Burger, dancing a little jig.

"The system is everywhere," I retorted. "I cannot believe that such an enormous tract of land is in total system twilight. That's nonsense."

"So where are her eyes then?"

I pointed silently skyward.

"I've never heard of anything like it," Jorann said as she joined us. "What about the twilight roads where the killers get away with whatever they want? Remember that freaking zoo?"

"The system is everywhere," I repeated. "But it is bound by certain rules. Convoluted and overly complex rules which hinder more than they help."

"Where do you get that idea from?"

"It's just logic," I said with a shrug. "Shitting paranoid goblin logic which asserts that you are always under observation. The system sees, but it also doesn't see."

"I don't get it," said Burger.

"I get it," said Jorann. "The system may well see, but it's forced to ignore much of what it sees due to certain restrictions. So goblins have the illusion of freedom."

"Precisely."

"The system has eyes in the sky. It sees everything, but it also kind of doesn't see… Ah, dammit, I'm confusing myself now. Do you think it'll work?"

"A message like this is difficult to ignore," I said, my smile widening as I looked down on the square from the rooftop. "Added to which, show me a lady who can resist red flowers smelling of ass and blood."

"I sure wouldn't be able to resist that. How long will we have to wait? Long?"

"I shouldn't think so. The machines always react quickly. And the system has clear objectives, since it tries so hard to establish its lawful rights everywhere."

"What rights?"

"The right to be everywhere," I replied, beaming wider than ever now, and sensing a powerful jolt from underground.

An artificial earthquake.

Another jolt, stronger this time. And another,

after which the earth simply began to judder slowly, making the carefully laid centuries-old cobblestones begin to separate, allowing compacted dark earth up through the gaps between them. From beneath the ordered tidiness crept a loose moist blackness, a neat analogy to the locals' fulsome souls, sleek on the outside, long rotten on the inside.

The prostrate ammnushiti howled their fright and began to congregate into groups all praying together. I did not interfere, for our business was done and their positions were of no importance now. Before the masterpiece was utterly spoiled, however, I did manage one final glance at it.

The square was adorned with a sign made out of bodies, both dead and alive, in a frame fashioned from useless fools. It was a picture of a misshapen flower with a message in the middle: DISASTER! SYSTEM CHALLENGE! URGENT! ELB! The sign was written in motionless bodies covered with fresh bright-red blood, and scattered around the square were the mutilated disemboweled corpses of people and animals. We'd also added a few severed heads so nobody would think we'd merely held a burlesque party in the good old peaceful manner of Paradise Promised.

Few would be able to ignore such a message.

There was the chance, of course, that the system would not respond, but considering its mechanical single-mindedness to establish its obvious presence everywhere (emphasis on the word "obvious"), it was worth a try. And here was the result...

With a droning sound, a familiar steel column rose from beneath the cobblestones and extended twenty meters into the air right next to the "control stone", accompanied by the protracted wail of a siren which spread over the village. Then silence. Then dozens of laser beams rent the dust hanging in the air and crept over the squealing ammnushiti, the defiled bodies of animals and people, and the roofs of the houses.

Then came the familiar words before my eyes:

Hero Erikvan!
Attention! *Immediate full verbal free-form report!*

"Prepare to return to barracks, goblins," I said with a snigger as I strode towards the dome.

"We should have killed them all," Jorann hissed softly.

"Far scarier things await them," I replied, stopping and looking up. "The system is a far more effective punisher than us. And the main thing is that Paradise is finished. They will not be forgiven for their transgressions."

"And there'll be people to interrogate," growled Wreck, inadvertently stepping on and breaking somebody's flimsy elbow. "The system can winkle out secrets better than any seasoned whore. The commander is right. It's curtains for this shitting paradise. Damn! I should have used a few of those fuckers' bodies to write 'Wreck was here' in one of the side streets.”

“What the fuck for?” I asked, gobsmacked.

“Fuck knows.” The orc shrugged his enormous shoulders and was silent.

And I began to speak, clearly and concisely listing the reasons which had incited me to breach the peace of the Eden that was Paradise Promised. And each of my words was like a nail in the coffin of that shitting place. Something I was only too glad of.

CHAPTER 5

IT WAS STRANGE TO SEE a turd smiling.

I even blinked in the hope of unseeing it, but when I opened my eyes again, the smile on his ugly lumpy mug had only widened.

Wormeus was smiling. Wormeus was smirking. Wormeus was grinning. In fact there was nothing he wasn't doing with his thin lips in his attempt to express the whole spectrum of mirthful emotions seizing him.

After taking my fill of the spectacle, I swept the smaller shards from the table, removed the largest one from my bowl of hearty soup, and picked my spoon back up. The proprietor of the Shiny Shack bleated humbly from the far corner:

"I'll clear everything up."

Nobody paid him any attention, and he fell back into happy silence and returned hastily to the kitchen, from where bowl after bowl continued to appear.

"Noisy," said the disapproving Klappa, who had been standing still as a statue behind me for two hours.

"Do you understand what you did, you mindless goblin?" asked Wormeus, shaking his head.

None of us paid any heed to the inn's smashed-in window, through which the deformed hero had dropped in on our squad dinner. Outside the window stood an exoskeleton, painted in screaming red and gold, its transparent reinforced gun turret open to display a comfy curved divan. It stood at a little over three meters, was excessively massive, and had a large letter M emblazoned on its abdomen. Two legs, four arms, hulking body, and pretty nippy to boot, the steel monster had made short work of traversing the sizable courtyard, on the way jumping over our medieval cart and the four freaked-out horses harnessed to it. And credit where credit was due: its guidance and identification system had pinpointed my location exactly, and I wasn't sitting by the window, and it couldn't have seen me through the glass. But Wormeus had definitely known where I was, and had jumped through the window, landing opposite me in the only free seat.

"Do you want one of those as well?" asked Wormeus, losing his smirk and catching my brief appreciative glance at the exoskeleton.

"Not my cup of tea," I said with a frown.

"You don't like the color?"

"Or the size. Too big."

"Like that is it? What would be your ideal size then?"

"That's not an exoskeleton, it's a walking machine," I said with a shrug.

"So what *would* you like then? Your mechanic is fiddling around clumsily over there in the White Hippo's asshole."

"That's not my cup of tea either."

"So, what then?"

"A Night Adder," slipped out, and I froze in astonishment and listened in to myself, trying to figure out the meaning of what I'd just said.

"Never heard of it," said Wormeus, shrugging and returning to the subject. "Have you any idea what you did? Oh, man!"

"The system doesn't tell me anything," I said, dropping a hint. "Although some things are obvious anyway."

"They are no longer independent!" the worm barked. "It's the end of the ammnushiti's freedom. Have you seen what's going on over there?"

"It's coming down from the firmament as well," I said.

We'd been returned here in record time. I didn't even believe it at first when the system made its offer, although it didn't occur to me to refuse. And so we returned to base, dangling in a net beneath the belly of an enormous cargo drone which carried the corpses of the ammnushiti in its main compartment. The worm food travelled business class, while we were in the hold, although we had no complaints.

Dem Mikhailov

As I said to the ginger mare, the system was capable and fond of acting quickly, even lightning fast. The ammnushiti lying there in the shit and blood didn't even have time to bleat a protest before three dozen flying machines entered Paradise. The first tribes actually arrived before I'd finished my report. It was particularly long this time, for there was much precise detail to impart so that none of the child killers would think about making wily excuses and trying to squirm their way out of trouble. I wasn't going to provide them that chance. I listed everything we'd witnessed, including the names of the teenagers rescued, and the savvy Wreck immediately found and presented them, smashing down a couple of doors on the way. The teenagers, scared witless by the laser show, dutifully laid out everything they'd been through, pointing out a couple of the fuckers who were still alive and who'd committed similar shitty crimes against their own offspring. I continued to speak, and the drones kept on coming, while my fighters gathered the dead bodies and threw them into the containers, and the system delivered them to the one-stop-shop medblocks/interrogation rooms. And so it began. Then the gallows arrived, and the ammnushiti realized Armageddon was upon them. They stood witness to a court-martial and the passing of sentence, followed by the immediate execution of the sentence. What is more, each sentence was repeated verbally, which is to say, out loud, so that the information penetrated right to the bone marrow.

At this point we split. But not before I received system confirmation of the completion of the task, despite us not having put ticks in all the right places or laid our hands on all the monitor stones. Nobody needed that shit anymore. No more ticks, no more interrogating respected elders. Fuck that shit.

On the way back we collected everybody from the shelter nobody had needed, and when we got back we found the main squad expiring from the unbelievable number of exercises they'd been made to do. Klappa had been bored and angry and taken it out on his underlings, forging steel beauties from squealing shit.

In celebration of the successfully completed mission, I announced a banquet and ordered the innkeeper to lay on a spread. And so we feasted. Until sundown, at which point Wormeus had appeared in his exoskeleton.

"The numbers of raped and murdered teenagers run into the many hundreds!" Wormeus mumbled, shovelling an enormous lettuce leaf into his mouth. "And how much more shit came out as well. The illegal imprisonment, disfiguration, and coercion into labor of the inspection squads, as well as the shockingly fantastic and imaginative gardening experiments carried out on the poor things. The genial old men, the fucking druids, drilled a hole in the skull of one of the rebel protesters, before planting a flower in it with slowly growing lower roots and fast-growing aerial roots, whatever the fuck that means. They tied the lad in a sitting position to some statue, fed and watered him regularly, and every day led crawling slaves past him so they could watch him slowly die. Yet at the same time they kept repeating that every sinner must work in the interests of sanctity, either by toiling in the garden or by becoming part of the fertile soil. Genetically modified herbs had antibiotic and other general healing qualities, so the lad didn't decay, he just went slowly out of his mind while watching light-blue flowers droop down from his forehead. Oh yes, the old men picked the flowers from his head and brewed an infusion out of them. Cool. And, by the way, the lad is still alive. They untied him from the statue and dragged him to the medblock. But he's nothing but a vegetable now. All he can do is smile and tug thoughtfully at his eternally erect and inflamed cock. Am I ruining your appetite?"

"Do continue."

"Well, obviously they're restoring order in the place. The lands will remain closed, but they will now be a small nature reserve, and the ammnushiti are going to stay there. The ones who weren't involved in any criminal activity, that is. But there will be no more twilight. They'll be bending low and digging vegetable patches, and the all-seeing laser beam will be able to peek into even the darkest sweet-smelling crevices. But that's all bullshit. The main thing is that my authority has grown. And do you know what the first thing I told the system was? Disguising it as an innocent question?"

"Mm?" I tore myself away from savoring my soup for a second.

"I asked why the hell the other groups of seven controllers didn't notice anything and reported that everything with the ammnushiti was in order and super fucking decorous. Do I kick butt, or what?"

"I don't give a toss."

"You might not give a toss, but I had to put a big fat dent in the karma of the higher heroes who've long been trying to strangle me in the political movement here. The system may not reveal anything to them openly, but all the same. Oh, yes, I forgot to say they're all being chipped. Any accomplice to any crime, compulsorily; anyone else voluntarily and with good bonuses, including daily payments of a couple of crowns into their personal account. They're going to put trade points on the outskirts of the village, with large enticing windows full of lipstick, underwear, and tools. The people won't be able to resist, they'll come running. It's rubbish, but they'll go nuts for it. And how many classy items they'll be able to buy, huh?"

"Beads for the aborigines?"

"Exactly."

"How do you know all this? I can't believe the system told you."

"Not me, the Highers."

"And the Highers whispered it in secret into your chubby little pink ear?"

"I know the guy whose ear they whispered it

into. I'm telling you, you raised a proper rumpus and stink. And it isn't the stink of evergreen freshness. Paradise Promised was considered serious evidence of success. And then this shit."

"Evidence of what success?"

"All this," said Wormeus, indicating our surroundings with his enormous paw. "All of this world. Paradise Promised was evidence of the fact that it is actually possible to live peacefully in this world — albeit in a slightly distorted manner, because they did reject progress after all — having children at a leisurely pace and raising them correctly. It was a utopia. But in actual fact? That utopia was a fallacy. Paradise turned out to be a scary twilight forest sprinkled with the bones of children. A total failure. The only remaining dream is the Lands of the Covenant, with their guarantee of a rich and happy life."

"Are you sure?"

"Well, after what you exposed in Paradise, I don't even know. I may be a fucking wanker myself, but what they did with those kids really got to me. Those bastards! They were given what was taken away from us: the possibility to have children. We were robbed off that miracle, the chance to continue our bloodline, but they were gifted it. Here, fucking take that! And what did they do? I don't get it. Children are a great gift in this world. When a child appears in a kindheart village — they usually give a minimum of two or three so they can interact among themselves — when that happens, and the news reaches here, many of the heroes

visit those villages incognito during their vacations, and spend days on end delighting from a
distance in the sight of children playing in the
sand, eating porridge, acting up, and sulking. And
then, towards the end of their vacation, they walk
around the outside of the village, combing the forests and valleys and destroying anything that
might threaten the children's lives. And on top of
that they shout out for all to hear, 'Mother forbid
that anyone should even fucking think about attacking this village. It's been blessed with sweet
young lives.' Then those barren women come back
here and go on one hell of a bender, weeping
drunken tears in dark corners, and then they start
shagging distractedly in the hope of getting preg-
nant after all. That's what children need in this
world. While those beasts..."

After a brief chortle, I reached for a bowl piled
high with fried meat with nicely browned edges
and griddle-pan stripes, and another of finely
chopped onions mixed with dill. Then I took a
crust of black bread and was one seriously happy
goblin.

"I see it means nothing to you?" Wormeus
asked rhetorically, having understood me correctly.

"Nothing whatsoever," I confirmed, "but do go
on."

"Why? If you don't give a toss about the
drunken tears of sterile women."

"The more you babble, the more fascinating information slips through," I said, not concealing my

interest.

What was the point of being secretive? Wormeus was no fool and couldn't fail to understand my desire to know the situation around here. Even the drunken tears of heroic sterile women were a part of the crazy bilious mosaic of the world.

"I'm glad to be babbling today!" said Wormeus, with a twitch of the shoulder and a glance at the orc shoveling food into his face. "Is the meat good?"

Covering his plate with his hands, Wreck mumbled almost incomprehensibly:

"It'll do."

"Chomp in my direction, if you like," said the worm, "so the delightful aroma of the meat and your caries fills my nostrils."

"Do you want me to spit a ward of meat phlegm in your face? So it drips aromatically…"

"Do you want a heroic fist in your pie hole?"

"You seem to have digressed from your gleeful babble," I noted, before glancing at the motionless slant-eyed statue that was Klappa and saying, "Sit and eat."

"Yes sir, lead."

Slipping in soundlessly between me and Tigr, brazenly shoving the hairy animal, Klappa produced some chopsticks and tucked into the meat. The nonmeat dishes, which kept coming, we ignored.

"You're getting another five mugs to add to your dozen," I said to Klappa, before shoving another chunk of beef into my mouth.

Klappa nodded indifferently in acceptance of the order. Wreck began to fidget aggrievedly and mumbled something indiscernible. I turned around and cast an eye over the interior of the inn, catching the eye of Rox, who was taking his time over his food, and satisfied my fighters were having themselves a good feed, I turned back to Wormeus and stared at him expectantly. He took the hint and willingly continued to pour his heart out.

"Over there" — once more he pointed out of the window to where the slope running down into the huge crater of Crontown began, on the other side of which rose the zone's "noblest" territories, those on familiar terms with the Lands of the Covenant — "they're all about gabbling, whispering, gossiping, and yapping. They send out messengers and beg for invitations. It's one of the reasons why I'm here, to let them stew in expectation of my return. How everything's changed all of a sudden! I was of no freaking use to anyone, even getting in the way, and now everyone's aching to shake my hefty hand, if not kiss it. Why? Because thanks to you I rose up a step in this cesspool of ambitious gleet. Bear that in mind, goblin. A mealymouthed someone might soon be extending an invitation to you."

"Presumably that was the main reason for your galloping arrival here," I said. "Otherwise there's no fucking way you would have dragged yourself out of your lopsided little house. You're worried one of the other heroes might turn their attentions on me."

"Lopsided little house? My pad is splendid, I'll have you know. And my fighters' lodgings are none too shabby either. But yes, you do understand whose attention you attracted with your boisterous mission, don't you?"

"Any cretin would understand that. The Highers."

"The Highers," Wormeus echoed with a grimace. "They will definitely show up under a specious excuse, maybe to grab a beer and tear strips off a salted herring. But the real reason will be to keep an eye on you loudmouth provincial upstarts. And above all they will be watching *you*, goblin."

"I don't give a shit."

"That's the spirit! But they won't be watching for long. They'll drop a couple of hints that they're not against chewing the fat about miscellaneous trifles. And naturally the first to come here will not be noble elves but bewitching she-elves, elegant, smelling of expensive perfume, sleek bodies arrayed in silk."

"Elegant, you say?" said Wreck, swallowing loudly.

"They are Highers," said the worm with a chuckle. "There are no gorgons among them. Nor will you see any fatties. And if you do see any fat, it will only be where it's meant to be."

"Where it's meant to be," the orc repeated after him. "Hmm. And when will they be here?"

"Calm down," I said. "When did you ever think a blobfish wasn't cute?"

"Uh-huh," he said. As far as I could remember,

Wreck had never once slept with a blobfish. A spider queen, yes. A green-eyed heroine, yes. But never a blobfish.

"Calm down," I repeated, slightly more harshly this time. Sighing deeply, Wreck returned to his food.

"Blobfish," said Klappa, suddenly perking up. Then, after a few seconds' silence, he added, "Some thistles even flower on the odd occasion."

"Oooo," said Wormeus. "I'll have to remember that. Those are beautiful words about your dreary life of luxury. I shall remember it and enrich my vocabulary. And speaking of enrichment, what did the system reward the valiant commander Elb with, if it isn't a secret?"

"Various insignificant bits and bobs," I said dismissively.

"Stands to reason," said the hero, nodding understandingly. "Promotion?"

"Nah."

"Talkative, aren't you? Good job I never stop talking. Anyway, if a high-society lady appears and you happen to strike up a conversation, don't deny, okay?"

"Don't deny what?"

"Well, in a conversation with some VIP mugs, I kind of hinted that I'd always sensed something scummy and unsavory emanating from Paradise Promised. And that before your mission I even warned you to keep your noses to the ground and not settle for a routine quick once-over of the control points. And I ordered you to find some putrid shit or die trying. And you managed to... ahem..."

"Have you fucking lost it?"

"Yeah, I've fucking lost it," said Wormeus, not denying it. Then he leaned in towards me, shifting plates of salad with his chest, and said, "And I'm willing to pay a hefty fine for my obnoxious behavior. Just name what you want, so long as it's realistic. I definitely can't get hold of a Night Adder, whatever that is."

"Spare parts for the White Hippo," I began my list. "A dozen boxes of bullets for our rifles and machine guns. I personally want three or four boxes of something sweet for my needle gun. A large caliber for the White Hippo, preferably something like a Gatling gun, or if you can find one, a heavy machine gun would be even better. And for dessert, mortar guns, at least three."

"Are you off to war?"

"I am indeed."

"Your rank isn't high enough for heavy machine guns for a vehicle. Mortar guns ain't happening for you either. The system will ask, and even if you can wangle it, the system will demand you hand in your weapons. At a rough estimate, your status is roughly that of an advanced town virg, trusted by the system, and with your reliability, trustworthiness, and psychological stability proven on more than one occasion."

"Stability?"

"Uh-huh. The system Mother is very fond of serial killers. There have been instances of heroes going apeshit and suddenly unleashing a hail of bullets on a peaceful village because the local inn didn't stock their favorite beer. No unfiltered dark beer, so raze the whole stupid village to the ground! What do you fucking mean, they didn't deliver any cornflower moonshine? Take this salvo then! So from that time on, all heroes below fourth rank have to seriously tense their butts in order to conceal from the system any overly deadly weapons such as mortar guns, cannons, and anything scarier than that."

"For example?"

"For example, something that might put a hole in the sky. Savvy?"

"And there's no demand from fourth-rank heroes?"

"Many times have we proven our fidelity and the psychological stability of our noggins," snickered Wormeus. "We are but a hop, skip, and jump from the Lands of the Covenant. Who the hell needs peasants who don't appreciate the dark unfiltered nectar? This is why the system regards our arsenals good-naturedly. Oh yes, we have also proven multiple times that we are in great need of military hardware for the completion of tasks issued. Have you ever come across a squad of wild prisms that have somehow been through triple evolution?"

"No."

"They open exo armor in no time at all. And their own armor will easily repel a machine-gun burst at short range. Armor piercing bullets will just about take them out, but you have to be very accurate, because those beasts are nippy. Smart too. They aren't dumb animals that charge head-on at riflemen. They fight according to all the laws of tactics and fucking strategy. They set up ambushes, use explosives, dig deep trenches with steel spikes at the bottom, and they attack from the rear and sometimes even from the air."

"From the air?"

"Let your prism pupate another couple of times, and the hatchling will be such a nightmare, insanely powerful, or maybe it'll have wings. Or just imagine yourself shrunken to the size of an ant and bumping into a sentient rhino beetle which couldn't give two shits about the popgun in your genteel frail little hands. Maybe you are right, goblin, not to be hurrying to Crontown."

"How can a wild criminal prism undergo several evolutions without the aid of the system?"

"Are you not impressed by my tale of terror?"

"Are you going to answer my question?"

"Fuck knows. If you find out, you'll jump all the way up to the highest hero rank in one go."

"Did you make that up yourself?"

"An official system notice which has been posted for twenty years on the central noticeboard in Crontown and other places besides. Anybody who finds out how wild prisms manage to accomplish it instantly gains the highest rank. And that is without exception. Even if you used to be a kindheart or a herder of goosed tunny fish, you will be given that status. That said, it is impossible."

"Why?"

"Because it's been attempted many times, and either nothing was found, or whichever group was trying to find out disappeared, to a man. And we're talking about combat squads under the leadership of third- or fourth-rank heroes, small well-trained armies supported by exos. And it was the personnel that disappeared. The only traces that were found were blood-soaked soil, burned-out vehicle wreckage, and the odd chunk of shredded meat, or in most cases mince. You presumably understand why the dead and the wounded were dragged away?"

"Meat?"

"Five'll get you ten. Everyone needs to eat, and the system doesn't hand out rations to wild prisms. A year ago something unimaginable happened. Two hundred errs attacked two villages at once on the border of the Crontown district. The villages were home to approximately a thousand peaceful peasants, among them children. Following a distress howl from the system, a squad of heroes was dispatched to each village, where they were sliced up. They did manage, however, to give a shriek into their walkie-talkies concerning the immense horde of errs, whereupon another ten squads were sent to help. Unfortunately they were late, despite the system airlifting them in. Fires, blood, machines emitting intoxicating fumes. They followed some footprints, but they hadn't gotten far before the footprints diverged several times, the groups of bastards becoming smaller and smaller before completely vanishing in the desolate wild forests of Biorez."

"Um…"

"Exactly. Awful shit."

"No, I mean, what are errs?"

"That's what we call those beasts. They seem to be some kind of beetle."

"If the system only sent two squads first time, that means there's twilight there and it couldn't see anything, right?"

"Correct. The first thing they did was knock out the domes and blind the system. Only then did the errs invade."

"What's Biorez?"

"It's a very long and narrow centuries-old forest, part of which grows on flat terrain and part on the mountain slopes adjacent to it. It's a biosphere reserve with some kind of unique fucking ecosystem, which it's so fragile you can't even take a shit under a bush because you'll destroy the natural equilibrium. Basically, you can't go there, it's taboo. Although the motherfucking errs don't care about that. They went marching into the twilight forest and got lost, while we stayed at the edge under the umbrellas of the wailing domes situated around the perimeter. Some of the domes, incidentally, had been destroyed beforehand. If only we'd known that right from the start. If the system had informed ua about the twilight areas, we'd have used a shortcut to get there quickly. As it was, we followed the tracks, but the errs were way faster."

"Faster than a running exo?" I asked, doubtful. "That's nonsense. A runner against a machine?"

"They have machines as well. Do you think it was a herd of beetles burdened with virgins scarpering from us? No fucking way! It was a column of armored vehicles escaping from us at full tilt. And they were obviously following a route planned in advance. The vehicles were off-roadworthy, and the path was prepared, ditches covered over with logs, and red rags laid out as markers leading the way to fording places over rivers. Can you imagine just how precise and extensive their preparations must have been?"

"So they live in this forbidden Biorez?"

"For sure. But the system outright denies it and doesn't permit anyone access to the place. If you disregard the system's forbiddance and enter the forest, you get shot by a dome. And if you force your way in, you'll be stripped of your hero status for violation of the taboo. If you do happen to make it back, there'll be a tribunal waiting for you."

"How did the errs get to the village? Surely not on foot?"

"If their footprints are anything to go by, or rather the near total absence of them, they were taken there covertly in small groups, in carts and commercial lorries, and by boat."

"And what about the military vehicles?"

"The exos and all the freight carriers arrived later. At great haste and just in time to start loading and greet the first two squads of heroes."

"I see. So that means intensive reconnaissance

was carried out in advance."

"That goes without saying. And here's another tidbit for you, you clever goblin. The domes were destroyed by human suicide bombers."

"So regular goblins work with the errs," I concluded.

"Correct. But only goblins, no beastfolk. All the errs are insects like your Gabby. So forget it, goblin, you're out of your league here. You don't have enough strength and your cock is too short. But anyway, what do you want, apart from mortar guns?"

"Mortar guns."

"Listen—"

"You can give them to us in secret. We won't make a big noise about it."

"If you don't know the science behind them, you won't be able to fire them. How are you going to find their range?"

"That's my concern. Three mortar guns, and a couple of armor-piercing guns with a decent supply of ammunition. They're a bit like antitank weapons, right?"

"Correct."

"Are they also forbidden?"

"No. It's perfectly feasible to get hold of them using a standard line. When the system asks, you say you're up shit creek, because yesterday you were digging around and you suddenly dug up... Oh, what joy! Given your status as a system favorite, it won't ask you any awkward questions. It will just ask once for form's sake, and then forget it."

"In that case, it's a deal. If I'm asked, I shall mention your immense wisdom and healthy sense of suspicion."

"Deal. So, what are your plans now?"

"For the next twenty-four hours, maybe even longer, I'm here and going nowhere," I replied, puffing in my satiation. "I have squad business to attend to."

"Be in touch?"

"Drop by," I said. "We're always glad to listen to the tales of a talking turd."

"That's what I love about you, your freaking compliments. Aren't you going to ask about Green Eyes?"

"Nah."

"Respect."

I didn't know why the worm had come to respect me so, but the insightful chat was now at an end. Getting ready to leave, he lobbed a couple of golden crowns the length of the room, and the landlord caught them dexterously. Then he skipped out through the broken window, jumped quickly into the exo, kick-started it, and slammed the armored lid shut. The machine stood up straight and sprinted off, startling the horses again.

I watched the walking machine run away off-road, deciding wisely to make holes in the soft earth as opposed to the paved road, and he soon disappeared from view. Judging by his direction, Wormeus was heading for Crontown. The slimy yet smart worm was in a hurry to continue spinning his web. If you asked me, they were too bogged down in this shit show with all its stage decorations and cheap talentless actors. They sprang around like obsequious puppets on invisible strings dangling from the Highers' hands. And what the Highers were playing at, fuck alone knew. But for some reason, I did not fucking believe that the elite of this rotten little world were overly concerned with its future prosperity.

"Shit," I said, looking gloomily at Crontown, sitting at the bottom of its enormous crater and bathed in peaceful sunshine.

"What's up?" Wreck asked, before producing a protracted burp which made a passing waitress shudder and frown.

"They could do with a small nuclear fougasse around here," I said with a sigh, still gazing at Crontown.

"Why, for fuck's sake?"

"These cankers need either cutting out or burning out," I replied. "I'd go for the second option."

"What about cold diplomacy?" suggested Klappa, laying his chopsticks aside.

"You can't beat someone at their own game by playing by their rules, Klappa." I shook my head and rose to my feet. "Right, it's time for us to get busy with important squad business. Get ready, goblins."

CHAPTER 6

I HAD A FAIR FEW PLANS after dinner, but my sated body demanded a brief respite. Listening in to my sensations and realizing my lumbago was playing up again, I went up to my room, where I lay down on the wooden floor and stared up at the ceiling. A bottle of water stood beside me, while a tiny tablet dissolved under my tongue and my gurgling stomach slowly digested the meat it had been over-stuffed with. I wasn't concerned about my digestion, for I had long ago noticed that since I'd gained my first combat status — while I was still roaming the steel world beneath the ground — I had begun to digest my food several times faster. I didn't know what the ferments were, or whatever else the system was putting in us, but my stomach now broke down stodgy food very quickly, and my intestines were even faster and greedier at absorbing their contents, before dispatching building materials to wherever they were required. My muscles were becoming stronger, my wounds healed rapidly, and my stamina levels were very pleasing. The system took good care of its heroes, especially those who justified its trust time after time.

The elven tear tablet I had swallowed quite consciously. I had memories to recall. I had to understand who I was and what my role in all this shit was. And judging by previous flashbacks, my role was sufficiently big, and my authority back then had been extremely high. And moreover, I had a certain reputation in narrow circles of power. I was revered. And feared.

But the most important thing was that I gave everything my all in the interests of this world. I worked neither for money nor for glory. I considered I was doing something very important. I considered my business a special mission.

But since I was such an influential hotshot, how the hell had I been born a volitional nullform?

How the hell had I found myself shut in a stinking steel asshole heaving with worms with human faces?

Why had my memory been deleted?

There were hundreds of questions. But no answers.

And right now there was only one way to fish even a few memories from the dark abyss, and that was these freaking drugs, which would long since have eaten away my mind were it not for the system constantly flushing out the toxins floating around in my blood.

Closing my eyes and continuing to concentrate on the sensations in my lower back as it began to relax on the hard floor, I waited patiently. I paid no heed to the flash of stupid mawkish glee which threatened to grow into inebriate delight. I did not swallow this shit for the sake of a cheap high. I needed something far darker and headier, which was to say, my own memories.

*　*　*

I made no bones about coming here. I arrived at a hazy midday in the middle of the last month of summer. The civilian flier I'd rented from a small dying transport company landed on a flagstone-paved landing pad and opened its door, jabbering dismally about how happy the company was that I'd chosen its services.

A similarly paved wide road led away from the landing pad, and I set off along it, impassively checking out the pristine wild landscape sur-rounding me. Old darkened birch trees, even darker firs, hazel thickets. The only telltale signs of care for and order in the forest were the mown grass and absence of litter. After strolling at a re-laxed pace for a kilometer, I saw the folks respon-sible for the order, a group of smiling men with scythes, handling those primitive tools most deftly. Not far from them, a dray horse harnessed to a cart loaded with brushwood was nibbling grass. Next to the cart was a spacious electrocar, sitting firmly on wide wheels suitable for any terrain. As I walked past, nobody asked who I was or where I was going. It didn't matter. Had I been an uninvited guest, the security system would have kicked in ages ago and I would have been surrounded by serious guys armed with more than scythes and sickles.

This area was special, at least for those who lived and flourished here.

After the very first — and almost unnoticed for the majority of the regular denizens of this weary planet — sudden global climatic shift, changes were noticed, albeit not so obvious as those that were to come. Minimal, you might say, changes, manifesting themselves first and foremost in permanent temperature rises, of one or two degrees, in those places where nothing like it had ever happened before and the climate hadn't changed for thousands of years. The climate had always worked like a well-oiled Swiss mechanism, but the shift was a major glitch which brought consequences with it.

The previously cold summers became warmer and sunnier, the springtime melt began a couple of weeks earlier than before, and fall now came a few weeks later. The winters were still long and snowy, but less severe, and extreme freezing temperatures were a thing of the past. The local flora was grateful for the gift and doubled its flower and fruit production. There had never been a paucity of nature's offerings here, but the place was true paradise now.

Another enormous advantage for the world's

tough guys interested in this area was that it had never really been settled, so vast was the north-eastern region of this mighty northern country. Hundreds and thousands of kilometers of dense untouched forest known as taiga.

When the second climatic shift was portended — and these portents were voiced by far from everyone; only the important, the rich, and "your" people — it became clear that in ten or fifteen years the winters in these parts would become even shorter and milder, and the joy of summer would be enhanced by greater warmth and increased sunshine. Obviously, these paradisiacal conditions would not last forever, but there would be a certain stability for fifty years, if not more. At least that was the prognosis back then. And it did the trick. Upon being told that the none too enticing cake over there was in fact very yummy, any enterprising person would be overcome with the sole possible logical desire: to immediately grab a knife and grab himself a large slice of said cake.

Trade was swift and, again, exclusively for "your" people. They even managed to preserve almost completely the indigenous population, and the region was settled by the most "your" of "your" people. Following this, the autonomy of the region was forced through, a process which took ten years.

Construction began long before autonomy was established, and it continued unabated for many years, although it was hidden from the view of the general public, only the estates being visible.

Dem Mikhailov

Landowner estates, that's what they were called. Massive fence-encircled mansions with colonnades, grand entrance halls, coach houses, stables, and many other household outbuildings, among which paled into insignificance the apartments for the security guards and serving staff. All the buildings were adorned in the antiquated style of gloomy centuries gone by. Some of the adjacent lands were allotted for the establishment of villages, where anyone who so desired could receive a house with a plot of land and a whole field. Till, sow, grow, reap, and don't forget to give a tenth of your harvest to the landlord! And no chemical fertilizer, only natural. No chemicals whatsoever, no asphalt or concrete, no internal-combustion-engine-powered transport. Beneath each estate pulsed the atomic heart of a reactor, generously providing energy for all those in need.

And so the ball was set rolling. For twenty years everything bloomed and embraced life, beets grew, children were born, and people lived happily and busily. The landlords competed with one another in superfluity and splendor, growing richer and richer through multimillion-crown deals. Although there were also business incompetents who were forced to throw in the towel and auction off their native lands. That was when the real battle began. Every landlord lived with an insane bizarre desire to keep expanding his personal acreage. Just as preteens compare their members and titties, so the landlords compared the size and condition of their holdings. Lands up for sale were bought for immense sums of money, and afterwards all the buildings, down to the very last one, were demolished, each worked stone removed from the earth, and adult trees planted in the newly plowed soil. A month later, where previously had stood the imposing estate of an unsuccessful landlord, now grew a thick wild forest. There was a particular swank to being the owner of woodlands, meadows, and rivers. And landlords also compared numbers of villages and the souls inhabiting them. They took good care of their peasants, and their peasants multiplied. Children were educated in a specific manner, so that when they grew up they would never leave, remaining in their native lands and receiving their own plots. In order to increase the population, the debts of insolvent poor folk of suitable humor would be paid off, and those subjects relocated here. In this way they were provided the opportunity to make good on their debts, adding to the population of peasant souls, who would soon come to be known unofficially as serfs.

At around the same time appeared the symbol, well-known around the world, of the vast region of estates, the Bear Mountain. The steep slopes glistened with gold and malachite, and on the summit, rearing up on its hind legs, an enraged bear showed its teeth. Despite its intimidating appearance, this emblem was beloved by all the world's children and parents, for expensive natural food products were sold with it emblazoned on them. No chemicals, everything guaranteed organic. And the fools who tried to fake the emblem to push their cheap chemicals masqueraded as an expensive brand were rewarded with a dozen intensely harsh and bloody punishments involving arms and heads lopped off with an axe and littered everywhere, so that everyone understood just how reverent was the attitude of the estate region to its brand. And so the landed gentry continued to get richer, gaining in influence and adjoining more and more previously unclaimed territories.

This idyllic situation lasted for quite some time. Then the planet was rocked by a second climatic shift. You couldn't help but notice it. It was hard not to notice a global natural calamity which took the lives of almost 200 million people in one fell swoop. And that was just the official estimate. Nobody knew exactly how many corpses were actually removed from disaster-struck ghettos around the globe, nor how many remained to rot beneath ruins lost to the seabed. These taiga regions, however, remained nearly untouched, which spoke of their geographical location. While crippled reactors throughout the world exploded and entire cities were washed into the ocean, and whole archipelagos and not insignificant chunks of continents disappeared at once under suddenly rising water, everything here remained in good shape.

The world survived a second cataclysm and continued to live its life.

The common rabble was delighted to have survived, and continued to ruin the climate with its existence alone, making no attempt whatsoever to minimalize its wastage of drinking water and paying scant thought to sorting its waste. Although it was too late to do anything about the waste anyway, for the moment was long gone and there was no way to halt the wheels of destruction. Let the simple folk live on with their imperturbable ovine confidence in tomorrow.

Meanwhile, the smarter and the richer began to prepare for the next inevitable strike. In order to survive the knockout right hook of an angry planet, you had to be prepared for it. And joining forces, the landlords invested huge sums of money in defensive measures and specific research, turning their region into one of the best protected places on the planet. Yet at the same time they managed to preserve the pristine wilderness, hiding all the most important stuff underground. There, at great depths, were the most contemporary of bunkers stocked with everything required for survival. Also located there were very specific and surprisingly successful research laboratories, about whose incredible achievements only very sketchy snippets of information were known. But even these essentially everyday rumors were sufficient to be of serious interest.

For this reason I came here shortly before the third climatic crunch. And I did so to make a suggestion that would be impossible to refuse. That said, considering the proud and stubborn nature of the local masters, they could easily throw a wobbly and reject even the most generous proposal. For which reason I was forced to bide my time patiently, secretly observing, calculating, supposing, and waiting for that single ideal moment.

As so often happens, the big chance presented itself thanks to a minor incident.

The father and czar killed his eldest son.

Well, it wasn't as though it had never happened before, was it?

In a fit of rage, the chief landlord Savva Lukich beat his heir to death, sending him, along with a couple of his male friends and three girls, to the big estate in the sky.

The reason? Fucked-up on fine-quality narcotics, the crazy kids had been racing each other in light swamp buggies created for the transportion of the folk who gathered the berries, mushrooms, herbs, and other edible flora growing in the fens. They began by racing over the marshland, but then the hijinks got out of control when they switched the vehicles into overdrive and flew onto the road leading from their village to the school, where it all kicked off. The lead swamp buggy careered at top speed into a gaily painted bus full of little children, who were being told by an elderly tour guide about the beauties of their native region, in an attempt to instill in the younger generation a love for their kind and generous motherland. The accident crumpled the bus and flung it aside, right into the path of the second buggy. The tiny passengers were strewn hither and thither, hung up on branches, and crushed beneath bits of machinery. Many died. But the problem wasn't so much the fact of the incident as the teenagers' attitude to it. When the six racers stepped out of their vehicles and surveyed the results of their actions, the wealthy landlordly offspring merely burst out laughing. They guffawed as they admired the mangled children's bodies, the elderly tour guide rent in half, the crepitating chaperone with her crushed belly, and the disintegrated onboard biotoilet, perched upon which was a now dead ginger boy, his trousers around his ankles and his hands gripping a tablet with a game in progress on it making jolly beeping sounds. The sly little carrot top had gotten bored with the excursion and the guide's bleatings about cedar and fir trees, and decided to sit awhile in silence and enjoy his favorite game.

Anyone might laugh in a similar situation, according to expert witness from thirty-three percent of gray-haired doctors, who would add that such behavior was not mockery in the true sense, but more a kind of hysteria. After all, the brain will understand what has happened and be appalled, and in order to block out any extremely strong negative emotions and maintain sanity, it will switch forcibly into another regime, a regime which made these killers suddenly roar with laughter as they pointed their fingers at the ragged corpses.

Well, yes.

Perhaps it was hysteria, for six people simultaneously. Perhaps. Pretty much anything was possible in this shitting life.

The thing was that Savva Lukich, who by unlucky happenstance happened to be close by and had abruptly parked his flier next to the scene of the accident, was in no way expecting to see the dead and severely injured children or the cackling killers. Still, you had to give him his due, for before setting out on his killing spree, he did send a distress call to all the emergency services, including a short voice message. Only then did Savva Lukich take up his twenty-kilogram steel walking stick, which he had not been without for twenty plus years. If you'd spent twenty years twiddling a twenty-kilogram doohickey in your hands every day for hours on end, you would be very strong. And the big-chief merchant man put this strength to good use, committing such acts on the murderers that, when not only the emergency services arrived in response to his call, but also the newly bereft parents, it did not even occur to them to accuse anyone of anything. Well why, when justice had already been done, and lying on the road were a bunch of bloodied and mangled sacks stinking of blood, shit, and fear? There could be no worse punishment. And prison didn't count, for we all knew the lap of luxury that the wealthy do jail time in.

There was one problem, in that aside from his own child, Savva Lukich had turned others' offspring into stinking tenderized steaks as well, and the other landowners were none too pleased about the iniquity that had robbed them of their sons and daughters.

It went without saying that children did stupid things in the folly of youth. No one was denying it.

But...

It wasn't *our* daughters behind the wheel, was it? The young girls had taken drugs and leaped gaily into the spacious interiors of the swamp buggies without paying particular heed to what was going on. At any rate they weren't controlling the vehicles and therefore could not be held accountable for the accidents. So why the hell did you kill our daughters? Their laughter was the hysterical laughter of fright. And it was only natural they were frightened because they were so young. Plus, the drugs stopped them reacting adequately. And where did they get the drugs in the first place? Your son provided them! I shouldn't be surprised if he forced them to take those tablets.

Only two of the lads was actually driving the vehicles. The third was a passenger, so what did you kill him for, you freaking executioner? Especially the eldest, he was an heir, and the smartest of them at that. You killed an heir who'd been trained in the family business from a very early age.

No matter which way you look at it, the only one you had the right to finish off was your own son. Your own! How could you dare to raise a hand to ours?

Not good, Savva Lukich. With all due respect to your accomplishments, who are you to kill our children? Do you reckon yourself a god?

Then Savva's wife left him, taking their six children with her and having a massive fit of histrionics before she did so. Mothers will be mothers, and their own offspring are always more important than others'. And so, disregarding the fact that all lives are precious and equally valuable, she bawled hysterically that even five buses full of riff-raff children could never be as important as her darling eldest. And that in situations like this, one shouldn't be killing one's own children, but rather sorting out the situation in good time and not begrudging wads of cash to keep dissatisfied loud-mouths quiet. They should be paying the peasants so they could have more children. Their son would still be alive, and they could have sent him to an expensive clinic for a long course of rehabilitation, and when the village rabble had cooled down a bit, he could have apologized publicly in front of the people. And that would be it, everyone would be happy. Why kill your own son? Maybe you want to exterminate us as well?

Savva Lukich loved his family. He had always been one of those orderly men who knew categorically that family always came first. Friends, colleagues, and other acquaintances were transient, but family was forever. This was why looking after his family had broken the veteran landlord. And instead of somehow controlling the situation, which had grown like a festering boil, he sat at home in his lair and hit the bottle.

And then up rocks me, strolling along the path.

I entered unhindered through the open gates, which were fashioned from multiple layers of steel disguised beneath wood. Savva Lukich was expecting me. During a brief prior conversation, I'd promised not only to return his family and solve all his little squabbles with his angry fellow land-lords, but also to make sure his beloved family for-got once and for all about recent events and came to love the head of the family again. And this was what won over the drunk Savva Lukich.

A silent servant in a rustic shirt led me to an oaken staircase, which I climbed to a dining hall where a gloomy Savva Lukich sat solemnly at the end of a long empty table. On either side of him lay an enormous brown bear, asleep yet at the same time not asleep. I got the distinct impression they had clocked my entrance.

"What brings you here, dear guest?" asked the landowner sullenly, raising his bulbous head.

"An exchange," I replied with a smile, taking a seat uninvited at the opposite end of the table to my host.

"You are sitting in the seat of my son, Savva Junior."

"Junior is dead," I shrugged, "and it is not him I am not here to talk about."

"Your proposal is impossible. Vasilisa will not forgive me. Neither will my children."

"That is true," I said. "If they remember, they will never forgive you, and even if you are eventu-ally reconciled, a dark grudge will remain in the family for ever."

"So why are you here then?"

"We can make them forget."

"Forget what?"

"All the really bad stuff. The last three or four days, let's say. They will fall asleep, and when they wake up, they will not remember these past few terrible days. They will awaken in a bright room, in comfortable beds, with you sitting alongside them. You will smile at them and they will smile back. Their smiles will be serene and joyful, for they will have no recollection of their father's filicide."

"That is impossible. Chemicals? Can they be guaranteed to work?"

"We guarantee it," I smiled, lowering a hand to the polished wood. "And we demand nothing in return until you are convinced of the result."

"But even if they forget, others will remind them."

"That is true. But what if the bright room in which they will awaken is not located here?"

"Where, then?"

"Somewhere where they do not know anyone, but where all around is just as peaceful and beautiful as here."

"You speak in riddles, nameless guest."

"The end of the world is nigh, Savva Lukich," I said, making an effort to pronounce his name properly, since it was so difficult to say in the common language everyone understood. "Sooner or later we'll have to either die or move to a safe place."

"What rubbish! I am still listening, though."

"That is a good start."

"And for starters I want to know what you demand in return."

"That's easy." My smile widened and my eyes pointed at the reason for my visit. "I need them."

I was looking at one of the huge somnolent bears lying like obedient dogs next to the master of the estate.

"Them?"

"I've heard you call them your guard beasts. Genetically modified animals with enhanced characteristics, resistance to disease, heightened in intellect, stuffed with subtle electronics. Your laboratories have created something truly amazing, and I have come here to propose an exchange."

"Rubbish," Savva Lukich repeated, and pushed away a glass containing some kind of amber liquid. "Rubbish!"

"I can add something else as a bonus," I suggested.

"And what would that be?"

"You will also forget the last three days. Clean forget. And when you awake and inquire after your eldest son, you will be told that he died, let's say, trying to rescue the unfortunate kids from the burning bus. You and your family will be overcome with sincere grief and will spread his ashes from a silver urn over a serene field of dandelions. Then you will continue to live a full and happy life, blaming yourself for nothing and not drowning your sorrows and guilt in alcohol."

"Who are you?"

"Nobody."

"Who stands behind you."

"Something I trust."

"Rubbish!"

"Well, if you're going to be like that," I said, rising to my feet.

"But do go on!" barked the landowner. "Do continue."

*   *   *

After waking from — or snapping out of — my bright and vivid dream-recollections, I lay for a while recalling every detail of what I'd seen. Then I rose and took a couple of steps. The floor flew up to greet me. I managed to thrust out my hands and cushion the blow with my elbows before blanking out again.

I stood in emerald rain of insane brightness. A Geiger counter crackled unpleasantly in my ear, demanding my immediate exit from the zone. Green water, with just a hint of blue, trickled down my near-black steel shoulders, and my legs were knee-deep in effervescent liquid mud. A prefab multistory building, as old as life itself, towered over me, reinforced by a steel carcass and topped with a rusted makeshift metal roof. The sunlight scarcely penetrated the black thunder clouds, and although the obscure toxic haze was difficult to call a bright day, by local standards this was fine weather.

Standing motionless, I observed fighters in body armor forcibly drag out stubborn yelling inhabitants, unscrupulously employing electroshock devices and persuasive cudgel strikes.

Above the courtyard sandwiched between black-ened buildings, a female voice rose from a multi-functional cargo plane, trying to make itself heard over the general clamor of the ghetto dwellers:

"Attention! For your own good, it has been de-cided to administer obligatory vaccination against the black flu. Attention! For the good of your chil-dren, it has been decided to urgently evacuate all minors to a safe location for further treatment and examination. Attention! For your own good, it has been decided to administer the obligatory implan-tation of microchips. Chips are beneficial. Chips are to be used for the constant monitoring of markers in the body and the timely warning of dangers to health. Do not resist! I repeat, do not resist! This is for your own good!"

A dirty brown object flew out of a third-floor window, flipped over a couple of times, losing most of its red-brown contents, and landed on my head. I didn't flinch. The toilet bowl smeared with shit and dried vomit smashed against my head with a ringing sound and drenched me with the remains of what was in it. The emerald rain instantly washed away the dirt, and the man who had thrown the ceramic object received a paralyzing needle to the belly from my shoulder-borne dart-flinger, slipped from his windowsill, and crashed down into the filthy muck.

"Attention! For your own good, it has been de-cided to administer obligatory vaccination against the black flu. It is an extremely dangerous disease. It takes thousands of lives every day. Attention! It is your public duty to receive the vaccination. It is for your own good. I repeat, for your own good. Ah, shit, why the hell are we wasting our time on these mindless bastards?"

Private Richardson marched heavily past me, dressed in an ExoDefender and dragging a large protective container with transparent walls through the dirt. Inside the container, some sitting, some lying, were frightened children, and running after it was a woman dressed in rags and yelling:

"Give Chris back, you bastards! Give me my child back!"

"Attention! For your own good, it has been decided to administer the obligatory implantation of microchips. This procedure is not dangerous for your health. It is for your own good. Attention! We ask you not to resist. Our actions are sanctioned by the law-enforcement and municipal services. We are acting within the law."

My arm was grasped and pulled by a huge man whose puffy face was crisscrossed with black veins. My arm did not so much as twitch, but my shoulder-borne dart-flinger gave a short click, and after receiving a bite from the Night Adder, the man collapsed into the muck. A fighter ran up and held an injector to the base of his skull, pressing the button three times: the vaccine; the chip; and a small smart capsule which would open up upon a signal and release a concentrated dose of Amnos mixed with a mega dose of sedative into his blood. The man, unable to stir, was picked up and taken to a second cargo plane which now landed. This one was simpler and of the sort normally used for the transport of large cattle. The plane only just squeezed between the buildings, and it occupied the remainder of the yard. The doors of a cargo hatch opened, a gangplank was lowered, and the fighters began hastily to throw limp bodies inside, where they were received by people in protective medical suits, who lay them deftly on the floor and hung them on special straps on the wall.

"Attention! Our actions are sanctioned by the law-enforcement and municipal services. This area has been declared unfit for living, and its inhabitants are being relocated. Attention! Do not hide inside the buildings. They are due for demolition in two hours' time. Anyone hiding will face inevitable death beneath the ruins of the building. Attention! Do not hide your children. It will not be safe for them. The buildings are going to be demolished. For fuck's sake, you freaking idiot woman! Group number three, fifth floor, left-hand door, go! The scanner is showing a fat woman trying to push the doors to some shitting box room."

"Roger that. We're moving out."

"Hurry," I added. "We've got twenty-seven minutes."

"Roger that."

"Damn you all, you murderers!" A mad old woman had ripped off her rags and was jumping up and down on a fourth-floor windowsill. "You fucked up this world! You fucked up our life! You killed us and ruined our children. Damn you all!

May God punish you! You fucked up this world! Fucked it up!"

"Twenty-six minutes," I said, and marched off towards the second apartment building. "Olaf! Don't forget to search the basement before giving the demolition guys the thumbs up!"

"Yes, commander!"

"You fucked up this world! Damn you all, you corrupt bitches! Damn you!"

* * *

Regaining consciousness, I spat a wad of acidic viscous spittle, raised myself cautiously, and sat on the bed wondering if I could walk yet, or whether I should be expecting another wave.

I waited a couple of minutes and it seemed to have passed. Okay, now I could go about my business.

Business. I felt a bit woolly for a while after such a vivid trip. When I realized I was still sitting and staring blankly at the wall, my mind in the distant past, I gritted my teeth angrily, and stumbled out into the corridor with a snarl in search of victims.

It did not take long to find them, as usual, this time by looking out of the window at the end of the corridor. Leaning up against the wall of a hostelry, two shaven-headed fighters were copulating. One of them, his ass thrusting back and forth, was muttering irately into the willing ear of the second, who on closer inspection did turn out to be a woman after all:

"I'm fucking you like Elb! I'm fucking you like Elb would!"

Toppling out over the windowsill, I landed beside them and asked with interest:

"Have you come yet?"

"U-uh-huh," said the withering but angry artiste, hastily tucking his root back into his pants.

"I haven't, as usual," replied the bald girl. "Ahem, but that's not why you're here, is it?"

"Did Klappa let you have a sex break?"

"Um, Sergeant Klappa sent us to get some bandages and medical glue, lead."

"I see. Well, you go back and tell him his leader ordered him to do something with you that would definitely make you come. Tell him that, word for word, and Sergeant Klappa will try wholeheartedly."

"But *I* came," said the fighter, displaying a tad of wit as he wiped his hand on his girlfriend's shoulder while she quickly pulled her pants up.

"Do it."

"Yes sir!"

Both goblins tramped off to the rear yard, from where the multitudinous roar of meat being drilled could be heard. It wasn't loud or passionate enough for my liking. Klappa was being too soft on them. Otherwise, these two fighters wouldn't have had the strength for sex. So if the sergeant couldn't be heavy-handed enough, the commander certainly could. Fixing a sneer on my face in readiness, I stomped after them, limbering up my neck and shoulders as I went. *I certainly can.*

When, four hours later, I left the yard, pulling off my ripped wet T-shirt as I headed to the shower block, I did not look back. Why would I? I was sure all the goblins lying in the yard, down to the last man, had come. We would see just how able they were to have sex today. And if I should catch just one of them — or anyone from the night patrol — I would definitely put a cross in my personal dossier, and tomorrow I would do my utmost to make sure that by nightfall they didn't even have the strength to strain their anuses for a long rueful groan.

Nonetheless I did find myself looking back, my attention attracted by suppressed mutterings.

The mutterings of Wreck, Klappa, Tigr, and Gabby, shuffling after me scarcely able to put one foot in front of the other. I chuckled contentedly; the sergeants had understood everything correctly. Any boss had to be stronger, smarter, hardier, tougher, and more ruthless than his gang. And when his entire gang were flat on their backs, the boss had to have enough strength to get up, square his shoulders with pride, and walk calmly away, wiping his filthy face as he went. It was the only way to go. A boss was not a desk pogue whose nimbleness was long gone, if it had been there in the first place. He was a constant example to his fighters and had to show them as much every single day. And that example had to be a cynical steel girder with an eternal evil grin drawn crookedly on it. Today I tried to ram that home to everyone. Including the insects and beasts, who even then weren't able to outshine me in either sparring or running. No, I lie. Gabby beat me at physical exercises, but that only added to my wrath. It's hard to compete in push-ups and squats with someone who can do a thousand of each without displaying the slightest sign of tiredness, aside from jets of superheated steam spurting from his shoulder nozzles. The prism simply poured a couple of buckets of icy water down his gullet and was ready for whatever workload was thrown at him next.

This set me to thinking again about the wild prisms which had somehow contrived to undergo multiple evolutions. If Gabby, after his second rushed evolution, had transformed into a real robot with a beetle's mug, what would they be capable of?

We had to be prepared. We had to be prepared for the one very simple reason that the system had already issued me with a notification of the task Wormeus had spoken of. The task was encircled in my interface by a thick triple frame, so that I, a dumb goblin, would not miss it. And just in case, those frames flashed from time to time. Ditto the heading: "URGENT."

When Wormeus had mentioned the wild prisms and their evolution, I already knew about it. I'd received the task from the system during our airborne evacuation from shitting Paradise Promised. At the same time I had also received all the promised bonus rewards for our inspection of the lands of the ammnushiti.

Bonus reward №1: a trusting blind eye turned to the quantity and type of munitions of hero Erikvan's squad.

On its own initiative, the system had ceased to stick its nose into the matter of my arsenal. Mortar guns or anything extremely long-range, I could take whatever I wanted without stressing my tush about it.

Bonus reward №2: full gratis medical care for twelve months for all squad personnel.

This solved many of my goblins' medical problems all at once. How could that fail to delight any fighter?

Bonus reward №3: emergency delivery of mobile medblocks to any point on earth, with the exception of forbidden zones.

And this solved the remainder of my goblins' medical problems all at once. Field treatment was vitally important, and its presence or absence could mean the difference between a fighter's life or agonizing death.

Bonus reward №4: the placing at my full disposal of two old but fully operative buggies of the same model as Rox had cobbled together from odds and ends. And along with them, a spacious platform with low sides, which even in off-road conditions could be used to transport not only goblins, but also heavy machinery such as the White Hippo.

Bonus reward №5: the release, demothballing, and preparation for the red-reward return of all the personal effects of hero Erikvan, which were seized before the deletion of his memory and the change of his status. (Activate the red-bonus-reward line of the urgent Wild Evolution task).

The task was issued at the same time, and I read it there and then. It was a long read. The description of the aims stretched to twenty lines, and by the end I'd already stopped concentrating and understood exactly what was demanded of us.

MAIN TASK.

Task: wild evolution.

Description*: find the location where wild prisms evolve, and report your findings.*

Learn how wild evolution takes place, unsanctioned and not medically supported/enhanced /instigated by the system, and report your findings immediately.

Learn the organizational structure of wild prisms, and report your findings.

Learn the approximate number of prisms which have undergone multiple wild evolutions, and report your findings.

Location*: unspecified.*

Deadline*: unspecified.*

Reward*:*

Fifth-rank hero status to hero Erikvan.

Increased status for all squad members.

+ 150,000 crowns.

+ 1 week's vacation for all squad personnel in the Beach Dawns special vacation zone.

+ Bonus reward

+ Bonus reward

+ *Bonus reward*
+ *Bonus reward*
+ *Bonus reward*

Attention! This task is especially difficult and dangerous.
Attention! You may not refuse the task!

I tapped the red line, and read the following:

Battle exoskeleton + all other personal effects of hero Erikvan.

Battle exoskeleton. The two words which had made the name Night Adder slip from my lips. And no sooner had this happened, no sooner had my brain shifted into first gear, than I realized my recollection of the Night Adder had been brought on by the promised battle exoskeleton, which, according to the system, was among my personal effects from before.

I immediately wanted to get tableted — strictly for the utility, you understand — and lose myself entirely in new flashbacks. Yet I was refraining from any action that wasn't strictly necessary right now, to maintain sobriety of thought. And soon that sobriety was very much appreciated, when Wormeus's prediction came true and the Shiny Shack suddenly gained a new clientele that was entirely at odds with establishment's character. We dung beetles' favorite haunt seemed to have become the object of fancy for a bunch of bright tropical butterflies who were doing their damnedest to give the impression that eating shit was absolutely commonplace for them. Their pretense was so unconvincing that they soon desisted all attempts and took instead to doing what they really were accustomed to, which was drinking alcohol. It was not every hero who could pour so much booze into himself. Except posthumously. But these butterflies downed bottle after bottle of the most expensive wine. And that was just to begin with. When the wine ran out, they started on the homebrew, which was far stronger. And the more hooch drunk, the less clothing remained on the extravagant hostelry-hopping butterflies. After midnight they generally wore nothing more than skimpy knickers, and headbands with thick gray veils, beneath which would occasionally be secreted a glass of hooch, and from beneath which burst laughter that was so increasingly more cynical and malicious that it was soon completely incongruous with their original entrancing blushing-maiden giggles.

Uh-huh, blushing maidens indeed.

I rocked up at the inn early one evening, having visited the medblock and received all the necessary and recommended injections. As I walked in, I spotted my goblins heartily chuffing thick porridge with generous helpings of meat. The innkeeper had religiously executed my order of maximum amounts of carbohydrates, proteins, and fats. Every single day! And don't forget barrels of my favorite drink in this shitting world: lemonade, chilled. And no booze. Categorically. And no drugs. If you can't live without getting high on booze or drugs, you've chosen the wrong squad and are free to fuck the hell off. It went without saying that I didn't trust any of my goblins. And after a short speech, in which I'd given them all to understand that anyone caught high on liquor would have all their limbs broken, I ordered the sergeants and veterans to keep the situation under round-the-clock control. And I was soon convinced it had been well worth my while to err on the side of caution, for by the time of my arrival, the butterflies had nearly paralyzed my goblins with their appearance.

It's hard for a hillbilly to maintain composure when he's got juicy tits with gilded nipples quivering invitingly in front of him. Not to mention the taut contorting midriffs and slender twitching thighs of inebriated ripe fillies whose near-naked bodies are tattooed with mysterious gold-and-silver patterns. And to add insult to injury, those patterns pulsed with an enchanting light, underlining or concealing in shadow the crucial bits of those ideally crafted bodies.

My entrance coincided with the erotic light show, and it made the goblins regain their composure and notice the prods from their ill-disposed sergeants. Taking my place at table alongside Rox, who was indifferent to the shimmering delights, I helped myself to a bowl of porridge and took a slow look around the room. There were fifteen spirited butterflies, of both sexes, but I didn't notice the guys with their twinkling butts straightaway, since they clung shyly to the walls, sipping cocktails from enormous glasses through the complex curls of excessively thick straws. And anyway, they weren't immediately distinguishable from the girls, what with their similarly long, groomed hair and thick veils.

"I'm too old for this shit," sighed Rox, placing his spoon in his empty bowl and reaching for a glass of lemonade.

"Who *isn't* too old for it?" I chuckled, ignoring the sudden attention on me of the uninvited guests, who had so swiftly been overcome with the desire not only to have a drink in the village inn, but also to undress there.

"Does the alcohol ban extend to me as well?"

"No. You know when to stop."

"How do you know that?"

"You didn't become a raging alcoholic after the death of your own squad," I said matter-of-factly. "You didn't fritter your money away on shit, but used it to buy parts for the buggy. Basically you're a dry sinewy old codger with a clear program in your gray head, and boozing isn't a part of that program."

"You're right there," confirmed Rox.

"So what's going on with the Hippo's ass?"

"It's ragged and stinky. And dead."

"That bad, huh?"

"I can disassemble it and make a car. But a robot—"

"An exo," I corrected him.

"Same difference. That's another level, Elb, and at my age it would be a big ask. It needs a real tech-head."

"That's very open of you," I said, looking in surprise at the old man. "Not everyone would risk admitting their incompetence so easily."

"You use more and more clever words with every passing day," noted the old mechanic, giving the nearest waiter a universal gesture. Nodding his understanding, and throwing me a quick glance to check I approved of the order for alcohol, the waiter headed for the bar.

"More clever words?"

"Uh-huh. It looks like you were smarter before, goblin. Before they erased your memory."

"Perhaps I was."

"And your flashbacks have returned not only some of your memories but also some of the clever words you forgot."

"Perhaps," I said. "But let's get back to the Hippo's ragged asshole."

"I can't sew it up. Or rather, I can sew it up, but putting all the large bones and cables back in place, or replacing them, isn't an option. Although I have fixed some things I do understand. I've patched up a number of armored tubes, others I've replaced, I've taken off and flattened out a panel dented in the explosion, and I've replaced all the broken bolts. If we're talking about little things, I can do some more replacing and tweaking, but it'll be more like embalming a corpse and touching up its blue face cosmetically. I won't be able to bring it back to life."

"I see. Well, old man, there should be another buggy on the way today, with a loading platform. Klappa will give you the names of four of our fighters who will be completely under your command. Plus you can take Jorann. Consider them your brigade, although I need Jorann more as a communications officer. You'll get another four a bit later, for combat purposes."

"Communications officer. I said you were remembering strange words, goblin. What were you in your previous life?"

"The same as I am now, a killer."

"Well, yes, I suppose you were. Anyway, I understand about the brigade."

"Teach all of them to handle the vehicles confidently, work with the platform, load, distribute, and secure any cargo correctly, and manage minor failures in a field situation. I'll deal with their combat training, show them who controls which sectors when we're on maneuvers. We'll put machine guns on the buggy and mortar guns on the platforms."

"Jeez. Mortar guns?"

"Indeed. Make sure you create armored compartments on the platforms for ammunition."

"Will do."

"The Hippo will go on one of the platforms, so make sure there's space for it."

"Will do."

"And I need all this by the day after tomorrow in the morning."

"Aha. I'll have to get to work straight after din-ner. If I understand correctly, you'll be in charge of the exo, right?"

"The Hippo," I said, laughing. "What the hell would I want with that hulking thing. No, someone else will be on Hippo detail."

"You surprise me," said Rox. "And not just me."

"It isn't a battle exo," I explained. "It's a fat walking barrel organ which can play music, attract children, and somehow put one foot in front of the other. It has been slightly reconstructed, slightly enhanced speed-wise, and equipped with certain weapons, but it has not been transformed into an instrument of war."

"You know best."

"I know best," I agreed, standing up and look-ing meaningfully at all the now silent goblins, and then the salacious guests.

I didn't say a single word more. Well, why would I if everyone understood my unspoken hint? I didn't really care who my fighters fucked. And I didn't care what they chatted about after fucking. They didn't know much of interest anyway, so let them get jiggy with the gold- and silver-plated but-terflies. But only in their downtime. And at present the squad was a long way from leave. The goblins didn't know they were going to be woken in the middle of the night for a fifteen-kilometer forced march, followed by the freshening effects of cross-ing the nearest river to train their fording skills, before returning to barracks via an irrigation channel I'd noticed along the sides of the fields and vineyards. Obviously I would be doing all this with them, and gladly kicking the lazy ass of anyone flagging.

I took the staircase up to the second floor in a couple of bounds. I waited there for a short while and heard one of the goblins who had so recently been smiling say bleakly:

"Lead was smiling, did you see?"

"We saw," said a short-haired ginger lass in the same bleak tone. "Shit!"

"Shit indeed," sighed the fighter. "We're not going to be getting much freaking sleep tonight."

This was how goblins got smarter. Next time I would have to monitor their ability to maintain a stony facial expression, so that a surprise would always be a surprise.

We returned to the hostelry at daybreak.

Some of us ran in through the gates, some walked, some crawled, and some were pulled on sledges.

Not bad.

Seriously not bad.

No more than a couple of dozen mild injuries, five slightly more serious, and seven or eight broken limbs. Broken fingers didn't count. Only two nearly drowned and had to be given artificial respiration. Only one sustained a serious head injury, when he jumped into the river not as he'd been shown (legs firmly together in front, hands raised above head to begin with then spread out on contact with the water in order to slow entry). Instead the goblin executed a beautiful swallow dive, dumb head first, shouting "Geronimo!" just before his head collided with a knotty floating log. I didn't even want to resuscitate the cretin, but his group felt sorry for him and I decided not to interfere. They also had to quickly cobble together a stretcher for him, and in response to their request not to drag the half-dead fool into the muddy channel, I merely laughed and helped the fighters lower themselves in with friendly kicks. Then, standing over the squad as they sat there in the mud, I explained that we did not abandon our own troops. We either dragged them on, or we buried them. So they had a choice to make. They could either quickly burying the idiot and continue running unburdened, or they could carry him. The weary goblins pleased me by contemplating my generous suggestion seriously, while glancing ominously at their unconscious comrade. They thought for a couple of minutes, before deciding to carry him on.

"Meat!" I barked. "Not good. But better than I expected. Listen up! Each dozen is responsible for delivering their wounded to the medblocks. Each dozen is responsible for all their collective equipment and weapons, and if the wounded cannot clean their own gear, then their dozen cleans it for them. So get a move on! Get your wounded to the medblocks, and get your weapons and equipment in order, shiny clean! Wash your asses, have a bite to eat, and get some sleep before reveille. Chop-chop, goblins. You ain't gonna get a lot of sleep tonight."

The moaning yard came to life. They wiggled their leaden limbs to get them moving again, and their shouting bosses helped them with kind words and gentle kicks. The first sledges were pulled in the direction of the medblocks, and the street showers for washing cattle gurgled noisily into action. Powerful jets of cold water struck the fighters, who began scrubbing their mud-encrusted skin.

Leading by example, I got into a shower and got busy with my equipment, starting with my weapons. About five minutes later Tigr and Tigrala ran into the yard, followed by Burger and Steak, who were coughing wheezily. After making them cross the water obstacle, I'd given Tigr an extra order to run around the fields surrounding the inn, and only then climb into the irrigation channel. Reconnaissance guys had to have double the endurance and speed, for they always had double the workload. Catching his breath, the beastfolk waved a heavy paw towards the gates, where a dozen unfamiliar goblins with stressed-out expressions were shifting their feet timorously.

"Some fresh meat wants to join our ranks," explained the beastfolk.

"Klappa!" I shouted, making the swordsman step out from his shower. "Have a word with those goblins and tell them how shit everything is around here. If they don't change their minds, split them up among the dozens and tell them to get their butts ready for action."

"Yes sir!"

At a plodding trot, the Asian approached the gates, while I looked up at the contentedly smiling guardsman in his lookout tower and gestured for him to come down and help carry the wounded to where they could be healed. With another hand signal, I ordered Tigr to find someone to replace the watchman, and soon Steak and Burger were on their way up there. Their backs were very expressive, but there was no joy in that expression. The smart goblins understood that sleep was not on the agenda.

"I'm so up for some debauchery," sighed a girl with golden eyebrows and lashes as she leaned out of a windows, looking surprisingly fresh and sober after a whole night's drinking. "How about some sex, hero Elb?"

"Heroes have no time for sex right now," I replied, removing my load-bearing vest, scrunching it up into a dirty ball, and throwing it into the shower. "Wreck! Turn your mug away from those golden titties and back to your rifle!"

"Mug turned away from golden titties, sir! Bah!"

"What a bunch of losers," huffed the golden butterfly in umbrage, drawing herself back inside the inn. "Waste of time holding out. Hey, peasant, fancy a bit of my body?"

"Hehehehe!"

"It's soft and supple."

"Hehehehe!"

"Come and get it!"

"Ooooh!"

The goblins chatting by the gates recoiled to the side when they saw a couple of enormous black bulls approaching them hauling a laden cart covered with tarpaulin. Following them slowly was a buggy with a platform. Rox strode hastily towards the long-awaited cargo, and after throwing a quick glance at Gabby, who was trying to wash the dirt from all his crevices, Jorann hurried after him.

Good.

While the exhausted goblins slept, I would pay another visit to the medblock to request additional injections for speedier recovery. I would hustle the rest of the goblins there as well when they woke up. And I would check my interface for less important tasks. Perhaps something seriously worthwhile would show up.

* * *

The White Hippo was revived by Wormeus's mechanics, who, while they were at it, also replaced the cheap-shit brain of the recreational exo with a smarter module. Thus the exo lost its ringing voice and its ability to attract little children and other unwanted attention, because the vocal software turned out to have been in the removed chips. The mechanics were not from my squad, but I was the one they reported to after they finished the job, handling themselves in a calm but businesslike fashion and not allowing themselves to digress to non-essential subjects. In a word, professionals.

Their report gave me to understand that the Hippo now moved fifteen percent faster, and its manipulators would have a slightly firmer grip, but no matter how much you busted a gut or how many new brains you fitted into the old metalware, you would still not be able to get battle-worthy speed or hardiness out of it. That said, it would ensure you a half decent fight, although as the senior mechanic confidently claimed as he dusted down his gray coveralls, if the machine were to prove itself in a combat situation, it would only be to fend off an attack by spear-wielding savages. Whereas if you used it for combat support and fitted it with more suitable weapons and equipment...

I was entertaining similar thoughts myself, but I didn't interrupt the mechanics, nor did I hurry them. Quite the opposite. After buying them lunch, I spent a couple of hours listening intently to their every word, asking them to clarify and give finer detail where necessary, laughing at their jokes, which I did not always understand, agreeing with their opinions concerning often shit-for-brains exoskeleton operators, and basically being as genial as I could. I asked hods of questions not only about the Hippo, but also about exoskeletons in general. As I listened to the technicians, I committed to memory everything I heard. And after the men had eaten their fill, and drunk their fill of the strange local tea, which was red and mildly acidic, we returned to the Hippo, which had been repaired using scrap metal, and I told them what I wanted. After hearing me out, the mechanics had a confab, before proposing some minor changes to my plan. I approved those changes, and they got back to work, first of all fitting the battle vehicle with weapons.

As a result, the exo's batteries were replaced with higher-capacity ones, which gave it four hours of autonomy as opposed to the ninety minutes it had had before, and that at a push. Exos were energy guzzlers, and knowing this, I ordered Rox to prepare a permanent space on the platform for the Hippo. Such machines spent most of the time in sleep mode and were transported by other vehicles to where they would be called into action. Only once it was in place would the operator climb into the machine, hit the ignition button, and stand up to begin building, transferring, or killing, depending on the exo and its set aims.

And anyway, that four hours' worth of autonomy was bullshit, nothing more than a theory, as yet unproven.

In a real combat situation, with a professional combat operator sitting inside the exo, the scenarios were always different, due to the picture on the battlefield. Sometimes exos would simply stand there, concealed, all guns blazing, spending no energy on walking, and recharging with the use of land-based sources or solar panels. On the other hand, such ideal situations were rare, and there would generally be lots of running, jumping, falling, rolling, clambering up hills, and felling young trees to clear a path, at which point energy would flow like blood from a slit throat.

The Hippo needed testing, but that was a job for later. First we would have to wait for it to be fitted with additional armored plates, its left hand to be enhanced with a ten-barrel shotgun that would pepper an elephant at the pull of a single trigger, and its right arm enhanced with an armor-piercing weapon to be fired by the operator, if, that is, the operator had a chip in his head. Extra cartridges and other ammo were to be stowed beneath the rear armor plating, and a mortar gun attached firmly to the fine-mesh floor of the cage on the back of its neck. The cage also had room for plenty of ammo and one or two goblins, whose task would be not only to fire the weapon, but also to reload the exo's guns.

A second mortar gun was located on the loading platform, where Rox was welding together an armored crow's nest of sorts.

The Hippo would soon cease to be white for ever, and had come to look like the kind of regular battle exo driven by drug-cartel gunmen. Drug cartels, who never needed money but never had access to truly elite combat technology, would buy up hundreds of any available model of exo or other larger walking machine, paint them in the cartel's colors and add the cartel's emblem, arm them with nigh prehistoric homemade guns, and set them loose on the perimeter of their territories. Similar exos patrolled the gang-controlled ghettos, denying entry to cops and outsiders, and were also used for fighting by the law-abiding citizens of independent communities living in the Abandoned Territories.

The Abandoned Territories. Shit! All this info was swimming up in my head all by itself, without any effort whatsoever on my part. I was simply remembering it, though I was absolutely sure I hadn't known any of it yesterday. Never mind. I would soon be chuffing another tablet. Just as soon as I got these urgent matters out of the way.

Yet how bright were the pictures in my buzzing head. I was inside an exo and moving through thickets of genetically modified plants whose giant buds were already open and effusing a thick "ether," which dripped right into the greedily gaping mouths of emaciated weaklings sprawled on the ground, who, no longer eating or drinking, were slowly dying in an everlasting high. Occasionally a limb or a flimsy rib cage would be crushed underfoot, but the ones I was walking over continued to smile beatifically even with fountains of blood pulsing from their mouths. They no longer cared. Whereas for us, these fields and flowers were absolutely vital, and me and my squad were going to seize them from a drug cartel, by locking horns with their cumbersome makeshift exos and larger bipedal machines. The ether produced by the flowers in this field was a component of the complex cocktail that made up Amnos. It wasn't only the harvest we needed; we needed these lands, and the people who worked them, for whom nothing would change. Nothing at all would change here after my visit. Except, of course, the ownership.

Exos.

Whole wars were fought using this kind of cobbled-together fighting mechanism, private, obviously, and secretly sponsored by greedy all-powerful corporations. They were also used in gladiatorial duels, where one of the operators would more often than not die. Such exos pulled trailers bearing eternal hobos traveling the dying world, recharging with the aid of solar panels which opened up on the roofs. These hobos, traveling chiefly in small families with complicated internal relations, rejected what in their opinion were dead concepts and laws, instead inventing a few of their own. They were peaceful and strange, and loved to smoke pungent homegrown marijuana sitting on the shoulders of the exos and the roofs of the trailers when they were parked-up, discussing the fate of the world, and looking from the highways at the low-lying, derelict, and abandoned towns, factories, and cemeteries. These hobos delighted in the death throes of the world, feasting their eyes for hours on the multicolored chemical sunsets and black clouds.

* * *

There was a memory. And then it vanished. Like a fish surfacing momentarily before disappearing back into the deep. And again. Never mind, I would wait. I had things to do in the present.

The curious mettlesome guests drank and drank, expertly pouring hooch down their throats. So as not to let their reserves run dry, the innkeeper hurried to replace them, ordering a whole wagon of various kinds of alcohol, from fresh, almost child-strength cider (his words) to spirits so strong that one look at the bottle would make your eyes melt (his words again). Wreck didn't believe him and went to stare at the bottles of spirit, but he soon returned, choking on his alcoholic's saliva and looking like the most wretched orc in the area. He didn't try so much as a drop. The squad was temporarily on the wagon. The squad was temporarily not permitted leave. The squad was temporarily not having sex. This last point was not actually a ban, but if I were to see any goblins copulating, I would return to the conclusion that they were not under enough physical stress. After tonight, we would see whether anyone had the urge.

It was unlikely, however, for I allowed them only five hours' sleep before waking them for more training. This time it was weapons and shootouts, and involved three hours of uninterrupted firing. I divided everyone into twos and threes, gave them weapons, and made them shoot, then disassemble the weapons, clean and reassemble them, fill magazines and load cartridges into shotguns, change position, shoot again, disassemble again, etc. etc. over and over. And all the while I reminded them poisonously that a fighter did not need to know the name of that cunningly curved doohickey in his machine gun, but he it was vital that he knew where to insert it and how to do so in double quick time. Scarcely was the shooting done than it was "Hello, long distance run!" Running ahead of the goblins, I didn't give them the chance to just brainlessly put one foot in front of the other and shuffle as slowly as possible towards the finish line. I made them sprint flat out, crawling and jumping into the bargain. And who said anything about roads? Nah, this was real off-road terrain, overgrown with barbs, dotted with burrows, and piled high with boulders. The only children's playground one would ever need for training. If you learned to play here, you would be good to play anywhere.

Our route brought us to a small hamlet, a tightly huddled group of five tranquil-looking two-story buildings with their windows removed and their roofs partly dismantled. The hamlet was not dead. On the contrary, it was flourishing off to the side, proudly adorned with the stone walls of recently completed buildings surrounded lovingly by flowers. Attracted by the racket we were making and the stink of our sweaty bodies, the master came out to meet us. A beefy old man with a stony glare and the mannerisms more of a murderer than a farmer. It took me just a couple of words to convince him we presented no threat, and a couple more to secure permission for my goblins to cool off in a shallow pool beneath an awning, where some pigs were wallowing in the heat. Just the ticket. As I sat neck deep in the murky water, in the close company of my blissfully moaning goblins, I also managed a brief chat with the reasonable old man, and we soon came to a simple agreement.

Half an hour later I kicked everyone out of the cattle bath, before calling the bosses for a brief explanation of the task before us. I did not look at the observation dome glinting in the rays of the artificial sun, but I knew the system was listening to my every word. The system was watching us sweat blood in preparation, and that was to my advantage, although right now I couldn't give a shit for the system's approval, for I had a different task in hand.

The old log buildings required breaking up into their component parts, but there was so much to do in the hamlet that by eventide, when the laborers finished their daily duties, they were in no state to be dismantling anything.

In which case, we would be glad to help.

I had promised we would disassemble one building today, but first we would indulge in some horseplay in it.

The task I set the squad was simple: take the building by storm. The task would be considered completed when all the building's protectors were "dead."

The youngsters against the bosses and me. Weapons: clubs, electroshockers, brass knuckles, and carelessly sharpened knives. I held back on firearms for now, but tomorrow I would buy the trade points out of rubber-bullet guns, and then... But I mustn't get ahead of myself.

After giving the command, I waited for the bosses to explain the details intelligibly to the meat, then headed unhurriedly to the building, ignoring gruff complaints about how unfair it was. Climbing the creaking stairs to the second floor, I selected a position at the far end of the corridor and waited. Curses! Despite myself, I felt like that same zombie leader who had holed up in the Calm Beeches infirmary waiting for the next gaggle of glory- and cash-hungry idiots to encroach on his territory.

The first goblin, who hared up to the second floor with a strange bloodcurdling shriek and came at me wielding a knife, turned sharply around with a little help from me, crossed the nearest room in a couple of bounds and flew out of the window, continuing to screech. He crashed down belly-first onto some planks lying by the wall of the house and was quiet. Moments later he was followed by a bald girl who attempted to creep up unnoticed, and whose perfectly straightened legs now sunk into the earth. She tried to jump to her feet, not immediately understanding that at least one of her lower limbs was broken. Then Wreck, who had settled in beside me, gave a mighty roar and put his boot into the face of a goblin who appeared at the window. The boot made contact with the goblin's visor, and upon landing, the irate fighter yelled and stubbornly repeated his attempt, promising loudly to rend someone's asshole with his beef bayonet. This time the vexed Wreck jumped out of the window to meet him, only to be jumped on by five wily youngsters who had clearly planned the ambush having studied the orc's character. With ringing and clanging sounds somewhere behind me, also on the second floor, the next fool took heroic flight earthwards, shouting Klappa's name on the way.

What were you expecting, cretins? And this is all without firearms. I didn't say anyone had to creep up to the building. I didn't challenge anyone to slink up unnoticed.

The log-by-log dismantling of the first building fell to us, the veterans. The remainder, loaded down with stretchers and sledges, sauntered back to base as quickly as they could, since a dozen or so goblins were seriously wounded and required urgent medical attention.

When we were done with our disassembly, leaving everything lying just where it was to be carted away later, the old man came over with a jug of lemonade and thanked me for a job well done.

"What's with the praise, old man?" I inquired, passing the half-emptied jug to Wreck, whose face was a mess of scratches. He'd come out of the skirmish victorious, but his helmet had been torn off and an especially malicious goblin girl had given his mug a good raking with her claws, before being launched backwards into a wall tailbone-first and losing consciousness.

"What am I praising you for?" the old man asked hesitantly, collecting his thoughts before explaining. "There are plenty of young guys among the workers, and a whole building was allocated as their living quarters. They are all single, and all eager to get somewhere and prove their strength to the world."

"And?"

"And today they watched you and your honchos bung guys and gals ass-first down onto logs and bricks from the second floor, and their rhetoric changed in an instant. They stopped talking about heroic feats, and started talking about watering allotments and clearing irrigation channels. So I am thanking you for correcting the youth. And tomorrow there will be more people coming from neighboring settlements, and rumors will spread. Let them see faces being squished against walls and rocks, blood spurting from smashed noses, and bones crunching. You will be here tomorrow, won't you?"

"Perhaps even later today," I said with a chuckle. "And you will give us more lemonade, old man."

"More than today," said the orc throatily.

"You will have your lemonade. And a couple of barrels of salted rye pretzels."

"Now you're talking!"

Nodding in parting, I strode away accompanied by my honchos.

"Bask wants a word with you, lead," said Klappa nonchalantly, refusing the lemonade but chuffing a mug of thick sour cream and a sizable chunk of heavily salted bread he'd asked for. The swordsman knew how to replenish his strength.

"What about?"

"Something to do with Cecil."

"Well let's go and have a word with him then," I said, breaking into a run. "Let's catch the meat up. What's with the sour face, Gabby?"

"Some cretin fell off the roof and landed on the back of my neck when I stuck my head out of a window," complained the prism.

"And?"

"He skewered himself on my shoulder spines and pissed himself from the pain, and now I've got to wash his piss and blood from all my nooks and crannies."

"An experience to learn from. That's what they're like," I barked, accelerating. "Get a move on! When we get back, five hours' rest. And then it's back here for anyone who's up to it."

We returned not five, but four hours later. This time there were twenty fewer of us. The remainder, nursing varying degrees of injury, were resting up beneath awnings in the yard and carrying out my orders to eat, drink, sleep, shit, and visit the med-block. And all of this as often as possible.

The Hippo came with us.

We arrived by the shortest route, which took us just one hour. I drove the exo, carrying the youngsters on its shoulders, and I took the girl I'd picked out for the role of operator into the cabin with me to observe and learn on the hoof. With her wet vest clinging to me, that is just what she did, following my actions attentively and staring un-ceasingly at the screens. On the way I explained everything in brief. And on the way I remembered what it was like to be inside a moving battle walker. The Hippo was too big. It was difficult to call an exo, which was basically just a souped-up spacesuit, whereas this was a walking machine built for strolling around an amusement park. Too heavy and too unwieldy, although at least it worked silently now.

When we got the Hippo to the hamlet, I climbed out, looked at the gray-eyed girl with the high cheekbones who immediately stretched herself out on the divan, and asked for the first time:

"Name, fighter?"

"Sebl."

"If you can handle it, the exo is yours, Sebl, understood?"

"Yes, lead! Thank you, lead!" she replied, her eyes lighting up in delight.

"But if you fuck up..."

"Yes, lead! Understood!"

"Get busy. You've got twenty minutes. Keep an eye on energy consumption and remember you've got to get back to base under your own steam. Don't waste energy on shooting. Do a couple of laps around the hamlet, and ford a few streams and channels on your way. And don't forget about weight. Your tush now weighs a couple of tons, which are being carried on two legs. Think about where you're going, think about where you're stepping, and steer clear of trees and buildings to begin with."

"Yes sir!"

The lid slammed shut, and with a churning of servomechanisms, the exo half straightened itself up, stood there for a moment, and then slowly about faced and marched away, becoming freer and faster with each step. Another thirty seconds later the exo was fully erect, its manipulators crossed, and striding more evenly; Sebl had pressed the auto-control button, and the Hippo had switched into the more economical cruise control, listening in closely to its operator's body.

"You," I said, poking a young lad who a few hours previously had displayed reasonable skill at throwing stones and bricks in through the windows of a hostel, thus covering the gatekeepers storming the building. "Catch her up and clamber into the basket on the back."

"Yes sir! And do what there?"

"Study the mortar gun. Get used to the motion on the back of a walking or running exo's neck."

"Yes, lead!"

"You go with him," I said, nodding to a still wheezing shapely chick, whose enviable tenacity and physical endurance had stood out, despite her approaching fifty. She was also not afraid to be on the receiving end of strikes, and she dearly loved any firearm. "Your job is to replace the exo's batteries and reload its weapons."

"Yes sir! My name is Lana."

"Make yourselves at home in there. And tell the others you are all forbidden from exiting the exo before you get back to base. Do everything on the hoof."

"Yes sir!"

After watching them go, I turned towards another building, studied it briefly, and ordered:

"Bosses on me! Everyone else into the building. This time we attack and you defend. Check your ammo. Everyone must have rubber bullets. And check your gear. If anyone's unprotected face takes a bullet... The task is the same as last time. Defenders hold your positions, stormers destroy all defenders. Do not spare ammo! Your job is to kill us."

"Put a rifle round in the boss's ass?" said one of the new recruits with a wink. He was a big lad, fair-haired, left cheek scarred. "With pleasure!"

"Oh shit," moaned another big lad, this one lying on a stretcher and holding his belly, which had been injured in a fall. "Oh shit, my ass is grass. Oh shit."

Nobody paid him any attention, for they all had their own concerns. The column, with a limping exo bringing up the rear, moved slowly towards base. The spectators waved us off, another building now a pile of logs and planks. Young guys thoughtfully rubbed their bellies beneath their white shirts, clearly having second thoughts about becoming heroes.

"We will be back here again, won't we, lead?"

"Did you like the sour cream?"

"Yes, I did. And the bread was tasty too."

"We'll be back," I confirmed, turning back to look at the limping exo. "The Hippo needs recharging. Then send it out on a raid around the base.

When they get back, make them change the batteries, and send them straight out on another raid. Keep the basket squad busy."

"How?"

"Is the basket full of bricks and planks?"

"It is."

"So get them to unloaded at the base, then load it again and return to the hamlet. Unload, reload, then back to base, via a different route. Unload there, etc. etc."

"Understood, lead."

"Good."

"Get them used to the exo?"

"Get them used to their new walking barracks," I said, correcting him. "It's their new home. Get ready for a small mission."

"Can I go this time?"

"I don't remember forbidding it," I said with a chuckle.

"Understood, lead. I won't lose to the orc at that game again."

"Have you got something else to say?"

"It's nothing serious, but…"

"Nothing serious?"

"It's about the fruit and veg the innkeeper gives by the enormous basketful."

"Get to the point, Klappa."

"It really is nothing serious. Probably something to do with the seasonal spraying of the orchards and allotments. Mild food poisoning, I had diarrhea for ages. It's nothing serious, but it's annoying and it puts the fighters out of action. Today six of them went down with it, when they could have been training with us."

"Get to the point, Klappa. What's wrong with the fruit and vegetables?"

"Well..."

* * *

"Now then!" I shouted as I stood in front of the awnings that were home to no small quantity of bunks and hammocks for those fighters preferring to receive treatment and recuperate in the fresh air. "Apparently you goblins don't like washing your fruit and vegetables and are quite happy to eat them along with the dirt stuck to them."

"There are vitamins in dirt as well, lead!" said a goblin of about thirty, swinging in a hammock, his arm bandaged and a weary smile on his face.

"Vitamins," I parroted. "That's right, vitamins. Come here, fighter."

When the goblin in question ran over to me, I handed him a piece of fruit.

"Take this apple."

"Thanks, lead."

"It isn't washed."

"I don't care, lead."

"Eat it when I tell you to."

"Yes sir. Get this, goblins, Lead Elb has given me an apple."

"Let me tell you a story, goblins, a simple life story. The harvest season is beginning" — I smiled a beaming friendly smile as I sauntered to and fro behind the goblin gripping his red apple — "and the master of the orchard announces to his pickers that today they will be picking apples. So, they fetch ladders and baskets and start picking the juicy ripe fruit. They grip them with strong dexterous fingers, pluck them from the trees, and drop them into their baskets, and when the baskets are full, they take them to the carts and unload them. It's not the easiest of work. The poor things sweat, everything itches, especially their asses, and the sweaty hardy workers stop for a couple of seconds to reach their hands into their pants and give their sweaty balls a good old scratch, really raking them with their nails, which have gathered a ton of stinking sticky crap beneath them."

"Shit," muttered the goblin with the apple.

"Then their fingers venture deeper, into the especially sweaty crevice housing a hole which excretes lord knows what, and which yesterday they didn't wipe particularly carefully. And there you have it. After collecting sweat and dirt from their hairy cocks and cracks, while they're at it adjusting their sweaty members, which also haven't been washed since yesterday's hurried root in a haystack with their fat girlfriends, they return to their apple picking, gently gripping the fruit with moist sticky fingers."

"Moist with shit! Shit!"

"So what's the fucking moral of this story? That peasants toil in the sweat of their faces and buttholes, and their toil must be respected! So, now, eat the apple, goblin!"

"I…"

"Eat the apple, goblin!"

"Is it washed, lead? Is it?"

"Nah," I snarled. "It isn't fucking washed. And it has passed through any number of hands. So, come on, lick its red skin."

"Bl… bleugh!"

"Lick the skin, fighter!"

"Can I rinse it first, lead? I beseech you in the name of Mother!"

"But what about the vitamins?"

"I need to rinse it first. I really need to rinse the apple."

"Everyone's going to rinse their fruit three times from now on," came someone else's suppressed muttering. "Disgusting clammy cracks. Ugh, I don't feel too good."

With a nod, I about turned and headed for the inn. It was time to grab a bite to eat before getting down to some particularly important business.

CHAPTER 7

THE CHANGES TO THE INN'S ATMOSPHERE were tangible as soon as you walked in.

The flowery gilded butterflies were still there, but they were now all huddled together at the end of the room closest to the exit and were unusually quiet. In fact the whole place was quite. The drunken shouts and squeals were gone, as were the affected sighs of passion and the demands for more food and booze.

The reason for all this was also evident straightaway: the middle of the room was occupied by knights. Just the two of them, mind, but such specimens as to immediately recall Arthur's tale about the celestial warriors. Their armor was an exclamatory masterpiece in which gold plating, silver, and precious stones skillfully masked the advanced technology of these exos stylized to look like knights' armor. Taking just a couple of paces towards them, I understood there wasn't a single chink in them, and what seemed to the naked eye to be gaps between armor plates were nothing more than false markings drawn artfully with black paint. The knights' helmets were decorated with luxuriant twigs whose leaves were fashioned from a transparent green material. Their visors were raised to expose manly faces.

The fact that I hadn't been informed of their arrival meant they'd only just gotten here. And in the short time since their arrival they had managed not only to have a good look around, but also to make a few changes to the interior of the inn, chief among which was the table for two placed modestly up against a blank wall not far from the bar. The table was not local to these parts. I did not remember the inn having round tables made entirely, or even partly, of crystal, nor even matching crystal chairs with openwork backs.

"Hero Elb," said the elder of the knights. "How good it is that we are not forced to seek you out."

Saying nothing in response, I looked their armor greedily up and down, also paying attention to their weapons: cold weapons fixed at their waists, firearms fixed on their backs. "Fixed" was the operative word, for the weapons were located in special slots rather than hanging from belts. Little bulges in the smalls of their backs and on their chests, thighs, and shins indicated technical nodes beneath the armor, housing batteries, servomechanisms, medkits, and other necessary items.

Any glinting knight like these would appear to the apple-knockers to be a hauntingly charismatic, powerful, and fine envoy from on high.

"You must disinfect and wash yourself forthwith, change into clothes we shall provide you, spray yourself with a light tangy perfume, and take a seat on the left-hand chair. You must leave your weapons and other equipment in—"

"In your asshole?" I suggested, before about-facing and striding towards the exit.

"Hey, hero Elb! I see you do not understand exactly who desires an audience with you."

"A Higher," came a barely audible squeak from the innkeeper, who stood motionless by the wall. "Holy Mother, a Higher is here. This is her bodyguard."

Turning back, I took in the knights once again, then looked out of the window, where parked on the grass was the flying machine which had ferried the messengers here noiselessly. With a tsk and a sigh of envy, I strode on.

"Hero Elb! You are obliged to—"

"I am obliged to do nothing for you," I retorted.

"But many are obliged to you." A tall slim figure stepping silently in through the doorway lifted the thick gray veil from its face, to reveal unnaturally large yet phenomenally beautiful brown eyes staring at me through a frame of thick black lashes. "Hero Elb, perpetrator of yet another deed. Hero Elb, who continues to lie low in a modest village inn instead of heading eagerly for Crontown. Shall we talk, hero?"

"Let's talk," I replied, averting my gaze with some difficulty from the improbably beautiful and purebred face. "Who are you?"

"I am Diltariluella of the West." The ashen-haired beauty smiled, tilting her head a touch and allowing a piked ear to peek through her hair. "A Higher. We are also known as elves. You may call me Dilya."

"This is a great honor!" exclaimed the inn-keeper, who reacted to too many things in an overly emotional manner.

Taking another look around, I nodded towards the table, puckered my brow lightly, and suggested:

"Pea soup with fried pig fat and onion, cold meat with salt and garlic, warm bread with a wee dram of moonshine. We can eat and drink to our hearts' content, and we can always move on to sizzling fried eggs afterwards."

"Sounds awesome," said the elf lady, favoring me with a smile.

"There's an awning with a couple of benches behind our garage."

"Lead the way."

"Mistress." One of the knights expressed his displeasure through gritted teeth. "Your status... This is somewhat... According to your schedule, today is day nine of your strict diet of crimson fruits. Well, and cranberry and seaweed smoothies."

With a snorted laugh, the elf lady turned around and walked briskly to the door, removing her headband and veil as she went, along with her pink elbow gloves. I threw a quick glance at the innkeeper, who darted into the kitchen to prepare the sudden order.

"Fuck smoothies," muttered the elf lady resentfully as she threw her gloves on the floor. "Give me meat!"

By the time we arrived at the awning, little remained of the elf lady's attire, most of it discarded in the dust of the yard to be hastily picked up by the knights, whose composure had returned. On the way, not only did she remove all her clothes, but she also found new ones, unashamedly robbing a clothesline of a drying T-shirt and sneakers, and flattening down the back part of the latter to turn them into flip-flops. The garments' owner, who was shaving and nearly cut his nose off in his anger at such effrontery, clocked my signal to chill and stood there paralyzed by the flash of breast which quickly disappeared beneath his commandeered T-shirt.

Taking a seat on a crate of bullets, the elf lady crossed her legs beneath herself with a flash of her snow-white panties, then gathered her extremely long hair into a ponytail reaching nearly to her knees. Just when I thought that was all, the Higher then wiped her face with a silk handkerchief. I offered her a thin pack of towelettes that lay on the table, and the gift was accepted gratefully. After wiping off her makeup, of which she wore surprisingly little compared to the puffy mugs of the visiting ladies of the night, she sighed with relief, knit her brow once more, and muttered:

"I knew I should have listened to Mother and Mother alone. But no, I listened to the snivellings of those who observe shitting etiquette and revere the pageantry of stifling attire."

"What did the system say?" I inquired, looking at the knights who now stood motionless a little way away. "She obviously said something about me."

"How do you know that?"

"Your knights aren't standing right behind you," I replied. "No matter how sharp their reflexes, they won't have time to leap into action if I decide to wring your neck. The system won't have time either, because we're hidden from the dome by the buggy and the awning, yet your bodyguards appear not to be bothered by the risk. The only alternative is that I am currently in the crosshairs of a sniper's rifle."

"That would be perfectly rational," said the girl.

"But the sniper would have to be airborne, what with us being surrounded on all sides by a fence. Yet I see no flying drones in the vicinity."

"If you should happen to see one, no one will be aiming at you."

"So what did the system tell you?"

"That you like simplicity. You don't like excess in anything. You are a junkie, hooked on elven tears, and your dose is slowly creeping upwards. You inject crimson-lime isocitrate. You are clever and practical, committed and ruthless, unafraid of blood, and you kill with the composure of an executioner. You treat your body like a mechanism, demanding seamless obedience of it and striving to always be at the peak of your physical potential, and you demand the same of anyone who follows you. You hate pressure and harsh control, and you are always waiting for an excuse to display disobedience. You strive for total freedom. Money does not concern you, or rather you see it as a means to an end, but the expression 'I am rich' absolutely does not warm the cockles of your heart. You do not kill for no reason, nor for the sake of trophies or fun. But at the same time there is much you are intolerant of. You cannot bear, for example, cannibalism, rape, or sadism for the sake of sadism."

"Hmm."

"And also, you do not exist."

"How so?"

"We are elves."

"I could tell that by your ears."

"Elves... What did you say? Wring my neck?"

"Uh-huh."

"Bear in mind for the future, goblin hero Elb, that it is not enough simply to wring an elf's neck. It is also not enough to slit his throat, and stabbing him in the heart is a joke. The only way to kill an elf is to chop his head off, and even then you must make sure the head rolls a safe distance from the body. Then you will kill his reason and personality, which happens ten or fifteen minutes after brain death. But the body, most likely, will stopper the neck stump approximately four seconds after decapitation, then it will stand up and move after the head, knowing exactly where to find it. We Highers have an especially ignominious form of execution, which has only ever been employed a mere ten times, no more. An elf is decapitated, his head is attached to a rope and dragged along the ground, and the headless body walks after it with its arms outstretched. The head is taken to the compost pit and thrown in a decent distance from the edge. Then the body follows it."

"Technology and chemicals?"

"The very same." The elf lady understood me correctly and touched her right breast, before continuing, "The Highers' bodies contain many things, and I'm not just talking about electronics and high-tech medkits. I'm talking about DNA. Just so you know, goblin Elb, the elves are what the goblins were supposed to become, every last one. We are the people of the future, a race of demigods capable of living in the very worst ecological conditions, and we toil stubbornly to change those conditions for the better. We are highly developed saviors of the world. However, I am not one of them. I may be resilient, but I am no super fighter and I have no super strength. I am merely beautiful. I am meant to stand on the veranda of a cozy house, watching with a joyful smile as my husband's flier lands, bringing him home after a hard days' work saving the world. You get the idea. But we never got around to trying to save the world. We merely lounge around eating fruit, fucking in veils, and yawning indolently in the breaks between."

"Jeez," I said. "Are you sure you're not going to have your clever head lopped off for sedition?"

"Nah. I was chosen by lottery to be a Scarlet Jester for twenty-seven days. Only it has already been thirty-three days. I can talk about whatever I so choose, and demand whatever I so choose, so long as my opinion does not coincide with the opinion of the other Highers, in any matter and at any time. That includes during important meetings, polls, and all the rest of it. I must always be in opposition. I must always do what I want, and no one has the right to stop me, because I am this season's Jester. If the Highers want to plant a small fir forest in the flatlands, I must be against the motion, and I must explain why. Using reason, intelligence, and detail concerning why we must not plant a fir forest, and why it would be better to plant a meadow full of orchids instead, or let the marshy flatlands drain dry so they can be plowed at a later date. But it is not easy to always be against the motion, goblin Elb. Although I guess you wouldn't know that, right?"

"I'm glad to have met you," I said sincerely. "I enjoy gathering information."

"As do I. I also like unusual characters. And I am easily bored. And I snap easily. Which is why I am here. Where are my peas and pig fat?"

"They're on the way," I said, pointing with my eyes at the innkeeper hurrying with a tray, and the big-eared waitresses running after him. "So anyway, why do I not exist?"

"When serious rumors about you started doing the rounds, after the Blue Light, everyone became interested in who you were. What do you think says most about a person?"

"His past?"

"Precisely. Mother was asked to disclose your case. Many people wanted to know who this incredible goblin had been previously. And Mother let them know. Take that and devour it! It contained your biography, beginning with your awakening as a Volitional Nullform, and a list of your incredible deeds, which truly were incredible given your past abilities and technical capabilities. Basically everything right up to the present moment. There was just one problem. There was absolutely nothing concerning the time before you became a Volitional Nullform. Not even your age. Fortunately, your sex was at least mentioned, and the fact that you are a man. And now you have no tasks or duties. Not a single active task."

"Not a single one," I confirmed with a slow nod.

That meant that the "urgent" task currently posted in my status could not be seen by the elves. Good.

"What about rewards for previous tasks?"

"Those are always hidden," said Dilya. "Rewards for tasks are always personal, so that no one can be envious, or conversely, have a laugh. Whatever Mother gifts is personal and sacred."

"Complicated stuff." I frowned. "And odd."

"That's as maybe. But it's one of the taboos.

And who cares about your rewards for tasks completed. The main thing is that it's a list of deeds done for the good of the world. And what's more important is who you are. You don't exist."

"And who are you?"

"Me? I was born a Higher. I can tell you my biography if you like. I have been a Jester twice. Never a Queen. I was born into the family of a Decision Maker, the only child. I graduated from all my educational institutions with distinction. In fact, I am sick of my own success. I do not have a regular sexual partner."

"A Queen. Who's that? Presumably we're not talking about chess?"

"A Queen is the opposite of a Jester. A Jester aggravates, a Queen resolves. Her voice is equivalent to the voices of ten Highers, and that's funny when you consider there are only ever a hundred Higher Decision Makers. But who are *you*, goblin Elb? You don't exist. Any inquiry concerning your past before your memory was deleted is returned with a note saying that such information can only be provided in the Tower."

"The Tower?"

"Who are you?"

"My memory was deleted," I reminded her. "Is that mentioned?"

"It is. It is the ground zero of your vital records, the first note without a reference date — already a violation, note — concerning your amputation and the deletion of your memory, following which you were cryogenically frozen. The first date concerns your awakening in the Nullform World. Then your first task, collecting gray slime."

"I was born to collect slime," I chuckled, shifting up to allow the innkeeper to place his tray the our table.

"Judging by your documents, that is true. You are a nullform, born to collect slime, clean tables, and mop floors. And you did all of that."

"I did. A guy has to eat."

"Don't bullshit me," said the elf lady with particular relish, her soft mesmerizing intonation vanished without trace. In front of me sat a beautiful cynical babe, her nipples bulging teasingly through the wet T-shirt, her enormous eyes twinkling with ire.

Taking a chunk of bread, she dipped it in the thick steamy pea soup, leaned forward, took a huge bite, and released a long and satisfied moan. I was not going to stop her having her fill of regular food. Smoothies and seasonal scarlet fruits? Fuck that shit. I followed her example, although I acted more professionally, rubbing a crust of bread with garlic first.

"Somebody like you..." A soupy finger pointed at me. "Somebody like you... You are strong and angry, a vengeful goblin. In order to provide yourself with an abundance of food, drink, weapons, and anything else necessary to prosper down there in the stinking shit pit of the Nullform World, your native Outskirts, somebody like you would not need to clean tables and toilets. Maybe you would have been a conscientious worker, and those few days would have been enough for you to figure out what was what. You would easily have been able to beat up cowardly workers for as many sols as you needed for a sweet life, or even the slightly less cowardly hoodlums. But you preferred to mop floors until you were able to level up just a tiny bit and gain enough strength to kill pluxes. You are cut from very specific cloth."

"What are pluxes?"

"I will tell you," said the lady, "although despite my years, I don't know all that much. I do not know your age. I am seventy-six. Another fifty years, and I will have to start dying my gray streaks. Or maybe do some exercise."

"You do plenty of exercise as it is," I noted.

"Indeed I do," she said, picking up her spoon. "I work my tits off in the gym every day, for three or four hours. It is only the mad restorative chemicals that help my muscles and nervous system recuperate from the workload. But anyway, goblin Elb, know this: you do not exist. You appeared out of nowhere, beginning your life at the very lowest and most secluded point of this world. And you rose so high that you are now almost within spitting distance of the Lands of the Covenant."

"The closer I get to the center, the more praise I receive," I said, grinning. "But at the same time it's obvious that the main line of defense is just here. The hardest thing is avoiding Crontown and the lower hero levels, and instead just going straight to the Lands of the Covenant."

"Do you think so? You're wrong there, goblin.

Why are you in such a hurry to get to the Lands of the Covenant? What do you hope to find there?"

"Answers."

"Answers to what? To questions about yourself? I have already told you there is no information about you. Or rather there is, but it's hidden in the Tower and the system simply refers you there. So, if you're banking on finding out about your past, your age, your real name, the names of your parents, forget it, goblin. You won't find any of that there."

"Hmm."

"What? Are you having a moment of clarity that your whole journey has been a waste of time? You've been looking for answers which nobody can give you?"

"I need multiple answers," I said with a shrug as I pushed away my empty bowl.

"For example? Surprise me with your questions."

"They're obvious. Where the fuck are we? What is this multilevel world of steel walls and pipes covered in shit? And what is behind those walls?"

"Fuck knows." Dilya beamed a smile. "But if the answers do exist, they are in the Tower."

"You're Highers! How can you not know?"

"That's just the way it is. We are all hamsters in this gigantic cage. Do you still not get it, goblin? Mother oversees everything. You want the answers? Ask her. But she will not tell you. And that's because she has the right. Because she is an ancient machine with a distorted software code.

She's a faulty tin can full of sparking cogwheels, which is trying to keep a rein on this world, but is doing so worse and worse with every passing year. That is why I am here, goblin. Do you think the Highers lead an untroubled life? Absolutely the opposite. Sometimes I just want to go and have my memory volitionally deleted, get a bit of work done on my face to be a bit uglier, and go settle in a quiet village full of kindhearts. Get reborn there, and be told I'm a buxom peasant woman destined to mow the grass, rake the fields, and gobble off my husband on Saturdays. Do you think I'd be disappointed with a face like that? No fucking way! I'd be delighted. Give me a pitchfork and my husband's dick any day! Oops, there I go! Yuck!"

Leaning back against the back of the bench, I watched in shock as the elf lady returned to her food, growling her anger and choking on cold meat.

"That bad, huh?"

"Worse! When you woke up down there in the Outskirts, you soon understood it's all somehow fucking wrong, but at the same time you could proudly ask yourself 'What can I do? I'm a goblin! A volitional nullform locked in a steel prison asshole.' And you can't reach the steering wheel from the asshole. Do you understand? Whereas we Highers, well, those of us who still give a shit, we are like the drivers of a car careering towards a wall. We have the steering wheel in our hands and the pedals beneath our feet, but it's all either blocked or just doesn't work. You try to turn the wheel but it doesn't budge. You depress the brake pedal but it just goes through the floor and the car simply accelerates, rumbling and jumping its way at full speed towards the wall, while we stare through the windscreen and wait for the inevitable fatal crash."

"Is it all really that shit?"

"I told you, it's worse! The world is falling apart. We are slipping into the red again, and it's getting worse and worse with every year. And there's no way of compensating it. The red figures are increasing."

"Explain that in more detail."

"The balance of the world. The old world used to be balanced. Then the balance was upset by human procreation. According to legend, we were a hundred years short of a scientific breakthrough which would have allowed us to rid the planet of hunger and pollution, of devastating developments by hungry corporations, and of murderous military conflicts which nobody has needed for a long time, the larger part of which affected the already dying oceans. Another hundred years, perhaps even less, and we would have been able to alter the course of events, but it didn't happen."

"Clearly not. The doughy gutbucket drowned a meter from the life raft," I said, "as always. Why are you telling me all this?"

"The situation is repeating itself here. When I was born, the figures were in the green. You could see them almost anywhere in the Lands of the Covenant. And I grew up under a green figure of +0.1.

My coming-of-age, my first love, my first sex, and my first conviction of the fact that all men are total selfish bastards were spent under the yellow figure of 0.0. And now, after many long years, which have come at great cost to me and made me realize I'm not perfect either, maybe even a bitch (but let them envy me in silence), the red figures show -0.9. And it's easy to explain. Every year we take more from our new world than we put back into it, more than it manages to recover. And it should be the other way around if we want a future for ourselves, we need to give more than we take." Having eaten her fill, the satisfied elf lady hiccupped and stretched. "Ah, that's better. Do you know when the old world collapsed, goblin Elb?"

"When?"

"According to ancient history, it happened in the years when humanity began to spend its entire annual supply of renewable global resources in the first two months of each new year. Do you understand? We wolf down a year's worth of provisions in just two months. And that's approximately what the figure -0.9 represents. And we are now on the road to catastrophe again."

Her slim dainty hand grabbed a shot of moonshine, and after pouring the fire water down her throat, she smiled a beatific smile.

"The perfect cure for hiccups and a shitty mood. Elb, do you like your time to be spent as productively as possible?"

"What do you want?"

"Would you like to go for a ride? You and me,

and you can take five of your fighters if you want them to have some fun. I'll take my despondent knights. In lieu of payment, I would ask you for some comfortable pants, some non-smelly boots, a couple of pairs of woollen socks, and a bottle of this hooch. Is that possible?"

"Where are we going?"

"Not far. To a place where intelligent educated people gain knowledge from past epochs."

"A dog-eared toilet book?"

"Nearly. One of the abandoned coastal museums. Well, this one is almost abandoned. There are still a few oddballs there. I feed and protect them. Oh yes, we shall have to put together a hamper of nice food for them. Do you think you'll be able to find some clothes?"

"How many are there?"

"Five ungainly weakling eggheads."

"Well the trip be worth it?"

"It's time you received answers to at least some of your questions."

"What do you get out of it?"

"I'll tell you that after the excursion," said Dilya with a smile.

"I'll be ready in half an hour," I said, rising and going over to Klappa, who stood motionless near the knights.

"In the meantime I'm going to have a snooze." The young old woman yawned and lay down on the crate, resting her head on the stock of a disassembled shotgun. "The smell of oil, gunpowder, blood, and shit has made me sleepy."

I don't know about other goblins, but when I hear the word "museum," my mind conjures up a picture of a monumental colonnaded building, wide steps leading up to the entrance, a profusion of twinkling glass, a very high roof, and a severe doorkeeper whose eyes gently yet blatantly express: "Piss off, kid." I also see a square in front of the building, adorned with artificial trees and hundreds of fat pigeons eating free sterilizing feed, and I hear shouts of alarm from comfortable benches, saying, "Hey, kid, don't eat that shit, you dummy, it's for the pigeons! Hey, whose child is that? Where's his mother?" Then the gleaming pavement rushes to meet me, a protective dome twinkles over my head, covering the center of the old city, and I run from the cops, who are not exactly busting a gut to catch me.

Yes.

That is what I see in my mind's eye when I hear the word "museum."

I also remember that it was my last day in a city, and they did, after all, catch me that day, and they threw me in a cell with other youngsters like me. A cell without bars, but with doors shut fast, CCTV eyes winking coldly, and regular shit food which tasted worse than pigeon feed. Then we were quickly assorted, and I found myself in the belly of a "passenger" drone speeding over the foamy blue-gray waves towards the distant towering colossus of an old beachside residential tower block whose lower floors had long since disappeared beneath the rising sea.

Shaking my head, I yawned, squirmed, and took a bottle of lemonade from Klappa.

"You do understand you have some kind of mass psychiatric disorder?" asked the elf lady sitting in a comfortable armchair. "I'm talking about the lemonade. It isn't normal, you know? Your goblins swill liters of it every day, and today I saw loads of your fighters dissolving salt, vitamin, and energy tablets in it, before washing down protein bars and burgers with the resulting brown gloop."

"It is much further to this Museum?" I yawned even wider now, returning the bottle half-empty.

"It's right beneath us."

"Really?"

I stuck my sleepy face out of a porthole and saw some little islands floating past beneath us.

We flew back to the ocean ring and away from the shore, decelerating sharply before flying over a neat chain of small built-up islands. Earlier, all these stretched-out scraps of land had been connected by bridges, now destroyed. A kilometer and half out from the coastline, the string of islands turned parallel to the shore, before eventually turning back towards it. The result was a long arc, no longer connected by bridges though nonetheless forming a large bay protected from storms. Jutting out in the middle of the bay was another small island, decorated by a mournful-looking male figure whose face was turned away from the land and out to the ocean.

"That's him," said the elf lady, "the Higher."

"You're all Highers."

"You don't understand. He's the first Higher, the creator of this world."

"The creator of this world," I said, aping her and looking down at the bizarre monument.

Normally rock-carved characters wore a cape, were often on horseback, and had a hand held to their chest. Right? Whereas this one… His vest did not conceal his scraggy sinewy physique; his face was partly covered by a heavy mask with wires stretching to the opened petals of a solar panel on his back; he wore gloves; and in his right hand he carried a bucket, while his left hand gripped a common-or-garden hoe. Not much of a Creator. He was more like a farmer, wearily contemplating his never-ending travails while looking at a dead animal.

Our flying machine made a slight turn, and I got a closer look at his face.

Something stirred inside me.

I squinted, leaned forward, and peered at the lower part of his face, which wasn't covered by the mask. Regular chin, with stubble superbly crafted by the sculptor and brushed to perfection by the wind and rain, but it was the mouth that really caught my attention. The coarse wrinkles around the mouth, the slightly down-turned corners of the tightly closed lips. This man really did look disillusioned. And what's more, disillusioned with everything and everyone all at once. And yes, he seemed somehow familiar.

Leaning back into my seat, I caught the elf lady looking at me.

"What?"

"Ah, nothing, " she said, shrugging her shoulders. "I was expecting some kind of reaction."

"A monument," I said indifferently. "Someday it will fall. Is that where we're going?"

"It is," said the girl.

Girl. She was young in appearance only, despite the fact that she'd already lived a long and peaceful life, full of abundance and not lacking confidence in tomorrow.

"Confidence in tomorrow," I repeated my thought, pensively and out loud this time.

"Are you talking about me and all the other Highers together?" asked the smart old lady with the looks of a model.

"What do you think?"

"I think it's a curse."

"What are you talking about?"

"Self-awareness. Understanding what's going on around you. Awareness of the fact that none of us has a future, that a new end of the world is close. And I do seriously think sometimes about having my memory erased and leading an unconscious peasant life, which would be much shorter, but at the same time far more carefree. They are content, Elb, all those kindhearts, the ethnics, and even the volitional nullforms. They are happy in their own way, because they do not see the impending death throes of the world that adopted them. But I do, I see them clearly. And I understand that my immortality will, in thirty or forty years' time, afford me every chance to welcome the new Armageddon, sitting on a terrace, drinking orange juice and watching the wall of fire roll towards me. And you know what? I'm not afraid of dying. Fuck death! I don't want to die, of course, but I'm not afraid of it. But to wait for the inevitable end of the world year in year out? That is seriously frightening."

"Thirty or forty years? Is it really that bad?"

"It's worse than that, goblin. The red figures accelerate with every year. We people are eating away at our new little world again, like rats in a wheel of cheese. All we can do is eat and shit. No offense. Everything I'm saying relates to the Highers. That's why I was looking at you as we flew over the monument." The elf lady leaned in towards me and looked me in the eye. "Maybe you are him? Mother help us if it's true, of course, but just maybe you are him?"

"Me?" I laughed. "The Creator? Nonsense! I can't create anything. I can only destroy, turn to dust. I can torture and squeeze out all the juice."

"That is a precise description of the First Higher." The elf lady leaned slowly back, drawing her thumb pensively over her lips. "What do you know about him?"

"Nothing."

"Let me open your eyes to something. He who stood at the head, who suggested the idea, and then realized it, creating this insular autonomous world, that person was a pitiless bastard. A surgeon. A butcher. You kill lone-wolf goblins and take out small gangs. Whereas he annihilated people by the thousand, and he did it every day. And all for the realization of a single aim: to build this world. He didn't pull the trigger himself, obviously, in most cases, but with a single word and flourish of a quill, he would kill more people in a day than you've killed in your whole life as a hardcore killer. So don't feed me any lies about how uncreative yet violent you are. And yes, I am inclined to think that you are him. You are too small for this role. No offense again. Maybe not even too small; you are merely different."

"Did you know him personally?"

"No. We're coming in to land."

The drone, clearly delaying its landing so we could finish our chat, lowered itself softly onto a concrete square next to a long and absolutely unremarkable two-story building which took up most of the largest of the little islands in this handcrafted linear archipelago. The central and biggest bead.

"There were museum halls on the smaller islands." Dilya disembarked the vehicle first and immediately began waving her hands around, paying no attention to the goblins hurrying towards us from the building. "Each island held a thematic exhibition of objects and screenings of short films, among other nonsense. But here, in the central point, was the most important thing to the curious fat kindhearts: a relaxation and repletion zone. A small hotel on the second floor, several cafeterias on the first floor, and massage salons and a lukewarm saltwater swimming pool in the basement, with glass walls affording a view of the underwater world. But that was before. Now the enthusiasts have taken anything that survived from the dilapidated halls and put them in the central building, as well as ruthlessly discarding most of the tables, chairs, and kitchen equipment. Some of it is on the second floor, where they live."

"What about the swimming pool?"

"The entrance to the basement is sealed-off."

"Why's that?"

"Because it's the first underground level and it belongs to the gnomes."

"The gnomes," I repeated after her.

"The gnomes," confirmed the elf lady. "But they don't show their faces up here. When I decided to take this place under my soft elven wing, the first thing I did was order all unnecessary doors to be sealed, after which I convinced Mother to bolster her defense of the place, under the pretext of protecting valuable objects of antiquity. I also managed to talk her into supplying some hearty rations for the wacko fanatics."

"I can see," I said.

"The fanatics?"

"The system."

The first observation dome jutted from the middle of one of the building's walls, partly concealed by the edge of the roof. Rising from the sides of the building were two steel columns topped with vigilant mushroom caps. All-round vision.

"Do bandits ever drop by?"

"They haven't done for ages." Dilya said, and

smiled a beaming smile.

"But they used to do?"

"They did. You can still see the bones in exhibition hall number five. Plus a few remain in number three as well. The jackals and birds haven't taken everything. And with these enthusiasts, it's easier with them, I suppose. They're not like you lot. And their attitude towards me is simple and unpretentious." With these words, she turned to the thin, bearded... goblins?

All of them tall, shapeless, bearded, with long unkempt hair, and dressed in identical ripped blue sailors' turtleneck sweaters and green boiler suits, they were obviously not the kind to yearn for pastures new, nor to thirst for spilled blood or a week's worth of push-ups.

"Welcome, mistress!" The tallest goblin, who also sported the longest gray beard, smiled a wide, wide smile. "Permit me to kiss your boot."

"Simple and unpretentious, my foot," I said, before turning away to study the shoreline, which was just over a kilometer away.

I wasn't convinced by the place's potential to defend itself. That said, the presence of system armaments balanced out all the negatives.

It was a bizarre place. Or it had been in the distant past, when there were still attempts in this world to teach people things and keep them on their guard, even if it did involve museum excursions like this.

Judging by what I could see, folks used to come here in land vehicles via the Path, or by sea, mooring near the first little island, which was furnished with a convenient quay. The crowd of fat lazy impudent kindhearts would slowly hop from island to island by bridge, led by a tour guide whose instantly forgettable monologue they yawned their disinterest at. The kindhearts would not perk up until in the middle of the journey when they approached the central island with its leisure zone. Why would they? It was here that they could stuff themselves silly with fat juicy double burgers with double mayo and cheese, discarding the token lettuce leaf. Then they would have an hour's nap, grab another bite to eat, and settle down to marvel sleepily at the denizens of the seabed while drinking sweet fizz through a straw. Then, overcoming a massive "don't want to," they would walk on to the very last island, where they could at last put a big fat tick alongside karma to represent "I studied, I perceived, I penetrated," before clambering back onto the boat or shoehorning their fat asses into the car. They could also continue on to the next burger with triple fries, which is to say, the next treasures of art and monuments to murky, moss-covered, days of yore which had long since ceased to be of interest to anybody.

How can I possibly know all this if I've never been here before?

I just did. Everywhere. Always. Perhaps it was a memory from very early childhood, something to do with noisy museum squares, hordes of tourists, dozens of street cafés, and similar numbers of garbage bins where you could always find a yummy feast. If, that is, you weren't beaten to it by someone nippier.

While I was checking out my surroundings, ignoring the amusingly silent elf-security knights as I peered over the edge and into the water to estimate how deep it was, Dilya finished her powwow with the bearded squatters and waved a summoning hand.

"It is time for you goblins to immerse yourselves in some culture."

"Culture," snorted Jorann, the first of my goblins to break their silence, as she glanced at Gabby behind her.

The couple had flown here in the next compartment to me and Dilya. And seeing the contented and serene expression on the ginger lass's face, one might conclude they had not merely sat in silence during the flight. I'd brought just three of my guys with me: Klappa, Jorann, and Gabby, leaving the other veterans with the squad. I raised my hand, flipped a switch, and asked:

"How's it going back there, Wreck?"

"Everything's okay, lead," came his crackly voice from the speaker of a new walkie-talkie.

In truth it was difficult to call that thing a walkie-talkie. It was more like a transmitter supported and amplified by the system, a gift I'd demanded of the elf lady. I was paranoid and quite happy to admit it, and I did not want to be out of contact with my squad. Prehistoric times were in the past, and it was high time to ramp up the technological infrastructure.

"Are you going to the museum looking like that?" asked one of the graying beards. "My name is—"

"I don't want to know your name," I said, interrupting him. "Yes, we are going like this."

The question from the weakling in his sailors' sweater referred to our appearance. We were fully armed and dressed in full combat gear. We even had backpacks on our backs. The reason being, again, my paranoia.

"I would ask you to follow me," said the beard, forcing a smile. "I will show you our dark and gloomy past. And I will—"

"Have you started already, Finch?"

"Um, we're not there yet, mistress."

"So lead on in silence." The elf lady smiled bewitchingly, and the quick-up-on-the-uptake beardo hunched his back, looked with tenderness at his mistress, and trotted ahead, leading us down a long wide corridor and waving us towards a staircase.

"You are stressed, Elb, very stressed."

"I'm angry," I admitted.

"What about? Although wait a second. Why did you suddenly feel the need to be in touch with your squad? And why are you kitted-out like that? Kind old Mother and my boys will always cover you from any trouble."

"You expect me to rely on a bunch of boys I don't know?" I asked with a snigger. "I'm not that stupid."

"Hmm. What about the transmitter?"

"Same reason."

"You don't trust me."

"You drop out of the sky, you call yourself a Jester, and you invite us to look at a bunch of dusty shit protected by a gaggle of scrawny bearded halfwits. Why should I trust you?"

"Hmm. But why are you angry?"

"This world has no balls," I grumbled, stepping onto the first stair.

"That's quite a statement. Are you going to explain?"

"Why? Read my biography again, from the moment of my awakening in the Nullform world. It might not all be there, but there is plenty. Do you want to know something that's been screaming at me at every step and stage of our long journey?"

"I'm itching to hear it."

"Women are in charge everywhere."

"Ha! So you don't like feeling pussy-whipped?"

"It isn't that. It's just the fact of it. This little steel world has no balls. Either they've been snipped off, or they never grew in the first place. And at the same time, which is also significant, there still remain strong and incredibly terrifying men. I saw one myself, clearly from my previous life. He'd set up home like a surreptitious pale tick in a steel cesspool down below, and he was clearly in no hurry to climb out of there. He's just fine down there in his dark bloody misery."

"Who could possibly be so terrifying as to frighten hero Elb?"

"He was gruesome," I said. "At that time he

could have squashed me with a little finger, like a slug."

"And now?"

"Now I might manage to get a couple of lunges in, but in a proper fight the outcome would be a foregone conclusion, and not to my advantage."

"And what if one of them were to lock horns with him?" Dilya asked, pointing over her shoulder to where the mechanized knights were tramping heavily up the concrete stairs.

"Them in full exo-garb with guns, and a him in bedroom slippers?"

"Let's suppose he has a gun with armor-piercing bullets."

"He would kill them," I replied without the slightest doubt. "That terrifying pale tick is from an old dead world. I don't remember much, but I'm sure I've met him before. And in those times, that killer who made himself at home among the goblins was way more powerful and influential. And he's still a leader now, albeit far more small-time. On the other hand, how the chicks have flourished! Nymphs, spider queens, pythias, elf girls. This world is ruled by babes."

"And that pisses you off? Don't you like it when a girl is on top?"

"I don't like it when men sit at home knitting gaily colored scarves while the womenfolk are plowing their way through bloody moaning shit. I don't understand men not lusting for power. It's in our blood! The yearning to be the leader of the pack, the chief of a wild tribe."

"Surely there aren't that few really hardcore men? And many of them have patched together their own squads and manage them successfully. What else do you want?"

"Do you know the limits of their dreams?"

"Undoubtedly. They all want to climb up to the highest hero status and gain access to the Lands of the Covenant, right?"

"No. Or rather, yes, they want to reach the Lands of the Covenant someday, but do you know why?"

"Enlighten me."

"So they can do nothing. Nothing at all. So they can lie on the couch all day, eating grapes, admiring the beautiful scenery outside the window and not lifting a fucking finger."

"And that isn't normal?" The youthful-looking girl eyed me in surprise with her overly wise eyes. "Isn't that what everyone dreams of? Valhalla, Paradise, a hero's pension. Do battle, earn some R and R for your war wounds and frazzled body, and then chill, warrior!"

"That's the whole freaking problem," I said with a chuckle. "It's a problem for the whole world if all the men ever do is dream of claiming their pension as soon as possible. Not a single gray hair on their heads, and they're already dreaming about retiring and doing diddly squat. I don't understand why. When a man makes it to the top of his brigade, crew, or spider kingdom, or he's the top dog in a bordello, he starts doing less and less real work every day and prefers to spend his time taking drugs or frying fish. Instead of continuing to shred zomboids, he sets up some bizarre school and makes no attempt to climb out of the sandbox of provincial Coal. He opens a trading post. And what about the gnomes? Their ladyfolk keep the pluxes under control while the men trot alongside them or sit astride the scaly backs of beasts driven by women. And the whole problem is that the men are happy with that. They don't want to take those beasts by the scruffs of their necks and steer them with an iron fist towards their targets. But if a chick gets anywhere near the rudder, she starts getting things done. She cultivates relations, she argues, she bangs her head against the wall over and over and seeks out new approaches. Women are never content. There's always something missing."

"Let me tell you a secret. It is hard to satisfy a woman, almost impossible."

"This world has no balls," I repeated gloomily. "And you are evidence of that. Why was it you who came to have a chat with Elb the goblin? Were none of the male Highers interested? Just be honest."

"Everyone was interested, and many were even planning to come. But 'just a little later.' You know how it is."

"I see."

"But this world was created by a man."

"So where is he now?"

"Nobody knows," said the elf lady, darkening. "Except for the Tower. But it won't share that particular secret."

"Even with the Highers?"

"Who knows? Maybe it would. Maybe it would even disclose a fascinating secret to a Nullform. Except nobody knows where the damned Tower is located. Why was I the first one from the Lands of the Covenant to visit you? Why was I interested in you? You just listen to the scrawny bearded half-wit's tale. No offense, Finch."

"None taken."

"That is exactly your fucking problem. And it's the rest of the world's fucking problem as well. You never take offense," I said dispassionately, before striding ahead and barging a weakling out of the way with my steel shoulder. "Begin your tale. And keep it short."

"But don't miss out anything important," said Jorann with a thin smile as she squeezed past Klappa and stopped by the first exhibit. "What's this gob of phlegm in blue icing?"

"This is the beginning of all beginnings," said the beard, drawing himself up ceremoniously. "This is what our entire world began from. The Tabernacle of the First Higher. Listen."

"Oh shit." I puckered my brow and leaned on the windowsill to gaze at the waves out of the window. "Here we go."

CHAPTER 8

THE BEARDED FINCH tried so hard to appear cool that he actually gave the impression of an effete two-bit dumb fuck without realizing it. Leaning on a table with a blue bumpy surface meant to represent the ocean, he knit his brow, his lower lip jutting out, and gazed fixated at a small patch of land situated slap-bang in the center of the stormy waters.

"How simultaneously small and yet great is the land engendered by—" he began.

"Get to the point!" I barked, knowing full well I would not be able to cope with even a minute of his warblings.

"I'd be happy to hear it," said the redhead.

Gabby nodded his agreement. Klappa remained indifferent, but leaned against the wall, giving silently to understand that he was willing to listen. With a heavy sigh, I waved a submissive hand and returned to the window to sit on the wide sill (the walls were a meter thick). I loved buildings like this, unremarkable yet strong and reliable. The elf lady joined me, leaning her shoulder against the glass and staring out at the ocean, while a few meters away the beard gradually began to enjoy himself.

"Concerning dates, the first significant date which in many ways determined the disposition and mindset of the inhabitants of the blue planet is difficult to pinpoint precisely. However, many agree that it was the twentieth year of the twenty-first century after the birth of Christ. It was then, at a run-of-the-mill science conference, that one of the more radically-minded scientists, tired of listening to the pessimistic admonishments of his brethren, stood up and publicly voiced a simple and terrible truth. He said the following: 'The extinction of mankind is inevitable, but that does not mean the death of the planet. That is an incontestable fact. When the planet currently being killed off by people goes into a fit of paroxysm, humans will possibly become extinct. Perhaps the oxygen-rich atmosphere will also disappear. All the ice will melt and cover all the landmasses, destroying all of mankind's achievements, including mankind himself. But this will not mean the death of the planet. For the Earth has already undergone dramatic changes on multiple occasions, and this has involved mass extinctions every time. We are not talking here exclusively about the dinosaurs, for specific epochs saw the existence of hosts of the most unusual creatures which were unable to negotiate the rubicon of change, dying quietly out. And humans are in no way better than them.' In conclusion to his short speech, the scientist added, 'Enough harping on about the death of the planet! It is going nowhere! It will simply be different, a sphere more accommodating to us. And that is perfectly normal if we look at the concept from a global point of view. The universe is constantly changing.'"

Taking an unnecessary pause, Finch wiped his wrinkled brow with a bitter sigh, cleared his throat, and after running an eye over us and his museum colleagues standing modestly and motionless by the wall, continued:

"His speech was informed and buttressed by the popularity of the ideas of those times, and he eventually switched his emphasis from the 'salvation of the planet' to the 'salvation of mankind.' But most importantly, in attendance at the conference was the man who would later come to be known as the First Higher. The man who got the ball rolling. The man whose actions led to the creation of this fantastic world and made it a refuge for mankind to be saved from extinction. That's right. Few remember that unmemorable July 2022 day, which is not surprising, for that year was rich with far more noteworthy events. Yet that date was the beginning. Because a little over a month later, a tiny dying atoll was visited by a very angry and extremely determined man in an old T-shirt bearing a picture of the planet Earth sliced into segments like a watermelon."

As my thoughts drifted from these facts, interesting to nobody, about the distant and unalterable past, I busied my mind with a more interesting time: the present.

"Why are you here?" I asked the elf lady.

"Would you like me to open your eyes?" She smiled her willingness to enter into conversation.

"My eyes are open," I said. "And all they see is bloody shit sprinkled with sugar and vanilla. Everywhere. Why are you here?"

"The world is dying," she replied simply. "Do you not have goosebumps running up and down your back? Right now we are sitting on a windowsill in a derelict museum and listening to a tale of the death of the old world, while all around us the new world is dying. Déjà vu? The crooked smile of destiny? Ill fate?"

"Go on."

"You, originally a completely unknown goblin called Elb, crawled from the nullform world like a tapeworm from the poop-shute of a dying cow. But even down there in the steel intestines, you advanced like a vicious clod of red-hot barbed wire. You are like a toilet brush, able to scrub off even the crustiest and fastest-stuck shit. The cesspool, the pig farm, the spider kingdom, Zombieland. Wherever you go, you kill. And what is more, you start by attacking the most bloated and troublesome spots and ignore the smaller problems. Some might call you a leukocyte, an antibody, but you are simply an asshole goblin, a spiky toilet brush.

No offense."

"Go on."

"Your exploits have attracted the attention and interest of many. And they have begun to place bets and to observe. While I personally could not care less for your Herculean labors."

"*What* labors?"

"It isn't important. You are nothing like that classical hero, despite also being his colleague in the business of destroying monsters and purging squalor. Although I lie, you are like him in one respect, your chief quality, which is what drew my attention."

"Be specific."

"You never stop. You push forever forward, never slowing down. And do you know what slows down any person? Don't answer that, I'll tell you myself. People are slowed down by junk. Property, furniture, fancy clothes, objects of art, fondness for friends and loved ones. All of this acts like a bunch of anchors, which will eventually shackle you firmly to a single place, and as a result you become sedentary, never leaving that place, ceasing to be yourself. After all, you mustn't shit on your own doorstep. Meaning it doesn't pay to get into fights, it doesn't pay to behave too boisterously, it doesn't pay to be too conspicuous, too flamboyant, too individual. It does not pay to offend anybody, because you never know what that person will become tomorrow. Do you understand?"

"You're digressing."

"Agreed. Basically, it's the same shit that is happening right now in the Lands of the Covenant and the ring around it. The Highers and their inner circle have become totally bogged-down, like flies stuck to poisoned sticky paper, still buzzing yet incapable of doing anything. They are not making any decisions, Elb! They are not moving forward! Why? Because they're afraid of making mistakes, and as a result losing status, possessions, and contacts. Which is why they prefer to keep buzzing, because when a fly stuck on flypaper isn't buzzing, that means it's dead. But they are not doing anything. And those sweet feckless buzzings serve only to attract more flies, which end up bogged-down in the same honey bog."

"How does that manifest itself?"

"In everything! Have you ever wondered why real leaders are compared to surgeons but never to regular doctors?"

"Surprise me."

"It's because sometimes you've got to cut off a small part in order to save the whole organism. If a finger is festering, it gets amputated. If a leg has gone black and swollen from gangrene, it gets amputated. That's what a leader should do. And the worst thing is when a leader is afraid to make a radical decision, afraid to operate on a living being, afraid to act. They are afraid to even make a tiny incision in an enormous disgusting boil on a nose, because they believe that sooner or later it will heal itself, so all they do is put a hot poultice on it. Not too hot, mind. A luke-warm poultice. They are shit!

Useless shit!"

"Are you talking about the hundred Highers of yours who have the right to vote?"

"Exactly. I am one of them. All hundred of us gather once a week, sometimes even twice. All dressed-up, stately, self-important, untouchable, and above the law, they spend ages taking their seats, adopting sophisticated facial expressions to flick through papers and discuss various notions in their factions, parties, and alliances. And then, if necessary, they give endlessly long and boring speeches bristling with words such as 'possibly,' 'perhaps,' 'preferably,' and 'probably,' and phrases such as 'sensitive subject,' 'more than likely,' and 'it doesn't pay to be hasty.' By the end of the meeting, not a single decision has been made, and the exhausted-looking Highers leave and make their way to their awaiting carriages, trying earnestly to look like important statesmen. Bastards! Useless bastards! The world is dying, rotting, trembling in its death throes, and yet no important decisions are made. Those beasts!"

"Nicely put," I chuckled. "And sincerely."

"More than sincerely!"

"And who of them know about your attitude to these gatherings? About your attitude to the other Highers?"

"I do not hide my point of view!" The elf lady drew herself up proudly and shook her head. "I do not hide it. Fuck etiquette! Fuck these veils! Fuck pussyfooting and beating around the bush! Fuck smoothies and seasonal fruits!"

"I see. Go on then, you still haven't answered my question. Why are you here?"

"Because! You have done something to put the fear of the System into three quarters of the Highers. They might not be speaking up, but they are afraid. Their butts are wet from instinctive fear. And they do not view you with the vague interest of celestial beings anymore, goblin. Now they view you as a fugitive from a shitty ghetto who has strayed into an affluent residential area. You are like a malevolent drugged-up vagrant, crisscrossed with scars and tattoos, wielding a bloodied hatchet and wandering along a quiet sunny little street which has never seen murder but very soon will. They are afraid of you now, goblin."

"Why the fuck are they afraid of me?"

"You wiped out Paradise."

"You mean the ammnushiti?"

"Yes. Do you still not get it? It's built on the same shitting model! An exact copy. What you wiped out is basically just a children's sandbox. What you did was crush underfoot a model globe of this world, and that was seen as a rehearsal before the real thing. At the center of the Lands of the Covenant are hundreds of Highers. And what was the situation in Paradise? The ammnushiti had a dozen elders and a smattering of chieftains. In the Covenant, each one of the hundred Highers has his own huge mansion, where his retinue of girls and men live in the safety provided by a superb security system. The ammnushiti are a herd of toadies who regularly went hunting for teenagers, raping the sweet young things and slitting their throats. Our Highers do not want to make any decisions, so they block each other's initiatives, and it's just the same there. I saw the shitting ticks on those worthless papers, and all the ammnushiti elders contrived to vote differently, as if they were snubbing one another. There wasn't even a majority vote! It is impossible, it would seem, to destroy the system. The closed, autonomous system. But then who should rock up but Elb the goblin? Who annihilates Paradise Promised in the space of a few hours. You shattered their very foundation, violated all their taboos, and opened their borders. But the worst thing you did was to reveal the elders' and chieftains' true colors. They seemed such wise, collected, and peaceful old men, devoted exclusively to benefitting their communities and Paradise Promised. And you disrobed them of their sheep's clothing, exposing that above all else they were freaking child killers, rapists, perverts, and fucking sadists. And in doing so you proved that they wanted to shit on the destiny of the world. You proved that all their lives they had cared for nothing but their beloved selves. That is why the Highers are now afraid of you, hero. Yes, obviously it isn't real fear yet, merely lazy pensiveness mixed with hazy apprehension, the kind of sensation you feel when you see a poisonous hairy spider in the corner. Logically you understand you are stronger than the arachnid, the pharmacy has a reliable antidote, your hand is holding a heavy wet cloth, and there's a hospital

right around the corner. Yet you are still frightened. Do you follow me?"

"You still haven't told me what the hell you're
doing here."

"I'll tell you. I have made my firm decision. The
seasonal Jester has sided with the goblin from the
asshole of the world! And do you know what just
happened?"

"What?"

"That poisonous spider, so hairy and terrifying, has suddenly turned out to be not over there
in the far corner, but very close, on the palm of my
hand extended to the rest of the Highers. May they
jump in fright!"

"I'm in the palm of your hand?"

"I was speaking figuratively! It's a habit of
mine, since childhood. Putting it straightfor-
wardly, I gave the other ninety-nine percent of the
Highers to believe that you are under my protection and that I share your interests and aspira-
tions. You have my full support, both material and
moral. Any Higher who takes a stand against you
will also be taking a stand against me. I told them
I would show you the museum, tell you about all
the world's weaknesses, and describe all the
jammed mechanisms. And most importantly I
would tell you that the world has already slipped
from the edge of the abyss and is hurtling head
over heels down into it. That is what I told them."

"I see."

"The time has come for decisive action. The red
figures are no longer merely scary, they are mak-

ing life a living hell. The world will soon be at an end. And I cannot permit the Highers to squish you like a bug. And rest assured they would try, for it is not only I who do not believe in coincidence. You are a man without a past, deleted from all databases, and it is not without good reason that you appeared specifically in this time of troubles. And it is with good reason that you began your journey so far away, in the very outskirts and primitive conditions of an almost primordial world. It allowed you, with your blackguardly cantankerous disposition, to remain intact among fainthearted goblins to begin with. It allowed you to gain strength and find your feet. It allowed you to—"

"Enough of the hogwash already! Who have you told about your decisive action? Everybody?"

"Everybody! Just as soon as I learned about the fate of Paradise Promised, about that stinking pustule that had been sliced open. I understood straightaway that they would not forgive you such an act. So I announced proudly that I fully shared your convictions. I recorded a video message addressed to every last Higher, in which I declared that it was the way forward, and that Elb the goblin and I were like-minded people and would be continuing his work in the same vein. Any lunacy would cease to be lunacy if it was in the name of salvation. If necessary, we will dissect every cyst, every swelling, and every zit with a sharp scalpel or axe. Bring it on!"

"Shit," I concluded, looking with sincere bafflement at Dilya's lovely head held proudly high. "I thought you were a clever girl. I was mistaken. You're a dumb bint."

"What? I am not offended, but what did I say wrong?"

"Have you got any experience whatsoever in standing up to anyone? And I'm not talking about bedroom games, where you can use your tush to upset the thrust rhythm of the short-winded goblin standing behind you? Or the elf."

"Gross!"

"Have you or not? How many Highers are there in your alliance, crew, crowd, interest group, or whatever?"

"I am alone! I am that bristling cluster which—"

"Shit," I repeated, springing down from the windowsill. "Klappa! Check the perimeter of the building!"

"What about us?" asked Gabby, moving keenly towards me.

"You listen to beardo's tall tales for the time being," I said. "I'm just being cautious. Dilya, your knights, how loyal are they to you?"

We looked out of the window, to where one of the steel statues stood. The other was inside the building, positioned by the staircase.

"They are former high-ranking heroes, selectively reset to zero. They are as reliable as a well-oiled mechanism."

"What's that supposed to mean, selectively reset to zero?"

"Memory," explained Dilya. "Those highest-rank heroes who wish to continue serving for the benefit of the Highers and the world, and do not wish to spend their lives in sumptuous idleness, have their memories partially erased and then become bodyguards. In common parlance they are known as 'resets.'"

Watching Klappa leave silently on his beat, I shrugged my incomprehension and asked:

"What exactly do they remove from the head?"

"The most recent memories. You know the conditions and eternal intrigue under which most heroes move up the ranks. Relentless political games, sympathies, reciprocal services and needling, accumulated gratitude and hatred. And that whole package is transferred to the Lands of the Covenant along with the heroes who head there. If they simply retire, then to hell with them. But if they have their sights set on becoming bodyguards, then their heads must be clear of sympathies towards anyone at all."

"Logical," I said. "And what percentage gets deleted?"

"Of memories? It's on an individual basis. It depends how many years you spent working your way up to the fifth rank. All your mental baggage is flushed down the toilet, along with all your emotions, agreements, obligations, and sense of duty towards anyone who has ever helped you."

"So just as you get right to the top, your past is flushed down the toilet again?"

"If you want it that way. Or if you want to, you

can live a chilled life in a smart settlement, enjoying a life of quiet satiation and flipping through the recollections in your memory. Naturally anyone who chooses service is protected from any interaction with the pensioners."

"That's impossible," I retorted. "There'll always be a loophole, some memory will always float to the surface. Those drugs..."

"The knights do not get involved in anything of that nature."

"Uh-huh. And you're absolutely sure of that, right?"

"I am."

"Shit," I repeated again as I looked out of the window. "Okay. Never mind."

"Shall I go on?"

"Give me a minute."

"Okay. I'll listen to Finch in the meantime. He actually prefers to call himself Acid Shark, although he doesn't know why."

"Acid Shark?" I threw a glance at the beard in the stretched sweater, who had by now moved on to the second exhibit. "What a strange choice of name."

"You can say that again. He is a strange character all around. He hates running for some reason, but he can talk for hours about its benefits. Never mind, I'll shut up. You get your thoughts together."

I nodded and froze again, still staring out at the blurry ocean view, and sifting hastily through what I'd been told, in search of an answer to the main question: when?

In the meantime, standing by a large canvas depicting a flabby goblin sitting at a computer screen, his fat fingers on the keyboard and a bowl of potato chips on his knees, Finch continued to spout his drivel.

"It was around this time that mankind's primal instinct began to sense doom drawing closer. And so what did mankind do? Did it rush to destroy the dams and free the shackled rivers? Did it rush to replant deforested land? No, it did nothing of the sort. Mankind dived headfirst into computer games, which with every passing year became more and more advanced, deeper, and more realistic. People spent days on end in front of twinkling screens, exerting no small effort to guide their virtual incarnation through all the hardships of a fictional existence. What an extraordinary twist! Instead of rescuing reality, people submerged themselves in virtuality with no regard for the consequences. It's mental, but that's the way it was. Naturally, this tension, this expectation of the impending end of times, caused changes in popular gaming genres. The most popular genre was now robinsonade, where a player had to survive in the hardest and most hostile of conditions. A desert island inhabited by bloodthirsty beasts or zombies, the shores of which you are washed up on after a shipwreck, for example, is one variation."

"What is this bullshit you're spouting?" said Jorann, unable to contain herself.

"I am merely telling you what happened and

how. I am telling you that instead of rescuing reality—"

"Yes yes yes. Bullshit!"

"Not at all! You just keep listening! The thing
is that this bizarre and clearly abnormal identification of the self with a virtual character led to no
less bizarre ramifications for survival methods. As
a result of a global survey, it was ascertained that
no small percentage of the planet's population
would prefer digital rescue to real rescue. Instead
of building a similar world with reliable steel walls
to harbor and protect us, they dreamed of digital
immortality and eternal life in some reliably protected server on which a made-up play world was
laid out, with its own laws. It tended to be a magical medieval world full of magicians, necromancers, rugged knights in armor, and pious paladins."

"Off their freaking heads," concluded Gabby,
cracking his fingers.

"Everyone has the right to make their own
choice," said Finch with a shrug. "And many chose
virtuality, in the full knowledge that first they
would have to die in reality. Despite the lack of
concrete proof, there is no little evidence to suggest
that serious investment was made in this area.
But we do not know the outcome yet, and so let us
move on. To the 2030s. The Atoll of Life Corporation enters the world stage, headed-up by that very
same First Higher. The Corporation claims, for all
the world to hear, that the planet will soon experience a global climatic shift, like a strike from a

horse's hoof. But this time it will not be a horse lashing out at us, but a very angry planet. The strike is inevitable, leaving only one question: do you wish to live or die? Those who chose life for themselves and their kin had the chance to choose, if they gave all their resources to the Atoll of Life Corporation. Resources including not only money and property, but usually their physical strength as well. Resources."

"Yes. What is there to think about? I'd strike right now," I said, mainly to myself, as I turned sharply to the elfin-eared Dilya, who was lost in thought. "Is there any protective equipment in your drone?"

"What for?" she asked, confused. "I am not a warrior. And I am in no..."

With a bright flash, the drone which had brought us here was launched into the air, flipped over, and thrown into the ocean.

"Attack!" hollered Klappa from below, just before a machine-gun volley rattled the corridor.

"Prepare for battle!" I shouted, drawing my sawn-off shotgun.

The old wooden door blew out with a crack, and in the doorway flickered the familiar figure of a knight with his weapon raised. I pulled my trigger and did not hang around to see what happened next. Grabbing the elf lady, I smashed the window out with my shoulder, and in a cloud of glass shards, we flew out of it. We were soon followed by Gabby, clutching Jorann, who was yelling fiercely. From the second floor came the sounds of frightened howls and thundering gunfire. I landed on half-bent legs to absorb some of the shock, but that did not stop me crashing onto my tuckus. Leaping straight to my feet, I sprinted along the wall, accompanied by Gabby, who had managed to draw his armor-piercing weapon from his shoulder.

"Fantastic fucking museum trip!" hissed Jorann, breaking away from the prism's grip and skipping in through a door ahead of the rest of us.

The second knight jumped out from around a corner and tottered beneath a hail of bullets. With a wild siren wail, one of the system domes came to life and brought down a barrage of fire on the knight who had betrayed his mistress. The barrage involved needles that were far from innocuous for his armor, which was battered, knocking the knight back around the corner, from where came the flash of an explosion. A second dome turned slightly and fired a couple of volleys through a second-floor window, knocking out the glass and frame and defacing the walls. The system was protecting the Higher with true maternal ferocity, sparing no ammunition. With a hiss and a snap, the dome launched a rocket, which left a smoky trail in its wake as it made for a dark dot skipping over the waves.

We threw ourselves after Jorann and came across Klappa. The swordsman was limping along a corridor, dragging a real knight's shield behind him and spitting balefully in a language I did not understand. I gave a brisk hand signal to show everyone where to go: away from the staircase, into the depths of the old building with its thick solid walls.

"Where are we going?" The scarcely audible squeak came from the stiffened body under my arm.

Nobody answered the frightened immortal girl, who was experiencing true terror for arguably the first time in her life. And true terror (not counting the feelings of a parent watching their child flattened beneath the wheels of a heavy truck or something of the kind) arose in the minds of goblins and elves alike in the same situation: a direct threat to their lives. And if it came out of the blue, like thunder from a clear sky, it was doubly terrifying.

The elf lady was in shock, testament to which were the dilated pupils of her unfocused eyes, her woodenness, and her fast shallow breathing. She was like a doe in the headlights of an oncoming vehicle.

"Wreck!" I suddenly remembered the transmitter and barked into its microphone.

"Yes, commander?" The orc's indolent and calm voice brought momentary relief.

"Everything okay?"

"Never more so. The goblins are doing push-ups and gasping for air with their sweaty ring pieces. While I'm thoughtfully eating a washed apple. How's your excursion going?"

"It's lively. Interesting."

"Yeah?" asked the orc in sincere surprise. "Really?"

"Keep your eyes peeled. Double the guard in the watchtower. Get the gleesome threesome into the exo and on standby."

"What happened?" The last crumbs of insouciance were lost from the orc's voice.

"Nothing yet. But that might soon change. If anything goes down, take shelter right up close to the observation-dome column."

"Roger. Maybe we should come join you? Although fuck knows where you are."

"Obey your orders, Wreck."

"I'm on it!"

"Out."

Having relayed my brief and ragged instructions, I brought our run to a halt, finishing by the end wall of the building, with its wide panoramic window, which Gabby immediately smashed out.

"Boat!" shouted Klappa, before turning back and taking aim at the corridor we'd just exited.

After taking a quick peek through two doors on opposite sides of the corridor, I chose the room which had another door leading from it and three narrow windows looking out onto the rear of the building. Shoving the almost weightless elf lady into the hands of Jorann, who had climbed down from the prism, I motioned with my head which way to go, then commandeered Gabby's armor-piercing weapon and knelt down by a windowsill.

Speeding towards us over the now abated waves was a somewhat odd-looking vessel, whose bow was adorned with a large black exo clinging fast to the steel sides. The boat was inflatable, multi-compartmental, and high-powered, and its bottom and sides were reinforced with metal sheeting. While I could not actually see the details, I instantly identified the nimble little craft and could not help but approve of the motherfuckers' choice, because you wouldn't find anything better for short water missions where speed was of the essence. Right now the boat was maneuvering violently, speeding doggedly on a zigzag course towards the island. It was managing to avoid the large missiles aimed at it, while the small sharp treats fired by the dome had little effect, deflecting off the sides of the boat and the exo's armor. The aft section of the deck was also covered with metal sheeting, and I was sure it was harboring the enemy fighters and helmsman. There was another boat, maybe even two, heading towards us from another direction, and try as the system might, there was no guarantee it would be able to take out all its targets before it ran short of ammo.

"Lead." Klappa's voice, as he stood behind me, spoke volumes.

"Both to the left," I commanded, turning around with my back still flush to the wall beneath the windowsill.

The barrel of my monstrous antitank weapon was barely aligned with the helmet of the knight staggering down the stairs when I pressed the trigger button. Shuddering from the recoil, I didn't even blink when his return fire peppered the wall to the right, creating a cloud of plaster dust.

A shot.

The knight slipped, his arms flailing, and he crashed to the floor face-first, his helmet smashing into the polished floor tiles. Some of the tiles cracked, and the knight floundered and tried to stand up, despite the bullet hole in his neck, and another one in the armored plate covering his belly, which had already taken a fair mangling from the system. Stretching out a hand, I caught a new missile thrown to me by Gabby, reloaded my weapon, and took very relaxed aim, this time my shot penetrating the bulging technical node on the chest of the knight's thick cuirass.

A second. Another second. And the momentarily motionless knight suddenly dropped his weapon, waved his arms around chaotically, and broke out some bizarre dance moves, clattering against the walls of the corridor, one moment coming closer to us, the next moment moving away. Apparently the medkit I'd struck had pumped all its contents into his dying body. The knight wheezed, and blood spurted from the hole in his neck protection, also with a hissing sound. But by now I'd lost interest in him. Turning around, I caught another couple of rounds and reloaded. My eyes were now fully trained on the boat, which had nearly gained the shore but was listing heavily and had taken quite a lot of water on board. It had lost maneuverability and wasn't going to make it.

The exo sitting at the bow evidently came to the same conclusion and suddenly jumped from the boat, which now stood up on end, at the very moment when my rocket struck its hull. Splinters of boat and scraps of body flew all around, while the exo landed with a heavy clang on the edge of a concrete platform approximately five meters from my position. What the cretinous exo controller did next I would never have expected from a fighter storming an enemy fortification: he turned his ass to me to see how the boat was getting along back there.

Shooting twice, I put bullets in instinctively chosen spots on the exo's very wide armored back: just below, and to the left of, the center. Accompanied by the squeal of a servomechanism, and spitting oil, smoke, and sparks from the entry wounds, it turned heavily around, used both its manipulators to crisscross the rear façade of the building with large-caliber salvos, and collapsed backwards, destroying a low concrete balustrade it landed on. A wink later, its tinted reinforced gun turret was flung open, and the operator was ejected from the divan, splatting down onto the concrete a meter from the window. I stepped back. Gabby moved forward, grabbed the lad, who was dressed in a stylish dark jumpsuit, by the throat, and pulled him inside the building, using an arm blade to chop off his right hand, which was reaching for a holster at his waist.

"Insect!" hissed Gabby, pulling the shrieking lad towards himself and clacking his mandibles, cutting most of his nose clean off.

To the accompaniment of the medkit's frightened squeal and the lad's crazed howlings, the disfigured operator was thrown into the room, where he was attended to by Klappa, who in a matter of seconds swaddled and gagged the prisoner and bandaged his stump. There then came an explosion, which produced a fountain of water that doused the patch of concrete outside, washing away the blood, oil, and severed arm. We scarcely felt the explosion of the black exo. I chuckled my surprise. Strange. Normally battle machines did not explode. There was nothing inside them that could explode. There was plenty of stuff that could burn, and burn very nicely, but explosions did not occur so easily, except when ammunition detonated during an onboard fire. And I had not noticed any additional mounted weapons such as mortar guns and rocket launchers on the exo. Only assault rifles attached to the manipulators, and a small cannon installed in its crotch.

I stuck my head out of the window just far enough to see the column hanging above us crowned with an observation dome. It was enough to be spotted.

Hero Erikvan!

Attention! *Immediate full verbal free-form report!*

"It's not just anyone who gets appointed as Jester!" I barked, reloading my weapon, which was showing its worth magnificently.

I didn't know how it would get on against heavy armored vehicles — it certainly wouldn't pierce the frontal armor of a tank — but it was just the ticket against these exo lites.

Hero Erikvan!
Attention! *Immediate full verbal free-form report!*

"The elf lady Dilya — fuck knows what her full name is — is alive and under our protection. My group still has its full complement. I have liquidated one of the knights who rebelled against his mistress. I do not know what happened to the second knight. We have captured the operator of an enemy battle exoskeleton."

Report accepted.
Familiarize yourself immediately with your new task, hero Erikvan!

I did not have to log on to my interface, because a description of the perfectly predictable task lit up right in front of my eyes, proving just how concerned the system was for its beautiful beloved children. A single glimpse was enough to understand what was demanded of us: to apply every effort, possible and impossible, to save the elf lady. "At any cost." The system also demanded we stay where we were, defending the position and awaiting the arrival of a flock of flying evacuation drones that were already on the way with reinforcements and extra ammunition for the system. Announcing an additional offhand condition, the system stated that it very much wanted the captured operator of the black exo to be delivered to it for questioning.

"I have familiarized myself with the task," I said, and withdrew my head back into the room. Listening in to the ringing silence that reigned both outside and in, I motioned Gabby towards the staircase.

We would take a look around.

While Gabby moved towards the stairs, I followed, dragging the armless and medkit-less exo operator into the corridor, my free hand easily holding my bulky armor-piercing weapon. The others followed. The operator bleated, using his eyes to indicate his chest, from where his medkit had been wrenched. He was concerned for his precious health, the fucker, and asking for the medkit to be returned. But there were no fools around here, if you didn't count the elf lady, and I was not about to return a medkit that was perfectly capable of injecting a cocktail which would increase strength tenfold. If he was going to die, he was going to die.

"What have you got over there, Gabby?"

"The bearded mincemeat in the torn sweaters. The storyteller's still alive, but..."

When I reached the top of the stairs, I saw what "but" meant. The goblin who had preferred to be called Acid Shark had been chopped in half obliquely at crotch level and his diced intestines turned inside out, and he also had a couple of bullet holes in the right side of his chest. Fatal wounds, but he was still alive. Wedged into a corner beneath a raggedy old banner, the beard smiled weakly and looked at the holes in his chest and belly, before croaking with a strange sense of hope:

"Is it really that bad? Or...?"

"You've still got one ball," I said encouragingly, stepping over his legs, which lay a couple of meters from him.

"It's so strange to view them from a distance," said the beard as he stared at his lower limbs.

"What's this medkit he's talking about?" asked Jorann pragmatically.

"It's a celestial azure," said the elf lady slung over her shoulder. "One of the best medkits. Put me down. Hang in there, Finch, take deep breaths."

Her voice expressed sincere sympathy. Slipping down from the ginger lass's shoulder, Dilya stood up straight, leaned against a wall, and looked around in a slight and clearly chemical torpor. She'd been injected with something. Or rather, she'd injected herself with something. Except she didn't have a medkit. While she'd been undressing on the hoof when we first met, I had snuck a glimpse of her perfect body. She'd been wearing her own white lace panties, and someone else's old T-shirt, pants, socks, and boots which were too big for her. Since then we had not been apart, and she couldn't possibly have had the opportunity to slap on a medkit. Which meant she hadn't needed to, because she had an internal one. Elves, huh? Not so easy to kill, or leave in shock for long.

Slipping to the floor next to the fatally wounded beardo, she leaned a shoulder weakly against the wall and muttered:

"Hang in there, Finch. Hang in there, my clever one. In seven minutes the drones will be here to rescue us all."

"Seven minutes?" I asked, interrupting their intimate chat. "Where'd you get that information from?"

"Huh?"

"How do you know it'll be seven minutes?"

"The timer. Mother keeps us informed. And information concerning survival lights up in front of our eyes."

"Keep us informed. Out loud," I ordered, stepping over the corpses and peeking into the rooms the interrupted excursion had not taken us to.

"There are only three points: Don't take any initiative; keep close to hero Erikvan; and obey any order from hero Erikvan."

"I see."

"How sweet," snorted the redhead, looking askance at the elite beauty, who had returned to her chat with the bearded stumper of near-dead meat. "Such affectionate concern."

"She cares for the wounded," said the prism, shrugging his chitinous shoulders.

"That's not what I mean. I'm talking about the system's concern for the elves," retorted Jorann, turning to me. "Commander, you saw the system cover her, yeah? Salvo fire, rockets, armor-piercing missiles. Jeez. Now that is maternal love."

"She's one of a hundred Highers, and they have the right to make decisions," I replied, and kicking away from the threshold a slightly flattened severed head with a protruding tongue, I entered a large room which had captured my interest.

Not so much a room as a hall, actually. An elongated rectangular hall with painted pictures of various birds and animals on its walls and ceiling. Actually, they weren't so much pictures as bright plastic mosaics stylized as jigsaw puzzles, judging by the shape of each fragment. One wall was almost completely occupied by a long panoramic window, which somehow recalled the Observer restaurant at the top of the protective wall encircling Zombieland. Except that there, the reinforced glass had provided a view of deceptively sleepy beech-lined alleys and dilapidated infirmary corpuses. Whereas here the view was of the ocean, the object of the cravings of the survers doomed to eternal incarceration. But it was not the pictures on the walls that interested me. Neither was it the panoramic window. My attention was chiefly attracted by a number of regular desks covered with piles of time-yellowed papers, books, magazines, and booklets. Around the desks were comfortable armchairs, whose very wide armrests bore plates, bottles, and cutlery.

No doubt the place had previously been a café where pudgy kindhearts, drowsy from their dismal tour guides' whinings, could catch their breath and placate their nervous systems with the aid of double-hamburger injections into their stomachs. The scampering children would contemplate the animals on the walls and the birds on the ceiling, shove their snotty noses up against the panoramic window, and squeak to demand more sweet fizz, while their corpulent and eternally dissatisfied mothers gripped hamburgers between their fingers and nagged at their husbands who were chugging sour beer. Cheap, fun, and insightful.

Now, however, the hall — the largest room on the floor — had for some reason been turned not into a museum hall, but into a beautifully decorated workers' canteen. But why?

The answer soon made itself known. Seeing that all the desks stood in an arc facing away from the panoramic window and towards the back of the room, I took a couple of steps, peered around the corner, and understood everything.

Mounted on the wall was a screen, an enormous active-matrix screen, divided into a grid of different -colored segments. Each segment showed separate video footage of the ocean, hills, mountains, valleys, settlements, and roads. Live transmissions from observation domes in various regions of the world around us. Logical. It was perfectly logical to show the citizens of the new world just how beautiful and varied it was.

Approximately three yards in front of the screen stood a short amanita muscaria toadstool with a wide cap. Stretching across the cap was a long glowing plastic squiggle forming a legend which read: "What are nature's protectors currently busy with?" The sign flickered lazily. I took the hint and pressed it, ignoring a second, small screen displaying pictograms of available commands.

No sooner had I done so than the screen went blank for a second, and when it lit up again, I saw an enormous brown bear plodding through a light old birch forest, its lumpy head lowered. With the ease of a tractor, the bear was pulling behind it the corpse of a naked goblin girl with her throat ripped out. Her head was bumping against tree stumps and roots, her fair hair catching on them and leaving tufts behind as if marking the route they had taken.

What a marvellous spectacle for the children!

A roly-poly angel boy pushes a button, and sees the decomposing corpse of a citizen of the blessed new world being hauled through the forest.

Laughing, I watched the bear for a short while, noting its considerable age, the bald patches on its graying fur, the twinkling blue lights in its tiny eyes, and the incredible strength it employed to fling a fallen tree into the river with a single swat. Then the dead meaty doll landed on the sandy embankment and was immediately set upon by squawking flightless birds.

An edifying video indeed.

What else?

Now the screen showed three large fiery-red vixens running in a sprightly V formation after a scampering goblin who howled as he tried to put pressure on his left wrist stump. The hand itself was in the jaws of the rear vixen. This time a multicolored explanation ran across the screen: "Protector beasts chase a frightened citizen to return his left hand, lost in an accident, and explain the right way to the nearest medblock using gentle growls."

"URGHAAAARR!" growled the lead vixen.

"RAKRAKRAKOM!" seconded the other two, the one with the severed hand in her mouth nearly dropping it.

"AAAAAA!" responded the running goblin, accelerating sharply. "AAAAAAA!"

"Interesting," I said, turning my attention away from the squealing goblin and concentrating it on the screen with the control pictograms. *Hmm, what to press?* Most of the virtual buttons had no words written on them, only rather bizarre curly symbols.

"If you'll allow me" — Jorann's voice reflected sincere interest — "I'll sort it out."

"Does this seem familiar to you?"

"Oh yes."

"Be my guest. Gabby, Klappa, anything to report?"

"We had a look around. The first knight's still lying round the corner like a crushed tin can. There are bits of boat floating on the water, and a couple of mangled corpses washed up on the beach. All quiet so far."

"Patrol the second floor, Gabby left-hand rooms and windows, Klappa right-hand."

"Yes sir!"

"It will be done."

The fighters left on their patrol mission, while I settled in to wait patiently, chewing melancholically on a protein bar fished from my belt bag, and paying scant attention to Finch, who was wheezing in agony by the wall. His death throes were dragging and I seriously wanted to put a stop to them with a boot to his croaking throat.

What value was there in these bearded goblins?

None. It was more likely they owed the world a debt. Cherished by the elf lady's warm breast, they lived in safety and wanted for nothing, and were not especially concerned about cleanliness. Sitting in comfortable armchairs in front of a huge screen, they kept a lazy eye on what was going on in the world, feeding on tinned food and washing it down with free beer.

They took no active part in goings-on, attempted to change nothing, and lived quiet as mice in a deep dark burrow, eating and drinking to their hearts' content. But I was absolutely fucking sure that when they saw something of interest on the screen, a discussion would immediately kick off, involving faux knowledge, commentary, encouragement, spiteful laughter, and the occasional idler comment such as "No one gives a shit about anything" or "They only think about themselves," or phrases beginning "I would…" or "If I were in his shoes…" Yet none of them would even so much as think about beefing up their body, learning how to handle a weapon, patrolling the museum's coastal areas, shooting sick animals, zombies, or scratchers, searching for fugitive rapists and murderers, helping animals and goblins trapped in snares, or shoring up eroded riverbanks.

No, none of that. But why not? Because that would mean actually doing something, wouldn't it? And they were so lazy, and it was so dangerous, and it was so much more pleasant sipping beer in front of the screen and providing caustic commentary on the live transmission.

After all, they did have at their disposal this incredible all-seeing tool, an all-seeing, well nearly all-seeing eye.

So, since they didn't need it, I would take it. And I wouldn't give it to anyone.

Rising to her feet, the elf lady threw herself at me and demanded:

"Bandages! I need to dress my wounds!"

It was nonsense. Her emotionally overloaded mind was simply trying to get her to do something, anything, pointless or otherwise, just so long as she could rid herself of some of the psychological stress crippling her.

"Jorann, give Dilya a pack of bandages and a tube of glue," I ordered.

Glowering a hint at the surprised redhead, I stepped around the back of the elf lady and kicked Finch hard in his bullet-pierced chest. The useless lump of bearded meat twitched, before dropping his head to his chest. A medkit wailed. Then immediately stopped.

"Finch!" shrieked the elf girl, throwing herself at the corpse. But I caught her, picked her up with ease, and carried her to the wall.

"He died with dignity," I said, shaking Dilya like a kitten. "Do you understand? He took courage from you and behaved stoically."

"My sweet little Finch. He was so awkward in bed, yet so tender, with his tickly beard—"

"I'm gonna be sick," said Jorann, unable to contain herself.

"I'll take him outside carefully, with dignity," I said. "You stay here. Take this, it's lemonade."

Sweet hogwash. The favorite food of any brain reared on sugar. When the tongue senses the sweetness, the brain squeals its delight, and is then calm. A mindless association, where sweet equals safe.

The elf lady took a slug from the flask and sighed heavily. She was recovering, aided by the medkit built into her slender frame. Good. Stepping towards the dead Finch, I picked up his torso and carried it carefully from the room, closing the door behind me. A few yards down the corridor, I flung it into the first room I came to and went back for his legs. I repeated the procedure with them, also kicking out of the room a single wrinkly testicle, and after wiping my besmirched boot on his corpse, I went back to the hall, exchanging glances with my patrolling fighters on the way.

Not satisfied with this, I stuck my head out of the window again and looked at the system's observation column hanging over the building, my eyebrows raised inquisitively. A minute later it transpired that the system couldn't give a toss for my goblin eyebrows, and satisfied now, I drew my head back into the safety of the thick walls.

Returning to the elf lady, who by now was cussing deliriously and recalling whimsical names (she was obviously running through all her potential enemies), I stood thoughtfully nearby, listening, safe in the knowledge that productive dialogue was not on the cards right now. That was why I preferred to do business with former asshole-dwellers, graduates from the school of hard knocks. They were so accustomed to fate's never-ending strikes that they would regain consciousness after a knockout and simply pick themselves up and march on. While the emasculated elves, who knew no barbarity, were so accustomed to living in a safe shell that such stress would unsettle them for a good while.

Okay then.

I spent the next five minutes walking around the building, studying every room and every dead-end. I saw the entrance to the basement levels blocked up with their concrete draft excluder. Somewhere down there, on the other side of that stopper, was the hidden kingdom of the omnipresent gnomes, who so loved looking at fish and sunken boats. I even found an exit out onto a flat roof made of thick concrete slabs. And it was on that roof that I was standing when the black dots that had appeared on the horizon grew suddenly larger and became five fast-moving drones.

The two more unassuming-looking of the drones, the worker bees, immediately latched onto the system mushrooms and began loading ammunition. Down flew plastic and metal shrapnel, accompanied by bangings and sparkings. One of the other three drones remained airborne and flew in a wide circle around the central building sheltering us. The other two landed on the roof, where one raised its door invitingly, and the other ejected five knights in identical suits of red-and-white striped armor and helmets with mirrored visors. In their hands they carried automatic weapons, two of them belt-fed machine guns whose belts were being fed from heavy backpacks on their backs. One of the knights had a small of metal box attached horizontally to his left shoulder, its small doors shut fast. A mini rocket launcher. Those bad boys, of which there were normally four, could cause an awful lot of different kinds of damage, depending on the kind of ammo they were loaded with.

"Where is Mistress...?"

"Get out of my way," I said, waving away the rocket knight and stepping towards a hatchway in the roof, from which Gabby had appeared holding the elf lady in one hand.

"Stay here," I said to her. "There's no danger. New knights have arrived. We shall continue the excursion."

"Home. I want to go home."

With a shrug, I stood aside and watched as the exalted activist idiot benefactress Jester was carefully loaded into one of the drones. The red-and-white knights squeezed their armored tushes in after her, and the drone took off and flew away, accompanied by three of the others, one of the patrols and the two smaller ammunition-loading ones. Only one flying machine remained on the roof, still holding the hatchway doors open.

"Nah," I said.

Raising my visor, I looked at one of the mushrooms battered by the system's bullets and beamed a wide smile.

"Shall we talk about bonus rewards?"

* * *

Leaning back in a hard chair, I put my feet up on the pristine tabletop and stared at the back of Jorann, who was fiddling with the terminal.

"Any joy?"

"Just a minute. There's a whole pile of cutoff functions. It's all very slow, difficult, and cheerless. Like most men."

"How long?"

"Another couple of minutes."

"Okay."

Removing my feet from the table, I replaced them with a heavy clanking armor-piercing weapon and began to strip it down at a relaxed pace. If I was sure of anything at all, it was that coming from the lips of a techhead, the phrase "a couple of minutes" might have meant anything from two minutes to three days of ceaseless fucking around with programs which had no intention of playing ball.

But there was no sense in hurrying.

I honored the drone passing laboriously by the former canteen's panoramic window with the most cursory of glances. The remainder of my crew had arrived, and the next drone would be carrying nets bearing thirty-six newbies who wanted to undergo training and join the ranks of Elb the goblin's squad of heroes.

For saving the elf lady, the system had impulsively promised a whopping five bonus rewards, not counting the five thousand crowns. It had no doubt wanted to get away with the usual chickenfeed, like free medical attention, but I was proactive and expressed all my desires before it had the chance.

My crew was given permission to use the museum archipelago as a field base. Plus, if only temporarily, responsibility for the territory was transferred to me, and I was ensured that anyone who even thought about poking their nose in here would be told to get lost. An army base is no place for prying loafers. Although one building I did designate as a buffer zone, the far one on the first little island from the shore, which was stylized as a lighthouse.

What else?

A decent supply of provisions for us. No drinks necessary, because clean fresh water flowed from the faucets and the showers worked, although the whole water system was in a majorly shit state of repair.

The transfer here of all my crew, including newbies, machines, and all our possessions, by air transport, at the system's expense.

The provision of at least three mobile med-blocks next to the main building. And if possible, the same number of trade points, so that drill-weary goblins could spoil themselves with mundane trinkets and treats.

And for dessert I wanted the terminal screen to remain switched on all the time. I doubted the system would turn it off, but I wasn't going to risk it.

After expressing my wishes, I immediately explained them. The one simple reason for my need to relocate here was that it would give me the chance to find out some necessary information and get busy with the Wild Evolution task.

Although in actual fact this was not the only thing that drew me to the place.

The Highers and their flunkies.

Each day saw more and more of them in the Shiny Shack. And each day their rakish drunken antics worsened. More and more hints, more naked sleek bodies, and more discontent. Another day, and serious fisticuffs would kick off. Given that the system had allowed us a couple of days to relax without any tasks, there was no point us sitting around near this notorious town if there was a more interesting alternative.

And there was a more interesting alternative: a derelict museum complex which could easily be a reliable squad base away from prying eyes.

So why waste time?

The system heard me out, spent ten seconds mulling it over, and granted all my requests. Excellent. After using the transmitter to tell Wreck to immediately prepare for relocation, I went back to the main hall, chortling to myself in my head. Who would have thunk it? We were back at the ocean again. Back at the Path of Purity. Closer to the fresh air which did not carry the stench of elite noble ass.

A parallel to Zombieland.

Perhaps this is the baseline so ideal for folks such as me?

I spent the next half hour jettisoning anything superfluous from the hall, leaving only the tables, chairs, and a couple of benches. Klappa and I discarded all the waste paper in one of the smaller rooms which was filled with all manner of crap. I would delegate the room to Bask just as soon as the half-blind zombie landed his scrawny ass here.

As we worked, I issued Klappa with the first dozen orders concerning the housing of personnel and other priority business. The Asian heard me out and gave a short nod. I did not repeat anything, since I knew he'd registered every word. He was an ideal adjutant, not to mention bodyguard.

Jorann returned to the hall and removed her helmet, and prior to busying herself with the terminal, matter-of-factly dropped a bombshell:

"Make me into a prism, lead."

"Like Gabby?"

"Like Gabby."

"Are you sure?"

"Sure as sure can be."

"So you don't want to be an enchantress anymore?"

"Fuck pseudo-magic. I want mandibles, blades, chitinous armor, and spines. No fucking fur, ears, or claws."

"I repeat, are you sure?"

"Yes. It will be to the benefit of the crew. And to my benefit as well."

"Speak to the system yourself first. Go up onto the roof and pour your sick heart out, present your reasons. If it works, that's fine. If not, I'll try."

"Thank you, lead. It's time to pull a full-fledged insect from its hideous meat cocoon."

"Terminal."

"I'm already on it."

Coming back into the hall, Klappa shook the dust from his gloves, looked around to see what superfluous junk remained here, and removed it for liquidation. On his way back out, he announced:

"The rest of the squad has arrived with the arsenal."

"What sort of shape are the fighters in?"

"Frazzled."

"R and R," I ordered, gently wiping an oily rag over the bizarre curved part of my armor-piercing weapon, which actually looked more like a punch card than a part of a weapon. Since when did firearms have so many superfluous bells and whistles? And you couldn't throw it out, or you'd be throwing out the bells and whistles, which were actually the craftsman's visiting card.

"Copy that," replied the swordsman before leaving with the last pile of old books.

"Bask, on me!"

"Yes sir!"

When the almost healthy-looking zombie entered the hall, he did not conceal the joy and restlessness gripping him. Realizing that the normally calm and cold-blooded Bask (as he had been before his first, arguably excessive, bout of passionate and languorous coupling with Yorka) was just about to begin telling me about the building we were in, just as the recently deceased beards had done, I cut him off with a brusque gesture and, setting aside my now reassembled armor-piercing weapon, spoke first:

"How's your health?"

"Okay. I'm back in training. Wreck's persecuting me just like all the others."

"Good. I've got a job for you. Klappa will show you a room piled full of waste paper. Have a dig around in it. Most importantly, look for anything connected with the technical history of this world."

"Technical?"

"Precise dates, names, jobs, lists of hard facts. All the rest of the ceremonial nonsense, the long boring worthless speeches by the chosen ones, feel free to cull mercilessly.

"Okay."

"What about the jolly legless bandit?"

"I have formed an opinion of him," replied Bask. "Should I tell you?"

"Later," I sighed, turning to look at Jorann working her magic. "From now on you will have double the workload. Choose yourselves some assistants. Dig for information. I want someone sitting at the screen around the clock, observing and noting anything of interest. By which I mean any monster activity: prisms, zombies, beastfolk. Everything must be recorded, including times, locations, quantities, weapons, whatever. And that applies to the movement of any serious machinery. Got that?"

After receiving their nods of understanding, I stressed:

"Twenty-four-hour monitoring. As for the waste paper, Bask, look for any records by those idiots who were here before us. Just in case one of them had the bright idea to record everything of interest."

"Like this?" asked Jorann, pointing at the screen, where a male and female deer were coupling.

"No," I chuckled.

"According to the logs, the Reproduction of Biological Species pictogram is activated way more often than the other ones."

"It may not be worth looking for useful records," said Bask, quick on the uptake. "But I'll take a peek anyway."

"Report back this evening about anything you find."

Nodding again, Bask went off to the waste-paper room. Meanwhile on the screen, the picture of the coupling deer couple had been replaced by one of killer whales approaching a seal that had shat itself. I shouted:

"Why did those shitheads use the screen to look for copulating monkeys and tunafish? That's like…"

"Using an atomic grenade to crack nuts?"

"Something like that. They could have made a big difference, but they wouldn't even agree to be witnesses to the important stuff, because they were too busy peeking at copulating peasants. Wasted resources. And a dumb she-elf totally off her pretty head."

"Why?"

"She provided them full board. Food, accommodation, safety. They must have listened willingly to her speeches about the dying world, about the need to act urgently to change things, yet at the same time they did nothing. They just ate, shat, and jerked off in secret to deer grunting with exertion. Nothing more. Why did she keep feeding the bastards?"

"Because they protected the Museum?"

"The system takes care of that. Those 'protectors' couldn't clean a toilet bowl."

"I noticed," said Jorann with a frown. "It's ready, lead. Most of the functions have been deleted, but there are still lots of commands available, plus I found a hidden command which brings up a search box. That's not trivial, believe me."

"I believe you. Get searching."

"What search terms should I use?"

"Oh yeah," I sniggered, wiping gun grease oil from my fingers. "Right."

"I'm listening."

"Calm. Total absence of criminal activity. No violent deaths among the local population. Generally an untroubled happy life for everyone, without exception, including fleas, lice, and tapeworms."

"I can't search for parameters like that. It won't accept them."

"What will it accept, then?"

"Well, judging by the hints here, cornflowers blooming, nectar being collected, arctic foxes moulting, seal courtship games..."

"Shit."

"There's that as well. Bears defecating, the study of black bears' excrement, dietary variations between predators and omnivores..."

"Shit."

"All this technology was not designed and used for police purposes, goblin. It's a kind of corner for young naturalists."

"Shit. Get Bask back here. Rack your brains, nipples, and tushes for a way to find the information I need."

"Maybe it needs indirect association?" asked Jorann, her thinking cap firmly back on now. "A chain of accessible sequential queries. Hmm. But what search terms?"

"Prison. Death."

"Great selection. Not."

"Wait. Rape. That's also sex, right?"

"It's a display of bastardy which deserves punishment by slow agonizing torture," hissed Jorann, stopping by the door. "First the bastard should have his freaking slimy—"

"Hey!"

"What?"

"Rape is sex, right?"

"Technically, yes."

"Forget about Bask for the minute. Try 'sex' as your first search term."

"And the second?"

"Death."

"Copy. But would you mind explaining?"

"We're looking for shady organizations," I replied, emptying out the contents of my belt bag and wiping it inside and out with a moist towelette. "They hide. They hide from the prying eyes of heroes and the system. But they are still serious large organizations. And what is the most important thing for any organization which considers itself serious?"

"Hmm. Profitability, discipline, a strict hierarchy, order in all its territories, decent living conditions for its employees, a place for the top dogs to relax in comfort. I think I get it. That's why you wanted to start with things like 'calm,' 'order,' and 'absence of criminal activity.' Any gang will maintain strict order in its territories. No murder, no rape. Wait! Why did you want me to search for 'rape'? Or 'sex,' rather?"

"Rape and sex might be synonymous in the

eyes of the system," I suggested with a shrug. "Folk do have sex, after all."

Jorann grimaced silently, then said:

"Fuck it. Although there is no synonymity. And why search for it anyway? There won't be any rape on gang territory."

"There shouldn't be," I replied, correcting her. "But it's far from everyone who can show real strength of character."

"Some gang members just can't control themselves and keep fucking full-bosomed big-assed peasant girls, right?"

"True enough. Basically, we're looking for any sex at the edge of our range of visibility with clothes strewn around."

"I'm confused."

"Nobody except a person is going to deliberately have sex right in front of the system's electronic eyes. Especially gangsters. They have to know all the twilight zones, and more to the point live in them, never surfacing in illuminated districts. But any gang member lives on a knife edge, always under pressure. He might be killed at any moment, and his work is bloody and nerve-racking. Although there are ways to calm the nerves and destress."

"Meditation," said the redhead, "herbal infusions, mild medicines, conscious chatter with oneself, contemplating the beauty of nature."

"Drink, drugs, and sex," I added. "And it is precisely during an attempted rape that a woman will do anything to reach an area monitored by the system. Even if she's in a blind panic, a rape victim will always try to run away, and there's always a chance she'll find herself slap-bang in the center of an eagle-eyed tree stump's field of vision."

"And her drunk pursuer will be in no condition to worry about being observed." The ginger lass understood me correctly. "The bastard will start fucking her wherever he caught her and knocked her to the ground."

"Get searching."

"Sex. We're searching for sex, all aspects of it, be they beautiful and natural, or perverted and goblinesque."

"Porn?" asked Wreck, suddenly interested and sticking his nose into the hall. "I can help—"

"Get on with your duties!" I barked, making the extremely disappointed orc slope away.

"What have clothes got to do with anything?" asked Jorann, absorbed in her work. "The clothes strewn around the copulating bodies."

"We might understand who is who by their clothes and weapons. Whose hairy unwiped ass is that twitching in the camera lens? Whose entrails are we looking at from this awkward angle? Is it a peasant? Is it a bandit?"

"What sort of fucked-up world do we live in, if the observation system refuses to actively seek out crimes but is still cheerfully willing to show us scenes of moist fantasy sex in all its variations?"

"Search for 'sex,' Jorann. And find as much as possible. When something interesting comes up, we'll narrow the search."

"I'm searching—"

"Shit!"

"You are on fire today," hissed the redhead. "What's the problem?"

"Do you know what the operator of the black exo told me before I chopped his other arm off?"

"What?"

"He said, 'Fuck it.'"

"A real man. All arms can be sewn back on."

"But then he added, with a certain devil-may-care melancholy as he watched the system drone landing, 'I've had my fucking day.'"

"Something poisonous sewn into the body. Alphabet."

"Alphabet," I agreed. "He died right in front of my eyes, before the steel medblock doors opened for him."

"It was his choice," said Jorann with a shrug. "If you're bored, lead, feel free to take some drugs and leave me alone."

I opened my mouth to respond, thought for a second, closed it again, and settled in comfortably to the armchair. I was an intelligent goblin and I knew when to be silent.

CHAPTER 9

SEX.

The desire for sex.

A thirst for fucking.

Lust enhanced exponentially by drugs and booze. Lust which becomes inflamed exponentially when your bloodshot eyes alight on a very sexy dolled-up girl with a sweet but timorous smile.

In these situations, later on, the next morning, the rapist will wake up to the fact of his crime and try to justify his actions using the single excuse that it was her own fault. She was dressed like a hooker, made-up like a prostitute. And she smiled at me. It was a fucking hint: Fuck me! So I fucked her. What did she expect, flaunting her tits and ass like that? It was her own fault. She smiled at me as she was walking past, hurrying home to her children, so I caught her up and forced myself on her.

A common ballad where the hero is guilty of nothing.

This was the story of a simple peasant girl and a smiley vagrant fellow, told to me by the chief of a small village, snivelled through his smashed-up nose. A small group of us had arrived at the village by buggy after seven hours of hurtling and jolting down the road. To begin with we followed the Path, then we veered off onto a narrower road, then took increasingly narrower paths before eventually working our way through brittle bushes full of various beasties to scare off.

And here we were at dawn, in the neat little village of Ventira, inhabited by no less neat, and also smiley, citizens.

And here was I, having barely slept a wink, standing with the chief, who was trying in earnest but failing miserably to fill my head with shit. I smiled and listened, while the chief, believing his streams of verbal diarrhea had convinced me of at least something, continued telling his tales: a completely unknown rapscallion was walking along, gawking at the beauty of the sky, when he tripped and fell dick-first onto a local girl chilling at the side of the road. The act was not exactly one of mutual consent, but what could you do? You had to forget it and carry on with your life, thanking your lucky stars every day for your quiet and gentle contentment.

By the end of his speech, I'd begun to subtly edge my way towards a log barn, and just as soon as we found ourselves around a dark corner, and just as he said the word "contentment," I punched him in the ribs. I followed this up with several kicks meant to break his ribs. Everyone had the right to be a coward, it was everyone's right as an individual, but when you became a leader, you were deprived of that right and could no longer behave in a cowardly fashion. But the chief of Ventira was still a pathetic freaking coward, and he preferred to turn a blind eye to the violent rape of young girls. On top of which, he'd been stupid enough to lie to me.

When the chief, struck in the face by my boot, zonked out and landed broken-nose-first in the dirt, I turned to Wreck, who had brought me a shaking rape victim with a face blackened from grief and battery. The first thing she said to me, moving her swollen lips with difficulty, was:

"My husband says I'm dirty now because I've had someone else's penis inside me."

"Your face…"

"My husband says he finds me repugnant now, so he beat me. And his best friend agreed and beat me as well. He said I wanted to be fucked, otherwise it wouldn't have happened."

"Wreck, go pay her husband and his best friend a visit. Inform the husband he's now divorced, and make sure both those jovial chaps become dirtied themselves."

"Get them to suck each other off with gusto?"

"Use your imagination."

"Ooh, those bumpkin perverts."

"And take the chief with you. Let him get some

tongue and ass consolation as well."

"Gotcha. Fancy giving me a hand, Tigr?"

"With pleasure."

When the fighters had dragged the moaning chief away, I turned to the girl, who was now lying on the grass, and asked:

"What do you want?"

"To kill the bastard. To kill the bastard who did this to me."

"What about your husband?"

"I loved him. Even yesterday I loved him with all my heart."

"And?"

"I don't want to stay here."

"What do you want?"

"Revenge!"

My lips stretched to a wide smile as I replied:

"Easily done. Do you know where the bastard came from? The one who clearly knew the area?"

"Take me with you and I'll tell you everything I know."

"Let's go," I said.

"I want a knife, a long sharp knife."

"Easy."

"If it's possible, that bastard—"

"He's yours," I said.

"Let's go." The girl with the blackened face stood up and strode fearlessly towards a buggy parked by the village fence. It was full of outsiders armed to the teeth and was towing a platform bearing an exo covered with a tarpaulin.

She was helped to a seat, then had a cheap

regular medkit attached to her, and after a dose of medicine and sedative, the girl began to speak. I listened intently, paying no attention to the faint moaning, wheezing, and whimpering coming from an ornate little house not far away.

Ten minutes later we left Ventira, travelling just over a kilometer before turning in to a downward-sloping meadow and making for a small dark wood. Faintly discernible above the treetops were the outlines of buildings which even at a distance looked gloomy.

Was the rape victim showing us something very important?

No.

A regular gang of amateur cutthroats. But it was a thin thread that I was pulling to see what was at the other end.

* * *

Sitting on a log, I kicked away a snake that was coming for me, leaned back against a cracked concrete wall, and studied the thing peppered with holes that hung over me by the roadside. I didn't even know what to call it. It had once been blue with thick yellow lettering, and was probably a list.

We were right by the main road, just like at the Wildlife Park, where visitors travelled past massive enclosures containing wild beasts living in their natural habitat. This was also some kind of enclosure, but the animals here were nothing out of the ordinary. They might even have corresponded to the list of ten indecipherable items on the wall.

Sloth: the mother of all vices. And somewhere like this, sloth was the belle of the ball.

Aggression, reliance on physical strength and violence: another of the terrible moral afflictions of those who dwell in places like this...

I didn't bother reading any further, worried I would feel aggressive sloth creeping up on me. I simply turned my attention to a seven-story building, whose form recalled a candle stub, and which stood in the center of a concrete circle with a concrete wall around it. The building's façade was inscribed proudly with the phrase "Common Slum."

"Jeez," I said, looking at the dilapidated regular apartment block. "What *isn't* a slum then?"

"Jeez," exclaimed a goblin skipping from the main entrance in a dirty gray vest and matching shorts. His hand let go of his fly and reached for the holster on his belt.

"Don't do it," I said. "From the rear, man, they're attacking from the rear. We're just watching from the stands here."

"Huh?" said the confused goblin, goggling.

"Don't give away your office's position, you twat!" hissed Wreck, waving a fist at the idiot. The attack is coming from the rear!"

"Huh?"

"From your rear end!"

"Watch out!"

"Oh shit," said the goblin.

The rifle twitched in the rape victim's inexperienced hands, but from this trifling distance, and with the gun resting on a concrete wall, the bullet struck the center of the gray-T-shirted belly and sunk into it. The goblin began to croak and collapsed onto his side, scraping his feet on the ground. We ducked our heads behind the wall and waited.

Waited for what?

The attack from a squad of heavy infantry.

Or alternatively, the Hippo's first attack.

A heavy strike from the other side of the building told us the squad had at last gathered its wits and was getting down to business.

"Exo! There's an exo in the allotment!" came a shout from above. "Oh shit! Get down!"

Machine guns began to batter the building, knocking out the few remaining intact windowpanes, destroying window frames, and crumbling concrete walls. To begin with we just listened. Then we saw the exo coming around the side of the building, barraging the empty windows with bullets.

A second.

Another second.

The operator snapped out of his stupor. Holding the manipulators high in the air, Sebl walked another few meters, sharply lowered one arm, and let fly with a short burst at a first-floor window, prompting a wheezy yell which soon turned into a groan. The exo's mortar gun fired at the wall. Twice. The shouts from inside the building intensified, and someone up top discharged a gutless rifle volley before hiding from the retaliatory barrage.

"Go!" I said, remaining where I was.

"Let's go!" barked the orc, leading his dozen away.

Tigr darted silently to the side, followed by his girlfriend and two potential scouts whose reactions were a tad slow.

Not counting myself and Rox, I'd taken twenty goblins with me. Three of them were in the exo. Wreck's dozen numbered nearly twenty fighters, although many of them still weren't match-fit. Tigr had five guys. Another two were inseparable from Rox and had two machine guns, one for the buggy and the other for the rear of the platform.

Chewing pensively on a piece of hay, I waited patiently, listening to what was going on inside the building. Doors being blown off their hinges, glass shattering, shouts of anger, fright, and pain, someone yelping as they flew down from the top floor, and the exo firing and stamping it steel feet while its manipulators occasionally crunched and squelched bodies.

After fifteen minutes had passed, two figures collapsed in front of me, a regular goblin in a red T-shirt and a partially scalped beastfolk with its ears and tail chopped off. They both stared at me with identical expressions of malice, doom, and faint hope. After looking them up and down, I turned to Wreck and asked:

"The rapist?"

"She killed him. He was hers to kill."

"Good," I said, before turning back to the prisoners and saying "Shall we have a little chat?"

* * *

Another twenty minutes later we left, taking with us a small number of useful trophies and no useful information. Diddly squat. Nothing concerning the gangs that interested me.

"Squat," I barked into the transmitter.

"Copy," came Jorann's voice in response. "Do we move on?"

"Yes."

"Copy. Bask? What looks most promising?"

"The village of Zmoraliye. It's two hours to the west of Ventira, but if you show me your location, we might be able to find a more direct route." The zombie was unruffled.

"Rox?" I said, turning to the old mechanic, my eyebrows raised inquisitively.

"Only back through the village." He shook his gray head. "We need to recharge."

"The village of Zmoraliye, via Ventira," said the transmitter. "What happened there?"

"A couple of surprisingly well-dressed, well-armed, and cultured-looking goblins got methodically drunk and proceeded to engage in passionate sex in a flowery meadow. We observed the sex, and what preceded that we gleaned from listening in to goings on in Zmoraliye. The villagers are devoted tongue-wags."

"*And?* How do this couple get to be of interest?"

"They've got identical strange symbols on their

weapons and clothes. Some kind of horned animal skull gripping a dagger between its teeth. The goblins themselves have an unholy world-weary look about them."

"Are they still there?"

"They've just finished up their sweaty business, drained their bottles, and are now sleeping in each other's arms."

"Good. Leave them to rest."

*   *   *

Spitting my anger, I wiped my boot on the grass and walked away, leaving the butchered lady's body lying there.

Another blank.

Bandits. There was a band of them. Or rather, there had been. They'd recently stumbled upon a squad of heroes, and their numbers had dropped from twenty something to three. One of the survivors died on the way; a mercy killing. The remaining two were taken unharmed to the tiny village, where they celebrated their miracle rescue with a merry feast followed by sweet sex, their first. And last.

"Squat," I barked into the transmitter.

Instead of Jorann, the reply came from Bask, whose voice was full of ardor:

"Predictable. Commander, I've just seen something seriously worthy of our attention. And really close by."

"Where?"

"On the road leading south from Zm... Zmo... Ah, shit! Basically, there's a buggy pulling a covered trailer heading towards the village, south. We spotted it by accident. The system showed us a pair of prisms fucking by the roadside, and this buggy just happened to be driving past them."

"And why is it worthy of our attention?"

"The trailer's overloaded. The buggy was quite happy pulling it along the flat, but there's a dip where the concrete is flooded. It was okay going down, but in the middle and then up the slope out of the dip, the trailer... basically the trailer got stuck in a thick layer of mud. The buggy was barely able to pull it out. And I distinctly saw the tarpaulin twitch, as if someone wanted to jump out of the trailer and help, but there was an angry shout from the buggy, and everything went quiet in the trailer."

"The road to the south? Heading south?"

"Yes. They're about twenty kilometers away now, moving slowly but steadily."

"Copy."

"Just be careful, commander. There are some serious folk in the buggy. I didn't see any weapons, but who knows what's hiding at their feet?"

"Okay. Continue monitoring."

"Copy."

Climbing into our buggy, I announced:

"We've got a new target. To the south of Zmoraliye. Put your foot down. We've got a small ambush to set up."

* * *

I stepped out of the thick undergrowth onto the road, and found myself five meters from the nose of the oncoming enemy buggy. In the passenger seat was a beefy man in camouflage, his uncovered face honest and kind. When he spotted the armed goblin dead ahead, all wrapped-up in armor and wearing a helmet with a tinted visor, he smiled a sunny smile. My response was to leap to the other side of the road, where we'd spotted a number of gray boulders.

Mowing down weeds and rattling against the boulders, machine-gun fire from the buggy and trailer confirmed my easy guess. Ducking into cover, and hissing my ire more ferociously than any snake, I crawled over the legs of the goblins lying in wait, until I found a convenient firing position.

Who the hell smiled when they saw an armed man dead ahead? Be afraid!

No normal trader, traveller, or even hero would smile at an armed man jumping into the road from cover. A character like that was clearly not to be trusted, yet the prick in the passenger seat spread his lips into a smile which made clear his intent to kill me.

The fusillade was relentless. No let up. I got the impression their ammunition was unlimited, and judging by what we could hear, I estimated we were under fire from at least ten machine guns.

"The trailer!" I yelled into the ear of the fighter nearest to the massive ugly exo sitting behind one of the boulders with its protective steel-cage hunch. "Fire!"

My order was passed on in a couple of seconds, and Sebl immediately raised the Hippo to its feet. The manipulators lay on top of the boulder, and the exo didn't so much as flinch at the dozens of rounds now striking it. I grinned my encouragement, and the exo operator did not totter backwards or hide behind the boulder in fear. She kept her emotions in check, took aim, and blasted the trailer with two machine guns. The goblins sitting in the thinly armored back basket did not move, understanding it was not worth showing themselves. They did not, however, sit there picking their noses. One stood ready by the mortar gun, his visor twinkling, while the other waited with one of our armor-piercing weapons.

I broke cover for a brief moment and let off a short burst. Assured the enemy was concentrating on taking out the exo, I nodded at the same goblin again, and he threw a stone wrapped in a red rag into the air. The signal was acknowledged, and the enemy transport, which had come to a halt (the cretins!) was now attacked from the other flank. The engine revved and the enemy buggy started slowly forward again, still pulling the trailer with its bullet-riddled tarp.

No conversation, no attempt to alter the situation. The buggy and trailer simply snarled and plowed on through the enemy fire. And something was rocking the freaking trailer, which I noticed when I stuck my head out again and looked at the rear of the enemy squad. Adding to the confusion was a wild scream which rang out in a pause in the firefight:

"The pipe's damaged! It's going to explode! Any second now!"

"Shit!" shouted someone hiding behind the armored buggy doors. Then we saw the momentary flash of a steel helmet, and the voice continued, "Left! Fire! Left! Fire!"

"Fuck it," I said, finding a more comfortable position and pulling my trigger.

A single shot struck the throat of a cuirass-wearing idiot trying to make a dash for it from the frayed tarp, throwing him back into the darkness. My fighters followed my example, and a storm of bullets thrashed the left side of the trailer. There was no return fire. To my incredulity the enemy fled, terrified and exposing their backs and the backs of their heads to attack. We finished most of them off, then I barked a command to shoot at their legs. Otherwise, the whole circus would die and there wouldn't be a single clown left to interrogate. The figure of Tigr appeared on the other side of the road and ran after the few who had managed to escape from the buggy.

Meanwhile, the trailer continued to rock from side to side, and increasingly violently. The wheels left the dirt and crashed back into it, and the whole thing threatened to tip over onto its side. With a wave of my hand I gave the signal to withdraw, then led by example, dragging with me a shaking comrade who had taken a bullet from a loud clicking weapon, something like an armor-piercing machine gun, only not as unwieldy. I'd seen it fall from the dead arms of the downed shooter, and just had to take it and have a good look at the thing which had taken out at least three of my squad.

We moved ten yards off the road, to the left, and hid behind the next tooth of the comb of rocks running down a long slope. The slope began here and ran down to a green valley, where a village was visible through the trees. It was like a gigantic stairway, and we were ants on its steps. While something mental was kicking off behind us.

A metallic moaning and rasping sound, accompanied by which a number of prisoners were marched past, emanating blood, sweat, and shit. Their wailing mouths were crooked with fright, and it wasn't us they were afraid of, at least not yet. They were afraid of something else, probably whatever was rocking the trailer, judging by the fact that all their eyes were on it.

After reloading, I nodded my encouragement to the exo plodding in retreat. I was again very pleased with the operator. She did not hurry, she retreated efficiently, and she shielded her small crew in its less-protected basket on the machine's back. One of its manipulators was lowered to the ground, and up ran a fighter with a monstrous cartridge for the new machine gun. Brand-new, for fuck's sake. We'd found it on the beach after the black exo exploded. Its caliber was surprisingly small, but its firing rate was up to par, it sprayed like a garden hose, and it would be just what the doctor ordered against meat that was not superbly protected or trained. A real zombie shredder.

This last thought occurred to me a wink later, when from out of the bushes, twigs crackling beneath his feet, came a naked burly young man with ripped-off lips, a chewed-off nose, and a bleeding hole where his genitals should have been. Had all his protuberances been chewed off? Without looking around, the zombie pounced at the recharger, only to be swatted away by a heavy strike from a jerking manipulator. His chest was then stepped on by the entire bulk of the overgrown-child exo, crunching his rib cage and spurting meaty porridge from every orifice with a squelching sound. Then a single shot put a hole in his crepitating head, before we all forgot about the zombie in an instant when the trailer eventually tipped over.

Crashing noisily onto its side, the multi-wheel vehicle spasmed in the mud as though alive. Something inside it was thrashing around with groaning and clanging sounds, and out flew a short length of steel chain which thwacked into the trunk of an oak tree. Then a near-naked zombie girl flew from the undergrowth and landed right in the exo's basket. Inside that restricted space, the mortar gunner gave fierce battle while his squad mate climbed quickly up the machine. In the confusion, these two events — the zombies and the trailer — might have seemed connected, but I'd already decided it was mere coincidence. We'd attracted the zomboids with the stink of blood and shit, while the trailer contained something alive and fucking big.

"Oh shit," said Wreck, discarding his a sawn-off and raising his machine gun. "Freaking fucking shit!"

You could understand him. Through a large hole in the tarpaulin of the trailer, which was still retreating, we caught a glimpse of something gray-brown-black-red-colored, segmented, and rattling its feet against metal and earth.

"Run, you idiots!" gasped a dishevelled gray-haired old man lying at my feet, his legs all mangled by bullets.

"Uh-huh," I said to him, before someone stuck a needle in his thigh and gave him a horse's dose of sedative.

Strike.

The entire top part of the trailer flew up into the air. Then, above the warped wheeled construction, throwing aside a giant muzzle fitted with hoses and a steel tube, rose...

"Oh shit," I said, aping the orc and gawping astonished at the most monstrous of monsters, which began squealing piercingly for everyone in the vicinity to hear and battering us with a wave of vibrating sound.

A crustacean. A gigantic crustacean. A wood louse with extra legs. Its enormous swollen body was covered with thick plates, old and new and bullet-pecked; some of its legs were either missing or fractured; and its shell was decorated with something that seemed to be numbers and letters. And as for the head, its deep dripping-wet maw was surrounded by tiny serrated mandibles, and above the mouth was a grotesque human face. A female face.

We all stared at the ginormous prism that had once been a woman.

Slinging my machine gun behind my back, I strode towards the exo with my arms raised and casually removed my own personal armor-piercing weapon from its steel fastenings. My actions were understood correctly, and the wood louse was battered by almost all of our firepower. The freaked-out goblins gave a hundred percent more than they ever had in training, emptying their magazines with incredible speed, reloading instantly, and continuing to mince the legs and pulverize the armor plates with a squall of bullets. Everything had to do with fear. The irrational primordial fear of small monkeys pitted against gruesome ancient monsters. And I would know, because that was what I felt for a few moments. A sharp voiceless shriek from inside me said, "Run or die, run or die!" There was no in-between option.

A shot.

An oozing hole appeared in the huge crustacean's head, shortly followed by a second. The shots were coming from the back of the exo's neck.

The thrashing beastie managed to free its backside from the remains of its manacles and, twisting and turning, scuttled towards us shriek-ing. However, when its face was pummelled with fire from two buggy-mounted machine guns at once, it crashed onto his belly and the exo was able to fill its mouth with lead. I also popped a few caps in its distorted face, which looked more like a pic-ture on the frontal armor plating of a living multi-ped tank. The shuddering beast collapsed, rolled, lurched ahead, and pounced on a couple of sleep-ing prisoners, turning them to mush. Its bullet-peppered face was now nearly upon us, so I let off one last shot, looking into its painted eyes. Then I reloaded and casually returned the armor-piercing weapon to its mountings on the Hippo's body. This action served as a signal, and the firefight died down, the sudden conflict at an end.

Tossing and turning on the rocks, the dying beastie gurgled, chomped, croaked, and pounded the earth with its remaining intact legs.

"It was chained up," I said, looking at Wreck. "That's the only reason—"

"That's the only reason the woman was not able to reach us and beat the shit out of us," said the orc throatily. "Just as I figured, commander. I saw it cast off the last chains from its tail."

"We're out of ammo!" Rox shouted from the buggy, his face gray from what he'd just witnessed.

"Noted," I said. Then I turned to my goblins. "Take everything from the trailer and the buggy. Put all the prisoners in our buggy, and the exo on its platform. Top up our ammunition supplies with whatever you take from the enemy. Then we move out. And fast! Set course for the system's nearest eyes. Tigr?"

"Yes?"

"Prepare to disembark the buggy at the bend in the road we passed on the way here."

"Where that old dark fir wood is?"

"Yes. Take your guys with you, along with the three prisoners I'm going to pick out."

"Okay. Where are we going?"

"Vultures," I said with a crooked grin as I looked between the treetops at the serene sky. "Fucking vultures. They always try to snaffle a piece of someone else's pie. Look lively, goblins, look lively!"

"Three zombies to the right!"

"Shoot them! And all aboard the vehicle! Quick smart!"

Encouraged by my fierce shouts, the fighters looked among the corpses for anyone still living, before loading the prisoners into the buggy and our dead and wounded onto the platform next to the exo's rear end. Perched on the end went the spittle-soaked muzzle and a huge canister entangled with tubes. Then heaped on top were a collection of bags, sacks, and satchels, all topped with clothes cut from bodies (there was no time for checking pockets). All this was covered with sleeping bags and blankets and secured with rope, before finally a jar of wood-louse meat was carefully placed in the buggy, in case the system might request a sandwich for testing.

All this took quite some time, but we eventually set off, accelerating quickly away from the scene of the battle. We headed towards a village, to the system mushrooms skewered atop their steel columns. Tigr's little squad, along with three prisoners, various trophies, and a supply of food, disappeared unnoticed from the platform. When we exited the fir wood, we flew past fields and orchards, and when we reached a twinkling steel mushroom, we braked sharply.

"Commander," said the orc, pointing in the direction of the Lands of the Covenant, "up in the sky."

Flying towards us were three smallish dots quickly gaining in size. The airborne cavalry was on the way to help.

How had they managed to react so fast?

How had they seen?

They couldn't have seen. That said, I had seen among the trophies a couple of completely smashed-up gadgets which very much recalled high-tech walkie-talkies, or even devices for exchanging text messages. And I very much doubted whether the fuckers we'd killed had been in a hurry to inform the system. They'd had someone else to tell.

But who?

Who knew?

But flying towards us were…

Looking up at the dome which was passing a laser beam over our dead and wounded, I smiled a beaming smile and waved a hand to hurry the buggy up.

Hero Erikvan!

Attention! *Immediate full verbal free-form report!*

This was becoming a habit, albeit one I was quite happy with.

And there was no need to even lie.

This particular report consisted of short phrases spat ever faster with the approach of our rude and uninvited guests.

We travelled. We honed our field movements. On a narrow path we met a buggy. For some reason the people in the buggy were unhappy with us. A firefight ensued. We hid and returned fire. We won. At the end of the battle, a massive crustacean crawled out of the trailer. We used all our firepower to suppress it. We spent much valuable ammunition. This was not our main task. Will the goblins be rewarded? I have every reason to suppose the small enemy squad was directly connected to our main task, Wild Evolution. I want to interrogate the prisoners personally. I also want to keep all trophies.

The system heard me out. Then its siren wailed briefly, and its laser beams blinked, making the approaching drones land not in the village, but a little way off, probably so as not to traumatize the gentle aborigines, for whom flying machines were exclusively the stuff of rumor. After all, the village was located quite some distance from the sleepy ocean ring and the coastal lands of the kindhearts. Here, somewhere between the Lands of the Covenant and the seashore, there ought to have been more traffic.

The system did not think for long before pronouncing its eminently predictable verdict.

The prisoners were to be handed over immediately to the fourth-rank heroes who had just arrived.

Anything unusual, including any gadgets there happened to be, were to be handed over to the fourth-rank heroes who had just arrived.

And well done to goblin Elb!

A week's free medical assistance for every member of your crew.

Free courses of all recommended strengthening injections for every member of your crew.

Free bonus munitions and weapon parts in accordance with your rank.

Free bonus energetics, isotonics, vitamins, and proteins.

To your health, goblin! Eat!

Oh, yes. Also, out of sheer system generosity, two thousand bonus crowns and free full ATM service, deposits and withdrawals.

"Is that not a bit too generous?" I mumbled, turning to look at the heroes running towards the village. "Lay the wounded on the ground. Then step away and do not hinder their collection."

Into the village ran a smallish crew. Fifteen overstimulated brutal mugs in armor. Two imposing overgrown-child exos remained by the landed craft, their barrels raised to the sky.

After picking up the wounded, and bags of

mixed teeny tiny electronics, the knights returned to their drones. One remained behind, a short stocky man with an unpleasantly judgmental look. After grinning crookedly, he tried to make his smile more friendly before asking:

"Are you not concealing anything of interest?"

"Nah."

"Be honest. You don't have an honest face."

"You've got me there. Rumbled," I replied with a smile. "We made a secret cache in your asshole, and my whole crew crammed it in with their rifle butts. Had you forgotten?"

"You've got a big mouth."

"Your moans were really loud."

"I would be delighted to give you all a cavity search."

"Let your second-in-command delight in giving you a cavity search."

"Big mouth," the hero repeated. "So what about the stuff you're concealing?"

"The weapons, the buggy, and the trailer are all mine," I said, without a smile this time. "And rightfully so, seeing as it was my guys who did all the shooting and being shot at. My meat."

"I'm not talking about that chickenfeed."

"What else is there?" I asked, stepping towards him. "Should there be something else? What do you know about this shit anyway? And how on earth did you get here so quickly?"

"What about you?"

"We were following those guys," I said, nodding towards the field where two naked dead bodies lay with broken limbs and mutiple burns and deep cuts. "Bandits."

"Was it a task?"

"How did you get here so quickly?"

"Good luck, fighter. I've heard much about you. If you don't get killed, let's have a drink together in Crontown sometime."

"Maybe we will," I said, shrugging my shoulders. "But you didn't answer my question, goblin. Why are you here? How come a routine altercation was so interesting to a gang of almost celestials?"

I did not get an answer. About-facing sharply, the knight sped back towards his drones. His running gait was comical, and he coped easily with the weight of his regular battle equipment without any mechanical help. His strength showed. The only thing that made me wonder was, I may have been a rank lower, but even carrying the same weight I would have run no slower than him, perhaps even faster. Yet the knight was trying so hard, as though he thought such speed was possible only for fourth-rank heroes and above. And judging by the local apple-knockers' reverent goggling eyes and mouths wide open in wonderment, that was precisely what he was. They watched him run in awe.

"That's cooler than Bulma's titties!" croaked a guy with straw-colored hair, leaning on a fence.

After thoughtfully watching the drones fly off, I looked at the system even more thoughtfully and shuffled back to the buggy, which was parked by the medblock where our wounded had been taken.

On the way, I stopped by the mammary connoisseur and asked:

"Have you got a cemetery here? Or do you take your dead to the medblock?"

"We bury them ourselves," replied the villager proudly, "with Mother's kind permission."

"Where is it?"

"The cemetery? Over there by that coppice."

Nodding my thanks, I moved on, shouting to my fighters:

"Leave the dead on the platform. Rox, take them to the cemetery. It's by that coppice over there. We'll bury them there."

"A virtuous thing," said the old mechanic, before asking, as though in passing, "Are we in a hurry anywhere?"

"No freaking way," I said, shaking my head. "We'll pitch a temporary camp by the cemetery. Where there's a bit of twilight."

"Understood. Strange goings-on around here."

"Strange indeed," I agreed, sinking my teeth into a protein bar and watching a smiling goblin with broken legs being thrust into the medblock. The painkillers had worked their magic, and the fighter felt nothing, joking with his friends and winking at the pudgy villagers sighing their sympathy.

"Do you think anyone's watching?" asked the orc as he walked up, his gaze fixed on a particularly shapely lady.

"Fuck knows," I replied, unhurriedly taking in the thick impenetrable beauty surrounding the village. "We'll get ourselves fixed up, have a rest, and take a good look around."

"Gotcha, lead. Do you think we'll come across any more beasties like that?"

"Undoubtedly."

"I wouldn't mind an armor-piercing weapon."

"And you shall have it."

"Thanks, lead. More grenades wouldn't go amiss on the next outing either."

"Oh yes," I said, "oh yes."

"The system doesn't like explosions."

"It'll cope somehow," I said, my shoulders involuntarily twitching as I remembered the enormous multi-legged bug.

"Lead?"

"Yes?"

"If it's the fourth or fifth of this kind of evolution—"

"Wild evolution," I said, "wild"

"That's right. But I'm talking about something else. Do you remember that slippery exploding banana? In the Stench?"

"What about it?"

"What exactly is the second evolution? If the first one was a demolition banana, is this second one an atomic coconut?"

"I don't know what evolution he's undergoing right now, but it's a form of prism, not a system choice," I replied. "The system has no reason to be engendering such dangerous monsters. That's presumably why it makes such very generous payments to heroes who are willing to go searching for that kind of beastie and destroy them. Well done, Wreck."

"What for?"

"You realized there's a connection between those two facts, exploding bananas back there in the asshole of the world and a gigantic muzzle-wearing wood louse here. It's not only your muscles that are growing, but also your brain. That's encouraging."

"Ha! I'm trying, I'm trying. So anyway, what about this armor-piercing weapon?"

"You'll get it when we get back to base."

"I could take one from the exo. Not yours, but the one behind it."

"No."

"Okay, I'll wait then. Listen, why the hell did we give them the prisoners?"

"They've got a Wild Evolution task," I said. "Or rather, not them, but whoever those spunky guys serve. And whether it's obvious or not, they serve one of the Highers. How did they find out so quickly? They must have received a notification and set off straightaway, but who did the notification come from? If there were no system eyes there, which there weren't, then the answer is simple: the notification was sent by whoever we annihilated back there. And we smashed their transmitters to smithereens. We milled them with our rifle butts, which no doubt... Shit!"

"Confusing stuff."

"No," I said with a shake of my head. "There's nothing confusing about it, orc, believe me. It's all very simple. Plain for all to see. It's just that the game is being played up there" — I pointed a finger at the sky — "and simple goblins like us either don't see anything, or they just see one or two pieces of the jigsaw, maximum. But we'll sort it out. We'll get to the bottom of it."

"Uh-huh." The orc sneered with glee. "I'll help you get to the bottom of it. My hatchet is already sharpened."

"No," I sneered back. "I'll do it myself. On my own."

It was only two hours later that was I able to meet with the prisoners and Tigr's crew. Two hours so long and unbearable that I couldn't cope, so I took a tablet. I savored the crunch and felt its bitterness flowing over my gums and tongue before the drug whisked me away. Whisked me away, but still brought back memories. The system would heal me. Were it not for regular visits to the med-block, I would have turned into a brainless giggling skeletal addict long ago, hugging my knees and staring out at the world through matted clumps of hair, and staring inward at the sick hallucinations of my dying mind.

While they were waiting, the fighters dug deep graves and lay our dead in hastily cobbled-to-gether coffins brought from the village. Real wooden coffins. They had time to spare, so the funerals were conducted according to all the rules, including a short farewell gun salute. I took no part in this, but I didn't interfere, only encouraging it. The death of comrades-in-arms could only hurt.

It must have been painful. It must have invoked a long-lasting dull anger and the desire for revenge, to take the lives of a dozen enemy in return for each of our guys killed.

I did not notice Tigr appearing alongside me. He was just suddenly there, sitting on a low stone wall and grinning joyously at me while simultaneously nodding towards the buggy platform.

"Move out!" I barked, rising to my feet.

A couple of minutes later we were moving at a relaxed pace along one of the roads leading to our distant base. I was in no hurry. For the longest time now, all our interfaces had been devoid of tasks. And there had been no word from base, where they clearly understood my need to get to grips with the tiny gobbets of information already fished from the sea of shit. Although that information, or indeed the sea of shit itself, had not been squeezed from the prisoners yet.

"Two still alive, one dead," said one of the fighters as he stepped away from the bound captives.

"Fuck!" spat a gray-haired old man right into my face. "Fuck! I shit on you! Death has its hands around my heart!"

Putting the wet gag back in his salivating mouth and paying no heed to his malicious mooings, I asked lazily of Tigr, sitting beside me:

"What did the prisoner die of?"

"I don't know," said the scout, "but I swear it wasn't our fault. He didn't die of his injuries, and he didn't die on the road. He was lying quietly under a bush, and suddenly he arched his back and started mooing wildly through the gag, which I had personally pissed on. Then he died. And he was frightened, lead."

"When he died?"

"Before that too. He was mooing and thrashing his head about, and he wanted to tell me something. He was pulling beseeching faces and rolling his eyes, but I figured he just wanted to pour his heart out, so I didn't start questioning him yet. Then he distorted his face a bit more and died in agony. Maybe it was his heart?"

"No," I said, not looking at the scout, but at the old man by my feet, with his distorted gray-fringed mug.

Strange.

The old man was both crying and smiling. Sneering and trying to appear indestructible at the same time. He was being pulled apart by contradictory emotions, but only one was genuine, and that was fear. He literally stank of fear. And that ancient emotion, that primordial fear, had made the second prisoner lying beside him also collapse.

"Something's not right here," I said. "Where's the dead man's body? Did we bring it with us?"

"No," said Tigr. "We threw it under a bush back there. We cut off his head just in case though."

"Not good," I said, frowning and reaching again for the old man's gag.

Then it started. His body gave a massive jolt, and his pain became so great that he was bent into an incredible arc, and for a few seconds only his heels and the back of his head were touching the platform.

"Wow," said Wreck.

"It was the same with the other one," said Tigr.

I ripped the gag from the old man's mouth.

"Aaaaaaaaaaa!" Squirming and writhing around, and smacking his head on the metal platform, he looked as though a powerful electric charge was running through his body, while simultaneously a chainsaw was carving patterns into his kneecaps.

"What's wrong with you, cocksucker?" I barked. "Huh?"

"Aaaaaaaaaaa!"

The screaming suddenly stopped and the old body went limp. He was dead. His head tilted to the side, and his sightless eyes stared blankly at the toecap of my boot, scuffed by the platform's dull scratched metal.

"Shit," we all said in unison. Then, also in unison, we turned to the last prisoner, who was kicking his heels furiously against the metal platform.

Pulling out his gag, I ordered him sharply:

"Speak! What the hell is going on with you? Huh?"

"Fuck! Fuck! Fuck! I don't want to die like this. Fuck!" said the prisoner, bawling his eyes out. "Not like this. I don't want to die like this. Suicide is a sin, but I don't want to die like this either! I DON'T WANT TO DIE LIKE THIS! Chop my head off, cocksucker!" This last phrase was addressed croakingly to Wreck. "I had you in the ass. I had you.

You choked on my cock, you axe-wielding vampire. And when I was fucking you, you hollered for your grandma and your pink ponies. So get chopping! Chop my head off, you fucker!"

His face contorted, Wreck gripped a handle protruding from the body of the exo sitting on the platform and shook his head from side to side.

"Keep calm. The main thing is to keep fucking calm. I'll rip his member out at the root later."

With a faint chortle, I slapped the prisoner around the face, and when he shut up, I said to him:

"You're not going to die that easily, louse. You're going to live until you tell me everything I want to hear."

"Me?" The young man laughed in my face. "I'm going to live? You fool! Fool! I'm already dead. I can already sense death. I sense it. Death has come for me. It's got its spiny hand around my heart. It's squeezing my heart in a deathlike grip."

"Woah," said Tigr.

"He hasn't got a medkit on him, has he?" I asked just to be sure, although the prisoner had been relieved of not only his gear, but also most of his clothes."

"Only if it's internal. Do you think they might die from an internal poison injection?"

"Unlikely," I said, looking at the old man's corpse. "Too painful a death. They're not enemies. And if you wanted to kill them with a massive dose of poison, it would be easier to give them a sedative mixed with a couple of spoons of something sweet and narcotic. It would be nice for others to know their impending death wasn't going to be so terrible. Maybe even pleasant."

"But the old man bent backwards! With a crunch!"

"Precisely. Check his mouth. Check his whole body. Wreck, help Tigr. Cut all his clothes off."

After giving these orders, I turned back to the prisoner, who was clearly itching to regain my attention.

"I'm a dead man. And since that's the case, there's no point me telling you anything. I'm better off dying a fucking hero than divulging secrets." Beginning to sweat buckets, the man laughed. "Do you know what your fucking problem is? I'm a cowardly vampire, afraid of pain, afraid of death. But you look pretty hardcore. You would easily be able to make me tell you what I know, it's true. But only if you had time. Get it? No, you don't get it. And also, I'm a patriot."

"What are you?" I leaned in towards him, astounded. "What are you?"

"A patriot!" replied the prisoner defiantly. "That's right. Maybe I'm a lousy patriot who will crack just as soon as you start to torture me. But I love my motherland. And since I'm dying anyway, I will die happy in the knowledge that my death will fuck up all your plans. Although I still can't figure out who you are, or how you happened to be on that road in the first place. I could ask, but why the fuck would I? I'm dying."

"What of? What are you dying of?"

"Death has come for me," giggled the prisoner, "and you can't do anything about it."

"And why is that?" I asked, smiling a wide cold smile and brandishing my knife. "Seeing as how death is taking its time, and since you're an inarticulate cowardly patriot, afraid of pain and death..."

"Huh? What? Aaaaaaaa! Fuck! Fuck! Fuck! My eye! You cut out my EYE!" howled the prisoner. "You bastard! You motherfucker! I'm dying anyway. Leave me alone! I just have to hold out for another couple of minutes. You're getting nothing from me!"

"That's heaps of time," I said with a shrug, making a long deep cut in his side.

"Aaaaaa! Shit! Shit! Fuck you! I can hold out! Cut away! Cut away, fucker!"

"Thank you," I said, wiping his blood from my cheek. "I think I'll cut off your dick next. It's not like you'll be needing it anymore, right?"

"Huh? Wait! Wait!"

"Come on," I hissed, leaning down to his blood-wet face, "spit it out! You're dying anyway. Let's do it this way: you tell me a couple of interesting things, and I'll help death come quicker."

"It's already got me by the heart." The man's one remaining eye dilated and his lips trembled. "Oh shit, death's got me by the heart. Its shadow's hanging over me. I feel..."

"Go on."

"Mama. Mommy. It's going to be so painful. I don't want it to be painful."

"Speak! Tell me at least one thing, and I'll help you die quietly." As I said this, I quickly attached a medkit to his thigh. The smart device clicked, hissed, and squeaked dimly as it injected its contents, which I had no doubt were an antitoxin. "Speak!"

"I don't want pain. I don't want to die. I don't want to! Ah!" The man twitched, shuddered, and looked in fear at his chest, blinking the sweat from his eyes. "I don't want this. I don't want pain!"

"Speak! Come on! Here's my knife, look. I can stick it in your heart if you like."

"Yes, stick it in! Right now! Go on!"

"Speak!"

"Agh, argh! It hurts! It hurts! I need injections every two hours. Every two hours! Agh!"

"Fucking speak! Speak! Tell me something. So that I can get the others as well. And you won't be so pissed-off at life. Come on, speak!"

"Squi... squir..."

"What?"

"Squirrel... Squirrel's... Squirrel's Acorn! Acorn! There! Tonight! A strike! Now kill me! Kill me!"

"Who are you?"

"We are nobody. We... Aaaaaa! Aaaaaa! Fuck! Fuck! We are the abandoned! Kill me! Kill me! You promised! Fuck! Every two hours isn't enough."

Shuddering, his bones crunching, and his voiceless maw gaping wide, the man lifted his butt from the floor and began to rise.

"Shit!" I barked, thrusting my knife into his

heart. And again.

The medkit began to vibrate, but was immediately ripped off. I nodded to Wreck, and the prisoner's head flew off his shoulders. I stood up and shouted:

"Open them up. The rib cages. We need the hearts."

"What's in there?"

"That's what we're going to find out," I said. "They both said something about their hearts, something about a spiny hand. It can't be just flowery language. Try the little window in his chest."

"Just a second."

Holding the transmitter to my lips, I said:

"Bask?"

"I hear you, lead. How's things going?"

"Okay. A brief rumble, a couple of small losses, and a small tip-off. Squirrels' Acorn. Repeat that back to me."

"Squirrels' Acorn."

"Correct. Mark us out a route to it, and fast. Do absolutely anything, possible and impossible, to get a visual on what's going on there. And report back immediately."

"Copy. I'm on it. What's your location?"

"We're still here. We're moving slowly towards base from Zmoraliye. We're waiting for directions. Estimate our location and the coordinates of Acorn. If you can do it so we don't lose time, find a route that takes us past base. We need to replenish our ammo supplies and personnel. But no wasting time!"

"What if Acorn is so far—"

"That's impossible," I said, cutting him off. "I don't even think we'll make it to base. Those meat-hunters were hunting in tiny crews, and in a small operating radius. A regular small operation to gather resources, possibly in preparation for something bigger. But again, in the same area. Look for Acorn in the vicinity of Zmoraliye. Maybe even abutting it."

"Copy."

"Tigr?"

"Yes, lead?"

"Send a couple of runners back to the village. Tell them to make inquiries about Squirrel's Acorn. If it isn't too far, the locals might know something."

"It will be done."

"Rox, pull over to the side and stop. We're going to wait."

"Yes, commander. I wanted to see what that knocking sound was anyway."

We returned to the subject at hand three minutes later, when the two runners came back along the road leading down to the lights of the village.

"Medkit in the chest," said Tigr confidently as he looked at the corpses now lying on the grass. "Well, technically it's a medkit, only modified to be a personal guillotine."

"How is it activated?" I asked.

"Maybe they send it a command? Although

how would they do that? They did have some electronic devices, but they smashed them up before we killed them back there on that road. Were they taking precautions? But they didn't know they'd be taken captive. Maybe there's an emergency protection button somewhere in the hand or the tuckus?"

"They didn't give a command to self-liquidate," I retorted, looking at the hulking orc as crouched over one of the corpses. "They're not even fighters, Tigr, not even meat. They're just techies and herdsmen, to look after that beastie in the trailer. All their heroism, all their cussing is born purely of fear and fatality. They knew they were going to die, and for once in their life they decided to be heroes. But they were still shit-scared anyway, because their death was going to be seriously fucking grizzly, even by our standards. For them—"

"Very extreme for regular peasants," the scout agreed, before pensively running his tongue along his arm from elbow to wrist. "So, fuck knows. They've got no friendly faces around here. And we're on the move. So who else could have sent a signal to the chest device?"

"He was shouting something about injections every two hours," I recalled.

"Yes, I heard that. What injections though? And why?"

"Festering motherfucker!" shouted Wreck suddenly, leaping backwards directly from his crouching position and slamming his back into my knee. "SHIIIIIIT!"

"Shit," I agreed."

"Mama," squeaked one of Sebl's crew, who had stretched themselves out on the exo in obeyance of my command: If you're a member of the exo crew, then you live in the exo, and that means you eat, drink, chill, and shit in the exo. That steel Colossus must become home for its crew.

"Interesting," I said slowly, watching a big fat caterpillar crawl slowly from the old man's smashed-up chest.

Or rather, try to crawl slowly. It was difficult to crawl if you were not created for movement.

The long thin snow-white body was studded with black spines which kept grabbing hold of the flesh and hindering the crawling process. Distinctly visible was the wide blood-filled mouth of the insect that had been disturbed in its nest of meat.

"Wreck, behead the other one."

"Uh-huh. Ah, shit! It isn't as though I've pissed myself, but..."

The caterpillar, inching jerkily a tiny bit forward but not making any headway, tilted the front part of its body and began sucking the old man's not yet coagulated blood. *So we know what you feed on then, parasite.*

Death, gripping the heart with its spiny hand.

"There's something oozing from the spines," noted the eagle-eyed Tigr. "Thick green stuff. Poison? I can see the heart as well, under the caterpillar's tush. There's blood everywhere, but there's a whole bunch of holes in him. I reckon the caterpillar's putting pressure on the heart, gripping it with its spines and injecting the poison. Zowie."

"It's growing," I said indifferently.

"We are all growing," said the scout. Then he boggled and said, "Wow, it is too!"

The caterpillar had grown in fast-motion and was now twice as big as a minute ago.

"Wreck, get away from the other corpse."

"Gotcha," said the orc, obeying willingly.

Taking one of my last protein bars from my bag, I sank my teeth into it while I observed the fast-track growth of the disgusting spiny insect chowing down on the dead flesh of the host it had killed.

Life was beautiful. And full of surprises.

The trussed-up motionless corpse of the second prisoner twitched briefly and was still again. It was the chest that had twitched, as though the insane dead heart had given a sharp start. Then there came another jerk, followed by crunching and chewing sounds.

"The hatchling's going to break out any minute now," said Sebl in a very hushed tone as she climbed hastily back onto the platform.

The rest of the fighters, huddled together by the side of road, were transfixed as they observed what was happening. You could understand them. It was a transfixing spectacle. Insanely fast swallowing, digestion not exactly tardy either, energy production increasing at a similarly insane rate. The first caterpillar had already gained a meter in length, and its spines had ceased to grow and

looked to be a perfectly sensible part of its abhor-
rent body. Then the second prisoner twitched,
likewise crunchingly and splashing blood, its flesh
also being rent apart, and in the new hole appeared a snow-white body furnished with a couple
of pairs of black spines. One of the goblins couldn't
hold back and skipped quickly to the side, where
he bent double and vomited up the contents of his
stomach. I continued chewing and waiting patiently for news from Bask, news of the runners
sent to the village, and the end of this bizarre story
with the caterpillars.

"Oh shit!" exclaimed Tigr, turning sharply towards me. "Lead!"

"Yes?"

"The third prisoner that died, we just threw
him in the woods. All we did was cut off his head."

"So live with it," I sniggered, then turned my
focus on the village in the distance. "Maybe they'll
think of a convincing and terrifying reason to call
for assistance from some heroes soon."

"Permission to get busy?"

"Our main objective must be your priority," I
said.

"Understood."

"Elb," said Wreck, "look."

The first caterpillar had raised its butt verti-
cally into the air. It strained. It twitched. And into
the sky shot a stream of liquid. It instantly solidi-
fied and fell back down as spider threads, which
covered the corpse and caterpillar, taking anchor
on the spines. These spurts began to repeat every

three or four seconds. The still fattening caterpillar was concealing itself and its feasting beneath a hardening spider-web umbrella, a cocoon. The insect was withdrawing into a cocoon which would protect it temporarily from predators and later serve as a bolt-hole in which to transform in peace.

Transformation.

Evolution.

Wild Evolution, uncontrolled by the system.

However, despite their very close similarity, these were not prisms.

A fat white snake crawled out of the prisoner's chest with a crunching sound and shot a spiderweb into the air.

Well, yes.

Life is still beautiful. And full of surprises.

CHAPTER 10

KILLING IS ALWAYS easier.

Fewer complications, less time spent, and often less mess. Twat the fucker, and he's gone. Not so much life, as a dream.

But nobody was going to sugarcoat my goblin life. So here was a new task issuing itself: take alive a few of the bastards crawling along the narrow paths.

Not only did they have to be taken alive, but we would also have to wait until the meat hunters received their two-hourly injections, whatever that meant.

The theory concerning the injections was simple and doubtless bang-on. The injections required the spiky beastie that made itself at home near the heart to remain there quietly. It was unclear exactly what was injected. It may have been a selective sedative which acted exclusively on parasitic insects, but Jorann suggested the caterpillar might receive, via the blood of the injected carrier, certain compounds which made it "think," which was still too early for the awakening and subsequent creation of the cocoon.

The reason for the system was obvious: so that the meat hunters didn't blab under torture. And since it was so strict and harsh, they had nothing to blab to regular fighting men. They simply knew nothing worth blabbing.

Which all made the task significantly more difficult. We goblins had to get our greedy hands on someone more serious than a regular fighter or herdsman. We needed the commander of a small squad, or a second-in-command, or a medic, or a driver; they always knew more than everyone else, being part of a solid core which usually kept itself to itself, slowly soaking up tasty secrets and not letting the lower-rank dipshits anywhere near them.

The village of Squirrel's Acorn was located quickly. As I'd expected, it was a mere twenty kilometers from Zmoraliye. I chose our route based on my suspicion that the enemy squad had moved out together from the same place and only then split up to take different forest paths. Despite my realizing we were going to be late anyway, we set out as fast as possible. No freaking way were we going to make it in time. The last squad was already very close to the village. How long would they have to wait? A couple of hours maximum, but every hour would increase the chances of local aborigines or interloping heroes discovering our position. We could not afford to be late. But we were. So it was safe to assume the village of Acorn was already under attack.

Assumption incorrect.

When we flew into the village, it was sound asleep. The odd light on, a drowsy tranquility filling the air. The peasants were snoozing. No hint of a threat. We tore on through the village, our engine roaring, and dived again into the ancient oak grove, dotted with its occasional squirrel feeder and bizarre formless sack hung on a tree. Without stopping we took down one of the sacks, cut it open, and looked inside. Hair. Human hair. No slices of scalp or traces of blood. Hair clippings, different colors, male and female. Our alarm quickly faded when one of the fighters, who had a bit of combat experience, announced confidently that the sacks were meant to scare animals, first and foremost deer. *Strange people these peasants.*

Decelerating and sending the scouts on ahead, we crawled slowly along my chosen path, the one which seemed to have the most potential. Not too wide, not too narrow, and hidden from sight by thick rose hip, bramble, and other bushes, it was a route which slowed our buggy to a crawl with its heavy trailer.

We saw nothing for a couple of kilometers.

Then, after another kilometer, the hypervigilant Tigr jumped out in front of us. His report made me grit my teeth in spite and signal to maintain our course.

The scouts had come across some wheel tracks. They had been swept over, but in a hurry and not diligently, so the recent presence of a heavy wheeled vehicle was still in evidence. The hawk-eyed goblins had also found a place where the buggy had turned around, which had involved reversing, weaving the trailer through under-growth and around oak trunks, and scraping off bark.

The meat hunters had crept right up close to the perimeter of Acorn, with just a quick dash left to go. Instead, however, they had turned hastily around and hurried away.

Why?

Simple: the beasts had received a warning.

It was anyone's guess who had sounded the alarm: the guys we'd recently minced, or someone a rank higher.

Shit. My least favorite situation was looming: a ton of questions, not many answers. And in or-der to avoid that situation, we would have to stretch our strength and machinery to their limit to grab hold of the fleeing bastards' slippery tail.

And we did it.

We grabbed it.

We caught them in the most unlikely place they could have chosen. They'd driven down into a wide gully, and were now straining the engine to climb up the other side. The goblins had squeezed out of their warm musty cracks and were pushing their tarp-covered platform with everything they had, their boots slipping on stones and tearing up grass.

An easy job for us. I indicated to Tigr and Wreck those goblins visible from our position whom I considered the most desirable prisoners. They already knew I wanted the commander, driver, and medic taken alive, plus anyone else who might have more information. The remainder were to be minced. Also given orders in advance, the exo did not even climb down from the platform. Straightening itself up, it fired from its manipulators, and the tarpaulin over the platform quivered from the hundreds of bullets tearing at it. The exo had soon shot off all its ammunition reserves, leaving us unable to finish the job, and with a freaking enormous beastie on our hands.

Letting the meat go on ahead to attack, I followed far enough behind that once on the slope, I could fire at the enemy over the heads of my own guys. I did not say a word. I merely put one foot after the other and fired, keeping an eye on the platform and listening to the commands of my squad leaders, all the while carefully evaluating the situation.

The first to reach the enemy vehicle were the fighters who'd been sitting in the buggy. They unhitched the trailer, and the now unsupported and extremely heavy platform shot back down the side of the gully, while the suddenly unencumbered buggy shot up the slope like a rocket. Spinning around and rolling over, knocked off their feet, crushed, and squished into the dirt, were no fewer than five shrieking goblins caught off guard by the turn of events. In his dying moments, one of them grabbed a sixth by the leg and pulled him towards him with a bloodcurdling howl, whereupon the platform smashed, coldly mocking, into his chest and knocked him off his feet.

Then something long, multi-legged, and armed with enormous mandibles slashed its way up through the tarpaulin and shot into the air, before crashing limply back down, crushing the platform, felling small trees, and spraying poisonously yellow slime everywhere.

After shooting a couple of the injured enemy, I holstered my revolver and walked calmly up the slope, sticking to the grassy edges that weren't so slippery. The middle of the path was now a churned-up mass of mud with spots of blood and slowly sinking chunks of flesh. On reaching the bottom of the gully, the platform flipped over with a dull thud and was quiet, showing the sky its belly and slowly revolving muddy wheels. Stepping over bodies, I kept going, and was overtaken by a couple of disarmed goblins being carried. Rank-and-filers; you could tell straightaway by multiple vague signs. I paid no attention, continuing on my way in the hope of finding something juicy up where the enemy buggy had hidden behind the young oak trees, unaware that our scouts had taken a shortcut and were nearly upon them.

Don't let me down, tigers, don't let me down.

Dem Mikhailov

* * *

Leaning back against my backpack, my feet stretched towards a small campfire (real, not gas-fired, and burning, with disregard for every law, in the middle of an old dark wood several kilometers from the road), I sipped sweet black coffee and looked expectantly at a nearby tree.

Beneath the tree sat an old woman doomed to an imminent death.

Well, given time to make herself look presentable, she could easily have adopted the form of a respected lady. But now, filthy, sporting disheveled gray hair and rocking a metal cup of coffee on her knees, she looked very much like a tired old woman.

I said nothing. I was also tired, and not dying yet, so if anyone ought to have been in a hurry, it was me. The old woman, whose name was Isfir, had already given me to understand she was the commander of this squad, and that she was morally tormented and spiritually exhausted and wanted to die in peace. She did not ask much in return, just hot drinks, humane treatment, and a regular grave right here in this black earth penetrated by oak roots. I had agreed, and here I was waiting. Meanwhile, everyone else chilled around two campfires a little way off, near to, but separate from, the prisoners. I had already gleaned the most important thing: they had received their two-hourly injections ten minutes before we arrived,

348

inducing a blood bath in their heads.

"In August, near Little Towers, I was shooting great snipe with old Mazai," said Isfir, staring into the crackling flames.

"Who's Mazai?" I inquired.

"A literary character. Convicted and banned."

"I don't understand," I said.

"What do you remember of the previous world, commander Elb? About the old world we came here from?"

"My head is nothing but a mishmash of snatches from it."

"Mine too. Drugs?"

"Uh-huh."

"That will do it. One recollection shines particularly bright in my old head. In it I am young, serious, austerely dressed, and standing in front of an audience of distinguished literature teachers gathered from various schools to listen to my lecture. The lecture was about authors and works banned in schools for being unacceptable, which in those distant times covered a multitude of sins, including, among others, racism and sexism. *Grandfather Mazai and the Hares* was one of those banned works. It is a kind and poetic tale of how the old hunter Mazai miraculously saves hares from little islands and floating logs during a deadly springtime flood. He gathers the hares in his boat and takes them to dry land where he releases the rescued animals. Some of them are frozen with cold, and these he warms in his house and releases later. It is a tale of the selfless act of a kind person."

"I see. And why was the tale banned?"

"Because Mazai saves hares," said Isfir with a sad smile.

"And?"

"He saves *exclusively* hares, *only* hares. Do you understand? Naturally other creatures also find themselves in trouble during a flood, for example foxes and flightless birds, maybe even wolves, but Mazai saves hares, and only hares, thereby displaying racist tendencies. The rest of the beasts he abandons to the whims of fate, before returning home to the warm."

"Maybe there aren't any other beasts?"

"That is not mentioned in the tale, so it's a reasonable guess that there were other beasts, but Mazai did not want to save them. And that is why it was prohibited for children to read the tale."

"Why are you telling me all this?"

"You are hares, and we are not." Isfir smiled again, and from her writhing internal pain I understood she must have had a reason for telling me the tale, probably involving certain direct associations. And so I nodded and encouraged her to continue.

"We are not hares," repeated the old woman. "We are beasts, needed by no one, a forgotten line, an abandoned world of wondrous attractions, a world of adventures lost to oblivion."

I was silent, taking in every word, just like Wreck, who sat on the other side of the fire digging lazily with his spoon in a tin of Bunkercat stewed meat.

"What do you know of heroes, hero?"

Shrugging my shoulders, I replied:

"They're regular goblins, armed, trained, and capable of managing a variety of problematic situations. The system issues them specific tasks with increased levels of danger, bloodshed, and murder. Basically, heroes are a kind of hellish hybrid of three services: the police, the army, and the lifeguards."

"That is exactly right," said Isfir. "Exactly fucking right! And you are the first to precisely define the essence of the heroes, by removing all unnecessary pathos. Correct. Now the heroes help by shooting bandits, rescuing people from floods, setting up roadblocks where the system demands, and surrounding problem areas with an impenetrable cordon. The army, the police, and the lifeguards all rolled into one. They are universal. Shit! Stinking shit! The heroes are killing this shitting world. You are killing this shitting world. You are a hero, are you not?"

"I am."

"Shit! Want to know why I say that? You and people like you know fuck all about this world's past. But I know. Perhaps not everything, but I know, because we were locked in, together with the knowledge, and we handed it down from generation to generation. And that knowledge is remorseless. Here's the first fact: there were heroes before. They existed in the old world from its very creation, from the very first day. But do you know who they were?"

"Do tell."

"Nothing special. A source of entertainment. Entertainment for infantile adults, whose beards were already graying, and who dreamed of becoming knights, vanquishing monsters, and rescuing comely buxom maidens. And also of becoming maidens in armored brassieres, sleeping and dreaming of hacking their way through the jungle to find naked men bound to crosses with huge welcomingly erect penises. That is what the heroes were at the very beginning: a frolicsome game."

"A frolicsome game," I echoed. "I understand. Do continue."

"It is strange that you do not ask any questions. You do not interrupt my tale. What if I am playing for time? The clock is ticking, and I shall soon die in agony."

"Do continue," I smiled, and extended my empty cup to Wreck. Understanding my gesture, he reached for the cauldron hanging over the fire.

"Where are you from? What is the name of your village?"

"He and I," I said, nodding towards Wreck, "are from the very asshole of the world. The underground world."

"The lower technical tiers," said Isfir. "I have heard of them. A dark enclosed space. Volitional Nullforms."

"Correct."

"So how did you end up here?"

"We sailed here on the backs of goosed tunafish."

"Funny. Did you fight your way through with copious bloodshed?"

"We squeezed our way out like spiky pieces of shit from a bloodied asshole," I replied. "Why do you ask?"

"To find out how widely you know the world. Where you have been and what you have seen."

"We've picked up a little bit of everything."

"Did you, perchance, come across safety areas down there in the dark tunnels? With trade points, where you can buy clubs, salt tablets, pineapple chewing gum, and fresh underwear?"

"Regularly."

"And did you ever see welded-up holes in walls, where previously had been cafés, taverns, little shops, etc?"

"Several times," I said.

"And have you heard of the bestiary?"

"Useless crap."

"Useless now, perhaps, because they destroyed it and tried to create it anew. And up here, have you seen the Path? Have you seen the safety areas? They are relatively common."

"Of course, they're everywhere. This world is covered by a fine network."

"Correct. And game challenges? Have you received them?"

"A long time ago. Down there in the asshole of the world they are issued as rewards. If you win, you get a bit of money or some other bonus, also useless crap. Something incomplete."

"Something killed and then incorrectly resurrected."

"Uh-huh."

"And what about hero statuses? You probably know everything about them, correct?"

"Yes. Five ranks, five being the highest."

"That also goes right back to the very beginning, to the creation of this world. Everything I have mentioned is connected. The game challenges, the plentiful taverns and inns, the safety areas, the trade points, the hero ranks, the bestiary. They are all part of a single big game which was endless, played in real time, and truly engrossed the minds of the world's entire population. Did you see screens everywhere?"

"Yes, but they were usually kaput."

"There always used to be crowds of folks gawking at them, because they always showed extremely interesting things involving heroes. Oops, I completely forgot, did you receive courses of strengthening injections?"

"We did."

"Incredibly invigorating bonus energy injections? Enhanced wound healing? Limb replacement?"

"Yes, yes, and yes."

"It's all part of the game. It's funny, but I used to dream about it all the time."

"About becoming a hero?"

"No! Fuck that! I dreamed of meeting a hero and being able to unload all my pent-up anger in his face, backed-up by hard fact. I dreamed of proving it was the heroes' fault that the world was coming to an end. The heroes have destroyed this world."

"Have you fucking lost your mind?" I said, shaking my head. "You all blame each other for everything, and nobody takes responsibility for anything. Someone sins against the languid kindhearts, and someone blames the Highers, the Highers blame you, you bastard herders of wild prisms and hunters of human flesh, and you — what jolly shapes! — blame the heroes. It's a vicious fucking circle. Well, nearly. All that remains is to blame the impending death of the world on the goosed tunafish, and then the circle will be complete."

"Us? Meat hunters? Wild-prism herders? Screw you, you impudent ignorant son of a bitch! You are too young to be drawing conclusions. You know nothing. The ones who ever knew anything are long dead. And the ones who aren't dead have had their memories erased. And if the erasure misses something, the process is repeated. Responsibility? What responsibility do we have? We are a discontinued line, prisoners left to die, disenfranchised prisoners merely trying to stay alive. Yes, I won't lie, many of us dream of vengeance. Others long for the restoration of order and a return to the old times. And I am one of them. I was one of them my whole life, until I became utterly exhausted. But whatever the case, we are guilty of nothing. We are jilted monsters, that's who we are. Do you understand?"

"I understand."

"How can you blame a tiger left to die in a cage for stretching out a paw and grabbing a fat piggy tourist who comes too close? Everyone wants to live. Everyone wants to eat."

"Uh-huh, I hear you, Isfir."

"You weren't even freaking listening? You don't give a toss about us!"

"I don't give a toss about anyone except my lot," I said, shrugging. "I'm an ill-natured goblin who is pissed-off with the whole freaking world. You're going to die soon, so go on with your story."

"I am, it's true," sighed Isfir, turning to look at Wreck. "Fix me up with a jar of greasy stew, would you, beast-boy?"

"Uh-huh," said the orc, starting. "Just a minute."

While he was digging around in his backpack, Isfir continued:

"Let me tell you about us and our woes, hero Elb. You just listen to how all the shit started and why it is the heroes who are guilty of everything. And, it goes without saying, the shitting Highers."

"Oh yes, you mustn't leave them out," I said. "Where there's power there's money. I'm listening."

"In the beginning the heroes were simply a fantastic form of entertainment. They received tasks from the system and the people. Everyday social tasks mostly, digging allotments, gathering the harvest, clearing ditches. Manpower was always in demand. Then new tasks appeared, involving the capture and elimination of zombies and sick animals, which were extremely rare back then. Then came the first woodland patrols, or 'raids,' as they were known, which involved groups of heroes being dispatched to places not monitored by the system, where they searched for zombies and sick beasts. When they returned, they had rewards waiting for them."

"Sounds good so far."

"Well yes. Obviously there was the occasional mano-a-mano between well-known heroes; bets placed, everything shown online, peaceful citizens covetously ogling the ringing swords and cuirasses, and the sawn-off shotguns shooting at cussing knights. The miscellaneous weapons, the confused epochs, the quality medical assistance. What could be more entertaining? Do not be shy of spilling blood! It is bread and circuses for the hoi polloi!"

"Again, so far so good."

"From the very beginning the heroes were spawned on the initiative of one of the first Highers, whose name has long since been forgotten. He forced through the creation of this global game, as well as supervising it, arguing with the system and using his influence to gain new advantages, incentives, and freedoms for the heroes, who responded with loyalty to, and glorification of, the Highers.

"Just like now."

"In those days there existed no few services. There were forest rangers, who somehow resembled bears and were responsible for the zoos. There were water services, which looked after the underwater observation decks, organized water-based excursions, and kept the aquatic creatures under control. There were highway services, today known as the kindhearts, who keep order on the thoroughfares. Every town had a police force, today's virgs, although back then there were many more of them. They were in charge of the whole area around their village, and they were in contact with each other via a communications system which enabled them to exchange information. Essentially, everything you would expect in a civilized world. There was also a separate and extensive rescue service based in a number of towns, which could reach any point in the world fast. One of those towns was Crontown. Heroes were not welcomed there before, being considered fools, disguised clowns, who had no place in an almost closed service settlement."

"I'd do the same," I said. "Fuck heroes, give me soldiers."

"That's right," said Isfir in reply. "Soldiers are always better, as are policemen. They are dutiful and do not have the heroes' hubris or burning ambition. They simply do their jobs, fulfill their duties, receive their pay, and take regular vacations. Whereas heroes... Well, you get the picture. Fuck heroes."

"Absolutely."

"Inevitable clashes began between all the services and the shitting heroes. Constant clashes. None of the services liked others encroaching on their sphere of business. Imagine you are a fire fighter, and you clamber in through the window of a burning building to rescue a child, and suddenly some dick crawls past you in a hero's red cape, literally pushing you out of the way and wasting your time."

"He would die," I said.

"Die, my foot! Who, in those times, would allow you to shoot someone in the head and go unpunished? No. A brawl would kick off, no one would get into the building, and the child would die. Situations like that were very frequent. Game challenges became more common, and in order to occupy the bored heroes, they had additional raids organized for them to dungeons, grim and dangerous underground worlds. Do you understand where the heroes were sent?"

"What is there to think about?" I said slowly as I recalled the underground steel corridors with their safety areas. "They were sent to the lower tiers?"

"That's right. In large groups and for weeks at a time. It relieved the situation somewhat, but did not correct it fully. The heroes' numbers only grew, the world is not as big as it might seem, and there are not enough problems to go around. They wanted to be doing heroic deeds every day, appearing on screens and being the object of the rabble's admiration. And then one day our world was begotten. The World of Adventures, the World of Monsters. Do you understand what heroes need in order to be considered true fearless heroes?"

"An opponent. An enemy. Preferably frightful

and formidable, so that a single look at him takes your breath away. Monsters. Heroes must fight—"

"Monsters, that's right. You are smart. And spiteful."

"Did the Highers create monsters themselves?"

"They did. First of all they created beasts for underground raids, and those beasts soon showed their worth, turning playful outings into real combat missions with real wounds and real death. I do not know what kind of beasts those first ones were, but they were created in a special laboratory, which later began to create monsters for us as well, a function which has since been discontinued."

"Am I to understand that you lot are some kind of territory?"

"We are a territory of sorts," replied Isfir. "When the hero thing proved its effectiveness in brightening leisure time for the world's entire population, when it became a worldwide hobby, the next step was taken: doors leading to the World of Monsters were opened. You do not look like a fan of computer games, which were popular in the past and are now a part of game challenges."

Silently I shook my head.

"In days of old there existed a line of games such as Monster Hunter, where the storyline was very basic and the hero or group of heroes would receive a task to destroy an especially dangerous monster. They would find its lair, attack it fearlessly, and come out of the encounter victorious. Well, or die. Then new heroes would replace the fallen. Except that back then it was a game. Whereas now... Well, in principle it is also a game, only with real and very serious injuries and deaths. Nearly all of the first heroes to enter died after failing to appreciate the danger. The monsters created in the special laboratory literally tore them apart. But with time the heroes' losses decreased, for humans are always smart. They worked together in teams and assigned themselves different roles, including medics, whom they called healers, who had advanced skills in field medicine and could summon mobile medblocks for bonuses or even simply evacuate the wounded. The medblocks were flown in by drones. Did you think they were offshoots of hospitals? No. They are a legacy left over from the heroic past."

"What bullshit."

"People love to play. And watch others playing. They love to take risks. And watch others taking risks. It has always been that way, and it always will be."

"You said the heroes stopped dying."

"That's right. People are smarter. Can you guess the next step?"

"Prisms. Beast folk."

"That's right. Gruesome monsters with human intellect. Fast, merciless, frightening, causing a frenzy among people by their appearance alone. Able to pose, able to kill with a flourish, holding a shrieking hero in the air with pincers and dismembering him slowly so that his hero's blood, guts, and internal organs dropped right into a gaping fang-lined maw. It was a fucking blockbuster. And everything for real. The world liked it so much that the ratings of the scriptwriting Highers skyrocketed."

"Monster hunters. Gladiatorial games."

"That's right. Of course not just anybody could become a prism. You can't turn a human into a monster without good reason. But if they were prisoners, you could. Those who had committed such heinous crimes that they were guaranteed the death penalty. And those same Highers forced through an amendment in the law, stating that prisoners who had committed especially serious crimes could choose their own punishment. The majority of them chose memory deletion and transformation into a nullform. Others, threatened with death, agreed to an injection and were turned into modified larvae. Volitionally modified, of course. There were no prisms as such back then. With criminality a constant threat, there were so many desiring to become monsters that they were plunged into cold sleep and dispatched to storage facilities in the World of Adventures. I am one of them."

"Old, wrinkled, and maleficent," growled Wreck. "In which case any old biddy is a monster."

"I wasn't modified, you fool!" barked the old woman, casting aside her emptied stew jar. "Can you rustle me up something sweet?"

"We can," I said. "Continue."

"Aside from the nightmare insects with human intellect, viewers also wanted something more canonical and sweet, and thus were born the beastfolk. In the early zones of the World of Monsters, peaceful zones appeared, with inns and trading posts, catgirls with big behinds and breasts strolling the streets, and bordellos plying their trade to satisfy any pubescent sexual fantasy. Then, satisfied, you could go on a monster hunt. The laboratory continued to churn out ever newer kinds of creature, both sentient and non-sentient, just so long as they were nightmarish, or at the very least unusual. The creatures threw themselves into the fray, and the heroes destroyed them with glee. The heroes' fame grew rapidly and they became stars. Stars of worldwide renown. They were revered, exalted. And, it went without saying, the heroes liked it. The other services, however, did not, because the heroes kept getting under their feet. Complaints, reports, and demands were submitted, and the system turned to the Highers. And the Highers, for whom the heroes had long since become obedient beloved toys, even objects of collectability and sexual desire, defended their underlings to the hilt. They began pushing through new rights for the heroes, and successfully. The heroes' influence grew, while the influence of the services dropped. The heroes demanded more and more tasks, because they needed money for equipment, arms, and strengthening. It was no good rocking up in the World of Monsters with bare arms, for they would soon be chewed the fuck off. And no one would arm you for gratis. Plus, experience was required, and it was better to gain experience in battle against an insane tigress than against a smart prism. Soon all the services were disbanded one by one. The first to go was the rescue service, whose towns were soon settled by heroes."

"Crontown."

"The closest, that's right," said the old woman. "The other services soon followed suit, or had their rights swiftly removed. For example, the rovers' right to stay in any one place for long was rescinded, forcing them to tramp the world's dusty roads indefinitely. The virgs, the urban police force, became the guardians, their numbers dropping sharply and their zone of influence narrowing, and they began to protect the towns themselves and their populations, leaving the rest to the heroes."

"Bullshit," I repeated. "Atrocious dumbass bullshit. Leaving important zones like that to glory-hungry amateurs?"

"Exactly. It was bullshit. And it went without saying that the bullshit could not last for long. One day — I don't know when, but a long time ago — when the situation had gotten completely out of hand and the whole world had turned into a fruit machine, the Taboo was imposed. Imposed by *him*. We, the inhabitants of the World of Monsters, know that day as the Great Erasure. And erasure is precisely what it was. All records were destroyed, nearly all terminals ceased to work, the bestiaries were cleared out, game challenges were cancelled, and the system simply forgot about us once and for all and exited our world. So there you have it. It was all down to him and his word alone."

"Him?"

"The First Higher, the creator of this world. Don't ask about the details, I don't know. There is no information. The only thing we know is that when he appeared in the world he had created for the first time in eons, he took one look at all the morbid shit and dissolved the entire fucking gaming and entertainment industry in a click of his fingers. The World of Monsters, the heroes' raids, everything vanished into oblivion, and the gates to the World of Monsters were shut for ever. There was just one problem: they locked all the inhabitants inside, including the personnel, which was made up of prisoners. The automatic storage facility for frozen numbskulls like me was also inside, and just as soon as one World of Monsters resident died, the fridge immediately spat out the next poor unfortunate. And thus I was born. And thus were born all my peers and everyone else. Some were even born already injected, with a transformation charge already maturing inside them, which would soon turn them into either a beastfolk or a horrible prism."

"I see."

"You don't see a fucking thing! It's dreadful! What about food? We learned to grow some things ourselves, but what about feed for massive prisms? That first squad you annihilated..."

"With the gigantic wood louse? What about it?"

"Her name was Melissa, and for the first four

years she was a simple smiley peasant girl diligently digging soil in the carrot and potato fields. She was a good wife. Then one day the dormant charge inside her body sparked into life, and she was rapidly transformed into a stage-one prism, an ugly and silent creature. What for?"

"But she was a criminal, right?"

"Once upon a time, perhaps, a couple of centuries ago. But are you sure? I'm not. Erased memory. If she did ever commit a crime, then her old criminal personality was wiped clean. She had already suffered her punishment. And then, after years of toiling away peacefully, she was turned into a beastie. And after another year she underwent a second transformation and grew much bigger, and became much more vicious. She nigh forgot us. Shit! Now do you understand why we came here?"

"In two squads?"

"That's right."

"To feed them. And to take a small supply of meat."

"That's right. The fifth transformation is obligatory, and it demands enormous quantities of calories, which only meat can provide. And our herd is already depleted, only youngsters left for breeding purposes. So we came to kill."

"For the sake of a single prism?"

"For the sake of many prisms!"

"Let's forget about innocent lives for the moment. Tell me, why the hell feed and transform dumb wood lice if they just go and turn into monsters?"

"Sometimes the next transformation produces surprising results and returns the intellect. And the capacity for speech."

"It's a very high price to pay."

"Agreed," said Isfir. "I am not here of my own desire. I repeat, there are many different forms among us. I am one of those who always advocated humility, patience, and diplomacy. But our leaders consider us victims, and they thirst for vengeance. Their dream is the removal of all Highers and the desolation of the Lands of the Covenant."

"Jeez."

"Exactly," said Isfir with a wan snicker. "It sounds terrible. But in reality it will be even worse if the amassed hordes come out into the open."

"Hordes? What do you feed them?"

"Nothing. Prisms who have undergone their final transformation can be immersed in a long sleep, a coma, very like death. They don't move and they scarcely breathe. Every now and then we wake them up to feed them a sheep or a cow, and then we put them back to sleep for a whole year. But that can only happen with those who have undergone their final transformation."

"Do you give them injections?"

"We do."

"Like the ones you give yourselves? So the beasties living next to their hearts don't wake up?"

"That's right. You are clever. It is almost the same injection. But when we are at home, we use a different injection. One injection lasts for a month."

"Why all the conspiracy, for fuck's sake? Are you afraid of an intrusion if someone discovers the coordinates of the entry point?"

"We are. And it is also an order from the great Daurra, who has ruled over us for two hundred years. By and by, her tear will awaken in my breast."

"Wait a minute. Is it a caterpillar?"

"It is."

"But it's going to die."

"That's right. A caterpillar does not live long after awakening. It grows, eats flesh, builds a cocoon, and dies."

"Yeah, we've seen them," I said. "They died twenty minutes after being born."

"Sterility has not been banned. Perhaps in the laboratories they also created monsters that were just too terrible, but were also too stupid to be allowed to propagate uncontrolled. Daurra stabs her stinger into our chests and deposits a 'tear.' While the larva is dormant, scarcely sucking its host's blood, it is alive, useful even."

"How so?"

"It improves the composition of the blood, accelerates regeneration, allows for faster resting time. Four hours of sleep per day is enough for me, and I normally only sleep for two hours twice a day. Everything has its upsides."

"A spiny caterpillar in the chest."

"We call it taking a pledge of allegiance. But you are not obliged to carry a tear in your chest."

"How so?"

"If you do not want to go out hunting in the external world, you can live a relaxed life working in the fields of the World of Monsters, looking after cattle, foresting, and taking care of the sleeping Horde. The larva in the chest is needed for just two reasons."

"So you don't do a runner from a hunting trip and stay outside to live. And so you don't manage to tell anyone else. Although you've managed to."

"I have told a lot of tales, but nothing concrete. Although I will. And do you know why?"

"No."

"Because I heard about you before. Rumors about the hero Elb reached even the World of Monsters. And I am not surprised that it was you and your people who reached us. It is fate. Or maybe not, but I believe. I simply believe."

"I don't give a toss what you believe."

"And what do you believe?"

"That this world is being fucked. Violently raped. That this world needs cleansing with sharpened steel and fire."

"Radical and harsh. But fair. Shall I continue?"

"Please do. But first tell me how you know so much? You were in a cold sleep and had your memory wiped. Did they tell you about awakening?"

"Among other things. But most of it I read in the Chronicles of the World of Monsters. And do you know who composed a large part of the Chronicles?"

"Sentient monsters?"

"No fucking way! It was heroes. And do you know when?"

"Tell me."

"They started it straight after the Great Erasure. After the Taboo. And for a very simple reason: what else was there to do for heroes who were now full-time captives in the World of Monsters?"

"Wait a minute. Are you trying to say..."

"On the stroke of midday, the voice of the system sounded in the World of Monsters. It was heard everywhere. The voice announced that all heroes must immediately vacate the enormous territory of the World of Monsters. The reason was of a technical nature, and the urgency was great. How many strong spoiled heroes do you think took the warning seriously?"

"Minimal numbers."

"No one gave a flying fuck about the system. The gates weren't going to close for ever, were they? So they could wait it out here for the meantime. Yeah right! Wait it out? The gates to the World of Monsters had been sealed forever. And the heroes, knowledgeable, strong, smart, and outraged at such tyranny and the realization that it probably was forever after all, fell into despair. Those were terrible days. But a week or so later, tired of letting the grass grow under their feet and deciding it was the end of everything, the heroes attempted to assuage their anger in the only way they knew: by killing. Only they did not start killing monsters, because they were afraid. The screens and terminals had stopped working, the mobile medblocks had not arrived, and the system had fallen silent. All their ire was taken out on the peaceful part of the World of Monsters, the sparse itty-bitty towns with their bordellos and inns. They delighted in raping women, slitting throats, and burning down houses. And it continued until the denizens of the world united to retaliate, harshly, pushing the heroes back to the Caves of Obscurity, located not far from the town of Golden Aura, which the heroes themselves had sacked. And they were shut in those caves forever."

"What sort of names are those?" growled Wreck.

"The incarcerated heroes were not refused food, although they were not fed often. The food stores were still full in those times. They had their own water source there, but even so, there were soon very few heroes left, because they turned their madness against one another and perpetrated a massacre inside the caves. Those who survived disarmed, and asked the beastfolk and prisms for medical assistance. They became much gentler and more polite. Most of what I have told you came from them, about this whole great game which ended so ingloriously, and it comprised a large part of the Chronicles of the World of Monsters. And that is how I know so much about this world's past. I would tell you about its further development, about how the monsters came to power, and about our castes, but my time is nearly up. I can feel it. The tear is awakening and I do not have long left. I will tell you one thing: the system has forgotten about us. It was told to forget, and it forgot. They tried to use the remains of the enormous infrastructure, and part of it was destroyed. Most of the safety areas have disappeared, and eateries have closed. Tasks for heroes continue to be issued, but there is no longer any centralized control, and services for the protection and preservation of the world have either disappeared, or become a travesty such as the virgs with their cavemen's clubs. We know this from news reaching our world via infiltrators such as me and those Highers who remember us and dream of a return to the old times. However, I do not know any details because I was never particularly trusted." The old woman smiled bitterly. "I am an outcast. But anyway, do you understand now why it is the heroes who are to blame for the agony of this poor little world?"

"How do you get into the World of Monsters?"

"What will you do if you get there? You'll be eaten alive."

"Are you worried about your people?"

"Screw you all! My time is at an end, and it was spent wastefully. I spent most of my life wiping up caterpillar shit. Shit! I want just one thing: an end to this nightmare. Stop eating people! Stop spawning beasts! Let the world recover!"

"How do you get into the World of Monsters? Where's the entrance?"

"Nowhere. And everywhere. You cannot get in

to us, the main hero magnet, just like that. It is only for the selected few, and for those who will not spoil the show's ratings by perishing on contact with the first newborn monster they come across. Even I do not know where exactly our lands are situated. A complex system of mobile platforms leads there. You stand on a platform and you travel. Doors open in front of you and close behind you. You rise and fall. You do not understand if the World of Monsters is up in the heavens or at the very bottom."

"And how do you get to these platforms?"

"Unless you are a resident, there is no way. The World of Monsters is a closed world. We found a back door almost by chance. But find it we did, and that produced new hope among the John Does like me, as well as engendering plans for aggression among the policy makers. As always. The back door used to be a service entrance, some kind of colossal cargo elevator. Our scientists, or magicians, as they are also known, were able to find a way out. It was something to do with the terminals. And getting back in was no bother at all. If you follow our tracks back there, you will come across some abandoned ruins. A little shop, or pavilion, with a wonky roof and a regular concrete floor covered with smashed tiles. That is our exit and entrance. All we have to do is stand on the floor and wait, and it lowers us to a platform which takes us home. Why is it so easy? Because of" — the old woman tapped her temple — "the chip. We are residents of the World of Monsters. The system does not see us. It looks right through us. And it remembers nothing. While the peripheral computer system knows full well where we are from and where to take us. It's funny, right? We arrive here easy as pie, to eat you, before departing with the same ease. There is just one problem: it is very rare to be able enter as a large squad. Usually the magicians manage to send only one small party at a time."

"Techies," I said with a frown. "Techies, not magicians. Enough of the shitting fantasy."

"As you wish."

"So the entrance won't work for us?"

"No. Even if you take a living resident with you, the scanner will see strangers on the platform and refuse you admission. That is why the World of Monsters is inaccessible to you. It lets us out, but it does not outsiders in. There are scanners at many of the transport nodes, where the platform changes its direction of travel, so you would not even be able to jump onto a descending platform. And there are checkpoints. Check after check. There is no way for outsiders to get in. It was not easy before either, for the World of Monsters only ever admitted the selected few."

"Heroes?"

"That's right. Hero status is one of the most important factors. You could only get into the World of Monsters if you were at least rank four. Then beginning at rank five you would qualify to cross the Hrebros, a rocky ridge in the middle of the World of Monsters. On the other side were the most fearsome monsters. And also on the other side, at the very edge of the World of Monsters, where no hero had ever set foot, was the highest reward."

"What's that?" I asked, my brow raised in surprise. "The highest reward for heroes is—"

"The Lands of the Covenant?" the old woman snorted in contempt, cutting me off. "Pfft! They used to let them in there starting from rank three. But what is the Lands of the Covenant? It's nothing. An elite area, home to members of the parliament or the government. It's all nonsense. Access to the Lands of the Covenant has only recently become the highest reward. It used to be the Tower!"

"Say that again."

"The Tower. Or to be more precise, the door to it. On the other side of the door is a passageway leading to the Tower of the First Higher. That is the highest reward for any hero: to meet the creator of the world, to meet a living god and to ask him questions. One legend says it happened once. It says a legendary hero, having lost all his comrades on the way, annihilated a legion of monsters, broke through, found the secret door, entered, and gained the Tower. He gained an audience with the First Higher. And, allegedly, whatever he said to the Great Hermit so incensed him that the Great Erasure happened that very day. And that hero has not been seen since."

"A fascinating tale," I said. "Is the World of Monsters really that big?"

"It is colossal! I do not know what was to be

created there initially, but the world really is very vast. And beautiful. Very beautiful in its own way."

"So how do I get there? Rank is irrelevant, for the World of Monsters is closed. And it's no good asking the system, because it doesn't remember anything, right?"

"You can try asking" — Isfir shrugged her shoulders and swatted away an empty tinned-peach tin — "but it will get you nowhere. We have been erased from its memory. The periphery remembers us, the computerised transport system, but the brain does not. It's funny..."

"How do I get to you?"

"I am coming to that. Do you know how the techies — again this is hearsay — managed to find a way out? Of course you don't. Well, it is said they found something in the Caves of Obscurity, the place where all the heroes who were locked in the World of Monsters were incarcerated and died."

"What could they possibly have found there? Dusty broken bones? Dry dead tushes?"

"A beast." The old woman smiled. "They found a mechanical beast, stuffed with electronics. To put it more precisely, they found the Rainbow Koala, whatever that means. It is a toy, one of the so-called "artifacts" of the olden times. A beautiful mechanical guide which showed the way to the mysterious World of Monsters. The artifacts were awarded for the completion of especially difficult tasks, and whole squads of heroes would square off for them. Each such beast can open and close the doors to the World of Monsters a certain number of times. There and back."

"I see."

"Every single one of the scouts and hunters who go outside, every single time, come back and tell us to look for the other guides. They describe a mechanical orange sloth, a powerful spherical rolling creature, a talking teddy bear, a mechanical owl, a deer with golden horns, a turtle with a crystal shell, a scarlet bird with a silver beak, and an otter wearing a diamond crown. We remember these descriptions by heart, and all these creatures are mechanical. And they were all created with the same aim in mind, but they are not all used for their original intended purpose. And now no one knows their true intended purpose. Hey, hero, what's with the wry face? What did I say?" As she asked this, Isfir massaged the left side of her chest. "Oh shit. The tear is stirring."

"You need some injections," I said angrily.

"Daurra is wise," smiled the old woman. "And precautious."

Well yes, too much so. The scouts received their "two-hourly" injections from a prism, which used a stinger or a barb to introduce a particular cocktail that would prevent the caterpillar from waking. The prism would gain this ability after close communion with Daurra, whatever that meant, and an enema bulb, of sorts, would appear in its body, with a needle, which it then used to inject a strictly measured dose. After we finished off the prism, we could forget about injections. After all, it was the prime target of any attack. And rightly so, for it was a monster, a serious threat. So that was just what we did. We finished off the beast, and in doing so, peppered the biological reservoir inside its body with holes.

"You have become dependent on the monsters," I noted, standing up and beginning to walk in circles around the campfire.

"That is not important now," said the old woman, smiling, the bitterness gone from her voice. "So what now, hero Elb? I see by your face that you have learned a lot."

"Indeed," I replied. "I have even seen a couple of the guides. Are there any differences between them?"

"There are. Some are able to open big doors leading to big platforms, which permits passage to big squads. Some only open little doors, enough for a squad of ten or fifteen fighters with not much machinery. If you have a number of them, you will be able to take a decent quantity of troops in or out. That is what our leaders dream of, but so far they only have two guides."

"Two?"

"Two. The rainbow koala, and literally a few days ago a teddy bear appeared. And on the square of the little town of Welcoming, which is right by the entrance to the World of Monsters, a cage has appeared, housing a furry and extremely potty-mouthed beastfolk."

"Oh shit!"

"Do you know something about them?"

"Do you?"

"About the beastfolk and the teddy bear?"

"I do. Almost nobody is allowed near the beastfolk, although it does seem to have been hunted in this world. Some people nearly ran down an evil lady with a load of butterflies. And out of fright, the beastfolk used the bear's abilities to escape to the World of Monsters."

"Why's it in a cage?"

"I do not know. But it is not an overly strict punishment. Perhaps it stole something, or offended someone. Oh shit, the spiny hand around my heart. Go look for a guide, hero Elb. If you find one, you will be able to reach us. If you don't…"

"Was the Rainbow Koala not meant to be brought out? It is a guide after all."

"The techies somehow solved that problem using the terminals. I do not know exactly. Tell as many people as possible everything I have told you. Let them know that heroes are an evil, a great evil! They are to blame for everything."

"Damn."

"Kill me, hero, I beg you. And make sure the caterpillar dies as well. I do not want it to eat my body."

"I've got more questions."

"Fuck off with your questions! I have had enough of these shitty worlds. Kill me!"

"Shit!" I shouted, plunging my knife into the old woman's heart and twisting it. "Shit! Wreck, chop her head off."

"Yes sir."

When the sweeping strike removed her gray

head from her shoulders, I clenched my fists and yelled:

"Not a word of this is to be repeated over the system channel!"

"Is that why you left the transmitter in the buggy?"

"Yes. And not a word to anyone until I say so!"

"Gotcha."

"Kill the rest of the prisoners. Then load up."

"Yes sir. Then what?"

"We move out."

"Where to?"

"Back to base. And from there straight to fucking Zombieland!"

"Hell yeah! It's time to bust some surver ass! High time! Can we still go there, according to hero rules?"

"Fuck rules, orc! Fuck instructions! This is a real hunt."

"Yeah! Elb? Commander?"

"What?"

"Do you really think anyone has reached the Tower? And seen the First Higher?"

"Fuck knows. Do you need to?"

"Well, yes."

"So get a wiggle on, Wreck. It's time we hauled ass for the freaking World of Monsters!"

End of Book Nine

Want to be the first to know about our latest LitRPG, sci fi and fantasy titles from your favorite authors?

Subscribe to our **New Releases** newsletter:
http://eepurl.com/b7niIL

Thank you for reading *Nullform!*

If you like what you've read, check out other sci-fi, fantasy and LitRPG novels published by Magic Dome Books:

NEW and UPCOMING RELEASES!

Emperor of the Borderlands
A Historical Progression Fantasy Series
by Eugene Astakhov & Alex Toxic

Backstreet Evolutionist
A Progression Fantasy Adventure Series
by Anton Panarin

We Are Legion
A RealRPG Action Adventure Series
by Dmitry Dornichev & Evgeny Fox

The Doctor from Nowhere
A Historical Progression Fantasy Adventure Series
by Anatoly Drozdov

The Artificer
A Portal Progression Fantasy Series
by Marcus Cass

Guardian's Journey
A Portal Progression Fantasy Series
by Roman Savarovsky

„Earth" Release
A LitRPG Adventure Series
by Vasily Mahanenko & Vladimir Koshcheev

Nanomachines
A Progression Fantasy Adventure Series
by Nikolai Novikov

The Afflicted
A LitRPG Apocalypse Adventure Series
by Konstantin Zubov

The Dark Summoner
A Portal Progression Fantasy Series
by Andrei Tkachev

The Last Paladin
An Action & Adventure Progression Fantasy Series
by Roman Savarovsky

The Other Side
A Progression Fantasy Adventure Series
by Rodion Korablev

Me and My Demons
A Portal Progression Adventure Fantasy Series
by Oleg Sapphire & Alexey Kovtunov

The Blood Code
A Historical Progression Fantasy Adventure Series
by Michael Borz

The Banned
A LitRPG Adventure Series
by Michael Atamanov

How I Built a Magic Empire
A Portal Progression Fantasy Series
by Konstantin Zubov

The Order of Architects
A Portal Progression Fantasy Series
by Oleg Sapphire & Yuri Vinokuroff

The Selected
A LitRPG Action Adventure Series
by Vasily Mahanenko & Yuri Vinokuroff

The Hunter's Code
A Portal Progression Fantasy Series
by Oleg Sapphire & Yuri Vinokuroff

The One Who Changes the Future
A Dystopian Portal Progression Fantasy Series
by Boris Romanovsky

An Ideal World for a Sociopath
A LitRPG Apocalypse Adventure Series
by Oleg Sapphire

The Healer's Way
A Portal Progression Fantasy Series
by Oleg Sapphire & Alexey Kovtunov

The Last Portal Jumper
A LitRPG Progression Fantasy Series
by Konstantin Zubov

The Dark Healer
A Historical Progression Fantasy Series
by Alex Toxic & Nadya Lee

Lord of The System
A LitRPG Progression Fantasy Series
by Alex Toxic & Furious Miki

A Shelter in Spacetime
A LitRPG Apocalypse Series
by Dmitry Dornichev

The Coming of God of Death
A Portal Progression Fantasy Series
by Dmitry Dornichev

The Village
A LitRPG Progression Fantasy Series
by Dmitry Dornichev & Alexey Kovtunov

Condemned (Lord Valevsky: Last of the Line)
A Progression Fantasy LitRPG Series
by Vasily Mahanenko

Living Ice
A Portal Progression Fantasy Series
by Dmitry Sheleg

Ghost in the System
An Apocalypse LitRPG Series
by Alexey Kovtunov

The Goldenblood Heir
A Portal Progression Fantasy Series
by Boris Romanovsky

Law of the Jungle
A Wuxia Progression Fantasy Adventure Series
by Vasily Mahanenko

More books and series are coming out soon!

In order to have new books of the series translated faster, we need your help and support! Please consider leaving a review or spread the word by recommending *Nullform* to your friends and posting the link on social media. The more people buy the book, the sooner we'll be able to make new translations available.

Thank you!

Till next time!